A Superior Man

PAUL YEE

A SUPERIOR MAN

ARSENAL PULP PRESS ✦ VANCOUVER

A SUPERIOR MAN
Copyright © 2015 by Paul Yee

ARSENAL PULP PRESS
Suite 202–211 East Georgia St.
Vancouver, BC V6A 1Z6
Canada
arsenalpulp.com

The publisher gratefully acknowledges the support of the Canada Council for the Arts and the British Columbia Arts Council for its publishing program, and the Government of Canada (through the Canada Book Fund) and the Government of British Columbia (through the Book Publishing Tax Credit Program) for its publishing activities.

Canada

Cover photograph: *Chinese work gang on the C.P.R., Glacier Park, BC, 1889* © McCord Museum
Design by Gerilee McBride
Edited by Susan Safyan

Printed and bound in Canada

Library and Archives Canada Cataloguing in Publication:
Yee, Paul, author
A superior man / Paul Yee.

Issued in print and electronic formats.
ISBN 978-1-55152-590-7 (paperback).—ISBN 978-1-55152-591-4 (epub)

1. Chinese—British Columbia—History—19th century—Fiction.
2. Railroad construction workers—British Columbia—History—19th century—Fiction. I. Title.

PS8597.E3S86 2015   C813'.54   C2015-903342-X
                                             C2015-903343-8

DEDICATION

This book is dedicated to the Nlaka'pamux First Nations people, on whose lands most of this story occurs, and to the memory of Yee Fook, a railway labourer who worked near Lytton, 1883.

NOTES ON WORD USE

1. In this book, the term "coolie" refers to workers who did heavy labour for low wages, such as the Chinese who helped build railways in North America.

In the nineteenth century, "coolie" also referred to indentured workers brought from India to Caribbean and Central American countries to replace slaves who had done work such as cutting sugar cane. Unfortunately, in some of those countries today, the term "coolie" is used to insult and demean people of South Asian descent.

The use of "coolie" in this book does reflect the racial and class-based disdain directed at Chinese and South Asian workers in the nineteenth century. But here, no offense is directed at people of South Asian descent. Instead, this story tries to educate readers about that class of labour and give those workers an honourable place in history and literature.

Word meanings change over time. In India today, "coolie" is a labour category for workers who are registered, licensed, and given uniforms to do the work of moving heavy luggage at railway stations.

II. As this book purports to be a translation of a memoir written in Chinese about Canada in the 1880s, many colloquial Chinese terms and phrases appear in English. The narrator came from the Pearl River region of south China and spoke Toisanese, a rural dialect. Therefore, for some Chinese words, especially in spoken dialogue, I have tried to provide a Toisanese transliteration.

However, this principle could not be consistently applied. For example, the city of Guangzhou (formerly Canton) is already well-known in English by its pinyin spelling for Mandarin pronunciation. As well, other Chinese terms (e.g., *fan-tan, feng shui, mah-jongg*) are now found in English dictionaries. We follow those standard spellings, even though they reflect different Chinese dialects. *Fan-tan*, for example, is based on Cantonese, while *feng shui* is based on Mandarin.

III. To refer to First Nations or Aboriginal persons, my fictional memoirist likely wrote Chinese words that sounded like the term "Indian," common in the English language at that time. Those Chinese words would have sounded like "Yin Chin," a term that doesn't appear in the Chinese language today. For this book, I used "Native" to avoid offending modern-day readers. However, because I wanted to make the book sound authentic to its nineteenth-century setting, I did not draw on contemporary terms such as First Nations or Aboriginal.

1

WHEN RUNNING, KNOW HEAD FROM TAIL (FALL 1885)

Victoria, British Columbia

Three in the morning, and it was time again to squeeze through the walking corpses.

Before the hordes of jobless railway men jammed into town, I had kept peace with a free hand. No one doubted my clout. Boss Long let me do as I pleased in the game hall. Taller than most men, I never feared a fight. Boss Long and his crony merchants craved every penny held by the coolies but shuddered to think of them smashing store windows, shouting with glee, and looting the stock. The size of the rabble meant that no one, not even squads of redbeard police and soldiers, could stop a riot. Last week, my turtle-head boss had ordered me to go easy on his shit-don't-stink customers and forgive their little sins.

Today, I shrugged when someone pounded the plaster wall into shards.

I looked away when men spat out green slime and rubbed it underfoot.

I walked off when louts pissed on the wall and not into the pails of the wet room.

The stink slid under the decent smells. The incense for the house gods was fragrant while pompous big-shots blew out spicy cigar smoke. Men oozing whisky and Ningbo liniment puffed sweet tobacco in gurgling water pipes. In a hall with no windows, these smells thickened through the night. Eager guests entered the storefront door, guarded by the ever-watchful Pock Face, before strolling past my post. During police raids, they dropped their swagger, scooted out the back, or dived through trapdoors into mud.

Shouting gamblers raised their clasped hands and pleaded for the dice and *fan-tan* coins to favour them. They had no shame, showing their panic to everyone. But these cockheads posed no threat. No, the risky ones had pinched faces and gaunt hands poking from threadbare clothes. They shut their eyes and muttered to gods and ancestors as the crowd jostled them. Their last bets each night played to the volcanos in their guts.

Jeers rang from the boss's *fan-tan* table. I peered through the haze. Oil lamps dangled over tables and swayed from the sudden smack of winners. The players noticed a man riding a lucky streak and tossed their bets onto the cloth to mimic his.

"Three!"

Winners pounded the table and jangled the *fan-tan* coins.

Boss Long scowled and paid out. He swept the coins under the lid and then heaved his belly onto the table.

"You played me clean." He displayed an empty cigar box, its cover showing a shapely woman with bare, creamy shoulders. "This table is closed."

He had slipped money into his pockets when the men were distracted.

"Screw!" The winning player blocked the way and lifted his jaw. "You never quit when the cash is creeping up your shit-hole."

His crooked nose was part of a stranger's face. A rail hand, for sure.

"You lose, you leave." Boss Long shrugged. "Same rule for me."

"Show me your pockets."

I thrust the tea basket at his back. "Honoured guest, have a drink!"

He turned just enough to let Boss Long grab his rice-sack stomach and sprint. The door at the foot of the stairs slammed. A bar thumped into place. If the shit spread, he could toss a rope out the window that, from the street, looked like layers of nailed boards, and then shimmy to the ground.

The winner yanked in vain at the door. Players shouted for Boss Long to show his ugly face.

"Better leave now." I held up two cups for the winner. "Cookhouse closes soon."

Everyone knew the custom. At closing time, each night's big winner took his fellow gamblers to dine, to share his windfall and assure Heaven that he was humble and big-hearted and therefore deserved future favour. The size of his win let him choose good-luck foods: fish, oysters, and black-hair seaweed. These dishes were costly and sparsely served, so hangers-on snatched them and filled their mouths with rice. Then they slept, pigs at peace, dreaming of hosting the next such feast.

"Lick your mother!" The winner pulled at the door again. "Show your face!"

The crowd surged and goaded him.

Didn't the fools know they were too late? By now Boss Long had emptied his pockets.

"Honoured guest, let me toast you." I lifted two cups, tilted them, and let tea spill onto my head. One stream slipped by my ears and spine to my waist. The other passed my forehead and nose and ended on my chest. I flexed my shoulders and let my shirt absorb the liquid.

The crowd laughed. One man raised a candle to let people see the tea was real.

I lifted my pigtail to give him a better view and grinned. "I bathe to smell nice for Rainbow."

The winner fetched two cups too.

"Dirty bastard, nothing can clean you!" He pitched tea into my eyes.

I grabbed and slammed him into the wood, letting the doorknob punch his back and rupture something. I bent my knees and waited. He winced and pushed himself along the wall. His eyes narrowed but gleamed. He rose into a crouch, legs out for balance, hands and arms sliding into a fighting stance.

He was stupid, showing that he knew *gong fu*. Before he could move, Pock Face seized him from behind. I grabbed the gambler's feet, and we swung the cursing, kicking fellow through the hall and heaved him onto the road.

Stray dogs barked.

The crowd streamed out, eager for a fight. Only the first ones saw the gambler run at us and get his head bashed by Pock Face's bat. He dropped to the ground, senseless. The witnesses fled, knowing it was time for order to resume. In a riot, any man could get maimed, easy as borrowing fire.

"Go!" I lit a lamp to move people along. "Nothing to see."

Railway men spat at my feet. I noted their faces for future payback. Friends clapped my shoulder. The slowpoke was Old Iron, self-declared spokesman for the rail hands. He glared at me with his one eye. When Pock Face shouted the all-clear, I slid heavy planks over the plate-glass windows and locked the wood into place.

Inside, the door to the stairs was closing.

"Boss came down?" I asked.

Pock Face was packing dominoes, clicking them like abacus beads. "Old Iron called you a traitor for beating the rail hands."

"The bloated beggars want this, want that."

"Old Iron said you look down on them."

"I get them to America."

"Not now." Triumph lifted his voice. Even he was gloating. "Your boats carry ghosts. Old Iron told the boss to fire you. Otherwise, they boycott us."

"And Boss said?"

"'Limp off, rotted corpse.'"

"Best!"

Later, I went upstairs, treading softly to acknowledge the boss's nod of support. I sipped whisky and let its heat embrace me. I swore to crumple Old Iron's eye patch and thrash him soft and spongy. I was no traitor, not me—I didn't even hold grudges. I was just doing my job. That cockhead Old Iron didn't see the ground crumbling like sand under him. When San Francisco merchants sent funds to ship railway workers home, Council gave the first tickets to the stir-the-shit-sticks. You want to get home quickly? Then shout for more handouts and proclaim the end of the world. Too bad rail hands were turtles with their heads tucked in.

Two months ago, sternwheelers had started landing the vermin here. The end of our stay in Canada thrilled the redbeards, gave them Christmas in July. When the first ship bound for China clanged its bells and lifted anchor, throngs of white men, women, and children cheered at the docks. They could only blow shiny whistles; the flags and marching bands that formed their usual parades weren't present.

The merchants of Chinatown, those kicked-in dogs and sons of concubines, crept home and murmured their secret charm: seven thousand, seven thousand... At any single moment, the Company listed that number of coolies on its payroll.

The king-high eyes of merchants had foreseen that road building would take a decade. Too bad the bottom dropped out four years ahead of time. Last year, they put up seven brick buildings in Chinatown and forecast booming rents. This year they let them at beggar rates to rail hands who carried in planks and sawhorses to make beds. The vermin ate at Chinatown's cookhouses and vowed to pay later. But when ships set sail for China, the men failed to board. They lacked passage money. Kicked out of their lodgings, they napped in back alleys and scuttled for shelter under the raised sidewalks. We laughed: *Maid-servants had gotten fatter than their mistresses.*

Our Chinese Council claimed the rail hands were no threat to city peace, even as they spread bedrolls and stoked campfires on the lawns of Beacon Hill Park.

"Ignore them," said our leaders, "they await ships for home."

Good thing the redbeards had complained; if not, no merchant would have dumped stocks of useless canvas tents on an empty city block. Those cloth walls now housed 1,000 men. Once sheltered, the vermin pressed their advantage and leaned on the merchants for free food.

Council demanded donations, but local residents couldn't be squeezed for cash they didn't have. Merchants deducted "gifts" from payrolls, which caused even more honest folk to resent the rail hands. Council begged the swelling mass of coolies to see that the mess was far beyond local means; even grand firms with twenty-five years of history in Gold Mountain crumbled at the iron road's end. On Cormorant Street, the Council president climbed onto a crate and used his oily mouth to praise the workers for battling cold and disease, sharp rock and black powder. I expected him to urge the gods to change the vermin into Immortals who could glide over the ocean on fans and palm leaves.

Council never gave me food or clothes. In China, one blind beggar tapping along the street was easy to dismiss. Not so when fifteen of them walked in a line, droning like pious monks, each one clutching the pigtail of the man ahead. When they massed at a store, its owner made quick payment to get rid of them. A plague of vermin had landed on Gold Mountain, but we didn't have enough hoes to smash them.

※

Stubborn banging awoke me in the morning.

"Open the door! Repay the money!"

I yanked a pillow over my head. Boss Long's flunky was still on the mainland. These blockheads would have to wait. Then I heard wood cracking and leapt from bed.

Boss Long's bedroom was also the office. The chamber-pot stink swirled with the sour of ancient leftovers. Today, the ratty long underwear was gone from walls and chairs. The boots, one black pair and one brown, each worn every other day, left a gap by the door. Papers and account books slid lopsided to the floor. I stumbled down the stairs, shouting for calm. The boss had bolted on four scabby legs to America on a rival's boat.

I raced to the back but stopped. Vermin were waiting outside to thrash me. Then they would brag to all of Chinatown that their mighty farts had hurled me to a back-door retreat.

I went and unlocked the entrance. Smirking, I lifted the first plank from the window. "Boss isn't here. He ran off."

They charged in. Across the street, shopkeepers and clerks peered from half-open doors, ready to slam them if my callers turned rowdy.

I squinted at the expanse of morning light, a golden glow that beamed behind clouds. The tang of ocean salt and fresh-caught fish rose from the harbour. Fearless, screeching seagulls swept down on massive wings before folding their flaps. They strutted to the corner where the cookhouse chef, during better days, had left buckets of swill for the hog farmers. A heavy wagon clattered by, pulled by two brown horses trotting side by side, straw-yellow manes as bright as their tails.

In the boss's room, the coolies were hurling chairs and dishes. I shrugged at the thumping and shattering. The boss had nothing worth pawning.

A shove sent me sprawling onto the road. "Where's your cock-head boss?"

"Don't know." Bony knuckles rapped my skull.

"You wipe his shit-hole, of course you know."

They started to kick me. I covered my head but left my spine exposed. I wouldn't surrender to puny vermin whose courage came from you-first-then-me-too numbers. I could battle three or four men at once but not a dozen. Fighting was crucial in this wretched life. Redbeards murdered us in America. We drowned in black waters at the border. Decent men such as me choked every day on the bile of our pride. If these fools killed me, then my ghost would stalk them all their luckless lives. They would never know a full night's sleep, no matter how powerful a god they prayed to.

When another horse and wagon approached, I started to uncoil, but suffered another ruthless kick in the gut. That heavy boot could have served a better purpose: pawned for passage home.

A sharp crack cut the air. Another. And another.

"Stop!" yelled a rail hand. "Ow!"

Wong Jun the stable keeper snapped his whip at the man, who cupped his cock and hopped about, dodging the snake.

Smack the road and die, I thought.

"Ten kicking one. Is that fair?" Wong demanded.

"That cockhead Boss Long owes us," someone said. "His book-man deducted return passage on each payday. Now they say no such money was ever taken."

"This one, he sleeps under Boss Long's bed." Wong pointed to me. "He knows nothing."

He cracked the whip. The men backed away but vowed to return. "Boss Long can't hide. *The tide drops and rocks emerge.*"

Wong crossed his arms and watched me get up. "Your vile boss ran off, and still you defend him."

"If they were just six turds, I would have squashed them flat."

He boarded his wagon and snapped the reins. "Your boss cheats them, you beat them, and your boatmen drown them."

Wong Jun truly pitied the railway hands, so it was my good fortune that he scorned unfair matches. Last month, unending rains churned the tent site into mud. You could hardly blame the residents for stealing wood from a nearby lumberyard to use as floors. Next morning, the enraged owner sought payment but refused the return of soggy planks. His workers led drunks and rabble rousers into the tent city to stake out battle lines. We had more men but our teeth had fallen out. We knew that if just one redbeard got even slightly bruised, then lines of guns from the naval base would blast out and chop us down. The hooligans needed only a small excuse to set Chinatown on fire. Wong had jumped on a crate and called for peace, offering payment to the lumberman at wholesale prices.

A cat slinked by, twitching its whiskers. Behind rain-streaked windows, store clerks watched me.

Screw your mothers, I thought, holding my head high and refusing to limp.

On the plate glass, gold-leaf words glinted from the light.

Bow Yuen, Import and Export. Its bank accounts were empty.

Kwong On Tai, General Merchants, fired all its porters two weeks ago.

Tai Wo Chong Kee, Dry Goods and Cereals, "donated" its last shipment of rice to the vermin.

Fook Lee Lung, Provisions and Supplies. Its head clerk went to the mainland to pursue accounts. Waste of time, as well as the steamer fare each way.

My business had failed too. I hired Native fellows, expert boatmen, to smuggle China men into America, onto empty islands and lonely bays in Washington. My oarsmen became rich overnight. Ticket sales were brisk until swine, redbeard and China men alike, started rival ventures. Two weeks ago, six bodies washed up on a beach near Port Townsend. Four of them had pigtails. It was my bad luck to have sold them passage. The other two were boatmen. Chinatown's wide-mouth know-alls warned of angry spirits rising to haunt me. But my passengers and I had done an honest trade, so I figured that burning incense and spirit money wasn't needed.

Then a week of fierce rain battered the town. Water gushed through the swollen ravine behind Chinatown and blocked our way to the downtown. In the rarely unruly harbour, stiff winds rose up and swept high tides over the piers. It was easy to imagine swollen hands reaching for me from the murky depths. I swallowed my losses and took to the pier some red apples, a simmered hen with head and legs intact, and six bowls of rice plus chopsticks and wine cups. Temple Keeper said four settings were enough, but I ignored him. Why not honour the boatmen too? This wasn't China; I could do rites any way I wanted. The persistent rain flattened the smoke from the sputtering candles, incense, and spirit money. Then the food offerings were cast into the water. Later that day, the clouds parted and the winds calmed. I slept well, but my business collapsed.

※

Wet Water Dog stepped from the teahouse, a cigar at his mouth. I pulled him aside. "When's the next ship?"

"Fleeing bad luck, Hok? Aren't you the one who has no fears?"

"Shall I go buy elsewhere?"

"Day after, and then one on Friday."

"Which is cheaper?"

"Friday. But the first boat is bigger. The ride is not so rough."

"I'll see you after I eat."

"Why didn't you get here earlier? I would have treated you to tea." When he waved his cigar in farewell, I grabbed it and inhaled my first bit of warmth this morning.

"Come," I yelled at his broad back. "Your fat stomach has plenty of room."

Not only was his trade booming, but he also spent his profits freely. One of the few men in Chinatown whose wife and children lived here, he didn't need our whores. Wet Water Dog had brought over his Second Lady, a woman of his choice and not his parents'. She was never seen on the streets, but rumour said she was elegant enough for Wet Water Dog to make good money by offering her to the brothel, if he wanted. That was good fortune: to have real choices.

The loud talk and dish clatter in the teahouse stopped for a moment. I blew cigar smoke into the meaty steam of the kitchen. Then, halfway across the hall, I exhaled at the men crammed at the window. They had dashed outside to watch with eager eyes as soon as those cockhead rail hands started banging at my door. The last public fight involving money and blood featured two whores cursing and clawing over a wealthy gold miner who enjoyed taking two women at once. Everyone in Chinatown had seen that.

A waiter slammed down a cup and filled it, holding the kettle high above my head, letting the distance cool the hot tea as it traveled down.

"Don't see you much these days," he said.

The lout had never been friendly, but now he wanted to know all my troubles and explain me to the rabble. I let the marble tabletop dull the pain in my hand and fingers. There was dried blood on my nose but no cracks in my skull, only soft craters. Another waiter shuffled by with a tray of leaf-wrapped sticky rice. I raised my hand through an aching shoulder. I could have called out, but that was for low-class men.

At long last, I was homeward bound. Time to perform a reverse salute: turn my back on Gold Mountain, bend forward, and release a caustic fart. I was no railway worm, trapped here without means to leave. I could go at any time. I wasn't a child, but men like me deserved coddling and comfort. I pictured Grandmother brewing old-fire soups to renew my strength, weaving sandals that fit me snugly, and scraping wax from my ears. She would thank the ancestors for my safe return and make sweet and salty puddings and dumplings for the altar. Villagers with clumsy excuses to visit would be greeted by my grandparents, fretting and ill-at-ease due to the rareness of guests. People would finally show my family some respect.

My thoughts were interrupted when a Native woman in a long

skirt came to my table to beg, a child in tow. I shook my head and cursed the slipshod cashier who let them in.

"Yang Hok." A familiar voice spoke the right tones. Then, in Chinook: "I am Mary."

I was on my feet.

My lips were moving but no words came out.

Yes, I recalled her. But why was she here?

She needed no invitation to sit and call for tea. The waiter grinned and gave me a knowing look. I nodded, trying to assert myself.

No doubt the fox wanted money. She would get none.

If only I had twisted away, declared "no" to my name, and shouted "no" to her. Then I would be soaring and cawing like a cocky crow. I should have shoved them aside and let the cashier evict them with his broom. Diners were watching, ears perked, awaiting my next round of shame.

Screw their mothers. They'd get no pleasure from me.

Bones jutted from Mary's taut, thin skin. Her face had lost much flesh. I hardened my heart. Her tattered shawl reeked of animal grease and wood smoke as she moved closer. I fought the urge to back off. Sipping hot tea with a toothy smile, she mentioned a brother-in-law bringing her from the mainland, a hardworking husband at home, and a third child on the way. She turned sideways to show me the bulge under her skirt. When I stayed quiet, she spoke of raising cattle during a dry summer.

I slid my food over. The rough under-edge of the plate grated against the marble.

She sniffed it and fed the boy, who grinned and swung his bare feet.

"Your son?" These were my first words, which I regretted.

"*Your* son." She pointed at me. "Peter."

She urged him to say the Chinese words for father, but he refused.

I shook my head.

No.

Was it possible?

How could I be sure?

She had said nothing to me three years ago. Now I wouldn't trust her even if she was the god that I prayed to. Of course the boy looked Chinese. Our two races shared black hair, small noses, and colour of skin and eyes. But she could have spread her legs for any number of China men, dogs in heat chasing Native women. I was just a handy basket for dumping the brat. The fox had likely heard about my steady job. But there would be no distracting me, no matter who the father had been. I was going home to get married. My children would be Chinese, not mix-blood.

"Want money?" I asked.

She nodded. "No food at home."

"Give you tomorrow."

"Thank you."

"Where do you live?"

"Lytton." And in her language, "Kumsheen."

"At the two rivers?"

I only knew about the Chinese temple in that railway town and the two great rivers flowing into each other, one blue and clear, the other milky and muddy. A know-all once proclaimed, "When you see those two rivers, you will know the soul of this land."

I waved to the waiter. While my guests stuffed their mouths, I could leap up and run. The eager diners could rush off to blab inflated versions of my panic. I didn't care: this bowl of water had been spilled already. In the end, all these men would stand side by side to champion me, even though they would never defend me aloud. The right thing to do was to take home all earnings. Nothing was more important than one's family. No Native woman should scoff at a China man. That demeaned our homeland.

"Trouble?" asked Mary. "Those men, they beat you."

The boy slurped oily juice from the saucers. When Mary told him to take rice, he gripped the spoon in a baby fist. No proof of me showed on the boy's face, so Mary couldn't plead her case by pointing to my forehead. Lucky me, I had no striking features, just faint eyebrows, even eyes, and a flat nose. The boy's teeth were white and solid; mine were piss yellow. People at home said Younger Brother was better-looking, so the two of us never got along. They said to him, "You're so handsome, you don't need a mirror."

Trying to learn how the fox had tracked me down would only waste my time. Native traders always passed through Victoria's Chinatown, where many people spoke Chinook. Finding me would have been easy. I cursed Heaven for choosing to help her. A few more days and I would have flown the coop. She must have noticed the great retreat of rail hands in the canyon and thought the boy too could go to China. Three years ago, she had vanished without a word. I went to call on her, but the engineer's missus had slammed the door in my face.

The boy was squeezing his crotch with both hands.

Mary pointed to the side door. "Hole?"

A chance to run. Not to Boss Long's; no doubt Mary had shrewdly tailed me for a while. In our days together, as soon as I mentioned the head, she smiled and knew the tail. She had also been learning to read English. Uncle See could hide me; she would search Chinatown in vain.

A teahouse customer stopped the mother and boy. "Someone squats there."

The boy moaned and hopped from foot to foot. Mary frowned. "I buy clothes for you," I said.

She nodded and danced the boy to the outhouse. I ran to the cashier, paid, and bolted.

All my money was marked for China. It was clear as rainwater in a barrel: I needed to buy gifts, after bragging too much to Grandfather about my success in hawking boat tickets. My years away had let ugly rumours fester in the village. Only lavish gifts and loud talk could restore the family honour. Cascades of shiny copper coins, scattered like fistfuls of chicken feed, would brighten Grandmother's lifelong gloom.

Heading to Uncle See's store, I cursed Mary. How dare she suddenly appear like this? I needed to dig up my caches of money and go demand payment of debts. Some borrowers would show a short memory while mine proved very long. Yes, I would prop my feet on the table and gloat over friends snared in Gold Mountain shit. I debated seeing Rainbow one last time, as well as the strutting need to buy her a farewell gift. If only I had fled the teahouse as soon as Mary had appeared. She wasn't the first woman to come chasing after the father of her child. At those times, even I had joined the lively taunting.

"Go wed a long-sighted girl. She won't see the boy's face."

"Let the mix-blood one grow a pigtail and learn Chinese. But will he eat stinky tofu?"

"Falling leaves land on the roots."

After the railway, I had gone to a town where redbeard and Native women sold their bodies to men. Not Mary. She kept house for a railway engineer and his family in a neat little cottage. Her hands got callused from chopping wood and washing clothes. Her employer, an oddly thoughtful fellow, told her to take the household linens to the laundry. The first time she lit up the dowdy washhouse, my boss had caught me eyeing her and warned me not to meddle.

On reaching Uncle See's, I slumped into a dark corner of the loft and fumbled under the cot for his opium pipes. The lamp was easy to light, but my hand shook while mounting the sticky black drug. Finally I stretched out, raised myself on one arm, and set the pipe over the lamp. Sweet fumes floated me into dreams and scenes where each moment was pleasing. The pain and shame from the vermin's beating and kicking eased as my mind and face loosened.

I'm with Mary, on a Sunday morning while her boss's family attends church. She puts away a huge breakfast to be re-served as the midday meal. I nibble at smoked fish and fried meats, kidneys, and pork chops. Eyeing the cutlery on the white cloth, I ponder which piece to steal.

We enter her tiny room and close the door. She giggles at the speed at which I strip off my clothes, the thrust of my eagerness. My lips press her ears and neck. She flings a ruffled underskirt at me and flees. I chase her, my cock a flagpole. Laughing, she dashes to the dining room and keeps me at bay across the table. She dodges each time I dart to one side. We knock over a chair. In the big bedroom, we land on the bed's satiny covers. We stand and stare at the mirror. We're brother and sister with our tan skin and dark hair. We're man and wife, mulling over our bridal bed and the number of children yet to spill forth.

We hear the front door slam and then the voices of the engineer and his wife. They're bickering. We rush to Mary's room. I duck under the bed, and she leaps into the blankets. The lady of the house comes to summon her. I poke out my head to watch Mary dress. After a while, I leave by the back door when the family is busy eating. On my next visit, Mary pulls me under her bed onto a blanket. Our bodies twist on the hard floor.

Dusk was falling when I went down to Uncle See's storefront. The cat scampered away from me, mewling. The boarders loitered on the sidewalk, bent over water pipes and pails of bubbling water. Boxes of vegetables were laid out for men returning from farms and brickyards. A stray dog crept close to the entrance.

"Yang Hok!" someone called. "Where did you run to? Your landlord nailed planks over every door and window at your place."

"I return to China." I basked in the murmurs of envy.

"Taking your son?" The waiter from the teahouse lurked in the shadows. He thrust the boy forward.

"What's he doing here?" I demanded.

"The woman pushed him at me. She said one word, 'China,' then she ran. She must have told the boy that more food was coming because he didn't follow her."

"You didn't stop her?"

"She was weeping in a loud voice."

I grabbed his collar. "You idiot, I'll make you weep."

❧

The next day, late in the afternoon, I went to the fancy headquarters of the Chinese Council, ruled by the slick talk of our merchant princes. Last year, they finally addressed the frightful mess of our streets. Hatchet-men chased runaway whores and threatened decent folk who sheltered them. Pickpockets plagued the game halls. Storekeepers fended off burglars. Every ship from China landed bumpkins with feet dancing in the clouds. They fell for oily words promising jobs and leads. Soon they were begging on street corners. Ancient grudges got settled with knives and guns in dark alleys. Worried travellers bypassed Victoria or cut short their stays. That dropping trade panicked the merchant princes.

They formed the Council to deal with shady China men and foreign bullies. The Council paid rewards for catching killers and quashed petty feuds. It bailed out the wrongly jailed and hired lawyers. Council preened itself like an actor singing the virgin's role as the redbeard police visited Chinatown less often. But this good work devoured stacks of cash. Council then levied a fee of two dollars on every China man, payable upon his boarding a homebound ship, the moment when he was most likely to have cash on hand. Taking money from hardened sojourners was trickier than extracting their diseased teeth, so the Council sent burly guards to the docks. Every man had to show a receipt for two dollars before being allowed to board. No receipt, no departure.

The Council managed its affairs from Tai Yuen, a general store with branches on the mainland. The grand old firm didn't bother with street trade, so its storefront was a stately parlour with brushwork scrolls on the walls. Rosewood chairs and tables, carved and gleaming, replaced bins and barrels. All was for show, because the tycoons met at teahouses and sealed deals there.

I joined the straggling lineup at Tai Yuen to pay my two dollars.

"My money is my blood," one man said. "Who needs Council?"

"I asked the police about this extortion. They call this a China-town matter."

"Did you see the guards at the docks?" asked a third man. "Bigger than Shandong men! No one gets by them."

No one dared voice the biggest complaint. Why didn't the big-wigs put in more of their money? All they did was sit and brag about their farts while scraping profits off the backs of coolies.

Of course, anyone who challenged those tyrants would get no help from Council should he ever land in trouble. The merchant who represented him on Council by virtue of surname or home ties gave a twisted warning: "If redbeards see that we China men don't stand as one, then for sure they will kick us even harder."

The business kings never figured that the rail hands would turn around and use that same phrase to extort food and shelter from them.

Mister Secretary, the old boor, was on duty. In the streets, he chased men for whom he might pen a letter or explain its words from far away. For him, any other fellow who could read and write was a deadly rival. He always chortled and asked for my teacher's name, well aware that my small-town tutor was known only as

"Teacher." Mister Secretary bragged about his learned bloodline being centuries long and studded with royal appointments.

"Clever boy, Hok!" A sly smile wormed out of his face. "You gained a son and saved the bride price."

"The woman ran before I could ensure he was truly mine." I held out two dollars, keen to leave, tempted to wave in his face my other wad of cash, just amassed for the trip home.

"Where's the boy?" He rested his brush and leaned back. He enjoyed making us wait; it was the only time a scrawny scholar held sway over the rabble.

"Mission School." I pointed at the lineup. "Hurry, here's my two dollars."

He took a sip of tea. "Didn't the Pastor tell you?"

"Tell me what?"

"That Pastor is a coward." Mister Secretary stretched his words. "You have three choices. To leave the child at the Mission School, you must pay it fifty dollars. If you want to save your money, then you take the child to China, or return the child to the mother. If the latter, you must bring back a letter witnessed by a manager of a Tai Yuen store."

"Fifty dollars? That's a man's life!" I turned to the men behind me. "You ever hear of this?"

"Council and Mission School work jointly now," Mister Secretary said. "You won't get a receipt until you settle matters about the boy."

"Dogs don't chase mice! The child is none of your business!"

He dismissed me with a wave of his hand.

"I just bought passage from Wet Water Dog!" I protested. "My ship leaves tomorrow."

The old man pushed himself up. He stroked the straggles under his chin. I wanted to use them to bounce his head like a ball on the table.

"We Chinese are a refined people," he said for all to hear. "It's best to not mix with lesser races, but if men cannot control themselves, then they must shoulder the burden of sons and daughters born in foreign lands. Council aims to restore order for everyone here; therefore all those children must be cared for."

Pompous ass. Before reaching the front door, I knew exactly how to sidestep him.

2

A SUPERIOR MAN MOVES SWIFTLY (1885)

The sternwheeler passed so close to the rocky islands between Victoria and the mainland that I almost shouted to the captain on the bridge. But no redbeard in a uniform would heed a China man squawking like a hen on the butcher block.

At the clang of the boat's bell, sea lions on pebbly beaches rose up on flippers to watch us. The giant slugs were strange creatures, bulb eyes of an ox, nose and whiskers of a wise cat, and gleaming planks for legs. I didn't fear them; they couldn't move fast enough to catch me.

A redbeard retched at the railing. My never-sick stomach did me proud. Me, I was born under Earth, so my stomach stood rock-solid. Peter likely emerged under Water, setting our Elements to war and foretelling a life-long battle between us. Earth blocked and soaked up Water, but floodwaters swept away months of backbreaking work on land. Worse, Earth created Metal while Water nurtured Wood, two more deadly rivals. Metal chewed into wood, but wood wore down steel edges. Water moved faster than earth, but when the boat reached Yale, I planned to drug the boy with Rainbow's sleeping potion, dump him with his people, and then buy the needed letter from Tai Yuen store.

I was hardly the first or only man to heave his mix-blood off-spring onto the Native mother. Men—Chinese, redbeard, African—all with proud names and upright cocks, prowled this land like wolves. They came from far away, where their mothers set standards high above the talents of local women. Low-level clerks like Mister Secretary shouldn't snigger. He and his Council superiors polished the boots of the redbeards, trying to make Chinatown shine. They wanted the Jesus men at churches to announce this scheme to help mix-blood children so that white ladies of standing would visit the fancy-goods shops of Chinatown.

When we left Victoria, the boy stayed close to me, as if he had guessed my plan. We took clean air at a side door, away from the murky stink of cattle. Wind spat stinging spray at us. The laden boat rode low and let the brat squat over the unending rush of white bub-bles. For once he made no trouble. In Victoria, we had taken beds at Uncle See's store. But the brat chased the mouser and yanked its tail; the cat ran off and never returned. The brat tracked mud over the just-washed floor and stole fruit from the patron god's altar. Uncle See whipped him with a bamboo switch and muttered, "*Young, he pilfers hens; old, he pilfers gems.*" I watched for a while, pleased, but broke them apart before the boy got hurt.

Peter darted away to the middle of the boat. I shouted for him to stay. Nothing. He hadn't said a word to me. Maybe he was mute, with secret ways to tell things to his mother. His sulky mouth worked fine, bolting meals at the cookhouse. Thank Heaven he hadn't wailed for his mother; I would have wrung his neck, quick as killing a hen. In fact, he ate quickly, letting us escape our fellow diners and their rubbish talk.

"Give the boy to Rainbow! Your whore has no other way to get a child."

"He's got Hok's eyes and nose. Grandpa will smile, even if the boy is darker."

"Look at him gobble rice! In China, he can grow all he can eat!"

The boy stroked the calves that tottered on skinny legs and chafed at their ropes. Cables ran from the walls to the animals' throats, pinning them in the boat's centre. Too bad the brat wasn't tied down the same way. Two cows bellowed and he joined in. Beasts on the other side of the boat answered. On the deck, red-beard cowhands played cards with a scrawny China man, probably their cook. A blotch of rough red skin marred his forearm, as if hot oil had scalded him. All morning he avoided my eye, fearful that I might join his game and raise the stakes beyond his reach.

The flat grey sea hinted that my coming trip to China might be smooth, but I knew better. On my trip over, rough waves rose up to delay meals—no great loss, given the slop that was served as food. Smells of shit and vomit swirled as gamblers bickered and fought. Scorpion "brotherhoods" harassed feeble men to extort cash. There were even one or two deaths. The trick was to spot the bodies before their fragrance seeped into the bunk as a lasting stink. Typhoons churning through the China Sea almost overturned the ship. In a month's time from now, when I reached Hong Kong, there would be hurly-burly crowds at the docks and in the streets. For Grandmother and Younger Sister, I needed to buy gold earrings, heavy enough to impress the neighbours but not too costly.

I didn't want to buy a gift for Younger Brother or answer his questions. I planned to ignore them. The sojourners who returned to our village never talked about life abroad. Instead they chased local news. Who died? Whose sons and daughters got married? Which fields changed hands and for how much money? What new shops opened in town?

Day after day, they asked the same questions, as if checking for liars, as if they trusted no one to tell the truth, as if what played out in front of them wasn't real life but a scene from the opera. The comforts of long-ago lives were lost. They had been coolies abroad but came home with no honours. They squatted in the market and waved at people, no matter how slight the acquaintance, or joined the tail end of conversations. Me, I planned to tell lofty tales to impress loyal followers.

This Fraser River, for example, swallowed harmless landlubbers as well as mangled corpses hurled overboard by boiler explosions. Hot-headed captains ordered stokers to shovel in fuel in order to fight the current, to brag about new records for speed of passage. But too much coal burnt too quickly, and boilers failed to contain the rising pressure. Villagers would laugh to hear about redbeard stupidity.

At the river's mouth, the sudden rush of water almost spun the boat around. The giant circle of paddles beat faster as black clouds burst from the smokestack. The brown river held trees with tangled roots, planks green with mold, lopsided branches, even a heavy wooden wheel. The debris floated past miners who mumbled to themselves as they shovelled river sludge into sluice boxes, sifting for grains of gold. These grizzled China men refused to believe that the gold was all gone. Truth was, if any treasure was left, then you would see greedy redbeards working right beside them, cursing and belching.

Flocks of ducks and geese lifted like dark nets, honking over the marshes. Along both shores, Native people landed fish with spears and nets, and hung the orange meat on racks. Dugouts with soaring prows were beached beside nimble canoes. Every summer, vast numbers of Native men and women passed through Victoria heading for these fishing grounds. They stopped again on their way home and were welcomed by redbeard and Chinese merchants alike. At New Westminster's waterfront, sailboats brought in gleaming fish. Fearless seagulls swooped down to the canneries to feast on the bloody, stinking offal. This was odd about Gold Mountain: no one should starve amid its abundance, yet jobless rail hands were too weak to fish and too poor to buy the needed tools.

At the foredeck, the boy waved and called to Native children on the shore helping to fish and picking berries. Toddlers skipped out from makeshift lean-tos, clutching food to their mouths. At least I knew now that my son could speak. Too bad it was not Chinese. He wanted these would-be playmates to turn sour on themselves and envy his travel. To their credit, they stared back, unmoved, and watched the upper decks of the boat where redbeard men flaunted brocade vests and ladies swayed in hooped skirts. I waited for a gust of river wind to snag those cloth bells, lift the women like kites, and show everyone their underpants.

A piercing whistle trilled over a train's steady chugging. Its long black engine swung into view, spewing smoke while pistons thrust and fell at the wheels, stroke after stroke, pushing and pulling the spokes. The cars that trundled behind were square and flat, meek as slaves cowed by a tyrant master. A train grew longer when cars were added, then shrank when they were removed. It was a snake that could not be killed, even after being hacked to pieces. After the train vanished around a bend, its dark fog lingered.

"Don't attack a snake if you can't kill it," Grandfather had warned. "It will tail you for a hundred years."

"Hey, you!"

A cowboy waved at me. His cigar hung over a grey beard, flecked with bits of straw.

His friend, sullen from losses, stomped away. Grey Beard grinned through his bushy whiskers. He took me for an ox-skin lantern, dim and thick. I had watched them from afar and seen no cheating. I went over and squatted into the smells of machine oil, fish, and redbeard sweat.

"Watch out!" he shouted.

I turned. The boy had fallen off. Grey Beard hurled himself across the deck. His friends leapt up and yelled at the bridge.

A bell clanged.

Grey Beard tore off his boots and dived into the river.

The boat lurched and slid backward at downriver speed. Sharp hooves clattered as cows bellowed. Passengers on the middle deck gripped their fancy hats, leaning out for a better view. Crewmen ran onto a ledge and launched a small boat.

I flattened myself against the wall. No swimmer, I was useless as a fart. Did the redbeards know the boy was mix-blood? The dogs at their feet got treated better. They were idiots to think they were saving one of their own. They would complain that I fooled them and then demand payment for the bother.

"Couldn't you watch your boy?" demanded the cook. "I was winning."

Mister Secretary and the Council in Victoria would laugh at me if I told them about my boy drowning, even though children fell off boats all the time and this river was known for death. In Gold Mountain, mud smothered even honest stories.

✳

The boy lived by clinging to river debris. Passengers cheered the rowboat's return, waving hats and handkerchiefs as if the sailors were a winning army. Then they swung around as one to send me a look of fused disgust. In Mary's absence, I soaked up the blame.

In China, no one ever panicked about river drownings. People might throw out a rope, but no one ever leapt into the water. They feared how fierce ghosts under the surface tugging at a thrashing victim might grab the would-be rescuer and pull him down instead.

"Bring a wet dog to shore and it will bite you!" Grandmother had told us children many times.

A crewman thrust a bottle of whisky at Grey Beard and pointed to the upper deck. Men raised their flasks and hollered praise. Grey Beard yelled back, laughing, as the sternwheeler resumed its trip.

The sailors brought me the brat, wrapped in a coarse blanket. I clenched my fists to keep from slapping him. My faults were exposed in public. I had lost face. I had failed to watch my child and failed to rescue him. I didn't know how to swim. I was a shining example for the redbeards' claim that China men brought no value to Gold Mountain.

The brat couldn't avoid trouble for half a second. The blanket belonged to the boat. It needed to be returned. He would go ashore naked.

He cried and whimpered, burying his face into my neck. I wanted to push him away but sat and held him. The China man brought a mug of hot water and told me to keep the boy warm, as if I had no common sense. He asked who the mother was and where we were going. I didn't answer, knowing he would dash into Chinatown's teahouses to shout this tale with his big cannon mouth.

Yale's China men would shake their heads. "A redbeard risked his life to rescue a China man's mix-blood child? You're dreaming! Those people hate anyone who's not their colour."

I went and thanked Grey Beard, who was also wrapped in a stiff blanket. He offered his bottle to me, but I shook my head and looked for signs of madness in him.

The brat seemed fated to live. Or maybe some cruel god had toyed with him, providing a bit of luck for now that would only be yanked away later. Maybe the boy's stepfather had taught him how to stay above the river. I was truly grateful to Grey Beard. If the boy had vanished into the water, then I would be doomed to spend the rest of my life glancing over my shoulder for the lad's half ghost, half shadow. At any time, a young man could stop at my table at a teahouse, kneel, and cry "Father!" to claim his birthright. If this happened in front of my trueborn children or my wife's family, then my face could never be recovered.

※

I carried the boy off the boat into the swampy reek of fresh fish. Crates of shiny salmon, their blue-grey eyes stilled, were waiting to be loaded onto a steamer. The same dull gaze clouded the eyes of Chinese rail hands who squatted nearby. They were as thin and pinched as their fellow Chinese in Victoria. Loose rags hid bony frames. Some wore flimsy straw sandals. Here, living near forest and river, these men enjoyed one small benefit. They could go shoe-less without townsfolk looking down their noses and calling them savages.

They didn't turn to watch me carry a naked Native child in my jacket. Those who crouched by the main road lifted grimy palms, seeking alms. I strode by without stopping. These fools needed to see that this town was too small, too poor to help them. Yale had been the hub of railway work but the road was finished. Soon skies would darken with rain and snow. The cold of a Gold Mountain winter crept in as quiet and deadly as an assassin. At least our Victoria merchants were pompous enough to seek help from China's Consul stationed in San Francisco. I doubted they would succeed: the emperor didn't sit high enough to see across the ocean.

A swirl of familiar voices and smells swept me to Chinatown. We bumped against giant draft horses pulling wagons over gouged roads. Flat roofs shot out from shops and saloons to shelter pedestrians from the weather. Windows were boarded over, and the paint on many walls and signs was faded and peeling. At a cookhouse, the sizzle of oil and garlic and black beans made my mouth water and brought China to mind. I wanted to dump the boy in a back alley and dash back to the boat.

Men rushed onto the road, hooting and shouting. They pointed to a second-floor porch with a wooden sign painted in black, red, and gold.

Clouds Clear Tower was Soohoo's building.

Soohoo last year brought in a woman who sparked a storm of dizzy glee, even in distant Victoria. Men dubbed her, in awe, Goddess. Her fame was due to her perfection. Raised since childhood in Guangzhou's most lavish brothel, she had been dismissed from the ranks of the elite courtesans after the Governor accused her of laughing at his "little precious" with her friends. At that time, Goddess's skills were not mature; otherwise her owners never would have banished her. Like the rest of us, she too was second-rate goods sent abroad.

Her secret talent was being able to sense when a man approached climax. She then forestalled it. She shifted her grip. She stroked his eggs. She twisted away. She kept his hands from gaining release. The detour was always blissful. Then she smiled and re-engaged, extending the session until the man gasped and begged for mercy. Men left Clouds Clear Tower beaming and smiling because no spurting meant keeping the male *yang* essence that prolonged life and produced sons.

The men in the road yelled and pranced like schoolboys at end of term. A woman emerged in bright silks but her bound feet tottered away from the broken railing. I craned my neck and caught a glint of golden jewellery. The brat's wriggling stopped me from seeing. Her tinkling voice teased us but vanished under a torrent of lewd remarks.

She was a prize tale for home, for men in teahouses, for idlers squatting around the market. Returned sojourners would revisit moments spent in her bed, summon memories to restore saliva to their now dry mouths. She alone soothed years of anguish in Gold Mountain because coolies could never afford a woman of her high calibre in China. Her day was just starting; the bed-sheets and her wit should be fresh.

I had to find a place to dump the boy.

She withdrew and a road packed with men's jutting hopes emptied out.

Any worm would gladly watch the boy for a few pennies, but a smart one might sell the boy for thirty cents.

❋

The dry goods store was dark as a latrine with a dank, airless smell. Pricks of light glowed from incense sticks. The house gods stood duty on their gilded altar, calmly watching the piled-up canvas, stacked blankets, and shelves of dishes and tools. By the door, when I hefted a grindstone, its shadow left sharp lines in the thick dust. What did this fool storekeeper think he was doing? Hoarding rice until a famine came along to raise his prices?

He prodded us to the back, crowing that no other shop in Chinatown sold children's clothing. "All Native people come here because redbeard shops scorn their business. Look at those people: lots of children running everywhere."

I used Mother's words to show my expertise. "Only well-sewn clothing, with room for growing."

"This your son?" The merchant beamed. "Strong ox, tall horse."

"I take him to his people."

"A superior man!"

"No choice." I mentioned Council's new rule.

"They're not the emperor." He would boost me onto his shoulders and wipe my shit-hole if asked to do so.

The brat shook his head at the shirts and pants that the merchant put against him. He grabbed brighter colours with thicker cloth and higher prices.

"How can I find his mother?" I asked. "She is near Lytton."

"Native people are angry there. Redbeards steal their land."

"Who can help me?"

"Everyone is leaving."

"And Soohoo?"

"He has time to die but no time to get sick. Go see Goddess and enjoy yourself."

Too bad I had just made a solemn vow to the boy, during the last leg of the boat trip. It was an about-turn. I planned to learn where Mary lived and take the boy there.

Not right away. My pole bobbed up at the prospect of Goddess. Good thing I wore snug western pants. If not, everyone would have seen my jut and known my eagerness.

"You can trust me." The merchant grinned. "Native women leave their children here while they visit the other stores."

I went off.

When the brat had napped on the boat, I didn't lay him down for fear of waking him. His breath was soft and steady as a maid fanning a tyrant mistress. He kicked and stirred in his sleep, thick eyelashes twitching. He smelled of river mud and fish. In China, village grannies used colourful sashes to sling grandchildren on their backs with heavy, dozing heads. The women stayed in the shade and avoided the river.

My son, my bone and flesh, would be dead if not for Grey Beard. That cowboy saved a life; he acted as a superior man. *When places lack law, heroes emerge tall.*

The redbeards here owned no dogs that would lick up smelly shit. Instead, they found scrawny cats like us for the dirty job. They claimed that fleas with diseases leapt from our clothes to infect everyone. They hated how we ate pickles from China instead of chewing local beef. They called us heathens for bowing to ancestors instead of singing songs to their Heavenly Father. They said our lower wages cheated redbeards of their rightful jobs.

Screw their mothers, we told ourselves. Our people had rules for trade and business, clan and country. Redbeards prospered in China; why shouldn't we do the same here? We knew hard work, and how to open a shop with scraped-together capital.

But, when Grey Beard had jumped overboard, all such thoughts flapped off like a startled bird. Up to that moment, I was set on getting rid of the boy. Even if I had known how to swim, I would have backed away and muttered good riddance. That brat had entered my life suddenly; he could leave it in the same way.

Now, I needed to become a superior man and soar with the gods. Had I learned nothing from five years in Gold Mountain? Did I want to bring home nothing but the shit stains inside my pants? Didn't I want to be better than the shit-hole redbeards? This would be the best story to tell, the one with a great surprise. The boy must be raised well, safe from spiteful stepmothers. He shouldn't be taunted about his Chinese father. He ought to be embraced by those aunts and uncles who loved him. He should be fed well, and have warm clothes to wear. The best and only person to do this was Mary.

※

The merchant proved honest about Goddess but not his child-minding skill.

"He ran off! I rushed outside but didn't know which way to go. His people live over there!"

China men were leery of Native villages, fearful of sudden death, or worse, being outsmarted by the locals. I hurried around cabins and plots of vegetables. A black chicken with a bright red comb scuttled through fresh laundry hanging among wood smoke. At weather-beaten sheds I smelled straw and dung, heard horses stirring. The village was quiet. People were fishing at the river. Maybe the boy had come here with his mother and knew people he could hide with.

I called out.

Did the brat even know that he had an English name? Good thing it was one that I could pronounce.

An old woman sat in front of a house, weaving a basket. A nearby dog barked and lunged at me, but its sturdy leash held.

I greeted the woman in Chinook. She calmed the dog and dismissed me with a wave.

By the river, I spotted the red and blue of Peter's new clothes. Children were pitching pebbles into a ring of white stones. With every toss, a child shouted.

I went from behind to nab the brat with one swoop and avoid trouble. His shoulder was thin as paper; his shirt was gritty with sand.

"We go eat." I spoke in Chinook, cheerful as possible.

He pulled away. His dark eyes hardened.

"We go to Mother," I said. "Go home."

I scooped him up. He screamed and punched my face. I twisted my head from side to side, wanting to slam him to the ground. How dare he hit an adult? Was he loose in the brain? This demon!

A man ran up, shouting in Chinook. "Put down! Let boy go!"

"My son," I declared.

"Boy not China."

He yanked the boy away and set him on his feet. I shoved the man aside and took the brat's hand. As we headed off, the man leapt from behind and threw me to the ground. We sprawled onto the rocky sand, hands clawing at each other's neck, bucking to get on top. The children squealed in delight. I rammed my fist into his face. He slammed his elbow into my gut. He was bigger and stronger than most China men. We grappled and twisted, panting with effort. He smelled of sweat and fish.

I was still trying to flatten him when the dry-goods merchant shouted, "Sam, this man buy clothes for boy! Sam, this man buy clothes for boy!"

We rolled away, cursing each other, as the children danced off. I grabbed the boy and checked my clothes for rips and tears. He brought nothing but trouble.

New voices arose farther down the river, where Chinese rail hands and Native men shoved and shouted, fighting over something. With faces painted red and yellow, the Native men and their beast-skin clothes were fearsome. They towered over my people, brandishing stone-head clubs that took both arms to wield. They could have saved their strength; sledgehammers weren't needed to smash sparrow eggs. My attacker ran to join them. Clearly the fool enjoyed fights. The China men backed off.

I dragged the boy away from the water. At the Chinese camp overlooking the beach, rail hands had emerged from makeshift tents.

One barefoot fellow muttered, "Hungry dogs fight for vomit."

"Whose vomit?" I asked.

Bare Feet opened his mouth, but a sudden wracking cough bent him over.

"Another stupid thing 'ran off,'" said a second man.

"The Natives, they don't care about us," I pointed out.

"Their river is holy. They keep it clean."

He pointed. A beam from a collapsed dock had snagged a corpse by a shirt sleeve. It floated face down, its pigtail sliding on the water surface like an eel. The feet were bloated and dark. Wide pant legs flattened out like oars.

"Last week, some stupid thing filled his pockets with stones, tied a rock to his neck, and walked into the river. Two brothers carried him onto land and buried him. Four days later, one of the brothers 'got fragrant,' even though he had been eating well and laughing. Now, another stupid thing ran off. Of course, no one will touch the body."

"They need to pay someone," I said.

"It's fish season. Any Native who touches something dirty can't go near the river."

"Three gone in one week means angry ghosts all around," said Bare Feet. "You don't know who sleeps beside you, a man or a piece of wood."

"Me, I like salted fish," I said.

"Don't call them that, you pig head," he said. "Those who run off, they have clout. Back home, my landlord passed away smoking opium in town. The grannies said, 'Dirty things will follow him to the village.' 'Hold the funeral outside the gates,' said the elders. But the landlord's people pushed their way in and brawled at the funeral. Everyone lost face. Then, three women gave birth and each baby died before a full month."

In my village, the pigs and chickens sickened and died, one year. The *feng-shui* man blamed a family after one of its members threw out corpse-washing water by the bridge. After a long quarrel, that family hired a priest to cleanse the village. Only then had the live-stock flourished.

At the river, the China men tried to leave, but the Natives blocked the way. As the shouting and shoving resumed, two old women hurried up, grumbling and shaking their walking-sticks.

I recalled my friend Poy and said, "A superior man doesn't fear the dead."

"That's why they're so few," Bare Feet sneered.

I marched the boy to the beach. The tallest China man wore a mashed brown hat.

"Let me handle that." I pointed to the river. "How much will you pay?"

Mashed Hat backed away, his eyes darting and wary. The Native men stared at Peter as though he was a three-legged chicken. They chatted and gestured among themselves. The boy tugged at me to go but I stood firm, unafraid to fight again.

"Your lucky day!" Someone clapped Mashed Hat on the shoulder.

"This one isn't scared to touch corpses."

The man called Sam spoke fluent Chinese.

He wasn't Native, he was *jaap jung*, mix-blood. He seemed to know Mashed Hat, or at least how to get him to take action on the matter.

"Get the big wheelbarrow. Let him bury that thing. Look at the sky, it darkens. But you need money to pay."

"How much?" Mashed Hat asked me.

"A dollar."

"No one has money."

"Something must be paid. You know that." I tightened my grip on the brat's hand. To slap him in front of his people would only bring me grief.

"Anyone with money has left already," said Mashed Hat.

"My shovel goes deep," I said. "I put heavy rocks on top."

"A dollar, it's too much."

"Animals won't dig up anything. The one who ran off, for sure he'll approve." I was certain of winning.

"No one takes a day to dig a grave."

"These people will harass you until you do something. *Pock-face lady looks in a mirror; the more she looks, the madder she gets*. It's time to put an end to this."

"Bury him," said another rail hand. "I'll go ask men in the stores to donate."

The crowd dispersed. I looked Sam up and down and said, "Who's your father?"

He squatted to talk to the brat, and patted his head before stomping off without answering.

Another win for me.

My friends and I often asked mix-bloods that question. We looked past the man facing us and inquired instead about his father, that man's name and village, and when he had come to Canada. All mouth and no heart, we pretended to have known his father, or kinsmen from his home village, or stories they had told. But both sides knew full well that most such fathers were long gone with little left behind.

Mashed Hat's men brought a cart rolling on a wheel squeaky enough to waken centuries of the dead. With a scarf around my nose, I waded into the water, using a rope and rake to snare the corpse. I held my breath against the stench. Even wet, the man weighed no more than a head of lettuce.

I loaded the cart and called for the boy. He didn't move, as if he was deaf. Chinese children knew better than to dawdle, knowing that a tight slap or hard knuckle waited close by. I looped a rope around my waist, tied the other end to the boy's wrist, and yanked him toward the graveyard.

I thought about telling this burial tale at home, in the market. People would cringe and slip away, of course, ever fearful of killing airs. But they also respected sojourners, who were hearts and lungs for families crushed by debts or crippled by bad luck. People knew full well that life abroad was bruised and swollen with the anguish of their men. Those lives were wrapped in far too much shame to ever be discussed, aloud or in whispers. It was much easier to listen to an account of a no-name stranger and picture his tragic end.

The China men at the camp scurried away, seeing ghosts ahead and thieves behind, so scared that they never thanked me for diverting the anger of the Native people. I should have let the Natives beat them soundly. Maybe the China men wanted that: bloody deaths instead of ones by starvation.

Victoria was home to mix-blood men and women like Sam. They looked more sullen than their mothers' people, whose men eked a life from fishing and chopping wood, whose women went door to door, selling berries and handmade baskets. Redbeard children hurled mud balls and rocks at them, and then ran to hide behind their parents.

The mix-bloods who lived among us had swaggered about with their noses high in the air. Some had Chinese faces but they never asked about China. I kicked them out of the game hall because they never had much money. Wong Jun hired one to tend his horses, but the fellow kept staring at the ground, as though fearful of seeing his own face among the men of Chinatown. He lasted two weeks at the job and left without asking for his wages.

Redbeards loudly disdained the Chinese as being one and the same as Native people. We China men never let that pass. They didn't weave cotton or silk but wore animal skins. They didn't grow rice or wheat to make noodles or bread. They ate instead whatever grew wild. Without earthenware, they served food on mats. Without writing, they didn't make books. Mind you, our esteemed homeland produced plenty of fancy cloths and dishware but couldn't stop the redbeards from trouncing us at war. We weren't even strong enough to piss at them.

3

A Fear of Corpses on the Railway (Spring 1881)

Fire in my stomach woke me. I lay among the snoring men and prayed for the pain to go away. I wasn't a coward, but the forest's rustling and crackling never stopped, not even during daylight. Creatures darted through the bushes and yelped after quick battles. Birds swooped in on silent wings. Strange voices wailed under the moon. Trees grew higher and fatter than those of China while tatters of white fluff hung from them like mourning banners. We heard stories of giant bears, as tall as two or three humans and as wide as temple doors, slashing open men's bodies from neck to cock with one swing of the paw.

I took a candle and went out, blanket on my shoulders, boots loose on my feet. The cool damp night hinted at more rain. At the latrine, I set my light on a log. It was still too dark to see my hands, but I squatted and held my pants off the mud. When hot liquid gushed out, I cursed Head Cook. He told us the drinking water was boiled, yet we crewmen always suffered loose stomachs.

Something hurtled through a crash of branches. A jagged howling pierced the air, rose and fell without stop. I covered my ears, but it sounded as though a woman was wailing, bent over a coffin and rubbing her hair against the wood. Her bawling lamented a coming life of anguish. It begged Heaven for strength and pity. It hung in the night until my candle suddenly went out. I lost my breath and then tried to run, but my body refused to move. The dark was so deep that I had to touch my eyes to see if they were open or closed. I forced myself to breathe and waited for death.

In the morning, Long Life brayed over the tents. "Hok, was that you weeping and praying like a little girl to the Ghost Subjugator?"

"Someone had a foul dream," I said. "Wasn't me."

The crewmen called me a maiden with dainty feet. It was my shit luck that Long Life had the bed spot next to mine. Poy slept on my other side but he kept quiet.

"Hok went to the latrine," Long Life said, "but got scared. He soiled his pants!"

"Screw you, it's mud."

When Pig Boy died that afternoon, I knew that last night's howling had foretold his death.

I had pegged him for an early end. He came here alone, so family and friends were avoiding him, for good reason. His eyes twitched. He talked to himself. If someone called, he stopped and squatted, as if he needed to think, no matter if he was walking or working.

We were at war with giant trees that fought back. Our work chopped down too many of them, draining and sapping the ground of its male *yang* forces. The day before Pig Boy's passing, a saw ripped through Four Square's hand when tree bark snagged his sleeve and his partner daydreamed. Blood spurted out. Poy fell last week from a springboard jammed high in a tree where he chopped at the narrower trunk. The pain in his shoulder still made him groan. And when Salty Wet pushed a giant log, the wedges sank into the ground and the tree rolled onto his ankle.

We itched to wager money on who would die first. Only time stood between one of us and death. Twenty-eight coolies tramped into the forest each day, so the odds, plus the size of the pot, were good. Then some cockhead whispered, "What if the man's ghost claims a share of the prize? What if his ghost climbs onto the winner's back for eternity?"

We dropped our axes and saws and turned to the safety of dice and dominoes.

Pig Boy died on a grey afternoon, dank and dim as any day in our outdoor prison. The forest hid the sky and screened the light. Treetops were unseen until they landed and we gathered at their feet like gloating hunters. Steady rain fell. A roof of leaves shielded us, but the damp caused axes and saws to stick. The chuk, chuk, chuk of blades chipped off thin wedges. Long saws grated through trees, bleeding them of sawdust that coated the ground in bright yellow. When the whistle announced a break, we heard whining insects and distant blasting.

On our first day, we got two orders. First, every tree must fall away from the railway path. Crew Boss looked at a map and thrust out his arms. He yelled at Bookman, who dragged a pair of men to each tree caught in the boss's sightline. We cut notches to mark the way our cuts should topple. Once a tree fell, we sawed off just enough of its trunk to make way for the path. The rest of the tower stayed as it had fallen. We stood in awe of tree trunks wider than we were tall.

The second order?

"Shout when a tree falls and look up when you hear the warning."

Too bad the noisy forest muffled human voices. Our shouts drowned under the din of axes and saws. No tree fell cleanly. It toppled neighbours and, like a barber's blade, sheared off branches blocking its way.

On Pig Boy's last day, Monkey and Long Life's tree tilted into a neighbour and stayed standing.

"Those two trees are old lovers," Four Square chuckled. "Let them be."

Monkey and Long Life cursed the giant's great weight and chopped at the second one.

Poy and I looked at each other. Those louts deserved to be slowed down. Monkey was keeping count of who cut down the most trees. His own name, of course, was always at the top of the list. Long Life labelled Poy and me as "big girls" for being last to fell our first tree, despite having strong arms. But our tower had been fatter than anyone else's. Seven or eight men with arms linked couldn't have circled its base.

Monkey's trapped tree gave way with a sharp crack and slid as if greased. No one got warned.

Pig Boy was crushed under the trunk, face down, flattened over a pointed stump. Sawdust soaked up the blood. When Crew Boss and Bookman said he was dead, his workmate ran to wash his hands. He had touched Pig Boy, checking for life.

Big trouble had arrived: we didn't have women to death wail or experts to conduct a funeral. This was the second year of the railway, yet no one had rules for dealing with the killing airs.

Crew Boss and Bookman pestered High Hat, back and forth in English and Chinese. Crew Boss relied on Bookman, a China man handy with languages. He in turn begged help from High Hat, Elder of the brotherhood. Pig Boy was a member, and High Hat spoke for all the crew, even though only a third were brothers.

I could hardly hold my glee; the brothers were going to lose face. They had long taunted us non-members as failures at saving money.

"Look at us, we pool cash to buy candles and laundry soap."

"Follow us, we go to town together to get a discount from the barber."

"We each take a turn to wash the group's laundry so that the others can rest."

We non-brothers awoke late on rest days and each man scrubbed his own clothes, if at all. Those giddy housewives wanted to turn copper into gold, so like the women fussing at home, they should have known all about killing airs.

There, villagers shooed children and livestock away from the tainted house. They slammed doors shut while someone raced to get coffin, corpse handlers, and funeral master. They hung a big lantern at the village entrance and lit it at night, telling strangers to stay away. The dark side of death had to be addressed by rules, and quickly too.

Could that be done here? Key to the rituals was the dead man's kinsfolk, but they were far away. Family was vital; those people couldn't be replaced by cheerful men who went around calling each other "brother." Dubbing dog meat "mutton" didn't improve its taste.

The brotherhood had formed as soon as we were shoved into gangs. That day, boatloads of coolies reached Yale. Sweaty redbeards unloaded crates from scows and steamers. Cows clattered down a gangplank so sodden that they squealed and slid into the water. Horses reared up, shaking shaggy manes, as handlers tugged at them. My crew got its marching orders, but men rushed off to bid farewell to fellow travellers and visit Chinese stores and Native vendors. The contract promised meals, but no one trusted the document. When Bookman found us, only the brotherhood men were there, all from around the river port of Sim Hoi. It took Bookman an angry hour to round up the stragglers, after which we marched for half a day under a hot sun before being allowed to sit and rest.

Each morning the brothers were first to want to trek into the forest. Extra sleep didn't concern them. They shouldered axes and saws and toted cloth-wrapped bowls of food. They obeyed all orders, no matter how stupid. In return, Bookman gave them the posts of Head Cook and Second Cook. The brothers got not only better food but also hot water for soaking their feet. When we complained, Head Cook claimed the brotherhood was paying for the heated water. I sided with the losers who had touted Old Skinny for cook. We had pitied his weakness for opium.

At last Crew Boss stomped away from the corpse, leaving behind the two Chinese headmen. Anxious workers squatted on the rank, soggy floor of the clearing. A knot slid up and down High Hat's scrawny throat.

"We all know that such matters must follow the proper order. If not, our friend and brother will not pass smoothly on his way. With what little we have here, we must do our best to soothe and settle him. After all, everyone wants our friend to watch over and protect us while we are far from home."

The dark and clammy *yin* side of the forest smothered us. Our eyes were swarmed by clouds of mosquitoes that no smoky fire could evict. Prickly bushes clawed at our legs while soft mud swallowed our boots. We yearned for a bright, solid worksite open to the healing wind and sun. At the nearby lake, we held our breath and tiptoed around lean-tos made from tree-fibre mats. Woven cords hung from tent pole to tent pole. We never saw any Native people. Any coolie who was sent to the lake to fill our drinking pails pleaded for an escort, fearing water spirits and Native people, human or other-worldly.

"Four men are needed," High Hat said, "to break that tree and free our brother. Then they will carry him home to camp. There are no corpse handlers to hire here, so our brotherhood will pay for four helpers. The payment confirms the business nature of the handling, and will protect those men from any killing airs. They will dig a grave, wash the body, carry it to the site, and complete the burial. Who will help?"

"Shouldn't the Company pay?" asked Little Touch.

"The agent said bodies would be sent home," said Four Square, "so that family members would see that their men hadn't been sold as piglets."

"We can discuss that later." High Hat lowered his voice. "Our brother should not hear us argue here."

No one volunteered. We didn't have rock for brains. Pig Boy had just died. His soul hovered nearby. He could hardly be happy, cut from life so suddenly, having just ended a stomach-rolling ocean trip of thirty days. His family in China was waiting for money. This death wasn't timely at all.

The brothers shrank back from tending their own, yet were too proud to walk away. No man wanted a sullen corpse to suck away his *yang*, his vital essence, and leave him open to illness and death. What did those cheeky fellows say now about the need to help each other while far from home? How were they going to show the barbaric redbeards that China men always rose above hardships in refined and superior ways?

The silence dragged on.

"High Hat, we don't see you raising your hand," Four Square pointed out.

"The longer that tree sits on our friend," he said, "the greater the danger to us."

"I wouldn't touch that dirty thing even if you gave me a pound of gold," said Salty-Wet.

"Hok and Poy," said Shorty, "you two bastards should help. Atone for all the people you killed. Regain the honour you lost."

"I told you," I said. "We never killed anyone."

"Who believes a bandit?"

At a recent meal, I had joined some men chatting about Centipede Mountain and spoken too much about its hidden trails and shortcuts. Shorty, much smarter than I had thought, heard me and asked how I came to know those long hills. After all, wasn't my village located far away?

"Hauled loads through the region," I replied.

"Liar! Bandits ruled Centipede Mountain," said Shorty. "I know you. Your gang raided my village. We fought and killed one of you."

I stated Grandfather's good name and demanded proof from

Shorty, but he insisted that I knew far too much about the region.

Damn my itchy mouth. I had only wanted to make new friends. Poy was tagged as my partner in crime.

I appealed to the crewmen. "When there is no rice, children still must eat. Can anyone here swear to Heaven that no one in his family ever stole?"

The brothers accused me of blackening everyone's name. But we all knew from experience that bandit gangs never had trouble recruiting new members. Of course my co-workers had spent time among robber bands. We all came from wretched backgrounds; we all faced the lack and losses that Heaven cast upon us. Few people dared to be as self-righteous as Shorty.

Each crewman knew war and hunger as surely as his own name. The Guest Wars forced my village to flee to the hills. Armed bands crisscrossed the counties, burning crops and seizing livestock, smashing docks and bridges. Walled villages were set ablaze as clouds of black smoke turned day into night. Grandmother and Mother huddled with us children, beseeching Heaven and the ancestors for help. Before this turmoil, the Red Scarf bandits had rebelled against the emperor and demanded food from everyone.

"Guard your back," Shorty warned me. "You set the shed on fire, so the oxen ran. You killed the boy guarding the rice. You threw a net over our chickens and carried them off."

"You have eyes that can see in the dark?" I asked. "You must see ghosts too!"

I confessed nothing and he proved even less. My gang had raided villages now and then, but only ones that were poorly defended. We attacked mostly merchant convoys.

After this, I had kept far away from cockhead Shorty, at camp and in the forest.

"Let me move Pig Boy." California's face was grim, darker than usual. He gave everyone a pained look. "One day, you might do the same for me."

High Hat beamed. California was the only man who had worked in Gold Mountain before, in America. He had walked 800 miles to this job, but so far, hadn't spoken more than twenty words to anyone. A relaxed air hung around him; his clothes were well-worn while all of us were stiff in starch-hardened denim pants. His shirt buttons were flat painted wood; ours were coiled from cloth tubing. He knew English but never argued with Crew Boss.

High Hat egged us on, saying, "Be kind, receive kindness."

Old South stepped forward. He and Old North had been coolies in South Ocean, in Malaya. They sneered that railway work was child's play compared to tin mines. Their pigtails were dry and brittle; any touch caused bits of hair to flake off.

"You see?" High Hat waggled his finger. "Men who have worked abroad, they know very well that China men must unite and take care of each other. We must learn from them."

Old North cursed and stalked to the back. On the first night of camp, he had denounced the younger crew members. At dinner call, they rushed into the cooking tent while Old North tried to stop them. "At my home," he said, "elders always go first. Isn't it so in your village?"

The young men paid him no attention until High Hat stepped in.

The cheerless brothers scratched itches and bites and looked away, their motto of "mutual help lifts everyone" all but forgotten.

At last High Hat broke the circle of shame and offered himself. It was the only way to attract another brother to help. He glared at his men and said, "Just one more fellow is needed."

"Me," said Poy.

I pulled him aside and hissed, "We're going to America! If we stay, we will die."

"Will you do my funeral?"

"I could die first. Remember how one man ruined my people?"

"The Five Tigers?"

"You're going to thrust something dirty into the soil. You think earth spirits here don't mind?"

"We're respecting the dead. What god would disapprove?" He walked away.

A hundred years ago, our clan had raided a no-name village. We expected its people to flee. But they stood their ground, armed with axes, pitchforks, and magic charms worn at the neck. They suffered the bullying of bigger villages because their small number had chosen to stay and protect an ancient god. Then their god regained its power. In that raid, a Yang man purposely stomped on one of the god's charms. At that very moment, the battle changed course: our raid leader was fatally stabbed. Soon the Five Tigers fields that once enriched the Yang clan passed into the hands of the no-name. It was all blamed on that one fool.

The no-names were renowned now but no Yang man ever spoke their name aloud. We kowtowed to them and donated prizes to their festivals and cash to their temple no matter how our harvest fared. When they paraded their patron god through our village, crowing all the while, we served them choice snacks. Anyone who refused got cut off from trading at the market. If they walked into a crowded teahouse, then we gulped our food and gave up our seats and tables. Redbeard bullies here were nothing new to me.

"Back to work, all of you!" Bookman shouted. "We can manage this."

As Poy left with High Hat, the older man clapped his back. "You and me, we will help this man and then fly through the skies with the Immortals."

The crewmen hurried away, glad the matter was settled. They were rarely so keen to grab their saws and axes. When the light caught their steel for a moment, a glimmer brightened the forest.

Old North pulled me along. "Screw those two, let them go. If they want to do noble deeds, then let them die noble deaths."

With my teeth, I cinched a strip of cloth around my blistered hands. I should have thumped Poy's head with an axe. Coming to Gold Mountain was my idea; therefore I decided the big moves. When Poy had fretted about going abroad, I explained the contract and told him not to worry. Now we couldn't sneak off to America: killing airs raised the risk of misfortune.

"Is he your brother?" Old North referred to both family and clan.

"Friend."

"But you know words. Shouldn't he listen to you?"

"He's older."

"Everyone should have someone watching over him."

"I take care of myself!"

We tested the two-man saw, but then Old North pulled and pushed too fast.

"Slower!" I shouted. "No need to die for the redbeards."

At the start of work, we had been too eager to show our mettle to Crew Boss. We made the long saws sing but crippled ourselves with blisters and aching backs. Next day we slowed down.

I looked through the trees. Poy should be strolling over, a sheepish look on his stupid face. He should regain his senses and avoid the corpse. That bumpkin needed prudent guidance, all the time. Me, I had gone to school for a few years.

We had met on Centipede Mountain. I was new to the bandits, whose youngest member was Shrimp Boy, a vicious thug of thirteen, younger than me. Gang leader Cudgel was a filthy lout with a fiery temper and rusty but lethal halberd. Shrimp Boy scouted out targets and didn't back off from missions that Cudgel deemed too risky. He chafed under Cudgel's rule and vented his anger on me. I had to empty twenty men's shit and piss each day and then wash the buckets with creek water. That was Shrimp Boy's job, but he lorded over newcomers. Only Poy helped me carry the stinking pails beyond the range of the men's noses. Even then, he never said much.

For my first time at the brothel, Poy found me a pretty girl, guaranteed to be clean. I returned many times to her.

At the opium house, Poy watched that I never smoked a second pipe, no matter what discount the boss offered. I did the same for Poy.

After the bandit gang fell apart, we always met at the day's end to share the food we had scrounged.

On payday in Canada, I checked Poy's earnings. He couldn't read and didn't know his numbers. The first time I got paid, I accused Bookman of stealing. I received a total of $6.73 for twenty-six days of work. I had figured three times that amount. Then Bookman listed the costs for rent, food, and ship's passage, plus payment for boots, blanket, and hat.

Right away I warned the men that no one would ever get rich here.

"You think saving money is easy?" they scoffed. "You need to suffer."

When I urged Poy to sneak off to America, he shrugged. "They'll break your leg."

Company guards in every town watched the docks. We had heard that any coolie caught running away got a crushing whack on the knee.

"I could break my leg strolling through the forest," I said. "You too."

"We owe money."

"Screw the Company. Only in America will we get rich."

In China, returnees loudly touted America with the vigor of road-side vendors peddling noodles and fresh fruit at day's end. American towns and cities with tall buildings and fancy mansions offered plenty of jobs. Workers stayed clean and dry inside machine-driven factories. On wide flat roads, people drove their own horse-drawn carriages. A thousand times more people lived there than in Canada, it was said, and America's great railway had been laid a decade ago, so its people had been starting businesses and getting rich there for over ten years.

Old North and I took down one tree and were halfway through another when we stopped to return to camp. There, crew members were in a panic.

We had none of our women here, yet only they had power to dispel the corpse's killing airs.

Where could we find swatches of bright red to wear, to fend off Pig Boy's ghost?

How could a stranger not related to Pig Boy go and buy water from the river gods to wash the body? It defied common sense. If the body wasn't washed, then Pig Boy couldn't cross to the other world. He would stay to torment us.

The fiercest debate was this: If we couldn't manage the ritual properly, then should we try it at all? If we started the rites and then fumbled them, that would enrage the deceased and cast ruin onto everyone. We were already seeing too many accidents. No one wanted more blood or death. This was why we needed experts to conduct the funeral. Everyone cursed the brotherhood for acting rashly, for telling everyone what to do.

"Didn't stink before but now it does."

I was walking away when Bookman shoved his penknife and a block of wood at me.

"Carve Pig Boy's surname," he said. "Scrape deep and make it pretty."

I thrust my hands behind my back.

"Don't worry, cockhead, you'll get paid so you'll be protected." Then he added, "No one else here knows words."

The name contained six strokes, spaced well apart, so it was easy to scrape them into the wood and make the curves wide and smooth. I asked for oil to rub over the rough surface, but Head Cook refused.

High Hat and the three others came back and ate dinner alone. They took turns that night stoking a campfire to keep wild animals away from the body.

In our tent, men were keen to talk, shouting loudly to assert our will to live, recalling rituals gone wrong that ought not be repeated.

In Up Creek village, Cho had no future because he was his father's third son. But his two hardworking uncles lacked heirs. When one of them died, Cho went to the river, bought water, and washed the body. That let him take the funds his uncle had left for this. When the other uncle passed away, Cho offered to do the same. The grannies cried out, "No, don't! You look greedy, not kindly."

But Cho was under the sway of Jesus men and said he wasn't afraid. He came home from the funeral sweaty and hot, and filled his mouth with ripened fruit. A pit lodged in his throat, choking him. He died flailing on the floor.

Next morning, High Hat announced, "The grave will be dug this morning. Bookman says we can return earlier this afternoon with no loss of pay. I will be Chief Mourner and buy water. Men with the surnames Chew, Jang, Gwan, and Liu must offer wine at the service. After the burial, we will burn the belongings of our friend. Each man can cleanse himself in the smoke. After that, seven days of mourning."

The rest of the crewmen took themselves as far away as possible from the funeral. They stayed in the forest and worked. I returned to camp with men who planned to nap.

"Your friend does the right thing," Shorty said to me, sneering. "He atones for his crimes. You should do the same."

"Who says he's a bandit?"

"He confesses by handling that dirty thing. Why else would a young man do that?"

That idiot Poy should have told me about wanting to amend his ways. How in hell could a chicken know the duck's conscience? I could have devised a way out. Now that shit-hole prick Shorty could pretend to be smarter than me.

Old North walked by. "Your quiet friend," he asked, "how do you know him?"

"From the docks of Hong Kong."

He was decent enough not to ask about the bandit gang.

"Your people know him?"

"No. No one else wanted to come. I didn't want to cross the ocean alone."

"You should have found someone closer, a kinsman. Look at that fool, touching everything. Only kinsmen won't betray you."

I veered into the forest and slammed my axe into a tree. My father hadn't been home in twelve years. Travellers saw him in Singapore where he tended a shop and raised children with a local woman. He was polite enough to answer to his name and home village but would not admit his true family. Visitors pressed him about money, duties to his father, and memories of his mother. No answer. It was the same with our many letters asking why he had left us and what it would take to get him home.

But a son had to obey and respect his father no matter how vile the man. Even here, thousands of miles away and among strangers, I dared not denounce him. When Grandmother blamed Mother's nagging for driving away my father, I ran from the house. When Mother hanged herself, the villagers happily took it as her confession of guilt. I had been glad to leave home.

Second Cook cut open a potato sack for High Hat to wear in place of the hempen clothes used at home for mourning. No piper blew a *di-da* horn to announce the burial. Instead, High Hat used Crew Boss's shiny metal whistle. He smacked his lips and tried high and low tones to imitate the women's wailing. He was wise to have chosen the men needed to offer wine. They were the only ones to go up to the makeshift altar with its meagre plates of food. As soon as the wine was offered, I heard High Hat blowing the whistle to ensure that Pig Boy's spirit followed the men carrying the body. As the sound faded, the workers in the tent breathed with relief and slept.

High Hat and his helpers built a smaller tent to shelter them for seven days. The thick clouds scattered. Sunshine and blue sky emerged, all good omens. When Poy came to fetch his belongings, all his tent mates, including me, hurried away.

We didn't say a word, but none of us felt any shame.

4

BETTER TO TRUST YOUR OWN? (1885)

The cookhouse was poorly lit but noisy. Rowdy diners flung out fingers and chanted numbers in a drink-you-under-the-table match. When flames shot out from the stove, the cook splashed food into a wok and raked it with a metal scoop. At a stump of wood still wrapped in scabby bark, the helper chopped meat cake, a meditating monk drumming with two cleavers.

The place was packed, a sign of decent if not cheap food. Men squatted in the low light of candles and small lamps, their knees up, and backs against the log walls. The cook yelled a dish name, a diner shouted his spot, and the helper rushed by, steamy dish in hand.

Then he jabbed a broom at me. "Get out, you're dirty and filthy."

"Screw you, you're no boss." He must have seen me wheeling away the corpse.

"All seats are full."

I retorted with Grandmother's words: "Sit on the floor, for sure you're poor."

Our family always ate at the table, even when the dishes were meagre.

"Mister, such luck to see you again!" someone called.

Soohoo of Clouds Clear Tower pointed to the bench by him and spoke to the helper. "They paid him, didn't they? He's all free and clean, no?"

They exchanged glances. Of course everyone in Yale kowtowed to the doorman to paradise, the one holding the key to Goddess's room. Only a yam brain would refuse. The helper cursed and left.

"Can we do more business?" Soohoo must have heard that I carried my life's savings on me. Goddess had seen the cash when I was undressing; maybe they wanted to rob me.

"Of course!" I swung the boy into the air and onto the bench. He giggled with delight, but the same brat had fled the store today. "Can you watch him?"

"We have pencil and paper and stones for *woy kee*. He can watch himself."

"People play that?" Coolies played chess but never *woy kee*, which used two bags of pebbles, one for each side. Who needed more deadweight on his back while tramping through snags and swamps?

The cook came by, hands at a grubby apron, cleaver tucked into a leather belt that gleamed like a strop. I named two dishes and then added a third.

"Yes, build your strength for a night of bliss!" Soohoo was peering at the boy. "This one fell into the river?"

I nodded and reached for a candle in my bag but yelped at the touch of cold flesh. A dog with a wet nose sniffed at our legs. I kicked it hard.

A man oozing whisky fumes patted the boy's head with a grimy hand. "A *Yin-chin doi* eating rice! Didn't I say that Chinese food is best of all?"

"He's no *Yin-chin doi.*" Soohoo's voice rose. "He's *jaap jung*, Chinese and Native. Call him Best-of-Two!"

"That's so, that's so." The drunk nodded to excess and poked at the boy's face. "Be good, Best-of-Two, hear? Listen to your father. Always obey him."

When the drunk lurched away, Soohoo asked if Peter had been given a Chinese name.

Who the hell had time to waste? Choosing a name required thought and study. What did the brat need with another name? Whenever I called him, he ignored me.

Two men in overalls sauntered up. One removed his hat and dipped his head in respect. "Boss, need some wood chopped?"

When Soohoo shook his head, the man planted a foot on my bench and pointed. "Too bad the redbeards saved your son. You'd be laughing if he had gone under."

"I take him to his mother."

"Won't anyone else spread her legs for you?"

"She's a married woman." I raised my fist at him. "She has land and a house."

"Can't dump the boy now, can you?" The man chortled. "Heaven protects him."

The cook shoved him aside and slammed my food onto the table. "We chop meat cake here. Want to add something to the stump?"

One hand hung over his cleaver. Firewood in his stove popped and crackled. The diners fell quiet as the pair crept away.

"Those monkeys enjoy yanking their own tails," said the cook.

"Are you really taking the boy to his mother?"

I filled my mouth with rice to avoid talk, wary that this one wanted to impress Soohoo by acting nice to me.

"What if the mother doesn't want him?" the cook asked. "You'll have wasted time."

"Won't matter." Soohoo spoke for me and gave the worst of answers. "This one, he's a superior man."

"Superior man?" The cook's bellow of doubt caused his customers to snicker. "Superior men stay in China. They don't come here!"

"That railway worm heard wrong," I said to Soohoo.

"It'd be quicker to find a needle in the ocean than to track down someone in that wilderness." The cook smirked. "Maybe she doesn't want to be found."

"No woman turns away from her own son."

"There's trouble up north. Redbeards are angry, looking for work."

Soohoo raised his bowl. "*Better to have a beggar mother than a magistrate father*, isn't that what they say?"

The proverb silenced the cook and sent him scurrying. No doubt he had crossed the ocean in a tight little group, a pot of mice and ants. If one of those men made a move of his own, his friends were sure to scoff. Back home, a fellow in a nearby village decided to take candles and sell them where prices were higher, across mountains and bandit territory. Everyone, even his wife and brothers, called him a fool, pointing to his arthritis and reminding him that no profit was guaranteed. And, the rains were coming. On the day he set out, he gruffly reminded his critics that this was a very taxing trip. They had laughed in his face. "If it was easy, why, then everyone would do it!"

I asked Soohoo who might help me.

"Lew Bing Sam, the mix-blood, he tracks down lost kin for people. He speaks all dialects, knows how to lead the way. People from China come to us first. But when a man truly goes missing, he's a runaway monkey that can't be found."

"People trust Sam?"

"He drinks a bit, but what can you do?"

The brat was feeding the dog. I rapped his skull. "I'm still eating!"

Soohoo later insisted on carrying my bag to Clouds Clear Tower.

"No need," I said. "Your place is thriving."

"People are leaving Gold Mountain."

"You'll go home a rich man. No dogs will bully you."

"I sweep floors and empty shit buckets, same as my workers."

The door of his shop swung open and out stepped the mix-blood.

"Sam!" cried the boy.

I jerked him back. *A father spawned him but no mother taught him.*

"Sam, your name just arose," said Soohoo.

"I told Goddess to keep quiet!" He grinned. "That woman, she pants and scratches like an animal. She says there's no other man as straight and strong as me."

"This man needs a guide." The brothel keeper pushed me forward.

Sam frowned, as if recalling our scuffle on the beach and my insult.

"I look for this boy's mother," I said. "She lives near Lytton."

"Why not take him to China?"

"He belongs with his mother."

"Who's that?"

"Mary."

"Mary who?"

"Don't know."

"That's how you treat the mother?"

Soohoo steered us inside, away from another fight. "Sam, your woman is about to give birth. Save some money here; use this one to porter."

"What? Did I ask you for advice?" he demanded.

Meanwhile, the door guard led a dazed, dreamy-eyed client to the exit and greeted his boss. The lamps threw round shadows and yellow light onto wall scrolls containing single words, seven-term quatrains, and long couplets. I hadn't noticed them the first time I was here.

"Pretty, eh?" Soohoo strutted before them. "My handwork! I'm a read-books man!"

"I sell goods along the railway," Sam said to me. "You carry my goods; I'll find your woman. We don't pay each other."

"Go hire a hungry China man," I replied.

"China men don't want the job," said Soohoo. "They fear graveyards."

"Me too."

"Not so!" exclaimed Soohoo. "We saw you bury that thing. Our Council pays Sam to stop at those places and pay respect."

"He shouldn't take the job if he's scared."

"He needs a helper."

"Let him hire one of his own."

"They're busy fishing. He needs a man to talk pretty with customers. Isn't that so, Sam?"

"All China men call us stupid pigs," he said. "You say we mix-bloods have no brains. The railway snot worms are beggars yet they look down on me. 'Those aren't clear beans,' they say, 'those are green beans. That's not pickled turnip, that's cabbage.' They sneer and call me a dirty mongrel, half a loaf of bread. But if a China man brings them supplies, they smile and buy large amounts."

"A man with self-respect doesn't porter for a mix-blood," I told Soohoo.

"You want to find the mother? Then you need Sam."

"I have money; I know how to do things."

"I'm a superior man too," Soohoo said. "So I help you."

The guard opened the door too quickly, trying to get rid of Sam. He noticed and stopped to look back at Soohoo and me. A rush of cool air caused the oil lamps to flicker, caused the shadows on the walls to jerk back and forth.

"You two fools go the same way," Soohoo said. "Why not travel together?"

"That one prefers his own kind," Sam said. "Even when they don't know east from west. He doesn't know how much horse shit covers the road."

※

A morning later, Sam tied a brick onto this mouse's back. Lurching drunkenly, I acted as if the weight of the pack was nothing and tried to walk alongside Sam, even march ahead. Anything was better than being seen trudging behind him. The Native people by the river would see me as the beast of burden, the plodding ass being led, or the master's loyal dog even though our packs were alike in size and weight. We were both long-legged, but my clothes were better made and cleaner so I looked like a boss. My hat was newer too. But Sam had the surer foot and pulled ahead without effort.

At first I hung back to let the distance declare that we were strangers. Then I wanted safety, wanted Sam within shouting range. I thought of returning to Yale, but its China men would cackle like grannies. "We warned him not to go! City men totter on bound feet."

This morning I hadn't touched my breakfast. Sam asked, grinning, if I was sick or having second thoughts. I rushed off and squatted in the latrine to clear my head. To go with the mix-blood would be like dragging a cow up a tree.

Late last evening, the boy and I had followed him to a house, far from the raucous noise and flickering lights of the saloons, to save a night's rent. Sam didn't live in Yale. And on his visits here, he stayed away from Chinatown and the Native village.

"Summers, I go to mountain caves," he told me. "Cover myself with tree branches and sleep on rock."

"Wild animals don't eat you?"

"They're smart and stay away." Whenever Sam spoke to the boy, it took longer than when he spoke Chinese with me. Of course he was giving him more details. I heard the boy laugh, but nothing that Sam said to me ever made me smile.

Then, when three redbeards came toward us, I hushed the boy, who was dancing and singing by my side, testing his new shoes on the sidewalk. Sam ignored my call for quiet and for lowering the lantern. I held the brat as he squirmed. Luckily, our two parties passed each other with no trouble.

"What, you wanted to fight them?" I asked Sam. Not much was needed to provoke a redbeard to violence, especially when China men were far from Chinatown.

"Fight who?"

After this, my son clung to Sam the brave warrior, not his nervous father.

In the empty house, Sam lit candles and lay blankets on the floor. The doors had no locks. "What if someone comes to slit our throats?" I asked.

"Then we make sure to slit theirs first."

He and the boy laughed and went hand-in-hand to tour the house.

"The boy asked how I came to own this house," Sam said, "without the fuss and noise of a big family. He wants a home just like this!"

The blankets were thin against the chill so I drew the boy close. He turned this way and that. I wanted to slap him to settle down. I slept poorly and awoke when it was still dark. The boy was gone. I sprang to my feet. The worm had crawled to Sam and slipped under his blanket. Those two shared a similar stink, I told myself.

※

"Come!" I forced the boy to trot along. He kept squatting and pressing his hands to the steel rail, his gaze fixed on its mirror-like finish.

Big and small bridges carried the railway across the creeks that fed into the Fraser. Clear water streamed glistening down the mountains but turned muddy in the swift wide river. On the iron road side of the waterway, only the upper reaches of hills held green trees, ones that had escaped woodsmen and forest fires. Below the tree line, broken earth and charred stumps drained into long dry gullies. The mountain slopes were steep; workers had let logs roll from high up down to the water, crushing and ripping at everything in their way like maddened bulls. During the Guest Wars, the wild lands and bamboo groves had burned along with human bodies. Our fields lay trampled as blowing dust and ashes blinded us. Those lands, too, had not been restored.

The river narrowed as the two shores reached for each other. In the middle sat a rocky island, a small mountain of trees braced against the water. Sam spoke to the boy before turning to ask me, "Know what that is?"

No.

"It's the home of the bear that swims under the water."

"Bears can swim?"

"It planted this great rock to stop war canoes from going upriver. But nothing stops the fish!"

The grey plank buildings of one village perched on the hillside. Below, its people leapt like mountain goats over the rocky bank of the river and crouched with long-handled nets on platforms above the swollen current. They watched the water closely with spears at the ready. On snatching a fish from the water, they heaved it into a stone pit where it was clubbed to death and then butchered. The Native tools were hand-made and bound by rough twine. I pushed the brat forward to see; he would need that gear in his future.

Sam backed his pack onto a boulder to relieve the weight and hailed a woman hanging strips of orange flesh onto a rack. Her white teeth gleamed when she turned around. The boy ran to join them, and she patted his back and ruffled his hair. But when I approached, she resumed her work and Sam walked away.

I hurried after him, annoyed to be shunned. "That woman, does she recognize the boy? Does she know his mother?"

He shook his head.

"Did you ask her?"

"There are four days to talk!"

He spoke with people fishing, children picking berries, porters old and young bent under laden packs. When I asked if these were friends or strangers, he claimed they were both. I expected him to be asking after Mary, but he never had news for me. I stopped listening to his conversations and trying to catch familiar phrases. There was no need to learn new words now unless they were fresh ways to say farewell and good riddance to this joyless place.

The brat begged Sam for stories and games but ran to me when he needed to shit. The mix-blood was the boy's friend, but I was the servant who fetched water and took him into the bushes. The little master needed a slave to light his incense, sweep his floor, fatten his dog, and make sure the tea was hot. I tried once to walk away, but the boy screamed for me to stay. That pleased me, to be joined by someone who also feared the forest.

"Mary could be hiding from us," I grumbled to Sam. "What if she isn't in Lytton? What if she lied to me?"

"People will know where she is."

"My ship ticket got extended by ten days. If I'm not in Victoria by then, I lose it."

❧

At mid-morning, I reached a site before Sam and the brat. Boarding halls that had housed a hundred redbeards yawned with missing doors and shattered windows. Chirping birds flitted in and out. They must have built nests in the rafters. Under its own little roof was a large outdoor oven, domed like an egg but cracked. The rubbish heaps held rusty tins, chipped crockery, broken chairs, and livestock bones, dried and white as paper. I thought of China men with their sweaty faces and white-dusted clothes, but all that remained of their camps were tent pegs poking like snouts from the ground and trenches of wildflowers and tall grasses that marked the latrines. They had been set far from the boarding halls due to redbeard complaints.

I quickened my pace. I hadn't thought of the iron road when I was deciding to take the boy to Mary. Who would have guessed that that cursed path would help me reach an important destination? Those wretched days were best forgotten.

The smell of a wood fire led to a cabin, its doors and windows intact, capped by a mishmash of shingles. Cockeyed timber enclosed a garden, beside which sat a man, chanting at the sing-song pace of bored schoolboys.

The garden was a cemetery, with rocks, fence pickets, and rough-hewn wood as markers.

"Good morning." I made myself sound cheerful.

The man staggered over with a body-twisting limp, introduced himself as Moy, and pointed to my pack. "You walk with the mix-blood?"

The fur collar of his greatcoat glistened in the sun. Much too big for him, the garment was cinched at the waist and stuck out like boards. His forehead wasn't shaved, and the unkempt growth was swept behind his ears toward the pigtail. He looked me up and down with his small eyes and said, "That cockhead Sam hires his own kind, often just a boy. Why do you work for him?"

"He pays." It was easier to lie than to explain things.

"A China man can do better."

I looked around, acting curious.

"I told him to limp off with his rotted corpse, never to come back," he said. "He wants you to sell goods to me, no? You know what that shit-hole fiend told people? He said I should go home, said I had no right to stay here."

His tangled hair suggested someone crazy-crazy. No normal person lived so close to graves, especially those of fellow workers who hadn't been ready to die.

"You the caretaker?" I asked.

"Where are the visitors? Everyone rushes south, as if boiling water scalds their feet. No one stops, no one asks who is lying here."

"What's your book?" I dodged railway talk.

"*Three Word Classic*. I read to my old bean."

I tilted my head. "In the house?"

He pointed to the graves. "In three years, I'll dig up his bones and take them home."

His look was so smug that I had to snub the boast.

"Don't you fear the redbeards?" I asked. "If there's trouble, you're here alone."

"To follow you stinking bastards across the ocean now means I will never come back for the old bean. What cockhead visits hell twice? Better to wait and make one trip."

"You'll pass up prospects in China."

"Huh! The latrine is full when everyone shits at once."

I reminded myself that he was a customer. "You must have been close to your old bean."

"That stupid thing? He gambled away the land, the house, even the shit bucket. Our kinsmen refused to help unless he came here to work."

"You were a steadfast son."

"He wouldn't come alone."

When Sam arrived, Moy barked, "*Jaap-jung doi*, I told you to stay away."

"Just showing my helper the route."

Peter darted into the cabin and I gave chase. Mother and Grandmother always warned us children never to enter people's homes. If we got invited, then we must stay in the courtyard and not visit any rooms. That way, no charge of theft could stick to us. Clearly, the brat had not heard this lesson. I pulled him out quickly but not before noticing a line of shoes and boots lined against one wall. They were black and brown, left and right, high-sided and low, with laces and without. Only one shoe from each pair remained, so no doubt the other had been lost or damaged beyond repair. With his limp, Moy could likely wear mismatched shoes without drawing further bad luck to himself.

We followed Moy as he hobbled to the graveyard clutching a metal bucket, scorched black from flames. Sam told me to light the incense. To him, corpses must have been all the same, no matter if the person had just died or had lain buried for a while. At home, the bones of the ancestors were revered while they watched over us like a woodblock print of the gods. The recently dead, on the other hand, were much feared because they raged with anger at being cut off from earthly pleasures. Someone who been near a fresh corpse would never be allowed near the ancestral tablets. Here, I raised the burning sticks and candles, bowed three times, and planted them in soil. Sam handed me the whisky, and I poured three shots onto the ground.

"Elder Uncles, Younger Uncles, kinsmen, and friends," Sam called out, "all of you who sleep here in this earth, under this green grass. On behalf of the firms and people of Yale, on behalf of your co-workers, we come to pay respects. We lit fragrant incense; it is the smell of home. We poured whisky; it will warm you. We send money to ease your travels, no matter which way you go."

I was impressed. China men in Yale must have taught him the words. I fanned the sheets of spirit money, dipped them to the flame and slid them into the bucket. Grey smoke swirled with moths of black ash and rose into the air. When Sam went to unpack the goods, I looked for my clan name among the graves.

A red and black bird hopped from marker to marker. I didn't chase it away; guardian spirits came in many forms.

In Victoria, every surname group bragged about having the greatest number of deaths, as if mass anguish was boast-worthy, as if buckets of human blood made a weighty claim against the iron road. Even when dead, railway workers were summoned into duty for clan honour.

"That mix-blood shouldn't be the one doing this," said Moy. "China men must protect our own rituals."

I nodded. "Redbeard men and boys hurl rocks and blow brass

horns to disrupt our parades. They toss our ritual food to their dogs and laugh when we warn them of bad luck."

"When outsiders do the rituals, the power of the rites is lost," said Moy. "When a man passes on, his honour should pass onto kin, not strangers."

He pointed to his father's grave. "We were drilling a tunnel. One day we went outside when the explosives were lit. They went ba-lum, ba-lum, ba-lum. We heard the all-clear whistle, wee, wee, wee! My father was first to go in. But then came one last ba-lum! Rocks shot out like cannonballs. One slab spun like a flying plate and cut off his head."

He took my frown for pity. "When I tell this, people don't believe me."

"Maybe they heard it before."

"Screw you."

"Me, I heard the man was surnamed Chan, then Lee, and then Mah. Some say he was a bookman; others say he was a coolie. Some say the head rolled down the mountain into the river. Others say wild animals ran off with the head, leaving a trail of blood."

"Screw you!" Moy limped off, his body jerking from side to side.

Sam had put rice, dark sausages, and stiff slabs of salt fish on a cloth over the ground. The brat squatted there, fingering this and that.

Moy stomped by. "Wet shit and stinking piss. Who wants your garbage?"

He slammed the cabin door. I pulled Peter away before he was accused of soiling the food.

Sam ran up and banged on the wood, offering discounts. When no reply came, he gave me a vicious shove.

"Stupid pig, can't you talk to people?"

"He spoke rubbish."

The cabin door creaked but nobody came out. Moy was watching.

"Who doesn't tell lies?" asked Sam. "You want to carry a full load all the way to Lytton?" He pushed me again.

I shoved back. No mix-blood should bully me. No father should look weak in front of his son.

The boy's gaze darted from me to Sam, his arms suddenly still. He should see that there was no fear in me. One day he too would need to fight for his honour.

Sam saw the door. "Many customers ahead!" he called. "Nothing will be left on my return trip. You'll have to walk to town yourself."

Moy didn't come forth.

⁂

We resumed walking. Sam was angry, but that was his nature. Moy was my countryman, my workmate. If he told a lie, then I had a duty to call him out. I had worked on the railway; I knew its stories. I wasn't like Sam, who only wanted to sell goods to Moy.

Distant clouds dropped a grey curtain to the horizon. The green and brown patches of mountain and forest curled into shapes of giant thrones, humans, and animals. I was a fool to have accepted Sam's offer, mortgaging my body without stating for how long. My legs trembled and my back ached, making it a strain to look up from the canyon floor to the sky. The walls were steep, bristling with sharp edges. These mountains had killed my compatriots, so many of us that we were like children who scampered into danger while daydreaming. In China, forested mountains housed hermits who spouted reams of wisdom:

Get a mosquito to carry a mountain.

One mountain is high; another is higher.

One mountain can't house two tigers.

Those proverbs failed in Canada like water slipping through cupped hands. The sages didn't know how to use black explosives; they didn't know that Fire could be alloyed with Metal to rip apart the mountain's core; they hadn't seen the horizon rearranged in a single day's work.

The iron road had been laid atop the old wagon road built for the gold rush twenty years ago. That trail had teetered on skimpy ledges above the surging river until the coolies had widened them.

Then the railway broke from the wagon road to cross a high trestle over a dried-out waterfall. The legs of the crossing were a sturdy cage of logs, splayed at its feet, braced by tiers of cross-tied beams. The ground far below was rubble, cast-off lumber, and white rocks the size and shape of human skulls.

As Sam and the boy ambled across, I paused in front of the old stream. Tree roots poked from soil and the moss-covered bones of the serpent. Further up the cliff hung twisted vines, remnants of an early Native route. I looked at it from all angles. It must have taken long planning and great daring to sling that trail over the high rocks. For a moment, the land didn't seem so new and untouched.

The two rails of the iron road merged at a single point at the bridge's end. I was halfway across.

Already?

My knees buckled. Out floated my hands. My legs folded, crouched. I reached for the rail but stopped, half kneeling. My load shifted, about to drop, like a ship's anchor. I was a statue in a crumbling temple.

"Squatting to shit?" Sam called. "Hurry!"

I clamped my lips. My mouth was dry as paper. My lungs heaved. I gripped my armpits.

Sam's arms were triangles at his waist. Wind gusted past my ears.

"Watch my goods," he yelled.

I tugged at the knots of my pack without looking down.

Sam ran at me, his steps rumbling through the wood and up my backbone.

I almost tipped over. "Don't come near..."

He grabbed my hand. I pulled it back.

He glared at me. "Turn your body. Walk sideways."

I didn't move. This coward couldn't be me. This was someone else.

"Look this way," he said. "Raise your head."

I whimpered.

"See the river?" His voice was a granny coaxing a reluctant child. "It's pretty, very pretty. Look far away."

His hand drifted in front of me.

I grabbed it.

His other hand shot out for balance.

"I take a step," he said, "and then you take a step."

We went sideways, tiny paces, one foot at a time. I was a toddler learning to walk.

Once off the trestle, I squatted. My hands clawed at the ground. Hard, sharp gravel never felt so comforting.

"Good thing you stood still," said Sam. "Other people, stronger than you, fell."

I looked away.

"That load on your back," he said, "it threw you off, didn't it?"

I nodded.

"Leave the load and take the boy back."

I burst out, "All I need do is look ahead … as you said."

"I need my goods," Sam declared, "not you."

"You can't move two loads."

"Someone will come. I'll hire him."

"No one passed us."

I marched on.

"Come back," he yelled. "Thief!"

That stinking bastard Sam was no bigwig merchant with money and men at his beck and call. I walked fast, head down, eyes on the steady thrust of my boots. He was a mix-blood; did he ever glance at a mirror? No doubt his father had run off long ago, not wanting this son, not leaving him with family or means.

My family had farmed in our village for three hundred years. All China knew my renowned ancestor, Yang Jun, the Upright. Two thousand years ago, he refused a bribe of gold. The briber pressed him to accept, claiming the secret between them was safe. Yang Jun replied, "Heaven knows, Earth knows, you know, and I know. How can you say that no one knows?" Temples and grand halls throughout China were named after his "Four Wisdoms."

Yes, that bridge spooked me. The iron road was death: the

passing of compatriots, the loss of friends, the mourning of men not ready to die. My own death had been close.

I should never have come back here. The iron road had defeated me before. And here I was, fighting a mix-blood who was superior to me.

5

A Dream of Riches on the Railway (1881)

Our first runaway was the cockhead least expected to show any backbone: Old Skinny, the opium addict. He waited for the full moon, then grabbed his blanket and clothes, and strolled off.

"Had I known that the bastard was leaving," Little Touch said about his friend, "I would have followed him."

In town, he had overheard the addict ask about the border but doubted the fool had the gall to go.

I kicked myself. I should have been first to leave. If I had been nicer to that cunning bastard, then he might have asked me along. He could have used my help. But he was a frail old man, and I didn't want to carry him on my back. America was about freedom. I wasn't his slave.

To reach America, all I need do was to follow the river. When it swung west, it was time to leave the water and go south.

When our ship had docked in Victoria, the men were thrilled to hear that America lay close by, just a short boat ride to the mainland and then a quick hop south. No wonder armed watchmen guarded the pier and locked us in a stockade of sturdy logs. They snarled at us as if we were slaves of war plotting to escape even after being dragged far from home.

We cursed Old Skinny on our way to work that day. He made us all look like one-legged ducks, and now the bosses would watch that others did not flee.

"That turd won't get far. He fears the dark, wouldn't squat alone at the latrine."

He had bought himself a tin lantern to ensure his candle stayed lit.

"A Native will jump out and scare him to death. He'll die without losing any blood."

In the forest, the cur had whispered to me, "Look after yourself first. Always walk in the middle of the line. Let those who rush to the front or lag at the back face the danger. Wild animals, redbeards, or angry Natives—who knows that they want?"

"At least he'll find better food out there."

That was the best reason to run. Head Cook, the other cockhead in our crew, was as useful as dropping your pants to fart. All he did was boil water, throw in rice, and add ground-up dried salmon, the cheapest meat. Second Cook mentioned one day that Native hunters had brought wild birds to trade for tea but Head Cook refused them. What an idiot: our tea was so low grade that we would have come out ahead.

Three days later, Bookman told us to pack, to leave that very morning. Poy crowed like a child, keen to see more of Gold Mountain as if he were here on a tour of scenic spots. He didn't grasp that the Company wanted to move us away from the border.

"Path hasn't been cut through yet," I said to Bookman. "Why move?"

No answer.

I dawdled over my scanty packing as men hurried to dig up caches of liquor. The bottles were heavy but no one thought to discard a drop. Salty Wet had carved himself a wooden pillow; it was too hefty to take. He left it by the fire pit for some blockhead in the next crew.

I prayed for a delay to let me dash to the border that night. It seemed likely at first when the men fought Bookman over carrying the tools. The long saws were awkward to move, but Bookman insisted thieves were lurking and ordered us to lug them to the warehouse in Emory Creek.

"Who would steal them?" we demanded. "They're only useful for the Company's shit work."

Then the men threw down their loads and denounced Head Cook. All the heavy cooking pots had been put in the packs of the non-brothers. He in turn quickly blamed Second Cook and shuffled the items around. We folded the tents, coiled the ropes, and started our trek at midday. We were idiots, moving too damned fast for our own good, always trying to prove to the redbeard bosses that we were hardworking and willing, as if they might suddenly smile at our efforts and treat us nicely.

I wanted every man to break off and run to the woods. The bosses were too few to chase everyone, so some of us would reach America. Too bad there hadn't been time to plan this.

I lagged at the tail, hoping to melt into the woods, but Bookman made a point of walking behind me. When I stopped at every chance, he cursed but couldn't force me to go faster. I was bigger than him.

Chinese miners stood knee deep in the river and shovelled for gold, rocking their battered sieves with quiet patience. I called out greetings, but no one waved back.

"They hate newcomers," Bookman muttered. "They say you cause redbeard tempers to explode and singe every China man's eyebrows."

The railway camps were quiet; the crews had gone to work. A boy squatted by the shore, scrubbing cooking pots with bare hands and sand. I asked for boiled water, but he shook his head, eyes wide, as if scared of strangers.

The river held low-riding barges piled with machines, and smoke-belching sternwheelers laden with fares. A few children shouted and waved at us. Native men and women paddled dugout canoes. Those boats took them anywhere they wanted, while we coolies obeyed like dancing monkeys the Company's every whim.

Wide fields of tree stumps, their white flesh bright against dark bark, led to a landing half-built on footings, half-floating. We crowded onto a small boat. I boarded last, hoping to be left behind. I thought to escape when the men wanted to kick me off, shouting in panic, afraid of sinking. Too bad we pushed off without incident.

Low hills closed in as the vessel slid sideways against the current. We gripped the bulwarks to stay standing. Around a sharp bend, grey-black cliffs rose straight to heaven, leaving no ledges for even the smallest creature to grip. China had failed to warn us of such menace. Back home, feeble brown paintings showed distant mountains and aged them into misty hollows that sheltered the huts of hermits. If cranky oddballs could clamber up and thrive there, then mountain ranges were hardly risky for normal men.

At Yale, we boarded a train loaded with square, smooth-planed lumber and then we choked from the engine's black smoke. When it cleared, great walls of mountains surrounded us. The railway was squeezed in a narrow throat of rock where the river rushed in a breathless gulp toward the coast, the ocean, and China. Along smooth cliffs, men hung from ropes and ladders, flies on a teahouse wall. They dangled long tapes and weighted lines to take measurements. Bold splashes of yellow and red paint marked key spots. They drilled holes and planted blasting powder. Their feet scrabbled for traction as they pulled on thick ropes and the goodwill of fellow workers.

We bemoaned our fate until Bookman assured us that our jobs were less daunting.

A crew of China men had already claimed the site. Their tents lined the narrow beach, latrines behind a low wall of boulders. My workmates hurried to pitch shelter, always keen to show the bosses how quick and clever we China men were. Screw them. I looked up to study the newly blasted rock face, a vast sheet of jagged edges, a steep slope bare of stops. The thud and crash of explosions boomed through the canyon. Our bandit gang had once rolled boulders onto a convoy of packhorses and caused panicked whining, so I knew the deadly mix.

The headman of the other gang came by, chewing a wad of tobacco that slid from one sunken cheek to the other. He told us to call him "Old Fire" and offered advice: "Inside the tunnel, when you little chickies hear a krrr-krrr sound, flatten yourself against a wall and make yourself thin. Stay still and don't run, unless you want to 'get nailed.' The ceiling is breaking loose, but it could be a few grains of dust or tons of rock. It has no conscience and crushes men and animals alike. When redbeards leave the tunnel, you always follow them, no matter if you hear their whistle or not. If you can't see them, let your nose track their stinking sweat. The tunnel is dark, so no one can see who is who, or who is moving. Stay alert and don't say I didn't warn you."

As Old Fire left, my workmates sputtered and spat.

"That bastard mentioned nails to pound them into our coffins."

"He wants us to get fragrant first."

"That old thing didn't come to help. He came to taunt new-comers."

Me, I was glad for the advice. The mountain mouth could swallow several houses at once. Arches of rock supported the craggy ceiling, ridden with humps. No telling which were anchored and which had been loosened by blasts. The ground was cratered with pits and ridges that maimed and killed those who fell badly. The tunnel was black as midnight mud, but oil lamps in small tins studded the floor. When they burned out, they didn't get refilled right away. We offered to top up the oil but were turned down. The Company needed to save money wherever it could.

We were ants being flicked at a fortress city. We drilled holes to poke black powder into the rock, but the granite let us advance only fifteen inches a day. It was the bosses who complained about that because we coolies saw no progress in the dark. We worked in pairs: one man held the drill bit in place while the other swung the sledge-hammer. We made sure to blow the grit from the hole. Scaffolds slung between shaky ladders let us climb the rock face. Higher up, even less light was available. Each blow rebounded with a shudder; the hammer man clawed the air for balance. Good thing I worked with Poy, not clumsy fools with bad aim who clubbed their partners' elbows and shattered them.

High Hat warned us, "Stand with your feet wide apart and bend at your knees."

Redbeards tamped black powder into the holes and installed blasting caps. When they were lit, three rules were supposed to be followed:

Blasters leaving the rock face must blow their metal whistles.

Blasters going to the tunnel mouth must alert any China man seen along the way.

Lastly, lamps at the rock face were to be brought out before the blast, as a final warning to men in the tunnel.

Trust the redbeards? Better to call a wolf to guard the chicken coop.

After the blasts, we filed in, convicts to the execution ground, our noses twitching from the acrid smell of explosives. With our shoulder poles, we took out baskets of debris, sometimes two loads to one man, sometimes one load between two men. We hoisted rocks with bare hands and ropes. Big boulders were drilled and blasted apart for removal. When they told us about a second crew digging toward us from the other end of the mountain, we shook our heads in disbelief. Two deaf mutes groping in the dark could only land on different continents.

Crew bosses and bookmen watched us at the tunnel mouth. To show fairness, as if it was commonly found throughout Gold

Mountain, every coolie got time drilling the rock face and lugging debris. This was meant to prevent complaints and unrest on the job because hauling rubble inside the tunnel was more dangerous. But men keen to keep their good health paid their way out. They cited prior injuries or poor eyesight and waited at the tunnel mouth to buy baskets of rock to lug to the dump. Redbeards disdained them, calling them cowards. We crewmen saw a fair deal, a chance for men to trade freely. In any business, a man willing to take more risk deserved more reward.

I took on extra duties but it was safe work: writing and reading letters for men willing to pay a few pennies. It was easy work, full of basic four-word phrases: *your latest letter received*, *hard labour long days*, or *best efforts press forward*.

Not everyone used me. Men guarded their lives from work-mates who gloated over the bad luck of others, who dwelled upon people's misery to lighten their own hardships. They read scandal into simple matters. A father urging sons to tend to their mother was said to have raised useless scoundrels. A son telling his old bean to eat well and wear warm clothes was said to be atoning for past cruelty. Someone advising his brother to replace the roof and repair the dikes was seen to be managing from afar a family damned by inbred madness.

There was one line that all my customers praised: *Received your keen advice, etched it on my bones, carved it on my heart*. They wanted this in their letters, even when the home folk had sent them no guidance. They were even willing to pay extra for the sentiment.

One day Poy and I plodded back to the tunnel mouth and found the two crews milling there. A man from Old Fire's gang lay moaning on the ground, dirty blood caked on his face and clothes. Ceiling rock had crushed two workers. Redbeards brought out the second man slung in a tattered blanket while another carried heavy pickaxes. They lay the body before the bookman and crew boss and pulled back the cloth.

I saw the torn shirt and flesh of someone's chest. Where a man's head had been was now a red, pinkish mash of bone, brain, and rubble. I vomited and regretted wasting my meal. When the bookman nodded, the men hauled away the corpse. We backed off, bumping into one another, and averted our faces.

High Hat was impressed. "The redbeards move it so quickly."

"Only to get us back to work," said Number Two, his second-in-command. "Otherwise we get paid for standing here and doing nothing."

"Time to move!" Bookman shouted. "Back to work!"

The wily agents in China had never mentioned danger. All they said was that we would be building a road. How hard could that be? We thought that meant outside work. I should have known then that a dollar a day was a dream wage. Yes, it sailed far above a coolie's pay in China. But the tunnel was dark and ghostly, all honed edges and rigid corners. Their silent master, the mountain, loomed over us, solid and menacing, all male *yang* power. It came alive when sudden light threw bobbing shadows against the walls. We wretches drilled tips of iron into the core, sapping its gleaming strength. Of course the mountain gods despised us. We were as doomed as piglets caught gulping golden coins.

That evening, workmates asked what had caused me to throw up. I refused to say.

"Hok, come." High Hat pulled me away. "I want to see Old Fire. If he needs a grave-stick, then you can earn some money."

✤

"The last man we lost," said Old Fire, "it was the blaster's fault. That bastard ducked into a new corner to dodge flying rock. He said he never saw our fellow walk by. We wanted to kill him; we chased him into the river and pelted him with stones. The shit-hole prick almost got nailed, shivering from the cold."

"Was today an accident?" High Hat asked.

Old Fire shrugged and offered a brown jug of rice wine. I accepted, politeness be damned.

"Redbeards take the body and we don't see it again," he said.

High Hat asked for details, but we heard, "Don't know, don't care. Three men got fragrant so far. Who can handle so many?"

"Do the rites and let their spirits protect you."

"The mountain is stronger. Better to light incense and kneel before rocks."

"You don't care if they throw grass on the body, leave it for animals, or heave it into the river?"

"Back home, bodies float down the water, bloated and blackened. No one buries them. They're lucky to get fished out."

"No one knows them. Here, the bookman knows every name."

"Go find a runaway monk," Old Fire said. "Get him to chant sutras."

I reported this to Poy, who looked up from washing clothes. "This makes you happy?"

"We need to get to America."

"We have debts. I want to do right." He wrung out grey water. "Otherwise my life won't get better."

"Our luck will change in America," I said. "Don't let Shorty frighten you."

"Forget luck. It's about right and wrong."

After Pig Boy's funeral, Poy and I grew wary of one another. He didn't hand me the Iron Hit liniment to rub into his bruised shoulder, and I stopped inviting him to toss garments into my wash bucket. If we worked outside, sometimes I partnered with Old North, and Poy went with Old South.

"You owe me," I insisted. "I saved your life on Centipede Mountain."

"You owe *me*. I saved your life in Hong Kong." He snatched his wet garments and walked away.

Damn him, a wet hen in a soup pot, kicking at the lid.

I needed to remind him about riches south of the border. What if the bumpkin thought America was the same as what we saw here in Canada?

We had glimpsed America's bounty long ago, when a bandit raid netted us fancy goods from abroad. A sojourner had shipped strange products, puzzles to me until I reached Hong Kong and Canada. A lightweight box on thin metal wheels served as a baby carriage. Two wooden rollers and a handle squeezed dirt from clothes. An iron barrel turned out to be a pot-belly stove. We threw away tinned food until someone took an axe and split open a shiny can.

One day I saw armed militia sneaking up Centipede Mountain. I ran to warn the bandits, keen to win their favour, but found only Poy and two others. The rest had followed Shrimp Boy and Cudgel on a mission. We four wasted no time fleeing. The militia, rival bandits who had switched sides to become law-abiding mercenaries, waited overnight in the forest to surprise our gang and slaughter them. All their severed heads were thrust atop poles in the county capital. Poy wept at seeing our comrades' surprised faces. When the most corrupt magistrate in the region posted a reward for the four missing bandits, Poy and I raced to Hong Kong.

We found scant work, loading and unloading the ships. Then, angry co-workers put aside their hauling ropes and wheelbarrows to go on strike against a new government tax. After police arrested the strike leaders, 20,000 dockhands occupied the harbour and halted all shipping. Hong Kong was a big port; cargo had to be moved. But streets and alleys were barricaded to prevent headmen and their thugs from reaching the piers. Wet sewage was hurled at the comprador merchants sent to placate the workers. Armed British soldiers barged in but were driven back. We China men welcomed any effort to regain face from the redbeards who had shamed us in war.

Poy and I were too new to be trusted by the strikers, so we let merchants hire us to bypass the strikers under cover of night. Our sampan drifted slowly to a great ship. We unloaded goods on the far side of the freighter, out of sight. But as we tried to return to shore, word leaked out about our contraband cargo. Angry strikers shouted and hurled stones and bricks at us. Our boat capsized, along with all the cargo. Poy, a swimmer, had kept me afloat in the dark until we were rescued.

※

Next day in the tunnel, the man ahead of me screamed and fell back. The gods in the roof were still dancing. I landed on the shuddering ground as my laden baskets tipped over. The floor lamps were snuffed. Blind and bruised, we crawled over mounds of rubble until faint light glimmered ahead.

It was stir-shit-stick Shorty who had heard the creak above and warned us.

"Had I known it was you," he sniffed, "I wouldn't have bothered. You deserve death."

He followed me around, whining to anyone who came close, "The universe has no justice. Hok should rescue me; he owes me half a dozen lives!"

Most crewmen ignored him. No one worked at his lazy pace; everyone sought to stay out of trouble with the bosses. His only friend, Onion, had fallen alongside us in the roof collapse and lay in bed for days, bleating in faked pain.

When I passed him by the latrine, he grinned. "Take time off, Hok. You work too hard."

Once, Bookman lost his temper and threatened to reduce Onion's wages to punish his tardiness.

"If you fine me," he said, "I won't work."

A coolie who didn't work didn't get paid. It also meant that the Company's long fingers couldn't claw back the ship's passage or any cash that had been advanced. Then, Bookman barred Onion from the cooking tent, trying to starve him into line. But Onion had his own money to buy food in town.

When Bookman got cornered and lost face, he said the contractors would confront Onion's family in China.

Onion chuckled. "You think they are rich enough to sway my people?"

Rumours of danger followed Onion. He had insulted a corrupt judge. He had seduced a general's mistress. He had caused officials to lose face after bragging about his windfalls from high-stake gambling sessions. Here in Canada, Onion laughed even when he lost money, no matter what the game, no matter what the stakes. If he hadn't been Shorty's friend, then he would have been mine.

※

In town, the general store was crowded with railway men gambling on a rest day. I asked about America.

"You need money." The merchant slid close and lowered his voice. "The ones who reach America, they hire Native men to guide them through forests and mountains. They avoid the river and railway where the Company has eyes."

"I'll be fragrant by the time I save money."

"You take risks?"

"Want to report me to the Company?"

"Sell whisky at camp. All you need is a hiding place."

The Company forbade liquor in the railway camps, so workers hiked miles to town to slake their thirst. Noisy saloons, open twenty-four hours a day, offered women as well as other delights. Chinese pedlars trekked through the camps selling bootleg but were driven off by crew bosses ordered by bigwigs to keep their men sober.

"And end up in jail? I'll get nailed there!"

"And the laws of China?"

He meant fight evil with evil. Our Emperor had issued bans against opium, but the redbeards unleashed cannons and dispatched warships to protect the shipments and maintain the trade. Lacking human decency, they sold the drug everywhere. Stricken wives and naked children of addicts wailed and starved in the streets. Fleshless corpses, all bone and skin, of addicts who couldn't buy another pipe piled up in front of opium shops as though those firms were also coffin makers. The Yen mansion and its famed rock-and-water gardens collapsed after the master died and his two sons, both addicts, lost the family business. Every stick of furniture, every rag of cloth, and every piece of art had been pawned by the time remaining family members fled.

So I bought my first case of whisky and tied it to my back. At work, I watched the redbeards until I saw one fellow sneaking a drink. I went to him with a phrase learned from my merchant supplier: "Wanna whisky? Two dollah."

I pointed to myself and said, "Me, Hok."

After that, redbeards knew whom to seek in camp. As for Native customers, the merchant passed my name and place to them. Onion was a client, but if Shorty came to buy, I refused him. He had to send someone else with his coins. My bag of cups and small bottles let me sell diluted whisky in smaller portions.

One day after dinner, Bookman yanked me from the tent. "Didn't I warn you not to trade with Native people?"

Government laws forbade anyone to sell liquor to them. My merchant had failed to mention this, so of course I was surprised. Didn't every man need a drink at some point in his life?

Two sturdy Native men were waiting. My buyer was the leading hunter of his tribe. He looked chagrined that evening, carrying no weapons. His men preferred to buy in the railway camps because informers in town helped the Indian Agent arrest drinkers and peddlers. My merchant had told the hunter that I accepted only cash and nothing in barter. The hunter always came in western dress, and the other man wore an animal-skin tunic, painted in colours and bristling with bear claws. Under a hat of fur and stiff feathers, his eyes were stern.

"Your customer told his chief about you," said Bookman. "The chief says stop selling whisky; if not, he'll tell the Indian Agent."

"It's hard to say no to this one," I said. "He carries a rifle and weapons. He won't take no for an answer."

"You can't say this to the chief," Bookman said.

"Then tell him what he wants to hear."

After the visitors left, Bookman grabbed my arm. "Don't sell to Native men. They have wives and children. Redbeard men don't have families here; they can spend their money any way they want."

"If I don't sell, then customers go buy elsewhere," I said.

"You make us all smell bad."

"I sleep by the latrine. I'm used to the stink."

❧

Poy and I were on ladders squinting into the rock face when we heard shouts that High Hat had fallen off the scaffolding. By the time we pushed our way through the crowd, his eyes were closed and his body limp. The dim circle of gathered lamps showed a deep gash on one side of his neck and blood on the ground glowing and slick. Number Two raised his arms and a hammer to stop redbeards from coming near. He promised to pay Old South, California, and Poy if they helped him carry the body to camp. The rest of us followed. I dragged my feet: Poy was going to get polluted by killing airs and infect me too.

Our cantankerous lot agreed that High Hat should not have died. He had set up the brotherhood. He challenged Old Fire over the death rites. He settled petty spats between Bookman and the crew. If gods and spirits didn't protect such a worthy man, then there was little hope for sons of concubines like us.

Near camp, Old Fire's men blocked the way, shoulder poles in hand, ready for a fight.

"Don't bring that dirty thing here," said Old Fire.

"I need to buy water," said Number Two, "for our Eldest Brother."

"Put him down and go fetch it. Don't bring him closer."

"He has to go past his tent one last time to tend to unfinished business."

"Do filthy things ever get carried through other villages?" Old Fire gestured at his tents.

Number Two conceded that they didn't.

"Then turn around and go bury him. Find a spot in the woods before it gets dark."

"We must set up an altar and pay respects. He was a righteous man."

"Do that here, and be quick."

"This is the road, not our home."

"That thing won't pass through and pollute us."

Poy stepped forward. "You won't let us through because you look bad shirking your duties."

"If we carried filthy things past your kitchen," Old Fire replied, "your cook would chop us dead with his cleaver."

"If you passed away, you would want a funeral," Poy said to the other crew. "You would want to cross safely to the other side. No one wants to wander between the two worlds, bothering common folk."

Old Fire addressed them too. "We are far from home and need to stay alive. People get fragrant here but we must keep a safe distance. It has always been thus."

"Everyone gets a funeral at home," Poy pointed out.

"The family gets benefits, so of course it does the rituals," retorted Old Fire. "But we have no families here, so nothing can be done."

Number Two turned to consult his brothers and Poy was pushed aside. No one talked to him, so he came to me.

"Why didn't you speak?" he demanded. "You have schooling!"

"Without a funeral master, nothing can be done."

"A few things can make it right."

This wasn't about right and wrong. These were scared men clutching at the frayed edges of dignity. They had muscles and brains, words and opinions, but were reduced to numbers on the payroll, ink scratches in an account book. They had families and abided by clan honour, but the rock was supreme here. It did not need to be kind or righteous; it did not need to recognize anyone. Men owed it respect but had lost their senses, thinking those foreign peaks were more powerful than those of China. In town, I had met men from other crews who followed Old Fire's ways and observed no rites.

"We only want to go home safely," was what they said.

Poy had scowled and stalked away, an old man who knew only one way home.

In the end, the brothers told Number Two to appease Old Fire. If this death wasn't their Elder Brother's, I suspected the men would have walked away without a backward glance.

"There's no grave-stick, so we can't bury him." Poy tried to delay things. "If the spirit isn't guided by its name to its owner, then it stays and haunt us."

He sent me a sideways look that everyone saw.

"His surname was Liu," I called. "The word has fifteen strokes. It will take time to etch it."

"Write it on paper." Old Fire sneered again. "Set it on the grave under a rock until the stick is done."

He went on to list how the rites could be shortened. Number Two nodded, as if he too wanted a quick burial.

"Old Fire, we are not animals." Poy spoke loudly. "We will do as you suggest, on one condition. You must bow to High Hat and toast him with a cup."

"We never spoke!"

"Liar," I said. "We talked after your man died."

Number Two ran to the river to buy water and dabbed his wet bandana on High Hat's forehead. He murmured words of comfort as fast as he could. The handlers tied the blanket around him, after placing slabs of wood under his back and atop his chest to take the place of coffin walls. Our entire crew showed up for the ritual, not for High Hat but to send Old Fire a signal never to meddle again in our affairs.

Poy called each crewman to step forward and pour wine at High

Hat's feet. I was surprised. Usually an older man called the order; his age showed respect to the deceased. Poy gestured for all to step forward and bow. He led us in three large circles around the body before handing each man a penny. Then the handlers lifted the wrapped body and headed to the forest. In the meantime, a small fire was stoked on the ground. Each man stepped over it before heading back to camp, where right away he washed his hands and face.

I had new respect for Poy. But before we could talk, two armed lawmen rode into camp on big brown horses and seized my bottles. In front of the crew, they emptied the liquor onto the ground and arrested me. Along the march to jail, I wondered who had fingered me, Shorty or the Native headman. Grandfather's words from long ago came to me: no revenge, no rest.

6

A FATHER NEVER SLEEPS (1885)

I marched like a soldier into the next tunnel, then turned about-face and went back to the mouth, a mule with downcast nose. Sam had set a goal of fourteen miles for the first day, and I figured I was about halfway to Big Tunnel, the stop for tonight. But first there was Spuzzum, the first railway station north of Yale.

No prick of light showed at the other end of this tunnel: *Don't know the depth, don't ford the river.* I should have gone back to Yale, to my first shrewd plan, instead of scurrying on, a witless child on a fool's errand.

No mix-blood could tell me which way to go. A return to Yale meant swallowing failure and letting Sam tell a juicy tale about some donkey dangling halfway between land and sky, far from its convoy, far from safety. His people would hear about China men as stupid pack animals, too stubborn for their own good. I might as well have ridden into town astride a horse but facing its tail.

I untied the pack and searched for the folded lantern, tossing out bundles of rice and dried beans and little earthenware jars wrapped in cloth. The lantern was tucked deep on one side. When

I repacked, the goods wouldn't fit as before, so I hurled a packet of beans into the river.

That must have riled Sam's thrifty gods, because winds rushed at me as I struck the matches. One by one, they sputtered and died no matter how my shoulders twisted to shield them. A whole packet of matches was wasted before the candle got lit. My heel crushed them into the ground. If Sam saw this, he would have a good laugh.

The tunnel mouth, wide enough to take two more rail lines, hinted at a long hole. Iron rings had been screwed into the rock, likely for moving skids, and deeply thrust into the mountain, otherwise thieves would have grabbed them already. I tugged at one and recalled a grand temple door swinging open in my childhood.

The wooden ties underfoot led me forward. The lamp's rust dulled the flame: it faltered and left me taking baby steps. I swung the lamp to the ground, trying to gain reflected light from the steel rail. The feeble glow cast no shadows. Drops of water landed in puddles and echoed—natural sounds, not voices. Men had died in pain here, before their time was up, and now their blank eyes watched from dark corners. They wanted justice, but I wasn't their hero. I stomped loudly over the gravel to assert myself.

Something sleek skimmed my face, a weightless flicker. I ducked, one hand at my eyes, the other steadying the lantern. Flapping wings hurtled past again. I hadn't heard them, hadn't thought that birds could fly in the dark. Maybe it was a bat with sharp claws. Ghosts held no power during the daylight, but the cool vast reach of this tunnel was a moonless night. People said you could tell a human from a ghost because a ghost had no chin and no legs. Here in Gold Mountain, that could be just another injured coolie.

Leaving the tunnel for fresh air in the sunlight let me speed up. Sailing to China would take a month, but when Wet Water Dog had handed me the ticket, the heat of home filled my lungs right away. The longer I stayed here, the more bitter the taste. Not because the shit-hole redbeards kicked us around and used our pigtails to pitch us into the mud. No, our homeland too held a fine array of bullies: ox heads from downriver insisting we took too much water, no-name clans demanding tribute, former militia captains with no squads left to lead. No, it was the grim prospects of Gold Mountain, sharp as a shrill opera voice, which left us sleepless.

The old ones who had never gone abroad said all you needed to do was scoop gold from the ground. That's how easy life was here, easy as flipping your palm. Only a snot worm with a yam brain would fail to get rich. Family and clan members wrung their hands and clutched at your sleeve to yoke a cartful of demands onto you. You were the one to pull down nearby homes and build a bigger house. Your money could carry a daughter or sister into a rich family where she dodged farm work, where she trumped you by pulling strings to get odd jobs for kinsmen. You purchased more land, so the clan collected more rents and hired better teachers. One boy might shine at the government exams and become a high and corrupt official who funnelled home even more gold. Hurrah! What I took back to China would never be enough. Soon I would go abroad again, as sure as late flowers around me dried up and dropped their heads.

A trestle as high and long as the one that had disgraced me crossed the next gully in a wide curve. I looked to see if Sam and the boy were watching, waiting to have a good laugh.

A superior man fears nothing, I told myself. *Watch the distant mountains; the horse gallops across.*

My feet dragged as if shackled. I clutched my sides to stop the trembling in my hands.

I retreated to solid ground and crouched. The blue sky was bright with certainty. An eagle with broad wings floated far above, a chip of wood skimming through the clouds. That creature was the true Best-of-Two of this land, with talons that inspired fear on land and then folded neatly to ride the wind.

My son was approaching, so this cornered dog had to leap the wall. I untied the pack and kicked it aside. I crawled onto the trestle, nose to the ground. My elbows pulled me ahead. My knees scrabbled over the ties. I wished my feet, my boots, were heavier. A sliver pricked my hand and I glanced down. Something flashed below me, an insect or animal streaking by. The joints of the trestle creaked in the wind and I felt it sway. I backed up like an ox getting hitched to a cart.

The gods must have laughed until their teeth fell out and pity filled them, because then I heard a bell clanging.

People fishing and picking berries at the river stopped and looked up. I ducked behind bushes. The railway behind me held loops and turns so the chugging of the train slowed. First came the pointed nose of the cowcatcher rack. Smoke drifted from the giant wheels. A red bandana tied to the cab door flapped in the wind. The train clanked to a stop and then the driver hopped down and went to peer under the engine. It pulled no passenger cars, just two flatbed decks, one stacked with lumber and the other lashed with coops of clucking chickens.

I lifted my pack, crept like a thief, and climbed aboard to lie flat beside the birds.

When the cab door slammed and the train rumbled to life, I grinned. It would shoot me so far ahead of Sam that when he finally caught up, I could say, "Been waiting so long that my neck got stretched."

Then I kicked myself. Now the gods were truly laughing, laughing so hard that you couldn't see their eyes, hiding their open mouths behind airy fans. Stupid me, I had fled the wolf to face a tiger. Now, if I were to turn tail and scuttle back to Yale, I would need to cross two high trestles with the brat tugging at me. I rolled to the edge of the deck, but the train was already on the bridge.

My death meant no one would restore the family's name.

The family name. I had gripped those words to my heart on leaving home. Now it was my wizened grandmother's beseeching that pulled me back.

I shut my eyes against the glare of the sky.

Beat the family hen, it runs in rings; beat a visiting fowl, off it flies.

When news of Father's refusal to come home was confirmed, no callers came to wish us well at New Year's, and we dared not take our bad luck to other homes. It was as if he had died and our house collapsed. Grandfather blamed Grandmother for spoiling Father since his childhood, peeling his oranges, pre-chewing his sugar cane, and excusing him from chores.

"Didn't spank him when he didn't listen, did you?" he muttered. "He ran everywhere, screaming like a monkey."

"Why didn't you let him bawl and starve from time to time?" he demanded. "Then he would have seen how our sweat is water for the rice crop."

"To keep his food warm," he sniffed, "you covered it with your own hands. So useless."

Grandmother in turn railed at Grandfather for sending her son too far away.

"The Yang men in South Ocean were too busy gambling and whoring to guide my son," she insisted. "*The dropped bowl broke, but not one good shard was left.*"

"Men must come home to teach their sons," she said, "and listen to their wives, not spend their nights in town.

"When only one nib of a son survives," she yelled, "you keep him close by."

Mother kept quiet: she was worse off than the children. We ran to our grandparents who sometimes stopped her from beating us and scolded her bad temper. But when Father slapped or beat her, she had no one to hide behind, seeing that our grandparents were the fiercest voices nagging Father to reproach her.

Then, during her persistent pestering, Grandmother revealed by mistake Grandfather's veto of the first bride that she had picked for Father: "Didn't I say that that girl was best of all? She knew sweet words, knew how to sew sturdy shirts. Even without rice she could cook porridge. She would have taught our boy how to be a good husband. "

Mother's neck burned as if roasted and she slammed our chipped dishes.

"*Second best, you're always a guest,*" she lamented. "I knew people were hiding a secret from me."

On and on she went. "*Out of ten matchmakers, nine are liars.*"

"They sneer at me even though I had two strong sons."

"*In good times, praise the pig's big litter; in bad times, blame the pig's big belly.*"

After her death, the neighbours quickly changed their tune and marvelled without shame at the care she had spent on her final deed. Her hair had been washed, then coiled and pinned up, as for a special event. She put on her best clothes and only shoes, saved for temple visits, knowing full well that no one wanted to wash and dress a suicide's corpse that seethed with rage and ill will. Her body hung from the main beam that ran the width of the house, making clear her anger at my grandparents. If there had been any thought of sparing them the stigma of a haunted house, then Ma's final trip would have led into the hills to a sturdy tree. Or she could have gone home to her mother, but that would only have spread our great shame even wider.

Neighbours on one side of us moved away and that house was left empty, but Grandfather refused to leave because our house was newly built after the Guest Wars. Grandmother nagged Grandfather until he begged help from a priest renowned for cleansing homes. He paced our courtyard in a golden robe and placed candles, wine, and a woodblock print of mighty Ghost Subjugator on an altar. His first weapon was a sword, woven from brass coins. Then he marched through the house with a bowl of smoky incense, chanting and swinging a horse-tail whisk. He chopped the tail off a small black dog and dragged the blubbing puppy through the house, using its trail of blood to draw out evil spirits. Long strings of firecrackers were set off. Then the dog was taken away and killed.

I planned to do what my rogue father should have done long ago: leave my mix-blood offspring with his local mother and return to my homeland. I saw myself telling Grandmother about taking Peter to Mary and letting Grandfather grin, sigh with extended relief, and rub his ever-aching neck. Only from his tight grip of my arm would I be able to tell how deeply pleased he was. He would inform the clan elders and all his friends about my gruelling quest, about Mary bursting into tears at regaining her son and dropping to her knees to thank me. Grandfather would loudly report this to the ancestors at the hilltop graves, hurling his words through the incense and ashes into the other world. My deed would be sure to attract their blessings, unlike the disgrace of my parents. Then, in secret, I would visit Mother's unmarked grave to tell her that I had helped her grandson Peter find a good home. That·would bring her a small measure of comfort.

She was not a woman who nagged Father for money. She only wanted tuition for my brother and me. When thinking of gifts for Grandmother and Younger Sister, I wondered what to buy for Mother, had she still been alive. She was easily pleased. Tiny earrings were fine, but I wanted something that would never be pawned on behalf of the family. She deserved something that belonged to her solely and permanently. Only she had ever set out to make us children laugh. After dinner, when the dishes were washed, she sang out:

Come, come sit,
Eat sweet bits.
Piggy pulls the wood,
Doggy tends the fire,

Kitty brings a bench

Letting Granny rest!

When she named each animal, we all pointed at someone in the circle. If every finger landed on the same person, we hooted and the victim stomped his foot and cried out, "Not me! Not me!"

✳

As the train slowed to approach Spuzzum, I dropped the pack to the ground, recalling too late the earthenware jugs on my back. The jump wasn't far, but I grunted on landing, as though leaping from a high wall. I hobbled on sore ankles into the town, cursing how everything in Gold Mountain brought pain.

Redbeard shops were built close to the station while Chinese ones lay farther away. Flimsy boarding halls stood as forlorn as those that we had seen earlier. The town was lopsided like a wind-tipped scarecrow: all buildings stood on one side of the railway, its mountain flank, because the tracks ran too close to the shoreline edge.

The cookhouse door was open, trading sunlight for greasy smoke and cheap incense.

Three men sat around a low crate, two of them eating and slurping. The wall's rough planks were cracking; small windows held no glass. The kitchen lay empty. I untied my pack and found cold boiled water at the counter. Speaking a hick Yenping dialect, the men glanced at me and then away to talk even louder, debating if winter would come early or late, based on predictions from the Chinese almanac. One man insisted the almanac was never wrong; the others disagreed. They were testing my patience over this petty topic, watching my temper, wondering if I might be provoked into a fight at being ignored.

Finally, one man shoved blackened feet into wooden clogs and stomped over. I called for rice and eggs, the easiest dish to cook. When he went to the stove, I called out, "I need a guide to take me to Lytton."

"Sam Bing Lew knows people and can talk," said Cook.

"People in Yale praised him too," I said. "But he's not right for me."

"Men want to be left alone. One fellow bought land and couldn't bear to leave it. Another man picked up gold dust, but just enough to stay alive each year. He had nothing to send or take home. Men use nicknames and keep quiet. It's easy to hide."

"Sam found them?"

"They still avoided their relatives. A rich man came one spring and stayed until winter. He walked up and down the railway line, into every camp and Company office, seeking his son. He trekked to the gold fields. People wouldn't help. 'Don't bother me,' they said, 'You make trouble.' Sam found the man, not far from here, in Similkameen."

"People in Lytton can help you." The diner wore a blue smock. "Don't listen to the cook. Sam is his customer; he eats here. His grandmother lives nearby, in the Native village."

"Sam's all right," said Cook. "But he gets no respect, like us Yenping folk."

He brought my food. "Last year, Sam went to the graveyard. He came running back, his face all red. His father's grave was empty. Everything was gone—bones, marker, rotted wood. The father's friends had dug up the bones, cleaned them, and sent them to China. Sam howled. He grabbed one man and slammed his head into a log wall. He pulled down shelves of goods in the other man's store. People didn't know who to help. The police dragged him to jail."

"Sam is a stupid pig," said Blue Smock, waving off a pesky fly. "His father's eldest son lived in China, so Sam had no need to fuss."

"Not so," said Cook. "The son at home was adopted, but Sam was trueborn."

"That cockhead can't go around beating our people," said a man in a knitted hat. "I would have smacked him."

"You have no spine!" cried Blue Smock. "Every time you see Sam, you run away!"

"Sam isn't Chinese." Knitted Hat gazed at me. "Don't follow him!"

"Look at old Yang's daughter," said Blue Smock. "All those mix-bloods are crazy-crazy."

"She'll come back," Cook insisted. "Wait and see."

"Yang the washman married off his mix-blood daughter Jane to Wee-yum, the redbeard hotel man." Blue Smock grinned at me, taking pleasure from Yang's mess. "A week ago, Jane ran off. Wee-yum demanded his bride-money back. Yang refused. Wee-yum shouted, 'You and Jane, you cheated me. You told her to run. Townspeople are laughing at me.'"

"Jane and Wee-yum are the crooked ones," said Knitted Hat. "They're cheating Yang. When Yang gives back the bride-money, then those two will be laughing in their bed."

"Wee-yum has a gun," said Blue Smock. "Yang should run."

"A redbeard paid for a mix-blood bride?" I frowned. "Never heard of it."

"Pretty girl," said Cook. "Lots of men were watching her."

"Will you use Sam?" Knitted Hat looked at me and gestured at Blue Smock and at Cook. "Who do you listen to?"

"Go ask Yang about Sam," said Cook. "You can buy a bath with hot water there."

I enjoyed my meal. No brat here to fuss and demand food.

※

Sam arrived, tugging the boy along. Peter's face was smeared with saliva, dirt, and tears.

"You made him cry," I exclaimed. Sam was wearing a different shirt and looked as if he had washed his face.

"He ran shouting to my grandmother as if they were family. She pushed him away. He fell and started bawling."

Sam wasn't carrying his pack. He must have left it in his village.

"Didn't I say I could gallop like a horse?" I opened my arms. "I crossed that trestle, no trouble."

"Liar. You rode the train."

"I walked my aching legs to death."

"Let me watch you run over the next trestle carrying your son and I'll believe you." He reached for my pack. "Go to Yale and take your boy to China."

"Listen," I said. "At the next trestle, I'll take off my pack, and you can carry it across. That way your goods are safe."

"My grandmother says the boy will have a better life in China."

"I'll give money to Mary."

"For what? One meal? One month? A whole lifetime?"

"One year at school," I said, "a sojourner enrolled his son, born to a dark woman in the South Ocean. Classmates chopped off the boy's pigtail and held him down and painted his face black with ink. They said he wasn't Chinese. They tore off his clothes and chased him home naked. Why? They said, 'His mother's people dance in the forest wearing nothing.' Complain to the teacher? The man snickered and called the boy a monkey, a bastard, a mule."

"When I was small, my father promised to take me to China."

"You must have looked like a China man then."

"My father said the man is the line, not the woman."

"What did his parents say?"

"Mister, want to play? Want to play?"

A Native woman chanted Chinese words in a high voice and tugged my arm. Her blouse was filthy, her skirt swept the ground, and her hair, though coiled in a bun, was coated with dust. She had a girl's slim body but an older woman's face, crumpled with wrinkles.

She frowned at Sam and kept her distance. To annoy him, I caught her gaze, nodded and grinned, as if pondering her offer. I strolled around her, peering here and there to inspect her. She lifted her skirt and showed callused feet, soles pink against the dark skin.

"Mister, want to play?" Her next words sounded like *good price for good time.*

Sam yelled and ran at her, his fist raised. She made a sour face and flounced away. When he headed off with my pack, I called, "When is the next train to Lytton?"

"You don't listen!" He stopped. "Go back to Yale!"

"A boy belongs with his trueborn mother."

"You just want to crawl between her legs." He stomped away. "Chinese whores are crying for customers. Go visit them."

He wasn't listening either. There was no stronger porter here than me. I could sell his goods with no effort. If he had seen me touting boat tickets in Victoria, he wouldn't walk away. I could talk to any man. I knew how to bargain, knew the lowest price, knew when to almost walk away. If he saw the roll of bills I was carrying, he would fall over. Who the hell could Sam hire out here? His people were busy, caching food supplies to last through the winter, not loitering. He and I, we could help one another.

But China men didn't beg from mix-bloods.

※

The bell over the washhouse door jangled, and I propped it open to let in more light. The building was battered, built before the railway, but the shelves holding finished laundry were glossy from a recent coat of paint. A pendulum clock and paper calendar hung on the wall. Beside the front door, someone had hammered a row of nails, their gleam long gone. An umbrella and a woman's straw bonnet hung on them. Toys lay in the corner, a drum with one stick, a mop-haired doll, a wooden block with holes for marbles. The brat ran to some crinkled, rusted tin soldiers that looked like salvage from the garbage dump and tried to stand them up.

Yang came from the back, wiping his hands on his pants. He was middle-aged, with forehead neatly shaved and thick short eyebrows. His face lit up on seeing the brat. He went to squat by him, fishing out scraps of wood to help prop up the soldiers. The boy knocked them over and laughed. Yang laughed too, and stood the soldiers straight. Again the boy knocked them over, this time clapping his hands as well. Yang looked at me. But instead of giving me a hearty welcome, he kept quiet, forcing me to speak.

"This is my son." I faltered. "I'm taking him to his mother. Children should be with their trueborn mothers."

He went behind his counter and clicked his abacus, which drew the boy to him. Yang put it down and let him flick the beads.

What an oddball! Few shopkeepers would let dirty children play with a tool so crucial to reckoning one's wealth.

Without warning, he barked, "You walked from Yale?"

"Started this morning," I said.

"All the way?" His snort called me a liar.

I lifted my chin and said, "We go even farther."

"North?"

"Of course." I said, irritated. "Is there another way?"

"The Native people of Spuzzum here have trails that go west over the mountains."

"Cookhouse man said you welcome travellers," I said.

He nodded.

"He said there was hot water for bathing."

The adjacent room contained lines of drying shirts and trousers, and the smell of soap and starch. Light from the back door showed grimy Hudson Bay blankets on the log walls, the gaps plugged with white plaster. Steam rose from a large bucket atop the stove.

On the back porch was a big tin tub, barrels of water, and bars of soap on a plate. I wasted no hot water on the brat, who yowled

at my scrubbing and flung soap suds into my eyes. I fought to hold
him still and wash his hair. After drying him, I tried to dress him, but
he insisted on doing it himself. I threw out the slurry and scraped
myself clean before refilling the tub. My last bath had been over a
week ago, in Victoria.

During my washhouse job, each day I strolled clean as a newborn baby, always bending over to sniff the sweetness in my clothes.
People on the street asked why my nose needed so much wiping. It
had been easy to toss my pants or shirt into the cauldrons of clothes
being boiled and bleached. It was easy to dry them too, with a roof
overhead when it rained and a hot stove when it was cold. Too bad
the coolies hadn't been able to afford the washhouse.

I pulled my knees to my chin and slid into the hot water, shutting
my eyes. A smarter fellow, I told myself, would have paid fifty dollars
to the Church Mission and left the country right away. If I didn't
need to cross those trestles, I'd turn around and head south at once.

The washman padded in with two large kettles of hot water.
When I thanked him, he nodded and turned away. But then he came
back and stood staring at my cock until I tossed my wash cloth over
it. There weren't enough women here, so men sometimes made do
with the backsides of workmates. He seemed sullen; a pretty daughter running off must have caused him much anger and loss of face. I
wanted him to be jolly and friendly so the brat could tell his mother
tales of kindly China men selling us food, giving us water, and playing soldier with him.

I pulled on my dirty clothes but washed my wet smelly stockings
and hung them to dry. In the storefront, Yang sat on the floor across
from the boy, the abacus between them. The boy flicked the beads

one at a time from his side to the other side, moving from row to row, shouting, "Shoo, shoo, shoo." Yang sent the beads clicking back as fast as he could go, calling "Woong, woong, woong" with each snap of his fingers. The only grown men I knew who played with children were simpletons who had never found their adult minds.

"I need a guide to take me to Lytton and find the boy's mother."

"Ask at the cookhouse?" He didn't look up.

"They said Sam Bing Lew, but he's not right for me."

"Sam helps everyone."

I should have expected a man with a mix-blood daughter to side with Sam.

"That Sam is a brave man. He went to get free land," Yang declared. "The office worm told him that China men couldn't have any. Sam said, 'I was born here. I'm Canadian.' The office worm laughed. 'You're Native, and your people can't take free land.' Everyone snickered, for days. China men said, 'Sam, you're no China man. Go claim the free land.' The Native people said, 'Sam, you're not one of us. Go get some free land.'"

"Sam told me to take the boy to China," I said.

"He'll find the mother. He speaks all languages." He saw my face and then said, "Don't want a mix-blood, is that it?"

"Hey!" The boy tugged at him to resume playing.

With no need for me to watch the brat, I left them to their gleeful shouting. I visited nearby Chinese stores and watched the games. None of the gamblers looked at me. When they paused, I asked about a guide. Everyone praised Sam, as if he had recently saved their lives at great risk to himself. I nodded at their advice and bought new stockings.

Back at the washhouse, the brat was bawling. He had run along the corridors of hanging clothes with his arms outstretched, grabbing items and pulling them to the ground. Yang had beaten the boy with the back of a scrub brush. The brat was still screaming and stomping his feet. A thread of saliva hung from the washman's mouth, glistening.

"Stop!" I grabbed the brush and threw it aside.

Yang picked it up to wave in my face. "No beating, no growing."

"I'll hang the laundry up." I wiped the boy's tears. "You don't need to do anything."

"He needs restraint." Yang lunged at the boy, but I blocked him. "These children get wild blood from their mothers."

I pushed him away. "That's why your girl ran off?"

He growled and backed off.

I brushed dirt and sawdust off a shirt, and then saw sap leaking from the floorboard. That was causing the trouble. "You should have kept a clean floor."

"You sweep it." He took bedsheets to the door and held them to the light. "You're no superior man. You drag the boy to his mother, saying it'll be better. Truth is, you don't want him in China. You'll lose face."

"Taking him to China would be easier than this!"

In the end, we rewashed several bedsheets and shirts, squatting side by side at a tub, using soap and washboard. Yang cursed the extra work.

"When do you go to China?" I tried to distract him.

"Can't go!" He answered as if my question was the stupidest thing he had heard. "I stay to watch my daughter."

"Her husband does that," I pointed out.

"Who trusts the redbeards?"

"You let her marry one!" I almost burst out laughing. This old stick talked in circles.

"Wee-yum has a good business. He's not old. He's friends with Native people. It was the best I could do." He glared at me. "I was good father, not like you."

I ignored him, but he went on. "Don't dump that boy at church. No one loves a child more than the trueborn mother."

"I know—"

"His people must get strong again. Redbeard sickness killed them by the thousands. You want the boy's mother? You need Sam."

"You think the boy should stay here? But Sam says he should go to China."

"The boy belongs here."

"Then we have no quarrel." I slapped the crate. "We can talk as friends."

"You'll go home *high-high-glad-glad*. I'll go home sad and weeping, never to see Jane again, as if she suddenly died."

"Parents cry when daughters are married out."

"Jane was as big as your boy when her mother died. I raised my daughter. You, you won't miss your son. You don't even know him."

"You said you're not going back to China."

"No one here respects me. China men pestered me, asking me to sell them time with my wife and daughter. In the next breath, they called Native people dirty and stinky."

I finished washing the shirts, and the boy followed me outside.

Two children ran by the iron road, giggling and bickering, using sticks to keep a metal hoop rolling between them. Children at home did the same, but their hoop was of bamboo.

Good thing I was taking the child to Mary. Raising a mix-blood child had driven this washman crazy.

7

THE ROAD AHEAD ALWAYS SLOPES UP (1885)

All night I fretted about paying Sam. Too little and he would brush me off or make only a half-hearted effort to find Mary. Too much and he would gloat over my dread of the wilderness, lack of common sense, fear of falling. Having money didn't make things easier. Squeezing too tightly crushed the bird in hand, but too loose a grip let it escape.

The store clerks had advised going to Lytton and then hiring a guide, but I wanted to ask about Mary's whereabouts before I got there. Her people moved around, from summer to winter camps, from hunting in the mountains to taking food by the river. They married into one village from another and travelled and traded between them. They weren't like China men, stuck to one village like flies to honey, from the day they were born until they were buried.

Yang could advise me what to pay, but I wanted to avoid him. During dinner he had asked how long I had spent with Mary.

"A year."

"Bullshit," he crowed, making me a liar, "wasn't more than six months."

This cockhead knew nothing about me. "She left me!"

"Of course!" His eyes gleamed. "She saw you with a Chinese whore."

To talk further with him would only invite more taunting. After railway work, I had stayed away from all China people, whores included. It was the only way to steer clear of the iron road and its unending noise: men coming, men fleeing, fights here, and blood everywhere, and all men cursing in foul and violent moods, trying with shit luck to make the best of an ugly situation. If the men were suddenly sullen and quiet, then someone had recently been killed, and no one wanted to discuss bad luck.

After dinner, Yang had shown me a photograph stuck to stiff cardboard. A middle-aged redbeard man sat in front of Yang and a young woman who held flowers and wore a white veil. Father and daughter peered with large eyes like doubtful servants into the camera while the groom's pleased smile stretched over a mouthful of uneven teeth. The creases in Yang's stiff Chinese jacket poked up in straight lines, unlike the redbeard's suit, which was rumpled as a baby blanket. Yang demanded to know who was prettier, his daughter or my Mary.

"They could be sisters," I said. "Mary was so pretty that I feared for her. I told her to run to our people in case of danger. I taught her to shout in Chinese, 'Redbeard chases me. Help!'"

"Why would she come to us?"

"She ran to me all the time."

"Did she go to school?" He pointed to a pile of books. "I sent Jane."

"She taught you English?"

"I taught her!"

In the morning, I awoke at the sound of the front door. Yang led in Sam, who held out a brimming wooden bowl. The brat whooped with joy and started stuffing red and purple berries into his mouth. Mixed in a white mash, they slipped to the floor. He picked them up to eat.

I burrowed into my blankets. No doubt Sam's grandmother had sent food to make peace.

He nudged me. "Do you want me to take you to Lytton?"

"No use. Mary doesn't want the boy. She dumped him once already."

Through half-shut eyes I watched him crown the boy with a furry hat. Two animal horns jutted from its sides; a thick brush of a tail looped down the back. The brat started singing in an old man's quaver as his little body turned in circles, feet shuffling from one to the other.

I pictured villagers in China screeching in outrage, yanking away their children, covering their eyes and ears, and cursing the boy as a demon spawn who called up ghosts and evil spirits. Good thing he was going to his mother.

"The hat is for older boys," Sam said, "but Yaya thinks Peter will like it."

Yang pulled me to my feet. "I told Sam this morning that the boy needed his mother."

I almost slapped his grinning idiot face. "I said I didn't want Sam."

"He's the best."

"Sam and his grandmother are right," I declared. "The boy should go to China."

Yang shook his head as Sam broke in. "My grandmother knows the boy's mother; she told me where to find Mary. She's near Cache Creek. Her husband is Secwepemc—a man called Louis."

"You changed your mind."

"Got to sell my goods."

"Mary said Lytton," I said.

"You think she wanted you to find her?" He paused and then added, "Lytton is on the way to Cache Creek."

"By the clear river or the muddy one?"

"The clean one, Thompson."

"If you have trouble before Lytton," Yang said, "we have kin in North Bend."

"I don't need help," I snapped.

※

"Today will be tough," Sam said. "We climb four hundred feet. I warn you, in case you get scared."

"Can't be that high," I said. The pack dug into my shoulders. "The trains would eat too much fuel going up."

"*Wah*, aren't you clever? Shouldn't you be prime minister?"

Pompous ass, I thought. Then I asked, "Do we go past *Ee Yook Moon*?"

"What's that? You mean Hell's Gate?"

"I want to see it."

"You haven't? Didn't you work on the railway? Everyone saw it."

"Nobody pointed it out."

"You were too stupid."

"We didn't want to step on horse shit."

Dark clouds threatened rain as we hurried along. Mountains at the horizon, steep cliffs along the river, and dark forests were all overnight rice, served a second day. The river flowed in a steady thrust, glistening wherever it caught the light. Sparrows and blue jays chirped and flitted in the trees. Grandfather told me long ago that when birds sang in the woods, it meant safety, it meant that no wolves lurked nearby. The memory made me grin; it had never risen before. I went to tell Peter this lifesaving tip but stopped myself. If Sam translated it, then the boy would see him as the expert, not me.

"Ever hear of a China man taking his Native wife to China?" Sam claimed that his grandmother had asked this, but I reckoned it was his own question and did not reply until he put it to me again, louder.

"No."

"Ever hear of a China man taking children from here to China?"

"Of course. He needed help raising his son."

"What did people in China say?"

"How would I know? I wasn't there."

"Do men tell their wives in China about the women they meet here?"

"Do you tell your woman about Goddess?"

"I tell her that Goddess whispers playful words in my ears, puts me into her mouth, and says that having me is like bedding two men of two races at the same time." He laughed.

"Screw you."

"You should have yanked out your cock if you didn't want mothers and children chasing you."

"I always pulled out."

"You couldn't control yourself!"

I marched out of his range. Lewd talk was a manly pastime but not with this snot worm. It was common during railway work, especially after the rest day when men had gone to town.

"Look whose pants are wet and sticky!" They chuckled and made piggish snorts. "He's dreaming of the sows at home!"

"Peony stopped bleeding. She's open for trade now. Better go see her soon."

"They fired Jade Face. The grass soups didn't heal her down there."

"Redbeards went to Old Chong's place. His women said they had wee little birdies."

We chortled about the women who were kind and gentle enough to temper our bluster. They reminded us that we weren't at home with wives, doing our duty to assert clan strength with more children. They saw that we weren't fully men here because even a redbeard drunk with a walnut brain was backed up by law books and rifles.

We tried to watch over our own. We rolled in and out of the beds of Chinese whores, after which we strolled to the brothels run by redbeards. We toured those noisy places only once, to bounce on the heavy mats holding coils of springy metal and to test ourselves against thick white flesh. At first we vowed to buy time only from China women so that everyone could go home rich. But they were costly. Doormen took a cut from each client. Owners poked noses to the sky and declared, "Goods from afar, pricey for sure."

Then we noticed the mix-blood people. They stood out, with

blue or grey eyes, and the big noses of redbeards. All, however, had black hair. Some appeared at first glance to be Chinese, and then not at all, depending on the shade of skin, cheekbone tilt, or brazen look in their eyes. Redbeard men had set up house with Native women, and these were their offspring, so China men thought we had discovered a custom of the land. Soon we beckoned to Native women too. But the redbeards stayed here while China men were forced to think of home.

During my washhouse days, Lotus was empress over a band of Chinese whores shipped over for the railway trade. Like Goddess, Lotus reigned effortlessly over a loyal crowd of men. She had quick wit and strong views, so clients found her funny and charming. She took all men, from crew bosses to rail hands, from cooks to tea boys, charging them what they could afford. Then, after seeing a China man get thrashed in the street by redbeards, she refused all their business.

"*Help a person, do your best,*" she recited, "*Dispatch the Buddha, send him west.*"

She told her Chinese clients that if they bedded white whores, then they needn't return to her. Of course, she couldn't keep track of where her customers chose to poke their fleshy rods, but her threat made news everywhere.

Boss Lew had a hefty cock and bragged about it. Word reached Lotus that he'd been sporting with a white woman named Rosalind. The next time that he called on Lotus, she turned him away. Boss Lew stopped going to see her rival who, rumour said, had taken much pleasure from the China man's time and gifts.

When Rosalind learned who had barred him, her face turned

black as ink. She burst into Lotus's place to punch and kick her. Lotus fought back with equal measure until some men pulled them apart. Weeks later, a fire at Rosalind's place took her life.

The town's men watched as her body was taken from the smoking ruins. Mary comforted a stricken compatriot who had worked for Rosalind. We China men expected to get blamed for the fire. A few merchants fled town. What a relief when the redbeards did not strike at us. House fires were common then, and no one could prove that we had been involved. Lotus refused to go into hiding and carried on her trade. The China men mused that Rosalind had lost much face among her own kind after owning up to a fondness for Boss Lew. This was a first-rate story to take home.

Not long afterward, I went to see Mary. We went to bed, and she clung to me long after we were spent. She left town soon after. I didn't eat or sleep for days. In my mind, we had made each other content, even though we couldn't say much to each other. We shared a quiet sorrow, nothing that was ever discussed or understood. Many of my own people also lived in that makeshift town that had sprung up around a railway depot, emptying the redbeards' chamber pots, digging their latrines, and washing their clothes. Both Mary and I were alone and lonely, even though our own people and languages churned around us. Some mighty force had shaken us loose from all that, like apples falling from a high tree and rolling far downhill. The first time that I had called at the engineer's house, Mary's dark face brightened when she saw my hat and ironed clothes. Our leather shoes were equally shiny. Arm in arm, we strolled back and forth in front of the hotels and drinking houses where Native women gathered. Mary never spoke to them. But neither of us was free—excitable employers, an error in language, a runaway horse—any simple event could crush us.

∗

A mile after Alexandra Bridge, Sam said, "Big Tunnel is near."

The wagon road had crossed that bridge to the river's east bank, but we kept following the railway on the west bank. "And Hell's Gate?" I demanded.

"Further north, at least seven tunnels to pass. You afraid of the dark?"

I stalked ahead without answering.

The slopes of Canada's forests and mountains climbed like pillars at a temple, like the walls of a city. In China, the landscape stretched the other way, flat and level. Our patchwork of fields flooded annually to extend the muddy rivers that slid wide and turgid under creaking barges and ferries. What little wild and useless land there was, was found on the graveyard hills, where only drunks and madmen lost their way. In Gold Mountain, a single misstep in the woods led an honest man astray for days.

At home, sunsets shot shimmering orange light from the horizon all the way to my feet at the dockside. Here, the Fraser River burst through its narrow channel like an enraged dragon, spewing steam and spray. The only thing its froth reflected was the broad sky, sometimes bright, sometimes dark. The land and water seethed with potent currents.

A smooth edge caught my eye. Something planned and man-made sliced down through the bushes and white stumps toward us.

At first I thought of coffins on display, but this was too narrow, too shallow. It was a wooden trough, carrying mountain water downhill over crates and sawhorses to a large boarding hall. As long as two city blocks, the trough's sections were bevelled for a tight fit. Bands of leather sealed looser joints. The brat jogged beside it, running his hand alongside as if it were a massive horse. Where one section had toppled, water sloshed onto a soggy marsh.

Nearby, sheds with toppled roofs and walls lay open to the sky. A saw blade, cracked and rusted, as tall as the boy, stood among blackened boilers and charred pallets.

Farther on, a man watered raised rows of greens from a big tin can that hung from his shoulder pole. He plodded along without looking up, deaf to my footsteps. His garden was no graveyard, but I wondered who would be stupid enough to grow crops in the frosty autumn.

"Three men live here," Sam told me. "The old one, One Leg, is crippled and refuses to go home. Falling rocks softened the skull of his friend No Brain, and left him strange. He follows One Leg all over. The youngster, Fist, of course, wants to go home."

"One Leg must love the rainy cold of Gold Mountain. Or, he has an ugly wife."

"Shut your mouth. He's a good customer."

One Leg stood by a chair, hanging wet clothes on a line strung between rundown cabins. Crutches leaned against a chair. He shouted good morning and waved us on to do the rituals.

We clambered around stumps and boulders to a large grave-yard. Someone had cut the wild grass and replaced the markers. Mounds and craters with different heights of weeds and overgrowth told of burials done over time. It looked like a redbeard graveyard, wide and flat, laid out in straight lines, a sturdy fence around it. One hand had brushed all the names on uniform markers.

Fools had died here. Fellow fools buried them. Newcomer fools tended to them. But no one would be left here to dig up the bones and send them to China. Had the brushwork man used an oily ink? If not, all his careful efforts were wasted; the sun and rain would triumph.

One Leg and No Brain approached. The crutches were homemade, sapling trunks with flaking skin, bound with wire. No Brain had only one arm; his shirt sleeve was pinned to his chest.

Sam hadn't mentioned this flaw; he must have wanted to knock me off-balance, to leave me speechless. After introducing me, he asked, "Where's Fist?"

"That bastard?" One Leg frowned. "Who knows?"

"That bastard? Who knows?" No Brain echoed him but grinned. "He sleeps."

He had been in the garden, doing the watering with one arm. He must have had lots of practice.

When I honeyed my tongue and asked who had tended the graveyard, Sam stomped off to do the rituals, as if finally assured of my nice manners.

"Very dirty work." One Leg's crutches gave him heft and height, so he was almost my size. "Only I can read and write. We had no paper or pencil, only ink and brush. Fist stood at the graves while No Brain brought the markers to me. You could hardly read the names that had been written on lumps of rock. Insects crawled out. I gave a jump! I thought they were ghosts. I copied each word onto new wood and then No Brain took it back to Fist. He planted it in the exact same spot as before."

"Did you count how many?" I sounded earnest.

"What, you are collecting taxes?"

"No, but—"

"What's your surname?"

I knew that he would snort at my reply.

"Tiny name! We, we are Chan, so thirty of us came together, in one gang. We looked out for each other."

"How many survived?" Lucky for me, he enjoyed the sound and volume of his words.

"First man left after two months. Mosquitoes bit him and nobody else. They sucked him dry." He chuckled. "When he got nicked by a razor, no blood flowed, as if he were already salted fish. After the first cold, five men went south, sailed for home. That was three years ago."

"I've been here four years," I told him.

"All railway work?"

I changed topics. "Today, we brought excellent goods."

"Time to start!" Sam beckoned One Leg and No Brain to join him.

Thankful to escape, I led the boy toward the cabin. Its chimney was a rolled sheet of tin, matted with orange-brown rust. At the wood-chopping site, I found stumps with flattened tops and laid blankets over them. When I unpacked tea leaves, two grades of rice, several kinds of dried beans, and pork sausage, it drew flies right away.

I made sure the scoops and scales stood out prominently, hoping for quick sales that would let us leave. Rail hands who were lucky enough to have quit the work with their bodies intact were less lucky on meeting their maimed comrades. Then they were obliged to listen and grunt kindly to all tales of missing limbs and gory injuries, even if some cockhead was spitting out stories laden with extra vinegar and salt.

One Leg wanted to stay here in Gold Mountain. To go home with only one eye, one arm, or one leg was to bend over and offer your naked rear end to everyone for a hefty kick. If you couldn't work, you were a pot with a burned-out bottom, a hand lacking a thumb, an army without a general. Not only would your wife be forced to tend to you, as was her rightful duty, but she would also continue to hire workers to grow and sell the crops. Your friends and kin would turn away, seeing that you had fallen from the favour of gods and ancestors. Those powerful beings had, after all, let their shielding gaze wander away from you. And if you were bad luck, then everyone was safer to avoid you.

I turned around and found the brat gone. I ran through garden plots, piles of rubbish, and log cabins with fallen roofs. The buildings had not been shingled, only covered by tree branches and long grass. In the cabin that was occupied, faint opium smoke greeted me. Of course: One Leg and No Brain needed help with their pain. I let my eyes adjust to the dark. The cavern had beds, crates, and tools cringing by its walls, its centre as open and empty as a recently harvested field. At the far end, firewood was crackling in a stove by a window.

The brat sat at a big table with wooden legs like smooth sanded balls or the thighs of a giant lady. The table was split down its centre by a crack, but the two halves had been pulled together by struts, nails, and wire looped tightly around the edge. The boy hummed and stacked low walls of domino tiles, peering at the red and black dots painted on the wood.

I yanked him away. He whined. Gleaming metal caught my eye. A rifle sat on a shelf.

A stern voice in a slow deliberate tone cut through the dark. "At last someone scolds the stupid thing."

I waited, but the man in the shadows did not come forward.

"Doesn't your boy know not to touch?" he demanded. "He's filthy and our tiles must stay clean."

"You know what they say." I tried to laugh it off. "At game halls, fathers know no sons."

"Haven't you any shame, being a coolie to that mix-blood?"

I tilted my head toward the graveyard. "Don't you pay respects?"

"Don't know any names there."

"You keep it neat and tidy."

"One Leg dreams up chores each day."

"Shouldn't you help him? He was hanging clothes."

"He insists. I don't argue."

I snapped, "Don't know how to write the word 'diligent,' do you?"

Outside, I flapped a cloth to menace the insects again. The men strolled toward us, slowly, for the sake of One Leg, whose crutches poked for solid ground. Behind me, Fist came to the door.

He was small, with the furtive look of an opium addict, keen only on his latest stupor. Now I saw why he kept to the shadows. He had survived smallpox so nicks and gouges covered his face and hands. A ruthless blotch by his nose twisted his face sideways. His baggy pants and loose shirt made him a child in grown-up's clothes. Skimpy whiskers dripped from a sunken chin, but his eyes were widely set, a good sign. All his limbs and fingers were intact, yet beside him, One Leg and No Brain looked clean and neat, with buttoned shirts, and handsome, with dark eyebrows and wide chins. This could not be a happy place.

"One Leg cooked rice porridge," called Sam. "He invites us!"

"We have customers ahead," I pointed out.

Sam was busy touting his goods to No Brain. When One Leg went inside, I recalled the domino tiles. If he saw the brat's little walls, we might get scolded again.

He was balancing on one foot to shove wood into the stove.

"Let me help set the table." I pushed aside the tiles.

He tossed me a cigar box.

"Not afraid, living so far from town?" I asked. "Remember Yee Fook?"

"Yee Fook needed a gun."

Two years ago, redbeards sought revenge over a perceived slight and raided a railway camp late one night, setting fire to it. Workers poured out of cabins but got pummeled with poles and heavy tools. Yee Fook was one of two deaths. Every China man in Gold Mountain knew his name, one that would be taken home and sighed over.

No Brain grabbed pots, clutched cloths in his armpit, and ran outside again.

One Leg stirred the food, tasted it, and slammed the pot lid. "Watch that Sam doesn't cheat your wages. Once the trains start running, the price of goods will drop. He'll lose money, starve to death."

"Stand aside!" No Brain lugged in a laden pot. Sam followed with bulging loads in the carrying cloths.

When I went to fetch the last goods, Fist leaned against the door jamb, smoking a lumpy roll of tobacco.

"Good thing you know how to write the word diligent," he said.

※

One Leg ladled the porridge into bowls and put out bits of flavouring: dried fish and pickles, sausages and salted egg, ginger and green onions.

"Let's all eat." He waved for us to start.

"Let's all eat." We echoed him but waited for the eldest to begin.

Only Fist failed to repeat the invitation. Yet, as the youngest one present, he was the one most expected to do so. Nor did he pick up his metal spoon.

"Today we have guests." One Leg looked at Fist. "Can't we be grateful for this?"

"Very sweet." I took several sips. "What broth is this?"

Fist refused to reply. We ate in silence for a while until One Leg pointed to the antlers drying by the stove. "Fist shot a deer."

I had mistaken them for tree branches because they lay in the shadow. "You three ate a deer?" I asked. "How did you carry it?"

"Butchered it in the woods and took pieces to town to sell."

"Some days we sit there until dark," said No Brain. "Nothing comes near, not even a squirrel."

"Look at him," said One Leg. "Won't talk, won't eat, won't do a thing, all to show his contempt."

I ate as fast as the hot porridge allowed, but Fist turned to me. "Uncle, can you ask at the Lytton temple for us?"

"Get Sam to do it," I said.

"He's not our kind." Fist pointed to a tatty print of Ghost Subjugator, ripped from an almanac and pinned to the wall. "He doesn't even know what that is."

Sam took a moment before speaking in a drawl. "I've been in temples. I can toss the charms."

"Ask His Holiness if One Leg should go home, yes or no," said Fist. "Ask if I should stay here or not."

One Leg slurped his food and muttered, "Pay him no heed."

"I won't come back this way," I said. "My ship to China leaves in six days."

"All China men go home, except this ox head," Fist said. "Tell him to be reasonable."

"The older the ginger, the hotter its bite," I said, resenting the sting of One Leg's tongue from earlier.

"You're no different from One Leg," said Fist, "leaving your boy here for the same reason he stays: fear of people laughing at you."

"*Mares need a stud, sons must be true-blood,*" I retorted.

Fist slammed the table and then ran outside.

Sam fetched more porridge as the brat chewed with false vigour, mocking my itch to leave. When Sam emptied the plate of sausages into Peter's bowl, the boy grinned at him.

"Go to Fist," One Leg said to me. "Tell him to go home. He can say our injuries will kill us soon."

"He won't listen. He hates me," I said.

"He hates proverbs. Tell him not to buy extra ship tickets."

"Why doesn't he just go?" I threw down my spoon. My bowl was empty, and I didn't want any more.

"He promised his father to tend his uncle, No Brain, who won't leave without me."

"His father waits at home?"

"He died here. But people in China know about the vow."

"Go talk to Fist," Sam said. "Aren't you a superior man?"

I cursed them all.

The sun had broken through the grey clouds, and the faces of tree stumps were bright yellow basins, adding light to a gloomy day. They floated above the broken ground. I skirted them, suddenly fearful that they were a part of the graveyard. Across the river, cloud shadows hung like giant blankets over the cliffs, broken by airy shafts of white light. The distance reassured me. We needed to get back to the road, to find Mary. My family was waiting. Grandfather wouldn't live forever.

By the graveyard, Fist had lit another roll of tobacco.

"Didn't learn much from the railway, did you?" I asked.

He exhaled smoke and looked away.

"*Trust the mountain, but mountains slide*," I said, forgetting One Leg's warning.

"What did the old man say?"

"That you should leave him and No Brain here. That you should not waste money."

The afternoon light caught bright and dark shades of green stirring among the trees. Just as I wondered if a deer might be watching us, a sudden movement crashed through the bushes behind us. We turned but saw nothing.

Fist needed to be an animal with sharp claws and fearsome growl. He needed to sprint through the forest like a hunted deer. Canada was a dense forest, with stiff branches and prickly bramble blocking your every step. The longer he stayed, the more this place would drain him, until he cracked and fell apart like that overlong wooden trough.

He shook his head. "That cockhead One Leg thinks I can make a life here."

"He should kill himself. Then No Brain can go with you."

"Tell him!"

"Those two are fragrant already."

"You don't need to enter the temple," Fist wheedled. "Just come back and tell that shit-hole prick to go home. Tell him you asked and His Holiness said he must go."

"Lies are no good." These cockheads were all liars. Fist claimed he was told to make a life here, yet One Leg said he told him to go home.

"You can save them both," Fist pleaded.

"Fools came for the iron road," I said, turning away. "The only bigger fools are those who don't know how to go home."

Back at the cabin, Sam had loaded up our packs with new goods, making them heavier than before. I cursed on hearing the solid clink of bottles.

"Good trading is ahead," Sam explained with a rueful grin. "I had goods stored here."

"Well-hidden?" Of course liquor was involved.

"A horse brings the stock. Otherwise the bottles are too heavy."

No wonder he had raged when we sold Moy nothing. Sam was a far smarter businessman than I had thought.

One Leg limped out to say farewell. "Fist listen to you?"

"Uncle, go home," I said loudly. "It's better for everyone, here and in China."

"I told him many times to go home."

"Fools came for the iron road," I said again. "The only bigger fools are those who don't know how to go home."

❋

"Do you fight your kind everywhere?" Sam demanded. "That shit mouth of yours won't sell anything."

"Stupid donkeys."

"Want to be a superior man?" He matched my pace step for step. "Then clear them out. Push your China men onto those big boats and send them home."

"You evict the China men but keep the redbeards?"

"China men are weak."

"Then so are you."

"Native blood makes me strong."

I stomped ahead.

He shouted, "You cockheads come with no money but kneel to the redbeards. They give you the shit jobs that even my people won't take. China men have no honour."

I walked even faster.

We China men had been plenty brave to cross the black ocean. We had rules for safety and politeness: "*Enter a house, greet your hosts; enter a temple, worship ghosts.*"

China had lost its honour to foreign armies and navies, but we knew that life went on. "*Family at ease, nation at peace.*"

Sojourners were not yam brains. We talked wisdom all the time: "*Don't beat a dog until you know its master.*"

Clearly, Sam's father had not taught him much.

As the path sloped upward, the load tugged at my shoulders. Sam had been right about the steep climb. At Big Tunnel, Sam called a halt, lowered his pack, and dusted himself off. Then he shut his eyes, raised his arms, palms to the sky, and started to chant. Turning slow circles, he tossed crushed dry leaves into the air. The brat watched with solemn eyes.

As we unpacked lanterns, Sam said, "This mountain suffered greatly. Redbeards packed in black powder and blasted its head, chest, and arms into the river. Fish were blocked from going upstream. Native crewmen urged the Company to take action, but it refused. We cleared the rubble on our own. Finally the Company sent some China men to help."

Big Tunnel curved and cut off the entrance light. I hurried into its cool darkness to show my courage.

"*Baba!*" Peter called. "*Ung mai ngoi.*"

He called me father, asked me to wait! I spun around. "Sam, ask how he learned that!"

"His mother, who else?"

I spoke to the boy in Chinese. "Have you eaten rice?"

Nothing.

"Good morning."

"Eat sweets?"

"Want to go back to China?"

Nothing.

"Doesn't matter if he speaks Chinese or not." Sam had strolled ahead. "You're not taking him to China."

"He has Chinese blood. He should speak Chinese."

"He has Native blood too."

The boy pulled me to Sam and took his hand, so the three of us walked together, trying to hurry but not stumble. The darkness didn't bother the boy, who hummed and skipped along. I breathed with relief: Peter would do well, no matter where he went. He would make his mother proud.

"And you?" I asked. "Will you teach your child Chinese words?"

"Won't be there. The mother doesn't want me. At first she said I was the father, but then she said no. Now she says the father is a Native man."

"You let her take claim?" I was astounded. "But it was your seed that made the child."

"Child is inside her."

"Will her family raise it?"

"Of course."

"The mother fears you are poor," I said. "Many women think that way."

"I can care for them, but she prefers her people."

"Funny," I said. "Mary came to Victoria and dumped a child on me. Your woman took the child away from you, even before birth. Yet the two are the same kind of children."

"Not so," Sam declared. "Mine has more Native blood."

"That's good?" Of course I was doubtful.

"Of course."

"Bullshit."

8

THE TRIALS OF WORKERS ON THE RAILWAY (1881)

To walk into jail was to die. In China, a scruffy convict shuffling through the streets with head locked into a heavy cangue was a walking corpse. If he survived harsh guards, cruel torture, and filthy cells, then angry brushstrokes at the clan hall would cross him off the family tree. If he managed to get released from prison, the guards sliced off one ear so that his record followed him forever for all to see. Death was no escape. If he died in jail, the body was burned among other corpses, the mixed ashes and bone bits dumped far away. Never buried by your family, without a spot on the ancestral altar, your soul was damned to wander homeless forever.

The four-storey stone walls of New Westminster's penitentiary held 120 prisoners in small cells. The fifteen sullen Chinese inmates mumbled welcomes and urged me to stick with them in case fights erupted against the redbeards. They warned me who among the China men were rivals. They told me about the two old-timers who liked to poke their cocks up each other's ass, saying that I shouldn't be surprised if they approached me. All that I needed to say was a polite no. Otherwise everyone left me alone. I wasn't the only rail hand there. Two coolies had been convicted of pilfering a Company warehouse, but they kept to themselves. No doubt they thought, *Close to a judge, get power; Close to a cook, get food.*

Me, I didn't turn into a killer. My cellmate Big Town was a righteous man. He admitted to killing a man, a gambler with a small surname who had cheated him of his savings. He had proof of the gambler's crime as well as witnesses, but getting justice in a town of lazy merchants was beyond his reach. He did the deed, he said, knowing that he couldn't stomach his own indifference. The fact that the victim's ghost never bothered him here meant that Big Town had taken the high road. He claimed that his family in China knew all the gory details and backed him fully for upholding clan honour.

When I complained about cold shoulders from the old-timers, Big Town chuckled. "You coolies came in throngs that filled the steerage deck while we sailed alone, just a handful of China men on the ship. Back then, most people went to South Ocean, to Singapore and Malaya, just a few hundred miles to go. But Gold Mountain was 6,000 miles away, across the world's largest ocean. We timid children prayed to every god and spirit we knew. You coolies arrive with a written contract for job and wages; we came with nothing but rumours of gold. Your bosses feed and house you; we scavenged for firewood and slept on rocks. We learned English and Chinook one word at a time while redbeards laughed. You coolies run to your bookman who calls in a translator."

I shot back, "We're all safer now that more China men live here."

Big Town talked late into the nights and confirmed that America was the best place to be. "My cousin and I trekked from town to town there, walking barefoot to save boot leather, doing odd jobs.

Skies were sunny and dry, not rainy like here. Nights were warm; we slept outside. My cousin got a job cooking for a redbeard. That man knew farmers and businessmen who needed workers, so my cousin put China men into work gangs and hired them out. He got rich, erected a two-storey building, and installed a telegraph in his office. He sends home $200 a year."

I smirked. "Yet you came here?"

"Don't laugh. Every success is followed by fourteen failures. Such is the way of the world."

When my prison term ended, a guard marched me to the gate-house for my clothes. The dust and smells revealed they had not been washed or aired since I traded them three months earlier for a brown and yellow uniform. Good thing mice and moths had stayed away; if not, I would have returned to work half-naked. That trek was the start of my darkest time in Gold Mountain.

The escort cuffed my hands to a chain at his waist. On our way to the docks, we passed Chinatown, where compatriots frowned at me.

"I sold liquor and sent money home." I raised my fists and jangled the chain. "I served my time! They shouldn't tie me up! Tell him to unlock me."

People kept their heads down.

I needed to break free for America, which Big Town had said was close by. I vowed to get there, sooner or later. But if I died first, then I wanted my ghost to stay and plague the railway so that crewmen would flee the worksite and go home sooner.

The shit-hole prick escort shamed me every way he could. A second chain bound me close to him. When I made water, he stood by me and did the same. We glanced at each other's cocks; no doubt each of us thought his birdie was bigger. When I needed to squat, he chained me to a tree, my back tight against the trunk so that the shit rolled or streamed onto my feet. If I winced at the foul smells clinging to me, then so did he. Along the iron road, we dodged horse-drawn wagons and covered our ears against pealing hammers. We hurried across logs and planks over gaping ravines. When China men pointed at me, the escort jerked me off-balance or let the chain between us tighten.

Gold miners headed south. Those ragged parties were lone men fiercely armed and groups huddled for safety, bent under packs and rusty tools. I could lug their goods and vanish into their dusty midst, going wherever they went. But I needed pocket money; tightwads like them didn't welcome freeloaders.

On the second night, I awoke in a dark roadhouse. To my surprise, the escort was gone. We had slept chained together the first night. Maybe the stink of my shit was too much to bear. Maybe he had gone for a squat himself. Maybe he went outside to drink and shoot the breeze with his new friends from dinner. Or he had stationed himself at the door, waiting for me to escape so that he could shoot me in the back. I groped for my boots.

I stopped. No money meant hunger and fruitless begging from strangers.

I pulled on a boot and paused over my cuffed hands. Someone needed to smash the iron without asking questions. Surely a China man would help me, unless he wanted to collect the reward.

The woods churned with wild animals. No one could outrun bears and cougars. If I went out that door, I didn't even know which way to turn. I could trip and drown in the latrine.

Voices and heavy footsteps approached. I lay down quickly, my heart pounding.

I kicked and cursed myself. I wanted to scream aloud, pound with both fists the taut boxes that my lungs had become. The shit-pit prison had softened me into a lump of overripe fruit. We inmates needed only to obey the guards, and then each day was as neat and orderly as a *mah-jongg* layout: Sweep and mop the office floors, even though they were clean, muck out the horse stables, weed the vegetable fields, claw at tree roots, and clear the land to plant more crops. We even built high wooden fences to better imprison ourselves. The guards checked them with care, banging the butts of their rifles on them. We tore down buildings from long ago. At first I feared the armed guards might shoot us for sport. Then it became clear that their jobs depended on herding large numbers of inmates.

A prison sentence stopped a man from earning a living so that his loved ones would starve and suffer. But my faraway family farmed and fed itself without knowing my fate. More China men should break the laws here, I mused, in order to get some peace and quiet in jail. For the first time in my life, I tasted a rich man's day, not fretting about the next day's work.

※

Heavy rains began the night I returned to the railway camp. By morning, the worksite was a long pool of mud and water. The crew had been relocated, so now we worked outside with no ceiling over us. Men rejoiced that death could not crush or bury us from above. Our job was to dig out the foot of the mountain. We pushed forward and down, drilling holes and removing debris to carve a path that led to a tunnel.

Rain soaked us and filled the cut. We carried the rubble up wooden planks that climbed along one side of the great pit. The water left the wood slick and slippery, but the bosses shouted insults when we trudged too slowly. Everyone slipped and fell. Poy warned me to drop everything and grab the boards in order to soften the landing on rocks below, where legs and backs got broken. The crew had haggled with the bosses to gain room between each coolie so that one man falling backward would not cause more injuries. Some men claimed they got a better grip walking barefoot, but the bosses stopped them because the men had to sit and remove their shoes, tie their laces to drape them around their necks, and then stop again at the other end to don their footwear. The bosses said this wasted time.

When we stopped to wring out our rain-soaked clothes, to wipe water from our eyes that blurred our sight, the Company brought in wide farmers' hats of stiff straw, varnished to be waterproof, but their prices were steep. We could have made these ourselves had the materials been on hand. Rain pooled atop the canvas tents and dripped inside. In the mornings, our wet clothes and shoes were still damp from the cool nights. But we kept our blankets folded, off the ground and under oilcloth, because sleeping in the damp led to sure death if warmth leaked from body and soul.

Patches of black mold spread inside the canvas tents. My childhood cough returned. When we children had winnowed the rice at harvest, the dusty air caused me to cough and spit. Grandmother tied a wet scarf around my mouth and nose, but I flung it away. Only fussy old women had worn those.

The coughing bent me into a weakling, hacking and spilling my guts. Healthy crewmen refused to sit near the sick ones at mealtime and set up a separate tent for us. "Illness enters through the mouth," they insisted. I argued that mine was a childhood habit, nothing contagious. But a man in my tent started to cough, and we both got evicted. In the sick tent, men simmered in silent resentment unless one fellow had medicine that he was willing to share. It was there that I heard my first railway ghost story, told by Monkey:

"One day, a washman hurried through a long tunnel, newly finished, with the tracks about to be laid. The washman hoped to get new customers at the other end. The flame in his lantern went out, and then he dropped the matches and couldn't find them. No worry. He saw a prick of light in the distance. Then someone came from behind, marching through the rubble.

"The washman called hello in Chinook and heard a reply in Chinese, 'Who's there?'

"The washman said he had lost his matches. The other said, 'Walk fast. Tunnels have ghosts.'

"'I'll fall,' said the washman.

"'I worked here,' said the other. 'Hold my shoulder and come along.'

"So they walked. The rail hand offered water from a gourd.

"'Your surname?' asked the washman. 'Where's your home village?'

"He got no reply. The tunnel grew brighter. He saw a shovel blade propped by the man's ear but couldn't see the face.

"The rail hand knelt to tie his shoelaces. 'You go on ahead,' he said.

"The washman reached the tunnel mouth where a railway crew was packing up, getting ready to move to a new site. A worker ran to him.

"'Is that your gourd?' he asked. 'My brother had one like that too.'

"'No,' said the washman. 'It belongs to the man behind me.'

"But no one came out of the tunnel.

"'Are you there? Are you alright?' The washman shouted into the tunnel.

"Two redbeards pumped through on a handcar, a lantern on the frame. The washman asked if they had seen anyone in the tunnel. They shook their heads.

"The worker grabbed the gourd. 'This is my brother's! I recognize this crack. He sealed it with sticky tree sap.'

"'Where is he now?' asked the washman.

"'Ran off. Rocks crushed him in this tunnel. He wore this gourd at his waist, but we never found it.'

"The washman fled, never to be seen again."

"It wasn't foul here, but now it is," muttered one of the sick men. "If no ghosts lingered before, then now they've come for sure."

"Monkey bought a charm to keep away the ghosts," said someone.

"Where?" I asked. "I need one."

"Get a dozen! Crooks sell them in all shapes, all colours, everywhere along the line. Their pockets burst from the booming trade."

I told them a far scarier tale that Big Town had told me:

"Twenty years ago, two brothers Yan came to gold territory and staked a claim near a wide lake ringed by forests. On the other shore were docks and shops, including a China man's store. Late one day, Younger Brother rowed a boat to the store for supplies. There he chatted with miners from the district. When he left, night had fallen, but there was a bright moon. The storekeeper urged him to stay the night, but he wanted to get home.

"The next morning, the storekeeper found Yan's boat bobbing by the docks. The supplies that had been purchased the day before were still aboard, but the oars were gone. The storekeeper quickly rowed across the lake. Older Brother said his sibling had not come home. The two men thought Younger Brother had fallen into the lake and drowned.

"The following morning, Older Brother marched into the store, all his belongings on his back. 'I'm leaving,' he said.

"Younger Brother had come to him in a dream the night before, he said, dripping wet with a greenish face. In the dream, he told him, 'Four years ago, miner Chang found gold nearby. On his way home, robbers killed him while he slept. They tied rocks to his legs, rowed to the middle of the lake, and threw him in. Chang's body has rotted, and now he needs a new body. Last night, he dragged me to the bottom of the lake. Older Brother, get out. Every few years, Chang's angry spirit will pull down a new body.'

"The storekeeper thought Yan was scared of being alone and shrugged him off. It was easy to fall overboard and drown, especially when a man couldn't swim.

"Four years later, the storekeeper had forgotten the Yan brothers. Then a miner went missing one night while rowing across the lake. The empty boat bobbed to shore, but the oars were missing. The storekeeper left town right away. He said the lake had no name, but he was sure that boatmen still vanished there."

I had asked Big Town how many lakes needed to be crossed on the way to America.

He didn't know.

⁂

Throat tonic was costly, two days' wages. Onion had seized my liquor trade and found new customers. I offered to take bootleg to sell at other camps.

"People know to come here." He dismissed me with a wave of his hand. "No need to beg for trade."

Though not a brotherhood member, Onion gave Number Two shots of free whisky. To show respect, he claimed. As for Native buyers, their headmen hadn't come to bother Onion. They had plenty of trouble of their own, as redbeard settlers moved onto their lands and claimed rights to their water and food.

Onion asked about bootleggers in prison. I hadn't met any.

He laughed. "Only you were stupid enough to get caught!"

Shorty's worsening pain from his injury caused him to smoke opium every day. He gladly admitted to ratting me out to the Company.

"Still won't confess?" he railed. "You will rot in Hell. Even if I die, I won't let you go."

"I told you, you have the wrong man."

In town, the merchant snorted when I asked for tips on making money. "If there were ways to get rich here, a hundred men would be doing them already. America? Men everywhere squat on the streets, jobless."

"At least they're warm and dry."

"They brawl to death among their own. And fight the redbeards. Last year, redbeards hanged one China man and chased the rest out of Den-wah city."

"Just one place."

"They rioted in San Francisco Chinatown. The army took three days to restore order."

In camp, I asked California about this.

"Redbeards in America hanged seventeen China men in one town," he said.

"Why do China men keep coming?"

"Better than home."

But it wasn't better here. Men fell, broke their bones, and worked through pain. The constant rain never let our feet get dry and warm. Head Cook still served the same slop of rice and fish bits. The price of goods in the Company store kept climbing. Any trip to the south would be a solo trip for me. Poy had let himself get swallowed by the work. He wore western shirt and trousers, all of the thickest materials and the highest prices. His boots, made of rubber to keep his feet dry, had ridged soles that he said gave him better grip on the wet planks. He ate with Number Two, who wanted helpers close by to take on any trouble.

On my return to camp, Poy's first words to me had been, "You stink of shit."

"You sent no letters," I retorted, half in jest.

"What, pay to get words written, and then find someone who knows English and Chinese to deliver them? The prison guards demand bribes but no one knows how much, so I must give extra money to the go-between and pray he can be trusted. You think I'm stupid?"

In my absence, Poy had sent money to my family, so my debts had grown. I didn't repay him right away, not after he harangued me in front of the crew: "You had peace but went out to bring home that liquor trouble. Why didn't you just keep working? Then you'd have more money than me."

I tried to do better. I avoided game halls. I shunned the whores in town and used my hand for release. Rags drying stiffly, starched with semen, waved like banners throughout the railway camps. I shaved my own head and nicked myself badly, drawing laughter and mosquitoes.

I thought about robbing a store. But plenty of men prowled for extra cash and informers lurked everywhere. I thought to follow a winner from a game hall one night, knock him down, and grab his money. Such robberies were common; men knew to travel in groups. I pawed at Native men sleeping off their drink by the road-sides, hoping to find valuables. I thought to pull down my pants and offer my shit-hole to men who fondled other men, but the Pacific Ocean didn't stop gossip from reaching China.

Grandfather's letter brought bad news. Grandmother was seeking a husband for Younger Sister. I hurled his words into the fire. They should demand money from Father, not me. That shit-hole prick was the one hurting her search, making the need for money more acute than it need be. It was his great shame that we tried in vain to conceal. The go-betweens would report back to Grandmother that people fretted about Younger Sister's motherless childhood and also feared that the suicide hinted at madness in our blood.

To get a better match, Grandmother needed to send cakes and roast pigs to the prospective in-laws. She must enhance Younger Sister's dowry before the wedding. If she entered her husband's house empty-handed, then she would be seen as a concubine. She needed token pieces of gold and jade, new clothes, a storage chest, and household items.

When fathers couldn't protect their daughters, then brothers embraced the duty. Villagers watched our family, seeking new bruises where we could be poked and prodded. Once Younger Sister entered her new home, she could never come back, no matter how sharp-tongued her mother-in-law was, no matter how the back-stabbing sisters-in-law ruined her cooking and gave her the worst chores. We had only one chance to make the best match. Younger Sister, timid and gentle, couldn't speak for herself in a strange household. She would rather stay home and take care of Grandfather. But a spinster in the house also shamed our family name.

Bookman refused to advance me any funds. "What if you fall sick and die?" he said. "Who will repay?"

Only Poy might lend me money, but first he wanted token payments against my earlier debts. He wasn't so stupid around money any more.

If I didn't get to America, Younger Sister might be forced to settle for some oaf who stuttered, bullied women, or smoked opium.

❊

An armed party waited at camp one afternoon. Soldiers had marched in, belts over their chests, rifles on their backs.

"Everyone over age eighteen pays the school tax," said the Chinese translator. "All redbeards pay it."

After coughing all day, I had no appetite and a bad headache. I would have gladly paid the tax in order to crawl into the sick tent. But the crew was set to fight: we had been threatened over the tax several times. Now, anyone who walked away was a coward and a traitor.

We looked to Number Two or Poy to speak. To everyone's surprise, Shorty called out, "We have no children here. Why should we pay?"

"It's only called a school tax." The translator sighed with impatience. "It's a provincial tax, only three dollars a man, a paltry amount."

"Go tell your boss that."

Shorty, Number Two, and the translator exchanged glances. The visitors strutted about, muttering. A captain barked, and the soldiers jumped into two lines. Men in the front row knelt, one leg up, the other down, their rifles pointing at us.

Time to run. Or give up. Redbeard guns had shown no mercy in China.

"Go on, open fire." Shorty crossed his arms over his chest. "You can pound the rock and haul it away yourself."

"The soldiers will kill one man at a time," drawled the translator. "Not you, you with the many mouths. No, you won't be first. You, you will stand and watch your workmates die."

"Screw you," Shorty spat out.

"Will anyone pay the tax?" The translator addressed us. "Won't you obey the rules?"

"Don't listen to him!" Shorty shouted. "He gets paid to trick you. He sells you out!"

Bookman pushed his way to the front. "I'll pay half the tax but the men must pay the other half."

"Two-thirds," said Shorty.

"One-half."

"Done." Number Two, quiet up to now, cited a proverb. "*At low doors, bend down.*"

After the soldiers left, crewmen surrounded Shorty to thank him. In a blink of the eye, the snivelling opium addict became a superior man. Now he had a high stage from which to denounce me.

"Brothers, I cannot pay the tax and buy opium at the same time," he said. "Who can help me?"

His accident had happened before coming to the cut. One day, Crew Boss grumbled about slow progress. In the tunnel, a redbeard tamped powder. Crew Boss grabbed the hammer and pounded the rock face. Shorty backed off, knowing that blasters worked slowly and gently. The redbeard argued with Crew Boss but got shoved aside. He and Shorty crept away. Crew Boss hauled them back. He banged the tamping rod again, and the wall exploded. Shorty was behind the two redbeards and not hit. He fell onto the rocks. The blaster died right away but not Crew Boss. They carried him to the tunnel mouth. His arms were bloody stumps. He bled to death in the sunlight.

Shorty returned to work but couldn't sleep. Head Cook said that opium would dull the pain. This helped, and the bosses were happy. Number Two saw that this left Shorty no money to send home. He was told to quit the job, but his list of debts was a long one.

At dinner, Poy stood to speak. "We thank Shorty for speaking against the soldiers. Everyone should donate a few cents to cover his tax. How much each man pays depends on how many men are willing. Let's make it unanimous." He looked around. "Who won't join?"

My hand shot up, and several men joined me.

A furious Poy avoided me for days.

※

Rain fell for a week, filling the cut with two feet of water. Cold winds shot through the canyon. The firewood got soaked so Head Cook served lukewarm food. The latrine collapsed and dumped two men into a putrid swamp of shit. On rest day, workers refused to hike into town because they would only get soaked. The smarter ones hurried off to find stores and game halls with roofs that didn't leak. The men who were left behind clambered atop the logs that raised bedrolls from the ground and then shook loose cloths for games of chance. Stumps served as chairs and to keep goods off the soggy floor where insects thrived amid the tree branches and scraps of oil cloth. In a corner, deaf to all the shouting, a man might be mending his boot or rewrapping a bandage around his elbow.

We heard a thunderous crash one night. Next morning, the skies cleared, as if to let puny mortals better marvel at the mountain's mighty power. A landslide had dropped trees, boulders, and mud into the cut and the river. All our work vanished under the debris. Bosses and workers alike groaned. Mud was messy and slow to remove. We waded through it without seeing the sharp rocks beneath.

From the top of the heap, we worked downward, tugging at rocks and chopping trees. The debris broke apart without warning, a monster suddenly opening its mouth, swallowing and crushing workers. No foothold could be trusted. We kept an eye on the mountain above, fearing another slide. When ancient human skulls and bones were found in the debris, we backed away. Word reached the Native people, who hurried to collect the bones. Crewmen predicted death.

I awoke one morning with a bad headache. It was the same pain as from too much sun so I kept working. My nose started to bleed. By the afternoon my legs were wobbling. I took to my blankets and dropped into a deep sleep. I had short colourful dreams where masses of people rushed around me, all on urgent tasks. I was running through China, Hong Kong, and Centipede Mountain.

Someone shook me awake. It was California.

"I'm going to America," he said. "It rains too much here. Want to come with me?"

California hadn't needed ship passage so his debt to the Company was much lower. I clutched his arm and begged him to wait for me. It would be no trouble to pack, I said, I had nothing to my name and would travel light as a goddess.

I awoke wondering if he had come in a dream.

My belly bloated like a ball, tender to the touch. The diarrhea that dripped green had been followed by bloody shit, so I was glad to be constipated and solid for a while.

A fever gripped me. Poy pressed cold cloths to my forehead. Other men fell sick too: I heard someone shouting, "Drink this! If it's not bitter, it won't heal you."

The men talked about the rain, about Native men being hired to help clear the mudslide. California's freedom to quit the crew was envied by all. They cursed Head Cook, who refused to boil the herbal teas, leaving it for the men to do after their shifts. He even charged them for firewood.

They brought bowls of bitter herbal tea to me. When Poy lifted me up, sharp pain surged from my abdomen.

"Drink while it's hot." He spoke like Grandmother. "If it cools, it loses its power."

"Let me die," I said.

It took three weeks before I could stand up. Seven men had fallen sick. Half the crew fled to town. No one knew if the illness was contagious or not. Monkey died and his body was taken to the forest. Poy said he had weighed next to nothing.

I was the last of the sick men to return to work. I had earned no money, only more debt. Charges for food and lodging never stopped, not even for stricken men. I slept in a tent and my meals were ready, even if they couldn't be swallowed or kept down.

Better to have died like Monkey, like my chance to get to America. Illness would have been a worthy end, a death ordained by the gods, unlike suicide.

9

Is It the Mountain or Railway that Kills? (1881)

We awoke one morning, shivering in the sudden cold of autumn, and found Head Cook gone. The bastard had grabbed his clothes, blankets, and a week's supply of rice and fish. That shit-hole prick never faced sharp boulders or black powder, so what the hell was he fleeing? Of course he needed money in a hurry, but who didn't?

Second Cook moved into that job and Little Touch replaced him, a fine change for the crew. Number Two had been too polite, too snivelling to confront Head Cook's bad temper and fondness to brawl. Men refused to drink the water that Head Cook claimed was boiled; they demanded that Second Cook vouch for it. Head Cook labelled the complaints fussy womanly nagging. Mountain water was plenty clean, he'd said.

Right away, Onion's Native customers brought fresh meat to trade. First to arrive was a flank of deer that flavoured a week of stews and soups. Two weeks later came Eighth Month Fifteen: the autumn moon at its fullest. Back home, children lit paper lanterns for an evening parade. Their fathers twisted long grasses into a giant snake, then jabbed the serpent full of incense sticks. The dragon swayed through the night, the ends of incense bristling in a million pin-pricks of orange light, summoning the stingy gods to hear our prayers for a better harvest next year.

We had no parade, but the new cooks stewed two wild pheasants stoutly seasoned with herbal roots and nuts. We feasted and cursed the former cook.

"At summer solstice," reported Four Square, "other camps sipped old-fire soup laced with Brave Yellow brew."

"If Head Cook had served us that," said Long Life, "no one would have died during the illness."

Dried salmon remained the staple, but now pickles, fresh herbs, and sauces flavoured it. A few men, never content, grumbled that the cost of meals would rise. Onion and I exchanged knowing glances with Little Touch. We three had slyly devised this miracle.

Onion had long challenged the former Head Cook about the vile food. During my illness, Onion visited me alone one day.

"Better meals are needed, my friend, healthy foods to dispel the winds inside you," he said. "Otherwise there is no healing and you will get fragrant while young."

"Is that so?" At that time, my appetite chased my diarrhea.

"Little Touch tended horses at an inn near Foshan," he said, "but loitered in the kitchen like a hungry beggar and helped the cooks. He and Second Cook can make better meals, for sure."

Little Touch yearned to work in the kitchen. He and Second Cook often walked to town and ate fine dishes at the teahouse frequented by the bosses. The smallest man in the crew, Little Touch was viewed as a weakling by bosses and workmates. "Shouldn't you be a tea boy?" they asked. "Why don't you come back when you're grown up?"

In the kitchen, Head Cook often complained about his family, woes that Second Cook brought to Little Touch and Onion during bouts of late-night drinking.

Head Cook was the younger of two brothers. Their ailing father frowned on the older one's plan to sell the family land and buy a shop in town. Tensions were thick at home. In the letters that I read aloud to Head Cook, the father often moaned, *Trust the earth, but not a merchant's words.*

Onion told me to write a letter that looked to be from Head Cook's mother stating that dear Father had fallen very ill and pleading for the younger son's help because his brother was courting eager buyers.

Second Cook slipped my envelope into the bundle of letters that Bookman brought from town. On rest day, I read the letter to Head Cook, who cursed and stalked away to think. Not long after, he vanished.

⁑

Bookman announced that we were moving back to tunnel work. The crew argued about everything and agreed on nothing. A few idiots cheered because they took Monkey's death as a warning to leave this site of illness. The wet air lingered among the coughing, along with fears of more landslides. But others did not want to work in darkness; outside work offered bright light and cleaner air. Coolies had no say, so two unwilling fellows slipped away. The ones who were left behind fell sullen, too proud to admire the deserters' bravery, too afraid that the runaways would be proven right about future dangers. Me, I enjoyed the better meals.

We trekked north through winds and pelting rain. The men complained that we should be heading south, given the dropping temperatures. Dark forests and mountains stretched into the misty distance. All along the river, rock yielded to hammer and black powder as massive slopes of breaking stones crashed into the water. The changing landscape promised future riches and better times, but the redbeards didn't expect China men to stay. Nor could we wait. Generations of people needed to be planted and settled before towns and cities could grow and prosper like those of home, those with hundreds of years of trade and history. When we laughingly asked Bookman which rich clan was paying for this road, he said it was the government. No wonder it had pressed us for the school tax.

Crews at the new site had clawed open a tunnel using machines that we had not seen before. Workers heaved coal and wood into a sturdy furnace linked to two thrumming metal cases. The heat was welcomed by all men. Heavy pipes snaked out of the cases and into the tunnel. At the dimly lit rock face, the tubes merged into a single narrow hose that fed into a small keg. It gripped a thin spike that started spinning, turning so fast that it blurred and vanished. The redbeard lifted the keg and pressed the spike to the rock. It bit into the granite and sprayed out fine dust. We covered our ears and noses until the redbeard pulled away.

We raised our lanterns and saw nothing. Then the redbeard pushed a hand drill into the fresh hole. It was deep enough to take the powder.

That machine disposed of two hours of hand work in less than a minute, using little muscle or sweat.

Only redbeards were allowed to use the marvellous tool, a

pointed reminder of whose people had invented it. In response, crew men cursed it and sought to avoid it.

"Redbeards will use it against China, just you watch," Long Life muttered. "It will topple city walls and slaughter our people. Now it flushes out dust and sand, but blood and bone will be next, just watch."

"The Emperor bought plenty of guns and cannons from the west," said Poy.

"So why do we keep losing wars?"

Poy had joined a campaign that was collecting money to buy a pair of cannons for Guangzhou. Our provincial capital had been looted during the Opium War. Now some braggart down the line claimed that if every coolie donated a day's wages, then it was enough to buy the big guns from Germany and ship them to China. Poy recited a bunch of tired arguments: China needed modern arms to defend itself; China must copy western methods; China needed to strengthen itself and fight back. If not, foreigners would soon enslave our nation.

Four Square shook his head. "Fight the west with something else, not cannons. If you fight the redbeards with their own weapons, then they will win, for sure. They built those things, didn't they? So of course they know how to use them best. You think they passed all their secrets to us China men? You think a master chef shares his recipes with his underlings? Don't be so stupid."

"The bookmen here are crooked, and officials in China are corrupt," said Little Touch.

When Poy asked me to donate, I told him that my every penny was being sent home. "Haven't you noticed? I avoid women, wine, and opium."

"You still gamble," he snapped.

Other men moaned that the machine drills would put an end to our work.

"They will pierce the mountain in a week's time and leave us jobless."

"More machines will be brought in to get rid of us."

Number Two tried to quell the alarm. "In America, the railway employed China men for three years."

"That was fifteen years ago! Did they even have machine drills then?"

Number Two didn't know. They asked Bookman how long the work would last but got no answer.

What did it matter? If the job ended early, then we would all have a better chance of getting home alive. We could stroll into our villages with heads held high, having built a great road, having handled steel shinier than our ancient mirrors.

When Old Skinny, the first deserter from our forest days, was found among the other crew of the new site, our crew mobbed him, jabbering about what a lucky omen it was, a direct challenge to the Company's steady loss of men by death or desertion. Old Skinny's return reminded us of the ungiving nature of Gold Mountain. He hadn't found gold or steady work in the north, so he came back. The Company rehired him with no penalty, so that meant we China men were badly needed. But that was because the work was shit and we needed wages.

After the well-wishers melted away, I went to him.

"Hok, you're still here." He seemed surprised. "You're not stupid, you could have escaped."

"You didn't go to America. You should be rich by now."

"That route went downriver, to the coast," he said after a moment. "Much too close to China. Only cowards went home so quickly."

"I would have rushed to America."

"Why didn't you?"

I shrugged and asked about his opium habit. He declared that he had quit, so I told him about Shorty, who was smoking more and more. Bookman noted the weekly amount of opium that Shorty's wages could cover, and asked the clerk at the company store to limit his purchases to that. The clerk refused.

Shorty was angry enough to spit teeth. The pains had worsened and he needed more black mud to gain any relief. Number Two urged the store to stop selling it to Shorty, to leave him no option but to go home. Again the clerk refused.

Shorty wheedled cash from everyone, like a peddler on a busy street.

"It's the first of the month," he trumpeted, even though no one followed the calendar. "It's the God of War's birthday. It's the ascension of Heavenly Empress. Good deeds today attract sacred favour and reduce your suffering in the eighteen levels of Hell."

Poy and Onion were two of the few men to give Shorty cash. Others, like me, refused to give him anything at all.

※

The furnace at the tunnel mouth fed only one machine drill, so we still used hand tools at the rock face. Before the machine drills were brought in, smoke and dust from each round of blasting settled to the ground between blasts. Now dust spurted out all day long, fogging the air and the low glow of lamps. Grit coated our tongues and chafed our noses. We tied wet cloths over our noses and mouths. My cough worsened. The only mercy was this: machine drilling sped up the work and led to frequent breaks when the ladders and scaffolds were removed for the blasting.

The bosses pushed us to go faster. They brought in wheelbarrows, but the ground was too rough for the narrow wheels. They lay down long planks, but the boards tipped and cracked and then the wheelbarrows spilled. The tunnel grew longer, so we trudged farther and farther with our loads of debris. The bosses clapped each other's backs with delight when they started a night shift, claiming that the men in the tunnel already worked in darkness. But a lack of moonlight outside stopped us from seeing the way to the dump.

Poy told me to quit and head to America.

"Haven't you heard?" I wanted to strangle him. "There are no jobs. It's too late."

"Here you will cough until you're fragrant."

"Takes money to get to America," I said hopefully.

"All my cash goes to the big cannons."

We worked side by side but followed different friends. I spent time with Onion, Little Touch, and others. Poy sat with the older crewmen: Four Square, Old North, Old South, and sometimes Shorty. They played dominoes without betting cash and shared their whisky. They relived battles from the Red Scarf Rebellion and the Guest Wars. Poy had little to say about those events but sat among the old fellows, hoping to absorb some of their wisdom, and trying to build up his own store of virtue by meeting their need for a patient audience. Keenly aware that their deaths might happen at any moment, those men wanted someone young to hear them out before it was too late.

※

After a second machine drill was added to the pipes, twice the amount of noise and dust filled the tunnel. The amount of falling ceiling also increased. Men worried that the redbeards were shaking the mountain too much, unfairly gaining the upper hand by melding the elements of Fire, Metal, and Air to hurl against the rock. You couldn't chisel at the feet of a mountain without causing its head to shake in disgust. We took to wearing metal buckets over our skulls. We poked the ceiling with long poles to dislodge loose pieces. Old South was carried out one day after workers fell over him and screamed, thinking him a corpse. Number Two was knocked down too and hobbled around on a scarred knee. It was just a matter of time before a massive fall of rock.

Bookman brought us a proposal. A team of Chinese workers was drilling from the other end of the mountain. They had two machine drills too. He proposed a contest. The bosses would measure the daily progress made by each team. After a month, the team that gained the greatest distance would win a cash prize. I thought the opportunity was clearly useful, but our crew split into two factions.

"The faster we run in the dark, the less safe it is," said Poy.

"We came to earn money," countered Number Two. "Now they offer more cash and you say no."

"This is a ploy to push us harder; we run fast enough already."

"The lazy ones need incentives. Their people at home will benefit."

"They treat us like squawking cocks thrown into a fighting ring."

"Even if we don't win, it doesn't matter. The Company won't penalize us."

"Don't know that for sure, do you? What if the prize for the winners comes from the losers? This is a wager, like any other game."

In the end, Number Two told Bookman "no," because those crewman who were willing to work harder clearly saw that they wouldn't get a larger portion of the prize over their lazier friends. Bookman cursed and stalked away. A chance to make more money was welcome, but even I could not stomach having co-workers yell at me to go faster.

Then Onion pulled me away to talk in private.

"A big Native family travels to a wedding on the American side of the border," he said. "Men and women, old folks, and young children are going. They are taking gifts, and riding horses and wagons. You can wear their clothes, hide your pigtail under a hat, and walk with them to America."

"You're Shorty's friend. Why help me?"

"We eat better now."

"Won't they slit my throat in the night?"

"These are trusted customers."

I didn't sleep that night. Sojourners couldn't squat and do nothing. That was like telling a man not to fight the blazing fire that was gutting his house while family members ran out with precious belongings. Men worked abroad but rooted their children in China. They enlarged their landholdings so everywhere the bamboo flourished. But sadly, there wasn't ever enough money. Families grew larger. The harvest was poor. A man with a barren wife needed a second one. Bandits attacked with greater daring. Land taxes went up. Orchards and dikes were swept away by the wind and waves of typhoons.

Sojourners were every clan's trusted hope, but if a man failed, it was his own fault. Kinsmen could rally and help, but they stumbled too. Those who depended on you, they called you kin and brother, they labelled you dependable, as heart and head to one shared body. They were always glad to raise bowls of warmed wine to toast you. When far away, when you couldn't look at the autumn moon without weeping; when kinfolk feasted and you were alone, you longed for their praise.

In America, I would be better placed to help Younger Sister, but only if there was work. I had no capital to start my own business. What if I couldn't learn English? When I was jobless in China, each night I wondered whether I would be eating or starving, laughing or weeping the next day; my worries kept me awake and praying, left me even more tired and wasted for the morning's search for work. It took me until the end of the next day before I said no to Onion.

✻

At the end of a day, the men dropped their empty baskets by the tunnel mouth and hurried back to get warm in the cooking tent. Autumns were never this cold in China, and the men complained of having to buy gloves and thicker coats. Bookman pointed to Four Square and me. "Go help the redbeards bring out the drills."

They never left the machines inside during night, for fear that falling rock might damage them. Company engineers were always fiddling with the machines, peering at valves, and writing notes.

Four Square headed into the tunnel as I was pouring water. It was still lukewarm. Onion ran by and tapped my arm. "You drink, I'll go!"

Everyone was keen and curious about the drills. One friendly redbeard had given Long Life a chance to push it into the wall, and he emerged beaming, as proud as the father of a newborn son. Now each crewman wanted to go home and brag about pushing the drill into solid rock, piercing it like chopsticks thrusting through tofu, like pressing one's stiff cock into a mountain suddenly turned fleshy. The men wanted to coax the power of a blazing furnace in their hands.

Four Square and a redbeard carried out the first drill and its hoses. The other blaster was drilling holes so that he could light the fuses next morning without waiting for the furnace and compressor to start. Too bad his generous work attitude wasn't rewarded with good luck.

Thunder rumbled from the tunnel as the ground shook. Storm clouds of dust whirled out, choking those at the tunnel mouth. Men ran, some toward the tunnel and others away from it. They shouted for bosses, Heaven, and friends.

Shorty crouched and bent over, his head to the ground, wailing for his friend. He had seen Onion take my place.

Bookman did a roll call, to see who else might be inside the tunnel. Our crew pressed in as Shorty pointed a trembling finger at me.

"Hok should be dead! I saved him once before. Today he switched places with Onion. That bandit killed my people. He deserves to die."

"No one has run off yet!" I protested. "I'm no bandit. If I was, then Heaven would have sent me into the tunnel."

Number Two ordered Shorty back to camp. It was time for his daily dose of opium.

Men shook their heads in disbelief to hear how Onion had run by and traded places at the very last moment. They also stood away, afraid to get too close to me. If Onion was dead, then I had been the last one to touch him, perhaps the one who had cast the curse of death on him. At least Shorty the mosquito was swatted and smeared by this disaster. I prayed for Onion to be alive, if only to save myself from his angry ghost.

When it was safe to enter the tunnel, our torches lit up a massive hole in the ceiling. The mountain had let its gut plunge like a mother releasing multiple births. Its core was as hollow as the inside of a fine porcelain statue. The debris was too close to the rock face for there to be good news about Onion and the blaster. We shouted for them, but got no reply.

Workers started to clear the debris that very night. They re-stoked the still-hot furnace and brought the first machine drill back into use. Shorty came to help, moaning that no man was a better friend than Onion. We brought out the rubble and dumped it nearby. Bookman reminded us it would have to be moved away later. As night fell, the bosses set up lanterns near the tunnel mouth. They, of course, needed a quick salvage in order to speed up our return to work.

I squatted for a rest and Shorty joined me. I wanted to edge away but to retreat was cowardly. It would give satisfaction to Shorty. I braced myself for savage words.

"Your lifeline contains luck, Yang Hok," he said. "The militia that killed your bandit friends failed to capture you. You went to prison but returned alive. The sickness that killed Monkey left you a bundle of bones, yet you regained your health."

"I'm lucky?" I snorted. "Then why do I squat here with you?"

We both started coughing.

"Heaven protects you."

"Then stop accusing me."

"I will. I want you to kill me."

"You're crazy."

"I wanted to go home and tell everyone that you died here in agony. But pain plagues me instead."

"I could die tomorrow, even tonight."

"I talk about me!" He seized my arm. "Let people think I died by Heaven's will. Smother me in my bed. I won't resist."

"I can give you money," I said. No doubt he feared losing Onion's gifts, which had let him buy opium.

"Do this, and my ghost will spare you. Refuse, and you will never have peace again. You owe me. You owe me a dozen lives."

"You are insane." I hurried away. Last time he said it was six lives. My sweat chilled me. The night had never felt so cold. Shorty was a madman. He still believed I was his enemy the bandit. He had longed for my death, but now he wanted me to deliver it to him. He was using his pain, his injury to doom me to hell. Why didn't he ask Poy for help? He was a bandit too. Maybe the gods were punishing Shorty for some crime that he had kept hidden.

Four Square came and threw a blanket over my shoulders. Workers were preparing for a long night ahead. "Heaven watches over you," he said.

"You too," I replied. "You got out just in time."

"Shall we make some money?" He bent close. "When news of this spreads up and down the line, workers will clamour for your protection, for a piece of your luck. Let's make paper charms and sell them!"

I shook my head. "There's no priest or temple to bless them."

"Get ink and press your thumb mark on squares of yellow paper, then we fold them up and sell them in town."

"Men aren't stupid. They want proof the charm works."

"Someone will tell a story, sooner or later."

He was right. "What's in this for you?"

"You can't do this alone."

I began to see the potential. "If only more men had seen Onion switching places with me."

"Those are your best salesmen."

"We tell people to wear it at their necks or burn it and swallow the ashes."

Next day, we made our first sales at our own camp, using gentle tones to tout our sacred product. Later, as we reckoned how much paper, ink, and string to buy, and how fast we needed to make the charms, Poy stormed up. "Can't you do better than fleece your workmates?"

"I help them."

"When the mountain kills, nothing stops it."

"I survived two tunnel collapses."

"How did you get Shorty on your side?"

"Gave him a charm for free."

"That rock brain said you were protected in prison by the gods, so I asked him why you landed there in the first place, if you were so lucky. Then he said you survived the illness, so I asked him why you even got sick. After all, half of the crew escaped illness. You could have worked all that time."

"The gods were testing me."

Poy laughed as he turned away. "If you want to be the chosen one, then go ahead. The bosses will send you into the dark tunnel whenever they can't see clearly."

Clearing the tunnel took three days. The stench of the rotting bodies was terrible. Poy asked me to help move the corpse. "If Onion blames you for his death, then you can redeem yourself."

I shook my head. "What if he wants to trade places with me again?"

Onion had given Bookman money for his own service. He was the only crewman who could afford it. There was lucky cash to hand out after the funeral, but not a single crewman attended it. There were hefty amounts to pay Poy, Old South, Little Touch, and Number Two to bury his body in the woods. I got paid to carve his name and home village onto a plank. Only then did I learn his real name: Choy Ming Chung, "Bright Pine." I cut deeply into the wood, drawing each stroke with rounded bumps and smooth tapers so that each word looked like brushwork.

On the day of the funeral, Number Two ran to me as we workers returned to camp.

"Poy got burnt. Badly."

He lay on the ground in the sick tent, shuddering and moaning as his eyes flicked open and shut. When his face, throat, and body had been set aflame, his clothing melted into him. The skin was seared red and dry in spots; elsewhere it was charred leather. Pus oozed from dish-sized blisters.

"Get a blanket," I said. "He's cold."

"I covered him," Head Cook said, "but he started sweating.

"I'll run to town for ointment," I said.

Number Two shook his head, stating that burns were hard to heal. He told us what happened: "We started the cleansing fire. We started to burn Onion's things, his clothes, blanket, wooden pillow, and chopsticks. Poy brought out Onion's stock of liquor and squatted by the fire. He was happy to destroy it. He opened two bottles, clear as water. He sniffed them and made a face. 'We should have poured this over his grave,' he called out. 'No animals would dare dig at his flesh.' He chuckled and tilted the bottles into the fire. Whoosh! Flames raced up the streams like mice running on ropes and ba-lam! The bottles exploded into Poy. He fell back, screaming. His skin and clothes and hair were burning. He slapped at his face and eyes. I ran for a blanket to muffle the flames, but when I lifted it, his skin came away too."

Next morning, a hard scab covered much of Poy's burns. More skin seemed to have been lost. He couldn't talk or swallow.

"That's good, isn't it?" I asked. "The scab means he is healing, no?"

I ran to town for ointment but the clerk frowned and said, "Don't waste your money. *Heal an injury but not a destiny.*"

Shorty brought his lamp and cooked opium. Head Cook stood nearby with a bowl of soup and a spoon. Poy couldn't lie sideways to smoke but Shorty pushed the pipe into his mouth, covered it with a blanket, and pinched his nose, forcing him to inhale. When he stood to leave the tent, I said to him, "On Centipede Mountain, Poy never killed anyone."

"And you?" he asked.

"Doesn't matter what I say. You won't believe me."

I sat with Poy all night, trying to recall how Mother had sought favours from the Goddess of Mercy or the Heavenly Empress. She promised to fast for days, chant sutras, or release caged birds. I had nothing to trade for Poy's life, no riches, no prayers, not even promises. I got very sick once, and Mother took a bowl of hot rice, covered with a cloth, and rubbed it over my face and head. I remembered her calling out, "If this sickness came in through the mouth, then let it leave through the mouth and enter this bowl of rice. If it came through the nose, then let it leave through the nose and enter this bowl of rice." Then she took the bowl outside and emptied the rice into the gutter. She never did this for my brother and sister.

Poy died three days later.

I left the tent and heard Long Life say to someone, "Look how he died. Wasn't a work accident. He touched all those dirty things, so of course he died during a funeral. That's why men avoid those events."

I clapped him on the back and rubbed my palm there. "I just finished carving Poy's grave-stick," I said. "His name is imbedded in your back. His ghost will follow you forever."

I paid California, Old South, and Number Two to help me move the body. I bought water from the river for Poy's hands and feet. My tears wet the cloth for cleaning his face. Then we carried him to a site with a view of the river.

Upon our return, Poy's clothes were tossed into the cleansing fire. I watched the flames die down, and then left the camp late that night. I thought Company thugs would chase and seize me, but nothing happened. Maybe Poy's ghost was watching, maybe not.

Shorty had been right all along. I deserved to die. If I had had the courage to join Onion's Native caravan, then those two men would still be alive.

10

ON THE ROAD, GENTLEMEN ARE RARE (1885)

The darkness within the Big Tunnel began to lift as a nib of light grew bigger in the distance. Our footsteps sped up and sounded lighter. Near the entrance we heard banging sounds, the thud of iron on rock, the ringing of steel on tempered metal.

The damn railway was finished, wasn't it?

Canada was linked from ocean to ocean now, wasn't it?

Weren't all China men heading home to safety and peace?

Loud cursing and the thrum of saw blades grew louder and then clearer. The boy darted ahead to the curved road and we stopped.

The railway vanished under soil and rock jumbled higher than a house. Leafy treetops that were once aloft in the sky lay under loose earth. Boulders had split open, showing jagged eggshell edges. Threads of white roots wormed through dark soil and layers of yellow clay. Shiny crystals in the newly exposed rock caught the light and glittered.

Yes, redbeards might bleed from the land's unyielding edges, but you would never hear them cry surrender. They sauntered away, hands in their pants pockets, hats tipped back on their heads, whistling cheery tunes. Why shouldn't they? China men were already on hand to do the dirty work and restore redbeard order. The King of Hell invited guests, and these fools rushed forward.

China men clambered over the wreckage, chopping at mops of hairy roots and sawing at tree trunks. They heaved rocks to the ground and drilled holes for blasting powder. Teams of horses dragged laden skids to the railway, to a flat-deck car piled with debris.

That Sam was right. If all China men left Gold Mountain and went home, then the redbeards would be forced to do all the dirty work. They would have to pay more for everything and stop strolling around like pigeons afraid to dirty their feet.

I asked Sam, "Turn back?" and pulled the boy toward the tunnel. No one could scramble over the treacherous debris while towing a lively child and carrying a heavy pack. At the start of this trek, Sam had said Lytton was four days away by foot. A delay now would render my ticket worthless.

He paced back and forth, his face dark. He must have had many customers ahead, awaiting his bottles. I suspected only small bunches of China men were left, mangy weeds like Fist and his uncles, and they couldn't afford to buy much liquor.

By the black remnants of a campfire was a kettle. Sam kicked it over the edge of the clearing.

"Stinking bastard!" someone shouted. "What's that for?"

"These jobs, they belong to Native people." Sam stood with feet apart, hands at waist, elbows out.

The China men peered at him, stung into silence. Such insults were not often issued in our own language. They yelled muddled slurs.

"Lazy worms. You slink off at the first word of fishing."

"After payday, no one can find you."

"Last to join the work, first to leave."

"We aren't slaves." Sam raised his chin. "We have freedom. We have families."

They told him to eat chicken shit and limp off with his rotted corpse.

"Did you know?" He turned to me. "These shit-hole fiends mock the China men who leave for home. These men say, 'We don't know the word death.' But they keep feasting off our lands."

"Go fetch the kettle," I said. "If they beat you, I won't help you."

"I look after myself."

"If they hear about the liquor, they'll kill you for it."

After a moment, he stalked off.

"Who was that turtle head?" One worker ran up. "Screw his mother!"

"We got work!" A man atop the debris waved his hat. "Our eyebrows got long while waiting, but the jobs finally came. There's work for weeks!"

"Can we reach the iron road ahead?" I asked.

The man beside him spoke. "Go to the river."

"Are there boats?"

"Go look yourself," said the man. "Don't you have eyes?"

"You're the blind one," I said. "When redbeards see this, all you dogs will fight for drippings of shit."

"It's the same work as before."

"Jobs were plentiful back then. Not now."

A sawyer atop the rubble knotted a rope at his waist and tossed the other end to workmates. He thrust a sturdy triangle of wood, its smooth sides planed at a mill, into the notched break of a fallen tree. He leaned back and slammed his sledgehammer into the wedge. The tree split with a loud crack and one end rolled off, sending rocks and boulders sliding and teetering. For a moment, the sawyer clawed at empty air, but his friends yanked him to safety.

Had such ropes been common along the line? Was it only my crew that had failed to use them and suffered the bloody results?

The first worker brought over a dandy who was dressed for town in a grey suit and blue tie. Only the top button of his jacket was fastened, revealing a checkered waistcoat.

"Boss Soon, here's the cockhead," said the worker.

I expected the Chinese headman to scream at me for interrupting the work.

"Need a job?" he asked.

I snorted. "The King of Hell marries off his daughter: nobody wants her!"

"Ah, you've worked. Where?"

"They never told us. Can we get to Lytton?" The boy grabbed my hand when the headman eyed him. "The boy's mother is there."

"Good for you. Usually she never finds the father."

"The trueborn mother is best."

He nodded. "My brothers and sisters were raised by a stepmother."

I looked him up and down. "You always dress this fancy?"

"Company sends a bigwig to inspect us."

"You speak English?"

He nodded. "Can't you work a few days? I need strong men.

These ragged beggars can barely stand up."

"Give Sam a job. Then he won't make trouble."

"Tell that stir-shit-stick to go die."

He wished me luck finding the boy's mother and sent a worker to fetch the kettle. As we headed down a narrow path to the shore, I asked where they had come from.

The town of Kee-fah-see was where Sam planned to make the third stop of our trip. These men would have been Sam's customers, but now the Company fed them. No wonder Sam saw fire and berated them.

The kettle lay at his feet, at the foot of the path.

"You're lucky they didn't stomp your bones," I said to Sam.

"Boss Soon kneels to shine the redbeards' boots. He doesn't know shame."

"You sound like a China man."

"They should all go home."

"When they're ready, they will."

Two Native men in a dugout thrust paddles through the water, ferrying three passengers. Around us, a steep slope of small stones rose straight from the river. We squatted and leaned back to let our packs anchor us. Sam muttered about wrapping his goods in blankets against water damage. I kept a tight grip on Peter, who wanted to play in the water.

If he could find gold, then I'd let him jump in the water all day.

In China, cheery tradesmen sauntered through the countryside, tools and kits on their backs, come to mend pots or bowls, to repair bricks and mortar. Some of them flagged rides from boatmen, others trudged over the mounded dikes. Women and children flocked like flies to the men's news and gossip. They voiced loud opinions while working. If there were no jobs, they sipped tea and ambled to the next village. They smiled freely, but Grandmother sighed for them, for how they lacked a wife, a home, and a waiting meal each night.

"Better to be alone." Grandfather puffed on his tobacco. "Sleep in peace, work in peace."

As a boy, I had thought that travel meant moving at your own pace, going wherever you wanted, and evading tiresome talk. I reckoned that explained Father's fondness for rolling up his bundle and leaving on another sojourn.

"Does the boat go to Lytton?" I asked Sam.

"Are you stupid? The current is too strong. The boat crosses the river but doesn't go north. We walk to Boston Bar on the wagon road and then come back to this side."

"You prayed too late to the mountain," I said. "When did that landslide happen?"

He shrugged.

I thought that the railway people in Yale should have known. Word would have gone down to the station through the telegraph.

"That boat will waste our time," I complained.

"Not so," he retorted, "we cross over, sooner or later." He caught my frown and hooted. "You didn't know, did you? Another bridge further north takes the railway over the river to the east side, just like the wagon road crossed over at Alexandra Bridge."

Heavy footsteps crunched beside us, and then two redbeards called and waved at the boat. One cradled a rifle while the other held a skittering dog on a leash. The animal flattened itself and looked up with keen eyes. The two men stuffed their stockings into their boots, laced them together, and slung them over their shoulders. Rolling up their pants, they showed legs as white as paper.

Being so careful, they had to be husbands with tiger wives. Peter eyed the dog and moved closer.

When the dugout arrived, three China men waded ashore. One fellow called to another but aimed his words at me. "Don't we have enough workers?"

"That's so, we've got plenty of hands."

"Stinking bastards." I spoke loudly to Sam for them to hear. "Boss Soon just asked me to work for him. I refused him."

The redbeards pushed forward and offered the boatmen more money, so they were taken aboard first, leaving us to wait.

But Sam and the two boatmen took time trading news and jokes, chuckling now and then. The redbeards fidgeted and cleared their throats. Finally they nudged the boatman to put aside his cigar and get going.

⁂

The other shore lacked a useful beach. We climbed to the wagon road, clutching at plants and rocks, hoping they were firmly anchored. Across the water, the jumbled wreckage of the land-slide stretched for over a mile. *Heaven punishes, the earth destroys.* A god had thrust a giant pitchfork into the cliff and yanked with supernatural strength to gouge the mountain. Over the railway and river below, rubble had swirled out as though from a spinning dancer.

Didn't the railway bigwigs expect more landslides? High steep mountains all along the canyon had been shaken, like clutches of fortune sticks jiggled by temple worshippers until one stick dropped from the holder. Did the Company call upon Jesus men in lofty churches to pray for protection over the iron road? Perhaps people all along the line went to church to send up massed songs seeking favour. Maybe there were eerie secrets to building an iron road that we China men never saw.

At the edge of the slide, two thick lines of gleaming silver thrust out, hems along a grand grey curtain. Redbeards had conquered cliffs and forests with the railway, lashing it like a belt over the seething ground. Even when angry gods let loose landslides, the Company pressed on.

"You like the railway?" said Sam.

"Never thought it could be built."

"Didn't redbeards use black powder to blast China's forts and win the war?"

"We fight back," I said. "Your people should do the same."

"We use guns now. Soon we drive train engines too."

"Redbeards won't allow that." I backed my pack onto some rock, groaned at the weight, and demanded, "Where's that Hell's Gate? Haven't passed it, have we?"

"Soon, soon."

After a while, we saw men coming toward us, kicking at pebbles on the ground, like surly children. We had been climbing steadily on the wagon road. In some places the path was carved out of the mountain, packed hard and flattened by wheels and animal hooves. We looked up to our side and saw trees growing straight up against a steep slope. In other spots, to cross deep gullies, the road was a wooden trail that bumped over layers of logs, trees crisscrossing each other in neat rows forty or fifty feet deep.

I frowned. The approaching men held the high ground. They could run at us, gain momentum, and shove us over the side.

One man with a walking pole dragged his right leg, thickly wrapped at the ankle. The fellows were spread out, looking in different directions, not talking, as though peeved with each other. They were China men in dirt-stiff clothes with bundles on their backs. Their dark faces were sulking and bitter as they passed around loaves of bread, tearing off chunks with hands and teeth.

They ignored Sam's greeting and his raised hand. He walked on with the boy, who turned to peer at them.

China men usually made minimal gestures of respect to Native people, aware that they were everywhere, armed and seething near boiling point, a huge mound of dry kindling about to be ignited. We took care not to offend them. Their poverty and suffering was everywhere, but what could we do? Redbeards, not China men, ruled here.

The lead fellow stopped me. "Where do you go?"

"Town ahead."

"Don't go. All stinking bastards." His blackened teeth were chipped; dried blood stuck to the corner of his cracked lips.

"Redbeards or China men?" I asked.

"We are railway men. The Company ate us up and spat out our bones. What do you carry?"

The men pressed in, reeking of stale urine and herbal oils. I tried to push my way through. "Is it better walking here, away from the railway?"

"Lend us some food," Black Teeth said. "The shit-hole pricks gave us stale bread. They kicked us out of town, even though the day is ending."

"No China men there?"

"Not even a shadow of their ghosts."

Sam was heading back toward me, strolling without hurry. He should have grabbed a sturdy pole. I didn't see Peter, so he must have been told to lay low and stay still. Hopefully the worm would listen. If these oafs around me had any brains, they would grab the boy. Bandits had won great riches holding sons for ransom.

"These goods have been sold," I said. "They are not mine to give away."

"Don't give us anything," Black Teeth said. "Just lend us a bit."

"Do good, receive good," his men called out. "Don't fear your good heart."

"What, lend pigs to hungry tigers?" I tried to get them to laugh.

"Better to give a mouthful of food to a beggar than a bushel of grain to a rich man," someone said.

"Screw his mother!" The men were suddenly aroused. "Grab his goods!"

They yanked apart my arms and dodged as I kicked at them.

"Stop!" Sam shouted. "Or this one dies!"

He held one railway man by the neck and pressed a shiny blade to his throat. It was the fellow who had hobbled with a walking stick.

"Leave those goods," Sam barked. "Walk away."

"Kill the cripple, go ahead," Black Teeth said. "One less belly to feed."

"Kill me," said the hostage. "I can die standing up or lying down. If my friends get to eat, then I'm content."

His friends shouted at him to shut his mouth.

"He wants to die for you stinking bastards," Sam yelled. "I'm happy to help."

The men fumbled in their clothes, seeking weapons, wanting to rush over.

"What are you?" I demanded. "Coffin makers praying for clients?"

"*Better a broken jade cup than a solid clay pot,*" said the hostage.

"Let him die." Black Teeth clawed at the knots of my pack.

"You so-called friends will leave him?" I demanded. "Old clothes have more fleas tending them."

One man stomped away. A moment later, the others followed him. Only Black Teeth was left.

I grabbed a teapot-sized rock and smashed it into his cheek. There was a crunch of breaking bone and bright red blood spurted from his face.

"Drink that, you bastard."

Rocks slammed into my back as Sam and I ran away. Good thing I had quit the railway long ago. It would have been easy to fall into that nest of snakes and scorpions or turn into spineless worms like One Leg or No Brain. I could have clung to that fool dream about hours and days being the only blockage to earning money and going home rich.

The brat ran out from nearby bushes. Too bad he had been too far away to watch me do battle and draw blood.

"You hit him too hard," said Sam.

"Damn your liquor bottles. I could have outrun them."

"I saved your life again."

"That man could have pulled a knife and stabbed you."

"End of my self-respect."

"End of your useless life."

How often did a bandit get robbed the same way as his former victims? As often as you saw a chicken pee. I almost shouted at those thugs, *You think you're tough? You ever hear of Centipede Mountain? That was my gang's lair. You see me walking behind a mix-blood and reckon that I'm a broken stick of firewood? Think again! You don't want to fight me! You want to die?*

⁂

The win over the bandits gave us energy, and we made good time until Sam suddenly stopped and muttered, "Screw those bastards, we passed Hell's Gate."

The river had taken a curve and now mountains on both sides dipped to the river, their jagged slopes cutting into each other like interlaced fingers. They cut off any extended view of the rushing waters behind us.

I shrugged. "I'll see it on my way back."

He pointed downward, at the opposite bank. "That's China Bar, where your people took the gold."

"Never heard of it," I declared.

Even from our vantage point, we saw that the river was running low. A dark, ragged ribbon slithered over the rock face and giant boulders, marking the reach of springtime water when melting snow and ice had raised its level. Now, a stretch of shoreline had emerged, cluttered with rocks and gravel. We had passed many such sand bars earlier, where miners had left behind lengthy pits as well as fields of overturned boulders. Those men had pushed their way inland too, tearing down bushes, trees, and Native buildings to get at the treasure underneath.

"'Course not, that's redbeard talk," said Sam. "My people call that place by its real name."

"We should have a name too," I said. But what? At home, every spot was China. We lived throughout the Central Kingdom, where fitting names for sites and cities had been handed down through time and everyday use. On this river, China was that faraway place mocked by redbeard miners as backward and barbaric.

"See that waterfall?" Sam pointed further north, along the railway tracks. A steep waterfall crashed through a violent crack in the brown rock. "We call it Sq'azix. The redbeards used that name for the boat that China men pulled through Hell's Gate."

I strode on. I knew about *Skuzzy* but refused to discuss it with Sam. He would only sneer at how we had been used as beasts of burden.

The road narrowed and then widened, broad enough to let delivery wagons pass each other. The grey and cracking telegraph poles would soon be removed from the wagon road in favour of the new ones along the railway. We flattened ourselves against the mountain wall when a stagecoach roared by. Six horses churned up clouds of dust over the twisting road. Finally, it opened into a clearing of farms and houses.

We set down our packs. Sam told me to wait while he took the boy into the Native village. Its people would be more helpful to a stranger who had a child by his side, he said. But, to my delight, the boy at first refused to go. Maybe crossing the river had spooked him. The boy had sat with Sam until the boatmen asked him to grab the third oar and help get the boat across. Sam dumped Peter on me, and the brat refused to sit still, kept twisting and fidgeting to go to his hero. He'd cried out for Sam, but Sam ignored him.

Now Sam whispered something into the boy's ear to convince him to go along. Grandmother once told a neighbour who had a badly behaved boy, "Better a mischief maker than a simpleton."

I looked down at the shoreline where children shouted and pointed to the foaming spray. With great patience, they squatted and watched for fish in the water. In the river's middle, fishermen stood braced on swaying boats, anchored by stiff ropes, waiting to swing their nets. When they succeeded, the fish dumped thrashing onto the shore must have weighed twenty or thirty pounds each.

Birds chirped in the nearby woods. In Victoria, sojourners about to return home were often asked what, if anything, they might miss about Gold Mountain. Many said, "Trees and forests." They liked the convenience of having plenty of firewood on hand. The trees of Gold Mountain had been one of the few things that China men could take without offending the redbeards, who wanted the giants chopped down and burned. Tall trees with grey, furrowed trunks bore three-sided leaves. They filled the springtime air with seeds of fluffy white snow. Other trees with rounded crowns and smooth white trunks put out leaves in the shape of straw fans. They were yellowing and dropping. The evergreens were laden with brown cones of wooden fruit and bundles of sharp green needles. Such pine trees were a sign of longevity in China. I had been away from there long enough that new trees, planted after the Guest Wars, were probably now taller than me.

Sam returned with two young men who unpacked the whisky. The bottles had been wrapped in grimy scraps of cloth. Peter munched on a cold boiled potato. Without a word, the visitors lugged away the liquor in gunny sacks.

I asked Sam if he had gotten a good price.

"They don't have any money," he pointed out.

"You trust them?"

"Can't wait all day."

"Isn't liquor bad for your people?"

"I don't sell to everyone."

※

We crossed a creek spilling into the Fraser and saw the town ahead.

Boston Bar was small like Spuzzum but its buildings lined both sides of the wagon road. Carts and horses were tethered in front of a roadhouse, two storeys high over a long covered porch. There, men tilted back on the rear legs of wooden chairs, with hats and caps pulled over their eyes. Across from them, a dour-looking bunch stood around a hitching post, puffing on cigars and pipes, fiddling with coiled ropes as if ready to chase cattle. A little boy ran out to point at Peter, but an adult snatched him up and hurried away.

"It's drier here," Sam said in his know-everything voice, "so watch for poison snakes. They rattle when attacking."

"Tell the boy," I replied. "He touches everything."

"China has no snakes?"

"Plenty. The big ones squeeze piglets and children to death and swallow them whole."

"They're dead by then, no?"

Then a burly redbeard stepped forward and shoved a rifle sideways into Sam's chest. Yellow splinters of tobacco were matted in the man's scruffy black beard. From behind darted a Native man, also armed but wearing a western hat with a long grey feather. His finger tapped the trigger of his gun while its barrel pointed at Sam.

Tobacco Beard spoke English. A lumpy jacket was stretched tight around his middle.

Sam opened his hands in a friendly way to Grey Feather, but shook his head at the same time.

Tobacco Beard picked at his teeth while Grey Feather spat out short terse phrases. None of Sam's answers appeased him. They must have been arguing over blackmail money, to let us pass.

The two men glared at each other. Grey Feather growled and tipped his gun skyward.

Bang!

I ducked and stumbled. The crowd laughed at me.

Sam untied his pack and set it on the ground. Tobacco Beard pointed his rifle at him while Grey Feather rummaged through it with quick hands. He pulled out each bundle, hefting it, guessing at the contents by feel. With a yelp of triumph, he found the bottle of whisky that we used at the graveyards.

"Take off your pack," Sam said to me. "Slowly."

His hands were above his head as Grey Feather patted his pockets and took his knife. "They are arresting us."

"These are lawmen?" They wore no uniforms. "What for?"

"Selling liquor to Native people."

Sam trudged ahead. Tobacco Beard and Grey Feather pointed their guns at the boy and me. When I didn't move, Grey Feather swung the rifle butt at my head.

"No sell liquor!" I shouted in Chinook. "I go China!"

The words had no effect. Pushed along, I looked through the crowd, hoping to spot a Chinese face. In Victoria, China men landed in jail along with redbeards on the same charge. The police harassed Native drinkers and threatened to arrest them until they pointed out Chinese sellers. What China men hated the most was wasting time in jail, waiting for the judge to reach town and declare his court in session. Sometimes that took as long as two or three months.

⁂

The police cabin in Boston Bar was divided into two rooms by logs as thick as those of the outside walls. On the window sill sat the long parched skull of a cow, its empty eye holes big and almost round. At least the bones weren't human.

Grey Feather stood in a corner and held his rifle over both of us. My hands were clammy. Our packs were rolled onto the floor.

Tobacco Beard thrust out a grimy palm. Sam handed over his money, telling me to follow. I gave up my coins. Tobacco Beard slammed them on the table and rifled our pockets. No more money was found, so he pointed at our boots. Tobacco Beard gave them a hearty shake and then ripped out the makeshift paper soles. Only sandy grit fell onto the floor. He pointed at our stockings.

Sam obliged but not me.

Tobacco Beard nudged me and then reached for his gun.

I didn't move. He pushed me onto a chair and yanked my stocking.

My roll of bills vanished into his pocket.

"No!" I cried in English. "Please!"

He waved the money at his helper, who flashed a toothy grin.

If Sam hadn't been there, I would have dropped to my knees and begged. Better to let Tobacco Beard kill me than to have him steal my $400.

The boots were returned. I could barely pull them on. As we shuffled into the jail cell, Grey Feather pulled the boy away before the door slammed.

"Bring boy here!" Sam pounded the wood, but it absorbed all sound. "Don't let them take your son!"

I slumped against a wall and dropped to the floor. A man dies, then his house falls down. The cell reeked of shit and urine, soil and vomit. I wanted to tie a rope and hang myself from the window, swallow gravel scraped from the ground and choke to death, or plunge my head into a bucket of urine and drown.

I couldn't go home without a prize to show for all these years. Now, the village was sure to snicker about the black fate of my family. They paid no heed to how much money I had sent home over the years. They knew nothing about rail hands dying on the railway or trying to get into America. I could have been arrested as a smuggler and sent to rot in jail. The neighbours wanted only to touch the costly gifts I brought back, hoping for something new that they hadn't seen before. If they couldn't hold or smell it, it didn't exist. One sojourner brought home a silver fork from a dining set. It got used to dig out weeds.

I should have spent longer nights in Rainbow's fragrant bed and spurted buckets of sticky bliss. Why hadn't I given Goddess a day, no—two or three days, to massage her heaven into me? Then I might have been content to die here. I should have devoured fine foods: abalone, mushrooms, roasted duck with crisp skin, the best grades of rice, and the finest aged wines. I would have swept any leftovers onto the floor for the scavenging dogs. Why hadn't I taken bigger risks at the game tables? Good fortune might have let me return home long ago. *A thousand days at home are fair; a morning away, hell to bear.*

"Are you crying?" Sam asked.

"No."

"Not leaking horse piss?"

"Shut your mouth!"

"Don't China men think that weeping is bad luck?"

Sojourners who had returned to China as sad failures babbled such feeble lies that friends and family were obliged to sigh and pine along with them.

"You earned piles of money but gamblers cheated you naked on the ship? There's no watching your front and your back at the same time, is there?"

"A thief crept into your room and stole everything? Ah, people have Buddha's mouth but the heart of a snake."

"Thugs in Hong Kong pushed you into a dark alley? Not even daylight frightens the crooks there."

The women of such losers insisted with fearless aplomb that

they valued their men's lives more than money and put on a cheeky show of thanking the gods and ancestors for their safe return. They armed themselves with taut proverbs to refute the smiling but spiteful neighbours come to taunt them:

"Sugar cane isn't sweet at both ends."

"Gold won't buy a breath of life."

"Man gets seven poverties and eight riches."

An aging mother hugged her long-away son with tears of joy, but her own funeral would be a small affair that sent her into the afterworld with no extra clothing or servants. A wife pulled her finally returned husband into bed after years of longing and virtue only to find that he was riddled with impossible diseases. Children found a sudden stranger in the house who cursed them for running and making too much noise.

Grandfather and Younger Brother had bought more land and improved the house with my money. They sang my praises to everyone. My grandparents had found an ideal prospect for my bride. I planned to buy Grandmother a new grindstone, one that turned with less backbreaking effort. I wanted to buy Grandfather a plough and a good steel axe. On market days, we would spend the entire day at the teahouse, calling for any dumpling or meat we wanted.

Even if I sprouted wings, there was no flying from this prison. I was trapped for months, waiting for the judge who carried his courtroom on his shoulders. He would fine me, but I had no money, which meant I would have to do hard labour to work off my time. There was no way to get word to the Council in Victoria. Even if I did, it might choose to ignore me, seeing that I was so far away and entirely beyond the community's sight.

I bit hard on my teeth and cursed silently. From our first meeting, Sam had only been trouble. He should have known about Tobacco Beard and stayed away from this town.

Damn that brothel keeper, that washman, that merchant in Yale. All of them, even that cookhouse man, had called Sam the best. Surely they knew that Sam carried bootleg. Surely they knew the eyes of the law would follow him. Shit covered his name. Those fellow China men were supposed to help me. I was the stranger here, after all.

"Don't blame me," Sam declared. "The liquor that they found, that was for your graveyards."

"You sell bootleg!"

"Those bottles were gone."

"You look like a Native, so no one stops you going into Native villages. If a China man tries to do that, he gets kicked out right away."

"They kicked me out too. Shouldn't you think about the boy?"

"What can I do? My money is gone."

"Children get dumped onto Native women all the time. Fathers don't provide a cent, don't bother looking back. You're no better than them."

I turned away. The only light came from a tiny window cut high into the wall. A horse and wagon clattered outside. I took what little running start the cell allowed and threw myself at the wall, trying to reach the window, clawing with my fingers and boot tips. I grabbed the window ledge but something sharp made me scream and fall to the ground. I swore and sucked at my fingers, spitting out any poison.

"Useless," said Sam.

"If a China man was outside, I would yell to him. China men help each other. Not like your people, who help the redbeards."

"We keep order. Redbeards use us to chase their killers and robbers. We know the hills and woods where they hide."

"And you arrest China men."

"Who quickly pay their way to freedom. Don't worry, when I get out, I'll tell China men to come fetch you." He stood up. "Time for a piss."

He didn't go to the pail. Instead, he faced the inside wall.

"We piss through the cracks," he said, "so the other side will stink."

I went to the wall and loosened my pants, peering through the dim light. We stood side by side and sighed. For a moment, the urine splashed away the fetid waste stuck to the wall.

That night, I awoke with a start and begged the gods to help me escape. Send a bolt of lightning to knock over a wall. Open a hole under me, a tunnel from long-ago breakouts. Unleash a gale to lift me and the ceiling into the sky.

At home, women were the ones who hurried to temples with prayers and offerings. That was the one activity that Mother and Grandmother had not fought over like alley cats. They returned home from temple visits praising each other and joking. Such peace ended far too soon. On second day, second month they tended the God of the Earth to ensure fair weather for farming. Third day, third month they cooked no meat, to cleanse the body. Ninth day, ninth month, they went to Green Dragon Temple on Pine Mountain to gain favour from the illness-fighting gods. Despite Mother's efforts, few gods helped her. Indeed, she had ended her life a day after the birthday rites for the Goddess of Mercy, patron of mothers.

I needed to show the gods some sincere intent but had nothing on hand. All I could do was promise good deeds. I had started this trip with one, taking the boy to his mother, and it had ended in disaster. All I could do was make another promise.

Then a ghost tapped the back of my head.

Simple!

Ask Fist's questions at the Lytton temple and bring him his answers.

Such generosity should win me favour.

11

BOATS CAN CROSS THE DEEPEST RIVERS (1885)

In my dream, Boss Long, Pock Face, and I were yanking at floorboards in the game hall, breaking them, and tossing them into the fire. Ours was an ancient building from the town's early days. Boss Long had just heard talk of how miners from the gold rush accidentally left precious gold dust in the cracks of saloon floors after walking through and putting their feet up for a night of drinking. Pock Face and I scowled; none of that gold would land in our pockets. For once, Boss Long worked beside us, tugging at nails and planks, his pigtail pinned atop his head. We made our way around the stove, which was too heavy and too hot to be moved. Finally the ashes cooled and Boss Long sifted through them.

He shouted, held up a thin yellow wafer, and flung it at me. I reached out but grabbed only empty air. He tossed a second chip that glinted from the lamplight. I missed again. Boss Long started scolding.

The squeal of rusty door hinges dragged me back to the jail where Sam and I were lying hunched at a well's bottom. Tobacco Beard kicked me. My legs were numb, even though the cold wasn't severe.

"Go!" Sam stumbled forward.

I groped for my boots. A hairy insect flitted through my hands.

In the office, Tobacco Beard jerked his thumb at the front door, but Sam shook his head. Looking for our packs, I grinned at the reek of our urine on the wall. We dirty dogs had marked our spots, leaving a stink behind. A black cat arched its back and padded over a wooden bench. The pot-belly stove was cold. With a roar of anger, Tobacco Beard grabbed Sam, hustled him out the door, and hurled him onto the road.

I ran to him. "We can leave?"

"China men stole our packs, if you believe him. All my goods are lost!"

"He stole them!"

"I told him that. He said, 'We'd rather eat shit than rice.'"

"He stole our money."

Grey Feather brought out Peter, whose grubby fingers rubbed at his eyes. His other hand gripped the hat from Sam's grandmother. The constable glanced at me and spat onto my leg. I ignored him, but Sam shouted and shoved him hard. Grey Feather regained his balance and cocked his gun in one quick move. Sam's fist sprang up, but Grey Feather brushed it aside and thrust his face forward to mutter into Sam's. They glared at each other, and then the constable chuckled as if pleased with himself, and ambled off.

I checked the boy for injuries. His gaze was unsteady and faraway.

"Ask your lawman," I yelled to Sam. "What did he do?"

He spoke to the brat instead, who shook his head at each question. They trudged away.

"What about my money?" I shouted. We couldn't leave without a fight.

"Want to die?"

May as well, I thought. At home, my grandparents would retreat to dark corners to curse me aloud without being heard. To go abroad was a brave act that lifted everyone's hopes, even those of the ancestors. To return empty-handed was to topple all those lavish dreams. A return needed to be a celebration of promises fulfilled, not a keening circle for hapless futures.

A redbeard merchant cranked an awning over a dust-spattered window. The wooden frame of a new building was pungent from fresh-cut lumber. Two dogs wagged their tails outside a shack that smelled of baking bread, probably where yesterday's bandits had gotten their food.

By the roadside, I dropped to one knee and pretended to be tying my boot laces. I mumbled thanks to the gods for our quick release from jail. If I had known they were listening so intently last night, I would have pleaded for the return of my money instead.

Freedom was nothing without cash. Money made you a dragon; without it you were a worm.

I would offer to do a week of steady labour for Tobacco Beard; I'd scrub clean his jail or pound down his dirt floor if that obliged him to return my savings. I wanted to stay and devise a way to regain my cash before the scoundrels spent it all. But Sam had rushed ahead with the boy, eager to leave town, keen to forget all this shame. Dark clouds pulled the sky down; we trekked under a bed's low-hanging and smelly underside, where no man could walk upright.

Across the river, long-ago crews had cleared away earlier

landslides that had churned and slid over the railway. Ragged borders of broken trees and grey rubble marked the former reach of debris along the mountain. In the river stood a newborn island, a square beast with a rocky spine of horns. Blackened trees with withered branches spread spindly fingers from under the water.

"Down there is a crazy woman," Sam said. "She digs out a fishing station from under the rocks." He clapped my back. "Old friend, which way now?"

Friend? What bullshit was he talking? I pulled away.

"This road takes me north to Lytton," he said. "Go south, and it takes you to Yale."

"I go north."

"You have no money."

"Kinsmen in North Bend will help me." The words flew out before I could think. To turn back now would drain more blood and muscle from me. The boy must go to Mary. It was absurd to head home with no money but with an extra mouth to feed instead. That redbeard cowhand on the sternwheeler had acted so quickly, so naturally to save Peter's life. Why in hell couldn't it be as simple for me?

On the other bank, the path of the iron road led to a redbeard settlement, small and tight with stores and houses. Native people crouched at the rocky shoreline, nets and spears at the ready. To me, the two banks seemed spread apart, letting the water broaden and slow down.

"You can't cross the river," Sam said. "Want to die?"

"Look at those two."

Two Native men were launching a battered old boat from the other side. I pulled the boy down a trail buttressed with planks and rock slabs. Keels and hulls of rafts and barges lay half submerged, skeletons spat up by powerful river gods. Years ago, oxen pulled railway supplies along the wagon road until the loads got floated across the water at a slow-flowing spot. The squeal of straining cables against pulleys had seemed unending.

By the time we reached the beach, the two men had crossed and were pushing ashore a small dugout. Sharp rocks scoured its bottom. The men grabbed spears and nets and ran toward a fishing post. I almost called out.

Rusty tin cans floated in the dugout, which was carved from a single log, painted red and white, its sides glittering from rows of inlaid animal teeth. Shiny patches of pitch had hardened in spots. I reached to test their strength but bailed water instead. The brat ran his fingers over the pretty patterns. Did he know any secrets to crossing this dark foaming river? Surely now was the season for a gentler current. In China, water levels fell during the annual diversion for summer crops.

"You won't get across." Sam squatted on a nearby log. "Not in that wreck. You lack strength."

"At game halls, I threw out men twice my size."

"You don't know boats." He pulled his hat over his eyes.

"Two young men just crossed over."

"They know the river, you don't."

I looked to the brat, hoping his boyish charm would win over Sam. My son paid me no attention.

I put him in the boat and rolled up my pants. He waved at Sam as I tugged at the boat, which was reluctant as a water buffalo. I removed the boy and looked for small round logs on which to slide the boat along. The beach was too rocky to let them roll, but I needed Sam to see that I wasn't all stupid.

With a shout, Sam came running. He threw his weight low into the stern, and the boat moved a few inches. When I pushed too, the boat gained momentum and grated over the rocks. I prayed that no new holes were added. I splashed into the river, shrieked from the cold, and pulled at the bow. Sam lifted the boy in, shoved the boat again, and jumped aboard.

We shot downstream.

"Paddle the other side!" he shouted.

I glanced back. The boy bailed with a tin.

The boat tilted. I jammed my paddle into rocks.

"Stand up!" Sam yelled.

In the river's middle, the current gained strength. Water surged aboard. Every stroke felt useless. The opposite bank was far away.

"Dig deep!" he shouted.

The boat was turning; its bow faced downriver. The river swept us along like a twig. Rocks rushed at us. My oar lashed from side to side.

"Paddle out! Push the rocks!"

The bow dipped and water crashed into me. I flung water off my face in order to see.

The boat shot upward like an arrow.

I shut my eyes and braced for death.

"Don't stop!"

I shoved the paddle through the water.

We slammed into land, bow first, no graceful docking along one hull like yesterday's finish. As soon as we dragged the boat ashore,

I leapt up and roared. The headstones on the ancestral altar at home were jumping for joy. My lungs and chest felt huge. This was a mighty river, but I was a dogged mule, plodding on steadily. This time Earth had defeated Water. I could rely on the favour of Heaven. I could saunter across any railway trestle, no matter how tall, no matter how strong the wind. When I lifted Peter onto the beach, he clapped his hands and cheered.

Sam bent over to catch his breath. "Almost died," he gasped

"We have big lives."

"My customers don't die," he said. "Never thought to see you risk your life for the boy."

He got it wrong. It was for my sake that the boy's life had been put at risk.

We flipped over the boat, draining it to thank the owners, whoever they were.

We hurried toward a campfire, shivering from the cold and wet. A middle-aged woman emerged from a tent, hustled the boy to the fire, and fetched towels and clothes. Red paint was dabbed onto her face. She wore only Native clothes: leggings and a smock of animal skin hung stiffly off her as her moccasins glided over the rocks.

She scolded Sam and returned to the tent.

He wrung out his pants over the hot rocks, causing steam to rise. "Sophie is the crazy lady who moves rocks."

"Who's crazy?" A third Chinese voice startled me. An old man brought more clothes, some new with creases, others well-washed and patched.

Sam pointed to the hill of rubble. "You think she can move all this?"

"No harm trying, is there?" The man's leathery face, burnished from sun and wind, was much darker than Grandfather's.

"You crawl into her bed?" Sam flapped his shirt over the fire.

"If I wanted women, would I stay in Gold Mountain?"

"She tells people that when she awakes in the mornings, the boulders have shrunk in size," Sam said. "Or they have split apart, so she can move the smaller pieces. I said to her, 'If the spirits help you, then why don't they change the rocks into birds that fly off on their own?'"

"She has never fallen on these rocks." The China man lit a roll of tobacco from the fire. "Isn't that strange?"

"She has fallen many times!" said Sam. "But she knows not to complain aloud."

The woman smiled and beckoned Sam to follow her. He scowled and refused. She went alone to the great spill of rock, hands outstretched, an opera actor in a wide ornate robe making an entrance. When small birds darted from a crevice, chirping in alarm, visions of seared seasoned meat arose in my mind. We hadn't eaten since yesterday.

Sam draped our wet clothes by the fire and went to fetch firewood. My son followed.

"You think Sophie is crazy?" asked the China man, whose surname was Lam.

"Back home," I said, "there are worse."

A madwoman had lived alone in our hills, while we children both chased and feared her. She tried desperately to hide, but her unclean smells betrayed her every time. Her family wrapped food in leaves and cloth and left it high in the crooks of trees. She shouted curses at everyone before fleeing on bony, grimy legs. Summer days she left her upper body bare, but her long tangled hair hid everything. People said that nests of mice and birds flourished on her head. Her distressed children, left unmarried by their mother's madness, prayed for wolves to attack her. Indeed, those with serpent hearts had whispered that the food was meant to lure the animal killers closer to their target.

When the kettle lid clattered, Lam fished out metal mugs for all of us and dropped in tea leaves.

I gave silent thanks. Sam's rudeness could have gotten us dispatched without a sip of clean water.

Sophie was chanting and swaying to the rocks just as Sam had moved in rhythmic circles at the mouth of Big Tunnel. Then she squatted and lifted a boulder. She held it at her belly, bending back to counter its weight. She strode by and smiled, heading to a wall of rocks so like the beach in depth and colour that it couldn't be seen. I thought she too might vanish.

"I'll help her after drinking tea," I said.

"We have food then."

The tea came, very hot. I looked for the brat, who needed to drink and get warm.

"How does she move the large rocks?" I asked.

"People help her. They've gone fishing now, that's all."

He dumped flour, lard, and water into a container, tossing in pinches of white powder. His fingers squeezed the dough. Today, bread was welcome. Lam's toes were scarred by corns and calluses, but all ten were present, even if some of the nails were black and thickened.

Lam sensed my eyes on him. "I was heading south last autumn when heavy rain started," he said. "I got shelter here."

"She was alone?"

"I make tea and you ask such questions?"

I shrugged.

He grinned. "I rested for several weeks. I helped her with the rocks. Then she went to her family so I went to New Westminster."

"You dig for gold?"

"Twenty-two years."

"When do you go home?" I wanted to howl at the loss of my cash roll.

"Maybe I'll stay."

"Redbeards will kick you out."

"I'll hide in the woods."

He put the pan of dough over the fire. Lam was unlike the miners who passed through Victoria, bitter with failure. They mocked the townspeople as cockroaches who had never seen snow drifts as high as trees. Those miners had faced down bears and travelled alone through forests. They'd lost noses and fingers to frostbite. One miner warned me, "We couldn't bury the men who 'got nailed' during winter because the ground was frozen, hard as rock. Good thing the bodies froze too and didn't stink. But stiffs of wood staying in our world until springtime meant that plenty of dirty things wandered about. When my hands felt icy, I didn't know if it was the weather or a bloodless visitor."

Sam and the brat dragged back a sturdy bough that had lost its leaves long ago. The boy broke off smaller branches. Sam swung an axe at the trunk and shouted as if Lam was deaf.

"Her family says she's insane. They don't pay her any regard."

"She makes tea," Lam said. "She moves rocks. We sit when we're tired. She smokes to regain her strength. Same as me."

"Does her family worry, Sophie being alone?" I mentioned yesterday's bandits.

"Hers is a warrior family," said Sam. "She can use a gun. Her father and husband were killed when their people warred with the redbeards."

"Who won the war?" I asked.

"Everyone." Smoke curled out of Lam's mouth. "They talked peace."

When I stood to go help Sophie, Sam stopped me. "Our clothes are half-dry. If we walk, they'll dry off."

I asked Lam, "You ever tell her about the old man who moved mountains?"

"Many times. She liked that story."

"Tell the boy," I said. "He's the right age for such nonsense."

"Long ago there lived an Old Man whose house faced two great mountains. They blocked the way to town, and his family members were always forced to climb over them or around them. One day the Old Man called his sons and grandsons together and they started digging at the mountains to remove them. A Wise One passed by and said, 'Old Man, you will die soon. How can you bring down these two mountains?'

"The Old Man replied, 'After my passing, my sons will keep digging. When they die, their sons will keep digging. With each generation, my family grows larger, but the mountains grow smaller!' The Wise One tried to think of a clever reply but, in the end, walked away with head down."

Later, I followed Sophie back to the campfire. We had moved

only a dozen stones, going slowly. I had walked barefoot, letting my soles grip the rocks. Sometimes I walked ahead of Sophie; other times, I trailed her. Sometimes the ground was cold to my feet; other times I landed on Sophie's rocks, warm from her steps. She worked in silence, didn't even look at me.

Sam shook his trousers over the fire. Sophie drew lines of red paint on the brat's face. On seeing himself in a scrap of mirror, he shouted with delight and raced off to play.

When Lam gave me hot bread, I asked about the Yang fellow who lived in North Bend.

"That man went back home."

"No Cache Creek for you," exclaimed Sam.

When I cursed him, Lam glanced up so I explained about Peter.

"Don't do that," he said in a stern voice. "Take him to China."

"That's what I said," said Sam. "This fool won't listen."

"In China, he will learn to read and write," Lam said. "Let him use his brain, instead of chasing fish in the river."

"His mother is a good woman." Why was Lam praising China if he was going to stay here? And who would pay for the boy's tuition?

"He's your bone and flesh," said Lam. "He could grow up and look exactly like you."

"In China, people won't let him forget anything, not even a tiny mole."

Sophie nudged the miner for a translation and then she spoke right away.

"She says if you want to leave the boy here, then give him to her," Lam said.

"The trueborn mother is best," I said. "We know where to find Mary."

"Doesn't matter if it's Mary or Sophie, he'll be raised the same," Lam said, shaking his head, "learning only to hunt and fish."

"He'll feed his family, same as us."

"What, you hunt and fish?"

"I can grow two crops of rice in a year."

Sophie pulled out money and offered it to me.

"She says to take the boy to his mother," said Lam. "She says go ride the train. The boy is tired, can't you see?"

I wanted to grab the money but forced my hands behind my back.

"She says it's your pay for moving the rocks."

I shook my head but he urged me to take it. Sam was muttering to Sophie, who nodded and spoke to Lam.

"She wants you to promise to ride the train," he said. "Sam told her that China men pinch pennies wherever they can."

"I was robbed! Every cent counts."

"She helps the boy, not you."

※

As we approached the buildings of North Bend, I said to Sam, "Can't we trek to the next train station?"

"Twelve miles away."

"The day is still early."

"You promised Sophie to take the boy on the train." Then he grinned. "From here, the walk is a day and a half to Lytton. What about your ship ticket?"

The station master doffed his cap, smiling to see customers, and chatted in English with Sam. We climbed the wooden steps into the passenger car and stopped in our tracks.

This was no wagon; it was a fancy hotel rolling on iron wheels. A row of oil lamps, each wrapped in sparkling glass and capped by frosted shades, hung from the ceiling. Brass fixtures held windows open at all heights. Above them, polished panels of wood curved to the roof where more light entered through the small windows there. Cushioned with thick red cloth, the chair backs dipped both ways to let passengers face either the car's front or rear. I pressed the seat padding and found it soft and springy.

Peter ran down the aisle, shouting with glee. When he skipped back, Sam flung out his arms, growled like a wild animal, and chased him. The boy ducked under a seat. Sam pretended not to see and let him escape. Peter came running, leapt up, and grabbed my neck. I laughed and recalled crossing the river this morning. But such a good mood could not last long.

Sam vaulted over the seats, his long legs swinging. "We built this," he crowed.

A bell clanged and the train started to move.

Peaks of distant mountains floated by, as did tall trees. This was my first time sitting inside, not crouched among a gang on the splintered planks of an open deck. From the window came the steady clank of pistons beating louder and faster than anything I had ever heard. As it gained speed, the train moved so smoothly that I was able to stand up and walk without losing my balance. I sat down, caught Sam's mocking gaze, and felt like a country bumpkin.

"Not your first time?" I asked.

Sam shook his head.

"You and your brother both worked on the railway?" I asked.

He looked away, even when I offered the bottle that Lam had filled with boiled water. I sat back and decided to enjoy myself. Few China men had ridden in such comfort over this road.

I had felt strangely content at hearing the brat's whoops of laughter. Happy times were hard to find. We sojourners never unravelled the mysteries of good luck, not even after debates around teahouse meals and late campfires. The rich were born into it while we poor fools had no choice but to chase it. At home, the family altar was central, even during the worst of times because only the ancestors had powers and direct reason to help us. Now my luck had fled and dropped me back to where I had started: a fifteen-year-old leaving home without a cent. Maybe the ancestors were angry that I had not paid them sufficient respect all these years. Twelve years had passed, an entire cycle of animal emblems.

We sojourners also discussed the proverb: "First, Luck; second, Destiny; third, *Feng Shui*; fourth, Virtues; fifth, Education." Of these, we humans could affect only the last three. That was why Mother wanted her sons to be schooled. Some men believed that the port of Victoria possessed good *feng shui*: hills enclosed its deep harbour on three sides in the classic Dragon Protects Pearl. Other men said that *feng shui* didn't work in Canada; foreign spirits ruled the land and waters. But everyone agreed that people with poor luck and weak fates could improve their lives by piling up virtue. That was why I needed to take Peter to Mary. But our own proverbs reminded us that personal goodwill had long been limited by larger forces.

Even the good-hearted get kicked by thunder.

Kind deeds see no rewards.

Have some luck, then go on back.

I reached down, fingered my stocking, and cursed those so-called lawmen: May all their sons be born without shit-holes. Police were corrupt no matter where we went. I should have leapt at the constable and his gun. I should have rolled out the door and ran, even without my boots. If they shot me dead in the back, my ghost would haunt them forever. The ache in my chest was a heavy iron beam. Nothing could be done to lighten or remove it.

Soon the train slowed. Trees and buildings that had vanished earlier in a blurred rush now gradually regained their shapes and lines. We passed a burial site with boxes and wooden figures, and then boarding halls, cottages for railway bigwigs, and false-front stores. Doors and fences raced by like hunted animals, leaving me behind. No matter how hard I might work here, there was no catching up, no regaining my loss.

The hillside forest hovered like an anxious parent behind the station. A bell clanged to clear the tracks. A crowd of men pushed and hollered on the platform that was oddly busy when compared to the peace and quiet of North Bend.

A redbeard boarding with a broom spotted me and rushed over. His shirt sleeves puffed over his elbows, held there by metallic arm bands. "Get off!" he shouted.

I showed him my ticket but he jabbered at Sam, who leapt up to cradle the sleeping boy.

"Go! The other way!" He pointed back at the station. "Those men, they didn't get jobs to clear the landslide. They're heading to Lytton to make trouble. If they see you, you're dead."

Our tickets were wasted. The clerk resumed his sweeping, head down.

Sam stopped. "Want to save money?" He caught my eye. "Give me a few drops of water."

He tapped red dust from a pouch into his palm. "We paint your face and make you one of us."

His baby finger stirred the mix. The dye was Sophie's, he explained, a gift to the boy.

He dabbed a mountain on his cheeks and drew two streaks across his forehead. The lines were like those on the boy's face. I thought of blood flowing from a gash to the skull.

"Blow on it," he said. "Dry it faster."

I shoved my pigtail under Sam's big hat as he rubbed red onto my forehead and cheeks. His fingers were warm against my face.

"It's easy to wash off, isn't it?" I asked.

"Good thing your skin is dark," he said. "At last, you and the boy look alike."

He wiped his fingers in his armpits and laid the boy over my lap. He sat and gripped the water bottle, heavy enough to break a man's nose.

Six redbeards came aboard, yelling and stomping, louts in stained pants and loose vests. It was their first time on a car too: they bunched at the door, tugging their beards and peering at the ceiling like porters waiting at a mansion's entrance. They pursed their lips and cheeks, seeking a spittoon. Two men removed their caps and held them tightly.

The pistons clanked and the train started to move.

"Look busy," Sam said.

I backed into the corner. Along the tracks were rocks with sharp edges. My hands, though wrapped around Peter, itched for a weapon.

"Talk to me," Sam said. "Be my best friend and tell me everything in the world."

"What place was that?"

"Keefers, where the China men got hired."

One redbeard used a penknife to cut furrows of white stuffing from a chair and then blew them away. Another fellow combed his beard, as if about to meet a pretty woman. Their chum sprawled sideways on a seat and whistled a tuneless air. His trousers rode up and left pale skinny legs dangling in the aisle. A fourth man scraped clean the mud-caked soles of his boot on the steps of the entrance.

I prayed that Lytton's China men were ready to fight. Yee Fook and another man had been murdered near Lytton. That year, anger in the railway camps ran so high that the trial was moved to Victoria. Three redbeards had been tried in court, Chinese witnesses were called to testify, but no one was found guilty.

Why hadn't the Company put guards on this train? It should have foreseen trouble when so many men were jobless and fretful.

The boot scraper nudged Pen Knife to stop. Then Pen Knife strolled toward us.

"Don't get up." Sam spoke calmly in Chinese, loud enough for the redbeard to hear. "Sit still and guard your child."

Pen Knife sat and thrust his legs at us. I met his gaze and looked beyond him. To show weakness would egg him on. My hands trembled.

"Yang Hok, you are a big-talking turd of shit," Sam said loudly, "and you hate my kind. But Heaven forces us to walk together. Tell me, is your father well?"

"He breathes righteous air." I matched his polite tone.

"He'll be happy you don't bring home a mix-blood child."

"Few people can please their parents." I shrugged.

"But you are a superior one. What about your friends who left their children here? Didn't they want to be superior men?"

"They were stupid pigs. Only fools come to Gold Mountain."

"And you?"

"I wanted to go to America."

Sam paused and took a breath before saying, "I want to go away too. I plan to go to China."

"Don't," I warned him. "A man brought home a mix-blood son and put him in school—"

"I heard you before," he snapped.

Pen Knife grinned.

"Why do people in China hate us?" Sam demanded. "Don't they care for their own bone and flesh?"

"You have your country and we have ours."

Pen Knife lit a cigar and blew its smoke at us. The wind from the window hurled it back in his face.

"We don't sail to China and dump our children there," said Sam. "You China men are the same as redbeards. You think you are smarter than us."

"We *are* smarter," I said. "That's why you want to go to China."

"I need to see my father's family."

"Strangers there get blamed for thefts and deaths."

"Ba promised to take us there."

"Don't be stupid. He just wanted to make you children laugh."

"He said we would feast from orchards of orange and banana trees. We would eat almond cakes and dragon's whiskers candy. We would climb Pine Mountain to the five-storey pagoda. He said our family owned land and ponds and never needed to worry."

Truly, that idiot father had been crazy to tell such stories. Chinese people guarded the homeland, now more than ever before. There was no worse time for an outsider to enter China. Our borders were long ones, and outsiders had pierced them again. Long ago, horsemen who shot arrows from galloping horses crashed through the Great Wall and turned the north into a wasteland. Now, gunboats sailed up to Guangzhou and fired cannons to crumble its walls. But trouble brewed inside the borders too: the Guest Wars were fought between China man and China man.

"Did your father sever ties?" I demanded. "Some men leave and never go back. Families disown them."

"Ba sent money home. Mother argued with him, said we needed the money too."

"You can't just stroll into a house and declare yourself family. They'll kick you out."

"I am Lew Bing Sam of the twenty-eighth generation. My father Lew Dat Kong was the twenty-seventh generation, youngest brother to Dat Joe and Dat Chen. My grandfather Suey Chaw was twenty-sixth generation, second eldest among five brothers. My great-grandfather Yuan Lay was twenty-fifth generation, he was the only son. His father Ho Fai was twenty-fourth generation; he was eldest of four brothers. His father Yun Tong was twenty-third generation, he was eldest of five brothers—"

I stopped him. Not even I, a full-blooded China man, knew my ancestors so well. "How many generations can you recite?"

"All of them. When Ba was dying he said, 'You must go to China. You have land and houses there. I did not forget you or Huey. I am a good father.'"

"His family in China will fight you."

"My father had no trueborn sons there, only adopted ones. Huey and I were his rightful heirs because we came from his body."

"You are a cup of water against a cart of firewood. You won't win."

"Can you help me find them?"

"Perhaps. Where's the village?"

He paused and shook his head. "Once you leave for China, I'll never see you again."

"Then we go together."

"Why?"

"I want to be there when you recite the family tree. I want to see the look on those peoples' faces. The villagers will talk about that moment forever, for generations to come. At first they will slam the gate on you. But when you stand outside and start chanting those names, the door will fly open. They will pull you into their courtyard, slide their hands all over your face, and dance circles around you. The story will live forever in your village. It will be engraved in stone for the entire county to see!"

Pen Knife propped his boots on the seat beside Sam. Mud and worse was smeared on the soles. His green-eyed gaze moved between us. He seemed to smile to himself, knowing that we were outnumbered.

I wanted to grab his beard and slam his head into the window.

I would shove his neck onto the edges of glass. Blood would spurt, for sure.

His buddy the boot scraper rescued him by shouting across the car and raising a bottle of whisky.

12

THE POOR FARE BETTER AT HOME THAN ON THE ROAD (1885)

At Lytton, the canyon suddenly became a dusty plain, ringed by dry hills dotted with bunchgrass. A wind hurled grit into our faces, forcing us to squint and turn our heads. The sky was a faint, scorched blue. On the slopes, lanky trees strayed from each other, as if each had a different plan to seek out water. The sun dried the sweat on my brow. I swallowed hard but my throat was knotted with worry. If people here were as hard as the ground underfoot, then it would be easier to float a boulder than to get a cash loan.

Of course I knew better than to travel without money. In Gold Mountain, if bad weather, broken wheels, or splintered axles didn't hold you back, then redbeard mischief would. You reached a distant town to find kinsmen gone and nowhere safe to stay. Old stores had closed and new crooks watched from doors. The redbeard roadhouse was open but dangerous. You had to buy food, shelter, and even directions to the nearest latrine.

Tomorrow, my path led either north or south, to seek Mary or to head home. North meant cheating at the game tables tonight, to raise some cash. South meant going home with empty hands and no rousing story for Grandfather. Fingers got scorched at the stove or over the fire; it didn't matter which.

"Does it get drier?" I pointed north.

Sam nodded.

"Cache Creek too? Shouldn't it get colder?"

Another nod.

Damn my fellow China men. Hundreds of them had passed through Victoria, but no one ever mentioned this barren landscape. They only exclaimed about cold stinging winters, or the merging of the two rivers. They said farms were few, but I had taken that to mean the land wasn't broken yet, the forests not felled.

Our train ride from Keefers had been brief so the landscape changed in the blink of an eye. Leafy thick woods gave way to grim wide desert. In rainy Gold Mountain, I never thought of drought. In China, rains involved ceaseless beseeching from feeble farmers to uncaring gods. One summer, the nights brought no cooling relief. Grandfather watched the horizon all day, waiting for clouds. The fields bloomed bright green at first but water levels failed the budding plants. Mid-season, when the rice didn't flower, fretful men joined their women at the temples and children were warned against making mischief or ominous talk. As fields yellowed far ahead of time, Grandmother bemoaned her lifeless vegetables. The pond dried up, leaving shellfish to broil and shrivel in the sun. That year, no one planted a fall crop or celebrated the mid-autumn.

Mary and her family must have led a tough life. No doubt that had caused her to bring Peter to me. How many children did she say she was raising? There could be more than three if her husband had offspring of his own. Taking Peter to her wouldn't be helpful unless there were cash gifts. The great pig of my plan had died and now its shit was leaking out.

The railway station with its bustling goings-on stood outside the town, so Lytton was quiet. Its hush, of course, concealed whatever foul planning against China men was underway. Two men on horses drove a sizeable herd of cattle. They could easily whip these heavy beasts to stampede through Chinatown and tear away anything not anchored. The old wagon road broke free from its narrow mountain thrust and opened wide, so the landscape left few hiding places. Hot winds fanned the anger of redbeards, curling it like old paint on the buildings. A blacksmith pounded at his forge and then hot metal hissed in cold water. How easy it was for the redbeards to arm themselves.

Carpenters nailed shingles onto a roof. Plenty of hammers were on hand. Picket fences surrounded cottages, where flowers drooped by the doors. Who knew how many pairs of narrowed eyes watched us? Buggies and horse-drawn wagons clattered by, spreading dust that pricked my throat. A gaggle of Native women in bright dresses ran laughing from a church, books clutched at their chests. Their people wouldn't help us. Had we ever helped them? We shunned them, avoiding them like street beggars, claiming we didn't understand what they said or wanted. Hotel porters heaved trunks and suitcases onto a stagecoach as the yeasty smell of beer drifted out from behind them. Someone banged on a piano. No doubt the thugs from the train had found comrades-in-arms and were raising ham-fisted toasts to each other. I picked up a sturdy pole from the ground, and the boy did the same.

"We should have fought that Boston Bar lawman," I said to Sam. "Instead, we ran like chicks."

"You would have done what?"

"Yanked his intestines, twisted his stomach. Thrust a broomstick down his throat."

"Wouldn't he shout for help?"

"Rip out his tongue."

"Wouldn't his helper have come?"

"Slit his throat."

Sam shook his head. "Nothing but talk."

And him? Knives bristled over his body yet not one was sharp.

Sam said that the train ran north to Ashcroft, forty miles away. From there, Cache Creek was seven miles further. There wasn't enough money for train passage.

"You said it was closer," I said.

"You heard wrong."

"Liar!" My fist sprang up.

Sam pulled Peter to his side, saying, "I only said we would pass Lytton on the way to Cache Creek."

As they walked off, I roundly cursed Sam and myself. I had been stupid, played for an idiot by these people.

In Lytton's Chinatown, Sam tried to leave us, to go see his woman across the river. He promised to bring a new guide next morning. "Remember," he said, "you need money to pay him."

No amount of coaxing could get Peter to release Sam's hand. It was good that the boy knew who he looked like and leaned toward his own kind. Sam ought to see this and stop insisting that Peter go to China. Indeed, tomorrow would be much better with a new guide. If Peter howled and held onto Sam when we met Mary, then she would see me as a fool who could not control his own son or win his respect. She had taken such trouble to unite us. No doubt she too needed a tale of an upright China man in order to impress her family and friends.

Sam walked us to the junction of the two rivers. Native people massed at the banks to reap its bounty. The river, no longer squeezed by narrow cliffs, slid around a jut of land where a second water way entered. At first I thought a wide cloud hung above, blocking the sun and putting half of the river in darkness. But it was no shadow: the water hugging the bank beneath us was many shades darker. For half a mile, the two colours ran side by side: the milky brown next to the greenish blue, until the latter dipped under the first. Clear and pure gave way to dark and muddy: that was the future of this place. In China, two such rivers would flow together for much longer, as the black and bright forces of *yin* and *yang* contended.

"This is the centre of our people." Sam pointed to burgeoning clusters of houses and farms along both rivers. "We call it 'Crossing-over.' The son of spirit-creature Coyote landed here after seeing the upper world. But railway workers blasted his spot."

Sam translated for Peter and then turned to me. "During the gold-miners' war, Native warriors from the rivers and mountains gathered here to drive the redbeards back to the ocean."

The boy shouted and raised his stick like a spear.

"Could your people have won?" I asked.

"Of course. It was before the sickness."

"And China men?"

"Kicked them out too."

"You wouldn't have been born."

"A blessing, then."

Two men loaded crates of apples and melons onto a small steamer. The sagging plank between shore and boat allowed one man to board each time.

"Is *Skuzzy* here?" I tried to talk up some goodwill that would get the brat to follow me.

"That's it." Sam lifted his chin toward the vessel.

The hull was bashed and splintered, a mass of patches covered by glossy layers of dark paint. The sternwheeler had three decks, each smaller than the one under it. The drum-like capstan at its bow, with thick ropes around it, was taller than a redbeard. The Company had built *Skuzzy* to carry supplies north to avoid paying tolls on the wagon road. Expert boatmen tried for five months to launch it through the Hell's Gate rapids. Finally, 125 China men used a thick rope and dragged the ship through, the way it was done at home.

China men in Victoria said, "Isn't the West more advanced than this? Couldn't they have used oxen? This is barbaric."

When those coolies passed through Victoria, everyone wanted to hear about the slippery rocks underfoot, the overseers' orders, and how the men had been chosen.

"No faster way to get downriver," Sam said, "for China men rushing to reclaim ship tickets."

"Those two rivers are lazy brothers," I said. "Shouldn't a huge waterfall have crashed into still waters to cause fish and water to leap up? That would be worth seeing."

At the bridge, the boy finally let go. Sam took the sky but I had the sun and moon. We both gazed at the brat, not each other.

Now I wanted Sam to take us to Cache Creek. Only he had seen my strength of mind to take Peter home. Only he could confirm the loss of my money roll. He could get us to Mary, if he wanted, maybe borrow a horse and wagon. Didn't he see how I was trying to help his people? He should witness mother and son brought together and observe Mary's kind and loving nature. She had not brushed aside her son like a tick and now she would welcome his return. She was probably standing at the door of her house, the gate of her front yard, waiting and waiting. Most of all, Mary needed to see how I had befriended a man like my son, proving that I didn't dislike such people and would have taken Peter to China if it were truly best for him.

"If you can't get money," Sam said, "you can always take him to Sophie."

"You call her insane."

"She's different with children."

"I don't hate the boy."

"You just want to save face."

"And you?" I snapped. "Does your grandmother want you to go to China?"

He looked away and shook his head.

"What does she think will happen to you?"

"She told me a story. You should hear it."

"Hurry," I said. "We need to go."

"Long ago, a transformer travelled through the land. He asked people to respect him and pray to him. He met a man who was making a canoe.

"'I'm busy,' said the man, 'and have no time to pray.'

"'That's a nice adze,' Transformer said. 'Let me see it.'

"He took it and pushed it to the canoe-maker's nose. At once the man was changed into a woodpecker. He flew to a tree and began to strike it with his beak.

"Then Transformer met a man who was sharpening a stone. He asked the man what he was doing. The man said, 'I'm making a weapon to kill Transformer when he comes.'

"'That's a nice knife,' Transformer said. 'Let me see it.'

"He took it and said, 'You ought to have this on your head.' He pushed it there, and at once the man became a deer with antlers.

"Transformer said, 'You won't ever make weapons again to kill people.'

"Then he came upon people playing *leha'l*. A man with two wives had gambled away his dog. Transformer turned them all into stone.

"At all the places he stopped, he met good people and bad. He scattered the good people throughout the land, and our families are descended from them. As for the bad people, they were changed into rocks, birds, and animals."

"Oh, so you think someday your Transformer will turn the red-beards into rocks?" I said.

"What someday?" He was annoyed. "Transformer came back and took the lives of workers on the railway."

"He killed China men too?"

"All invaders."

"Then your brother should have been saved."

"It was a warning to me to quit the job."

I thumped my stick on the ground several times. Time to depart.

"In China, people prayed for the gods to strike dead the redbeards."

"Heaven didn't listen, did it?"

We fell silent as though we agreed on that point. Then he said, "Do me one favour? Write your name and village and home district. That way I can find you in China."

We had no paper or pencil so I offered to leave a note in the temple store. "I'll write the words big and clear. Anyone can read it."

The pained look on Sam's face said he didn't trust me.

"You don't think I'll reach China, do you?" he asked. "Too far-fetched, isn't it?"

"I said I would help," I snapped.

He was shaking his head as I pulled the boy toward Chinatown.

Farewells involved the squaring of debt, to give the two parties some peace, to reduce the distance about to separate them. But leaving didn't free a traveller. In fact it tied him closer to everyone and everything he left behind. After I left home, my village's grey-black houses, straw-fed fires, and livestock smells became closer than my shadow. I sent money for building a new home, buying firewood, and adding meat to meals. My letters always asked what meats the family had been enjoying, but no one ever replied.

Only after I left home did I recall events from long ago: as a child, one day I dropped my bowl of rice to the dirty floor. The dish broke and Grandmother cried out against bad luck. I started to cry, expecting to be beaten. Instead, Mother scolded my clumsiness, swept up the mess with her fingers, and gave me her bowl. She ate my rice and spat out the earthenware chips. One year, bandits raided the village while Grandfather was away, so Grandmother crouched by the front door, the kitchen cleaver in her hand, waiting. I was hidden in the cold stove, covered by a mound of kindling. I peed in my pants, but Mother didn't grumble about washing them. When a wily shopkeeper cheated Mother, Grandfather dragged all three grandchildren to town to watch him gain redress. When a crowd gathered to watch the unruly dispute, Grandfather realized he was shaming the entire family.

"Don't meddle with troublemakers," was all that he said at our parting.

Grandmother added, "Write plenty of letters."

They left no room for tears or regret. To show fear was to be weak. To stall the departure was to revisit earlier decisions, all laboured, all painful. Better to think ahead. Look after myself. Get food. Find clothes. Stay healthy. Send money home and then return in person bringing even more. Go back grinning and laughing, and tell tales to dazzle the villagers.

I had met Sam Bing Lew, what, four days ago? We saw no matter eye-to-eye. He was a fool carrying an earthenware purse, clanging it when he had a few coins. He was a slave who thought himself smarter than his master. Yet I was stricken, a fly with no head. I was ginger that lacked heat, vinegar with no tang. Not only had Sam helped me cross the river in that creaky canoe, but he had also saved me from the trestle, the bandits, and the thugs on the train. He was entitled to receive prime favours from me and my family. My entire family and I should be on our knees before him. But this parting meant that those debts would never be repaid. I had slipped like a determined eel from his hands, and we would never see each other again. He had fallen, and a hundred men like me were trampling over him.

꒜

Chinatown was anchored by the great barn that held Boss Joe's general store, warehouse, and boarding hall as well as the famed temple. Gold paint announced in English and Chinese the firm, Tai Wo Chong, which was connected to Victoria's Tai Yuen Company. Its storefront was crowded. In the sun, under awnings for shade and by water troughs for horses, China men loitered and watched passersby. The size of the gathering made me hopeful about borrowing money, but first I visited a smaller shop for some background.

"You Chinese?" asked the man in English and then Chinook.

"Ever see a redbeard with one of these?" I replied in Chinese and held up my pigtail.

Two men stood at a basin of pungent vinegar. One man gave a startled look and hurried out, as if I was a thug for a loan shark. I quickly put down my stick.

The one in a long apron was stirring pickled greens. "What a face! Never wash it?"

At the trough outside, Peter howled, but I showed no mercy.

"This is for your own good!" I shouted. A dirty face was dangerous at bedtime because the soul flew off during dreams. Upon returning, if it failed to recognize its owner's face, then it did not re-enter its proper home. Parents in my village had woken in the morning to find healthy babies dead, streaks of vomit dried around their mouths. Grandmother said that scrubbing our faces at bedtime was more important than washing our feet. If the boy died while in my care, then I would be cursed forever.

Inside the store, I tried to regain my honour. "Redbeards on my train wanted to thrash China men, so my guide painted me."

"No ladies' skirts to hide behind? You're big and tall; you didn't brawl?"

"Anyone surnamed Yang here?"

"I am Yuen. Close enough?"

"Boss Joe in the Tai Wo Chong store, is he here now?" If not, I would return later. Low-level clerks were a waste of time.

"A railway bigwig and his wife came to town. The churchman mentioned our temple, so they insisted on a visit. Boss Joe took his oiled lips and slimy tongue there."

"Those rabble-rousers want the bigwig to fire the China men," I muttered.

"You just arrived and you know everything? Are you Prime Minister?"

"Why else would they pay train fare to come?"

"Then those fools just boarded a ship full of bloodthirsty pirates," said Yuen. "It's Ancestor Day for Boss Joe. Plenty of China men have come to town."

A din outside grew louder. Someone banged together pot lids, clang, clang, clang. A dog barked, high-pitched and without stopping. Boots crunched on hard ground and gravel. Eager voices cheered the marchers. I thought of the English Queen's birthday rallies in Victoria with military bands and high-stepping horses, crowds and children waving small flags. It had been terrifying to see all the redbeards of the city lining the streets at the same time, vastly outnumbering the China men. I wanted to run but forced myself to stay until the end. In Chinatown, people had asked if I was looking for an early death.

Yuen hurried to the door but not me. My thieving eyes looked for a cash register. From the front, he called to me. I trudged by a row of flattened ducks, glowing from grease. They were doomed to a second death here.

When Grandfather took me as a small boy to town, he avoided parades, unless they were sponsored by temples that he knew. Gong beaters and snooty callers led stately marches, shouting for crowds to make way and fall quiet because a judge presided over a public beheading, or a general led troops to the frontier. Common folk never watched if they could find a handy alley for escape. No telling when a sergeant might grab a harmless bystander and press him into the army or cuff and kick him for a lack of respect.

A ragtag line of redbeards, including Pen Knife and his friends, followed a man waving a red, white, and blue flag on a pole. The man beside the flag bearer walked at a casual pace. It was too hot for suit jackets, but he wore one over a shiny red tie.

They stopped in front of Tai Wo Chong. Fewer China men were left now, while those who remained were brandishing shoulder poles. The men crouched at ease, chatting in small groups like porters taking a break during a job. Poles were propped against their necks, across their laps. Too bad there hadn't been time to set planks over the plate-glass windows. Those sharp edges were deadly too.

"This is death." Yuen hurried away.

I slipped two small jugs of rice wine into my jacket and let it fall to the floor. The storekeeper returned with a sturdy hoe and a pitchfork. I gripped my stick from earlier.

"See the red tie?" He pointed. "Boss Joe owns horses to rent and deliver goods, so does that one. Boss Joe sells cloth and clothing, and so does that one. Boss Joe sends China men out to work, and so does that one. Up to now, both men had plenty of business."

"No policeman here?"

"Left town."

"Just as a railway bigwig arrives?"

He shrugged. "This one inspected the iron road, but now the Company sends him to look at the rockslide."

A scream ripped through the air. A China man ran at the redbeards, a shoulder pole raised over his head, ready to crack skulls.

"Stinking bastards!" he roared. "I take your lives!"

The redbeards fell back, their mouths open.

A second China man sprinted from behind them and crashed into the first man. They fell to the ground and then compatriots raced out and dragged them away. They vanished in a second and the two sides stood as if nothing had happened.

"That Seven could have gotten us killed." Yuen cursed the hothead. "He is surnamed Jeh. He lost three fingers during railway work."

"Can't they kick him home?"

"We donated money for a ticket, but he sold it. He is crazy-crazy."

From the temple came the bigwigs, led by a churchman. A round white collar capped his dark garments. Mrs. Bigwig sailed by, her bustle up and poking out, yards of cloth draped into a skirt, and a pointy prow of yellow hair at her forehead. Mr. Bigwig fanned himself with a hat. Boss Joe wore a mix of western and Chinese finery. The last man clutched a box with folded bellows, three thin legs, and a shiny glass hole. It was the machine that took pictures.

A man bowed to Mrs. Bigwig. He offered his arm, she took it, and they strolled toward town. She stopped to shake Boss Joe's hand. What a three-legged chicken. Most women of her class couldn't bear to go near China men, much less lay a hand on one of us. But she did wear gloves.

Red Tie spoke in earnest to Mr. Bigwig, who tucked his thumbs into his vest pockets. The churchman and Boss Joe stepped back. Mr. Bigwig shook his head and mopped his forehead with a handkerchief. Red Tie dabbed his cuff under his chin and across his neck. Finally, the railway man strolled away with the churchman. Red Tie yelled to their backs. There was no response. He ran and blocked their way, but the men swerved around him. When he went back, palms up in failure, his followers gave a roar and started to hurl rocks.

Right away, Mr. Bigwig was hit and stumbled forward. Luckily, they missed his head. The churchman spun around just in time for a chunk to crash into his chest. Good thing he was sturdy and young, not an old man. The rock throwing stopped. The churchman hurried to Red Tie and pointed at his men, who punched at the sky and booed. Red Tie lifted his hands to calm them.

Could the Jesus man call on the powers of his god to strike down those who didn't obey him? A gust of wind swept through and raised a cloud of dust. If Pen Knife and his friends recognized the boy and me from the train, then more trouble was coming.

Finally, the talking seemed to cool the anger. The tension loosened and the redbeards walked with Mr. Bigwig into town. I sagged with relief, but Yuen shook his head and predicted certain death. "Redbeards lost face in front of us. They can't live that down. Soon, they'll come to nail us."

He twisted brown paper into a cone and filled it with peanuts for the boy. I hefted the extra weight in my jacket and felt like cat shit on the altar, hated by both gods and ghosts.

In the street, two men in mock battle swung shoulder poles at one another, hitting and spinning through a *gong fu* set. Around them, China men clapped each others' backs, jabbering and chuckling.

Those fools should have been planning their next defense. They weren't squatting to shit right away, but the latrine needed to be dug now. Instead, they circled Boss Joe, asking stupid questions. What was discussed inside the temple? Were more railway jobs coming? Did firecrackers need to be burned at the temple to drive away the dirty evils left behind by the redbeards?

The boss's high-collared tunic was cut from heavy brocade. It poked out from his hips like a judge's jacket. His face was fleshy and well-fed.

"Boss Joe?" I was dusty and badly needed a genial introduction. "Sorry to disturb you on this busy day."

He noticed Peter. "Did you find the mother? I can write the letter for you."

"Not yet. She lives near Cache Creek." I mentioned getting a guide tomorrow.

"A superior man knows the way." He smiled but his gaze went elsewhere and he nodded at someone.

"Boss Joe, I have no other way to say this. Great men have great capacity, so please excuse these poor manners. I need help."

"Cash?"

"A redbeard lawman stole my savings, four hundred dollars. I was heading home to China. Then he threw me into jail."

"I don't even know your name."

"Other people, strangers, helped me along the way. *A good heart never fears action.*"

"Those people were better men than me." Boss Joe turned to leave, but the brat held up his cone of peanuts.

"Decent boy!" He took a few and patted Peter's head. "Come to the banquet, both of you! Out-of-town visitors pass the night for free; you can join them."

"Did anyone come from Cache Creek?" I asked. Such a person might offer a free ride.

"Fish Eyes! Go into the temple and ask for Fish Eyes."

Thanking him politely, I stepped back with lowered head, and almost turned to leave. Then I pressed the two bottles of liquor into his hands.

"You lack money but carry wine?"

"Pinched it from Yuen's store."

He laughed.

If Boss Joe was also pushing me to the temple, then clearly the destination was fated. I had, after all, made a vow to go there while locked in that shit-pit prison. *Man proposes but Heaven disposes.* Sojourners viewed His Holiness, the god in Lytton, as far more potent than the lesser gods in the temples of Yale and Victoria. It couldn't hurt to ask Fist's questions. A lane along the main building led to the temple entrance. Spades and hoes, rakes and shoulder poles leaned in the shade against a log wall. The China men of Lytton were ready to brawl. They knew a thing or two about honour.

A guard by the door let me enter. The vast hall had few windows; oil lamps and candles gave light. A small crowd gathered around a *fan-tan* table while men at two tables of *mah-jongg* were mixing tiles and shouting their way through a match. The boy and I crept to one side. Fools who approached a table in the middle of a match and opened their mouths could easily get lambasted for changing the flow of luck.

We drank tea at a side table. My stomach rumbled. I marvelled that the boy wasn't whining about hunger. Perhaps he was used to food shortages. Maybe the stepfather liked his own children better and starved my boy. Did Mary's husband resent her life among the redbeards before she entered his?

It had been a long time since my last *mah-jongg* game. My play would be slow at the start but I needed to be running, even flying, before walking. The key move was to palm the flower tiles while we were mixing them. Then, from watching the dice roll, I would know where to plant my tiles. The cast-off tiles would tell me who was playing what hands. Hopefully no one would notice in the dim light that the wall in front of me was short by two tiles.

An expert once said to me, "Hok, there is no such thing as a bad hand of *mah-jongg* tiles." He lay open his hands and spread his fingers, palms up. Then he tapped his forehead. "It's what you know that lets you win."

By the tea table, a man hunched over a water pipe lit his tobacco with a long, glowing taper. Scrolls of brushwork covered the logs of the walls. I wondered if Soohoo's work was here too. Two short lines from the Master caught my eye: *"Brave men fear naught; the wise don't fret."*

A steady trickle of men paid respect to the statue of His Holiness. I watched because it was rare to see so many men in a temple without women fussing around them, insisting on the proper methods. On the altar, the wooden carving of His Holiness was small and dark, wrapped in stiff, faded garments sparkling with gold and silver threads. The statues of guardian gods were larger, their porcelain bright from fine paint. They held spears and war-axes. Their beards hung long and smooth, unlike those unkempt bushes worn like coarse bristles on the faces of redbeards. The urn of sand before the altar was full of red sticks, the tail ends of incense.

Guan Gung, the God of War, sat with his red face alert, eyebrows raised, the green civilian robe over his armour, a great halberd by his side, and an open book in his hands. My family worshipped a statue of him, even Grandfather. When he went to town to sell rice, he nodded and muttered at Guan Gung, seeking his protection. In the bandit gang, Guan Gung was the patron god of brotherhood men, setting high standards for loyal and righteous actions. My railway gang paid homage to him too, hoping that his courage and endurance would course through our veins. In secret, Grandmother prayed to him to extend her life, at least until my father returned. Always last to go to bed, she was the one who took a final look down the darkened lane, drew our front doors shut, and dropped the bar in place. She claimed she was checking for robbers, but we knew she was looking for Father, certain that he would accost her first of all in order to decide how to approach Grandfather.

I lit incense and poured wine. I murmured a prayer and tried to recall One Leg and No Brain's faces. They failed to emerge. I only saw a pant leg pinned up, the glint of a steel pin piercing dark cloth, the bib of the overall with a missing button.

Should One Leg go home?

I tossed the wooden charms to the ground. The two sides landing face-up advised yes. I threw them again. Same answer. No need to ask a third time. Fist should be happy.

Should No Brain go home?

This time, yes and then no. The third deciding toss was yes.

Should Fist go home?

Yes.

I thought of my own question. Should I take the boy to China?

It would be grand to have the Will of Heaven on my side, a shield to my back and a steady wind behind me. I raised the charms, but then clenched and stayed my hand.

I was afraid His Holiness might order me to do something that was within my power.

I prayed instead for big wins at tonight's game tables.

13

FIRE CAN WARM YOU OR LEAVE YOU IN THE COLD (1885)

Boss Joe climbed atop a wooden crate with a lamp to his face so that all in the hall could see. No small-town merchant would miss a chance where everyone had to look up to him. He loudly praised his esteemed forebears for packing their meagre goods and leaving central China 600 years ago, after barbarian hordes had crashed through the Great Wall and laid waste to the region. His ancestors walked for months and crossed high mountains to reach the southern frontier. There, dense jungles and swamps had to be tamed and shaped into working farms while hostile tribes armed with poisoned arrows surrounded them. He wondered with a chuckle if China men in Gold Mountain had any of the same gumption to claim new lands for their clans and families.

Stupid ass. His ancestors had travelled with wives, children, and parents, all over many generations. They possessed better tools and weapons than local enemies. They carried useful goods that could be readily traded along the way. They could have stopped on any available land and built a flimsy, self-contained village. Here in Gold Mountain, redbeard invaders held China men and local Natives with the same brutal regard: runts from a diseased litter destined for death and disposal. Now Boss Joe sneered at them too.

The brat drummed the table with chopsticks, causing men to frown. I stopped him. There was peace for a moment until he started kicking the table leg, which set the bowls and spoons rattling. Chopsticks landing on the dirty floor brought bad luck so the men at my table muttered among themselves, loud enough for me to hear.

"No spanking, no growing."

"Fold the young tree, not the old."

"Kill a small fire before the mountain burns."

If these cockheads were like Father and Grandfather, then they were just crickets in the night hills, all noise and hazy air. They expected their women to feed the children, teach them manners, and smack into them an abiding fear of their elders. Never could these men persuade a wayward child to eat a cold rice breakfast before a long day's journey.

"Today, many strangers in town asked me how His Holiness was brought to this desolate place," Boss Joe bragged. "So I want to tell everyone the story."

"You know us merchants," he started, "we are as lazy as any worker."

He paused to let people laugh, but no one did. "Once the goods are received and unpacked, we sit around, swatting flies and awaiting clients. Rail hands come to my store to drink tea and pass the time. Every day, another one asked me for advice:

"'Boss, a worker in the tunnel got fragrant; shall I leave to be safe?'

"'Boss, the washman in town is quitting; should I buy his shop?'

"'Boss, there's work at fish canneries; do I go?'

"'Boss, is it better to winter in China or in New Westminster?'

"They asked me, they asked each other, they worried themselves silly. 'Is it best to take half a pound or sixteen ounces?' 'Is it best to leave on the first of the month, or the fifteenth?' That was when I went to China and brought over His Holiness. He made everyone's life simpler."

Who in hell did Boss Joe think he was fooling? The little statue of His Holiness had cost next to nothing to bring over. Boss Joe spent a few measly coins in order to rake in the big money, that's what he did. He knew his customers well. China men here were nervous; having seen ghosts, of course they feared the dark, so by all means they sought holy advice. Normally, clan elders mapped out every path and every direction for each clan member, but here we were far from the village.

I made better use of my time by asking guests about the host, seeking ways to approach Boss Joe again for a loan.

Did he have children?

Did he trade at Cache Creek?

Was he friendly with Native people?

The guests were as lazy as rich men and didn't care to talk to me. One man tapped his fingers on the table and muttered, "Start the meal, stinking bastard, start the meal. Night comes and so does trouble." He looked around at us. "In America, redbeards attacked us again. Coal miners' cabins got torched, but thirty men escaped."

"Good thing Boss Joe has guards outside."

The guests were divided half-and-half on whether to stay the night and gamble or to eat and run.

I needed everyone to remain and play. "Much smoother to smile among friends," I wheedled. *"In harsh lands, men laugh whenever they can."*

I asked who among the guests was an expert gambler. They snorted and refused to say. They had claimed this territory far ahead of me, an upstart newcomer whose cash should flow, by right, into their pockets. The less I knew, the better for them. But it ran both ways. The less they knew of me, the better for me. They didn't know about my game-hall skills or that I was penniless and desperate.

Seven, the crazed attacker of the afternoon, dropped into the seat by me. He grunted at the diners and, frowning, looked Peter up and down before asking about him.

"What?" He scrunched his face at my reply. "What damn use is that?"

"The boy will be raised by his mother."

"Nothing changes for him." His left hand stayed inside a pocket to hide the missing fingers. "Those people have wretched lives."

"Trueborn mother is best."

"If her people suffer, then so will she. What about your boy then?"

"You fought the redbeards," I said. "We need more men like you."

"No one joined me out on the road," he noted, "not even you."

My head tilted at the boy. "Who looks after him?"

When the food arrived, the men complained loudly. The chef hired from New Westminster never reached Lytton due to the landslide blockage. Amateurs in the kitchen overcooked the soup, melting the strands of bird's nest into mush. The rose-flower chicken was dry and stringy from being simmered at too high a flame. The eggs scrambled with tomatoes were soggy. Guests with feeble teeth spat out the too-tough beef brisket. Seven refused to eat and stalked off to squat by the teapots where he fished out a jug of liquor.

Soon we swept food scraps to the ground and summoned the town's stray dogs to feast. The gambling resumed: shouting and bluster filled the hall, as loud as that in Victoria. Men with no money unrolled blankets beside a darkened wall and pulled out tobacco pipes. I went from table to table to assess my chances while watching the sleeping boy from afar. Well-wishers besieged Boss Joe so I waited to broach the subject of the loan. When my low-risk bets at *fan-tan* failed several times, I regretted not pouring a larger quantity of wine for His Holiness. I hovered over the *mah-jongg*, looking for the careless players. The amateurs never bothered to track discarded tiles. I would let them settle into a rhythm of carefree gaming before joining.

A glass bottle shattered, and then another. A rush of air whipped by.

"Fire!"

The floor at the side door was burning, fuelled by straw and clothes left there. Yellow and orange flames shot up. Guests raced toward the store, overturning benches and tables, causing oil lamps to crash and spread the burning. Money fell to the floor, but it was too dark to paw around, even for me. Men beat the stubborn fire with shirts and blankets. The scrolls burst into flames, but not the logs of the wall.

I yelled for Peter, who was no longer lying on his blankets. Men at the door were twisted into a seething mess, unable to move. I peered through their legs but the smoke and flickering shadows hid everything. I kicked the blankets by the wall. No, the brat wasn't playing games and hiding there. Maybe he was outside already.

Flames at the entrance reached higher and higher, burning so fiercely that the rest of the hall fell dark. The boy stood in a trance, eyes and mouth wide open. Flashing light threw an eerie orange glow on his face; he looked otherworldly. He thrust his hands at the fire, as if needing warmth, as if drawn to the flames for some grand purpose. He was born under Water so Fire was the enemy that could evaporate him, reduce him to nothing. I seized him but he screamed, "No!" and broke away. He smacked into Seven, carrying one of the statues of the gods.

I grabbed Peter and ran out the door.

The massive fire lit the moonless night and unfurled sparks and embers that sailed north, away from town. I had never seen flames wide and tall as a village wall. Brick houses in China did not burn as fiercely as wood, and this timber had baked through months of hot sun and dry winds.

Boss Joe ran by, dragging a heavy sack and shouting orders. Clerks stumbled through the smoke-filled store to heave goods to the front, where lines of men passed them on to safety. Bags of rice swung through, followed by bins of beans, jugs of wine, and pails of dishes.

I prayed for safety for Boss Joe's gold and money. Otherwise he would be in no position to lend me anything. The building next door was alit; its windows swallowed a sharp crack and then the glass shattered.

The boy pulled me back toward the fire. I stopped, lifting him to my shoulders where he could watch. The rest of Chinatown's people had filled the road, fleeing their nearby homes for safety outdoors. The enemy was all around, but why hide inside if the walls were about to burn? I groaned aloud. We were mud Buddhas crossing water: ones who couldn't even protect ourselves.

Firecrackers banged in a rat-tat-tat of a rooftop hailstorm, followed by a run of loud explosions. Tins of kerosene must have ignited. The last clerk ran out just as one wall collapsed. The burning logs slumped to the ground and rolled away before the adjacent walls tilted. We backed away from the intense heat, coughing, hands over our noses and mouths. The finer the kindling, the bigger the fire. If Boss Joe rebuilt this Chinatown, maybe he should try smaller buildings.

Rumours spread through the crowd like ticks in a ragged bedroll. Redbeards had upended the horse troughs and barrels to deprive us of water. They subdued the guards and trussed their hands and feet. Flaming bottles of kerosene had been tossed into the temple and onto the roof. The store's front entrance burst into flames, but our men beat out the fire. Otherwise the hall would have become an oven and roasted everyone. The river was too far and the slope to the water too steep for any bucket brigade to be formed. Most astonishing, the holy statues were carried out without a single smudge. People praised the gods for a wondrous rescue.

"*Fire can't be wrapped in paper,*" they said. "Justice prevails."

Someone pointed out that no redbeard spectators had gathered. In Victoria, water wagons and pumper cars arrived promptly at blazing buildings, bells clanging to summon policemen, drunks, and eager children from nearby homes. This quiet was eerie. Were the townspeople cowering in fear that we China men planned to take revenge? Or were they waiting with guns and pitchforks?

I resolved at that moment to take the boy to China. At the fire, he was ready to leap into the flames. His future had exploded into danger and ruin. My boy, any boy, deserved better.

Seven was trying to rally men to take the fire to Red Tie.

"His thugs await," Boss Joe protested. "You fall into their trap!"

"We must show them that we're not scared."

Angry voices backed him up.

"They have guns," said Boss Joe.

"But they can't shoot in the dark. *Strike iron while the stove is red!*"

I held Peter tightly, afraid that Seven might grab him to pull me along. That fool needed to calm down. Our bandit gang had often rushed out of the camp livid and eager for battle. We forgot about all-night sentries or new guns the enemy had acquired. We failed to confirm the latest news received, or to recall how recent rains had turned paths into mud. Then, as we retreated in shame and confusion, our leaders shouted, "Death takes us home!"

This fire might have made a grand story to tell to my villagers: we burned the houses of the redbeards after they attacked our temple. We fought to the death and defended the honour of our nation. But Boss Joe was no flag-waving general, while Seven was crazy-crazy. We were China men in a lawless redbeard town. The fire was a colossal insult but no one had died. Should we consider ourselves lucky, grab our belongings, and run? We had seen, after all, plenty of deaths on the iron road, and now that it was finished, even the merchants were in retreat. Boss Joe had lost goods in the fire, yet he loudly urged restraint. Most of us had lost little or nothing; why would we invoke new dangers? We didn't even know each other's names.

Yuen, who had not attended the banquet, opened his doors and invited people into his storeroom. The crowd surged away.

In a corner, I lay down with the boy. Smoke lingered on his clothes and hair. Despite the panic and noise, he was asleep. I thrust my ear to his nose to ensure that he hadn't inhaled poison. He had been a willing traveller on this trip, showing little fear. Maybe panic was normal; this ruined and troubled land was the only place he knew as home. He may have trekked up and down the canyon and seen how rudely the redbeards treated his people. I should have praised his efforts, told him he was a good lad. I had expected him to wail loudly every morning for his mother, but he hadn't done so. Had Mary prepared the boy, telling him over and over that one day his true father would take him away? Had she drummed discipline and restraint into him, as tools needed for daunting times?

Boss Joe sternly advised his restless guests to stay far from town. Nothing could be done until the full extent of damage was known. He preferred to talk in daylight when the enemy's faces were clear. If the guests wanted to pursue redress, then they should list their losses with his clerk. Everyone would be treated fairly. Men shook their heads, doubtful of justice, wondering if Boss Joe might be playing some selfish game. Someone cursed Boss Joe for sending the crew from Keefers to the landslide. That had caused all this trouble.

Sentries crouched by the doors and windows with shoulder poles and hoes. The farm tools stockpiled at Boss Joe's store that afternoon had gone up in flames. People were lighting incense before His Holiness. A man prayed loudly.

"If we flee outside, we'll get clubbed like Yee Fook," said Yuen. Friends told him to shut his mouth.

Yuen wandered around, resting his forehead against the walls and scraping his knuckles against the wood.

"Death," he muttered. "Certain death."

"We all die," someone said, "sooner or later."

"Not at the hands of the redbeards. That's too low an insult."

The smells of dried beans and salted fish lingered in the storeroom. I lay stiff and tense, counting Sophie's coins over and over. They were too few to get us to Victoria. Yale was four days away, by foot, and my boot soles were getting thin and soft. The boy and I needed to walk the day and a half to North Bend. At Sophie's fish camp, I would loudly agree with Lam's advice to take the boy to China, and then press the miner to put some money behind his words.

"Talk is easy, action is not," I would say. *"Can't boil water by stirring it."*

Same thing for Yang the washman in Spuzzum: *"Better to set sail than stay in port."*

For Soohoo the brothel keeper in Yale: *"Superior men seek justice, not food."*

Voices in the dark revealed two factions among Boss Joe's workers. One side had expected the store to go bankrupt, sooner or later. In the morning, those men would head south. The men who opposed this view planned to stay, hoping Boss Joe would buy out Yuen, who had put his store on the market right after the railway's completion. Yuen was old and soft like a piece of wet cow hide, they noted, and keen to go home. Boss Joe could make a future here, especially if he also bought the other shop with two whores among its assets.

Overnight, Yuen stoked a fire and simmered pots of rice porridge. A few farmers and miners departed at dawn without eating. Boss Joe's men fetched river water to let us wash off the grime and soot. The boy and I needed to look clean in case we were forced to beg for food on the road. Too bad the red paint that Sophie had dabbed on Peter still showed.

The men were squatting, eating in the storeroom when Seven declared, "Tonight, I'll go burn that new church. Anyone can join me."

Someone jeered. "You can light matches with two fingers?"

"I'll do it with one."

"Screw you," said a miner. "Trouble circles back to us. Where we work, no crowds give us safety."

"Native people built that church," said a clerk. "They didn't burn us."

"No wonder redbeards burned the store," said Seven. "China men here did nothing after Yee Fook was killed."

"Redbeards have guns," said the clerk. "Want to send us to hell?"

Peter was tugging to go to the outhouse, but I wanted to hear this.

"Fire burned you out." Seven looked around. "Clothes, blankets, your letters from home. You lost everything and you're not angry?"

"You'll light a match, then flee, and leave a mess for us."

"I give you a lofty status. People will applaud. You fought back when China was insulted."

Boss Joe called for silence. He squatted among his men, eating porridge.

"Have children?" He glanced at Seven.

The firebrand shook his head. His thick pigtail, heavy as a chain, hung to his waist.

"Wife?"

"None, but my parents count on me."

"Then no matter what you say now, you want to go home safely."

"I'll do this alone." Seven's face twisted with scorn. "Then you can all puff up and brag about what *we* did here."

"You're crazy and people will die," said Boss Joe. "Tie him up."

His men surrounded Seven, who thrashed about until they pinned him and fetched rope.

"You're no magistrate!" He hurled his face from side to side, strong but no match for four men. "You serve no laws!"

"This is what I know." Boss Joe put down his bowl and grabbed a hammer. "I should smash your ankle, hand you a box of matches, and watch you crawl to that church."

"You disgrace all China men." Seven struggled to free himself. "None of you have face!"

"Anyone want to set a fire?"

After a pause, Boss Joe announced he would send Seven to Yale on the stagecoach and get rid of him once and for all.

Peter dashed to the door, one hand at his crotch. I ran after him, afraid he might fall into the pit below.

Seven was right about revenge. After our village was raided and burned during the Guest Wars, Grandfather had joined an overnight raid. I wanted to go too but Mother said no, even though other boys of my age went. The men dragged back weeping captives, fine furniture, and a crate of fine porcelain wrapped in cloth.

"Find kindness, respond with kindness!" they shouted. "Find hatred, respond with hatred."

The enemy struck back. They burned several fields of ripening rice and the ancestral hall, as well as the 200-year-old banyan tree by the fish pond.

Grandfather and his friends vowed, "No revenge, no rest." They set to work honing spears and axes.

They crept out on another raid, jointly planned with clan and village allies. This time, they returned with the corpses of our own people. The deceased were buried as heroes; their names were etched onto plaques. The raiders brought back less booty this time, explaining that other raiders had taken the best treasure. They bragged about scores of deaths, including the slaughter of women and children. No wonder people at home feared angry ghosts: among the trees and bamboo, on narrow paths, and anywhere near water. People had been bound and tossed into lakes, chopped down from the back as they fled, or burned alive in stockades under siege.

"If you don't kill them now, then they will slaughter you later," said Grandfather's friend. "Even if you kill them, their eyes don't close. They're watching you! And if you don't murder their children, they will grow up and chase you for revenge."

Grandmother had disagreed. "Wolves and snakes sneak around to swallow pigs and chickens."

When we returned to the storeroom, I found the cold porridge hard to swallow. Railway coolies were workers held in thrall by our wages. When redbeards spat on us, we let the spit dry. We shrugged off shame and swallowed pride so that daily life could go on. There was nowhere for the disgrace to go, only deep into our guts to be stirred into bile. No water could cool the burning hurt. We dreamed of revenge, of honour restored.

But no one had ever thought it through, had dreamed what exact form the revenge might take. Did it mean arresting arrogant bosses and having them beheaded? Would we receive back wages equal to what the redbeards had earned? Did it mean ordering redbeards to carry out burials with no expense spared for rotted corpses found in the river? Would the Queen of England kowtow to the Emperor of China? Did it mean rounding up foul-mouthed little boys and spanking them until their teeth were jarred loose?

That man Seven knew exactly what he wanted to do, but not the rest of us, and certainly not those who had gone back to China to forget everything.

It wasn't until Boss Joe took Seven to the stagecoach that we trudged outside. The sky was a faint, streaky blue, cut by thin clouds. A pink light, tinged with yellow, slipped through the dark trees. Smoke rose from several chimneys in town; it was the start of another day, business as usual. The lines of buildings were sharp in the clean morning air. In the west, layers of grey clouds massed over distant hills and hinted at rain.

The cool air reminded me how far I was from south China. I gripped the stick that had been with me ever since my coming to town. The mountains loomed higher and closer now that a gaping hole shrank the town. Fallen timbers, charred and whitened, lay helter-skelter in the ruins and on the road. Shabby rags of smoke rose from the blackened site. A sooty iron stove sat lopsided among the ruins. When two horses that had galloped off last night found their own way back, sniffing at the ground, the men shouted out lucky wishes.

"*A good horse never lowers its head.*"

"*One spear and one steed, that's all you need.*"

"*Dragons and horses bring brisk forces.*"

The men bound for Yale tied bundles to their backs and reached for walking sticks. To keep pace with these men, I would need to carry the boy.

Boss Joe walked with me. "You didn't say much this morning," he said.

I gave him Grandfather's favourite saying: "*To cross the river, raise your pants; to open your mouth, get the facts.*"

He chuckled and asked my destination. On hearing it was Yale, he asked, "Not Cache Creek?"

I shrugged. No need to talk to this demon with a rat's head.

"Take the boy to Hong Kong," he said. "Lots of mix-blood people there."

His advice was useless, so I asked politely about Mary's husband, Louis.

"That's Louis at Lopez Creek," exclaimed Boss Joe. "He and his first wife had three little ones, I think. Then he and Mary had more children."

He left abruptly to greet the churchman. They shook hands, as if no disaster had occurred last night, and spoke quietly. The stagecoach driver waved the passengers aboard, frowning when two escorts shoved in Seven, hands tied at his back. The firebrand was sullen and resigned, but he lunged, cursing and spitting, at Boss Joe. The merchant recovered right away to chat and laugh with the driver as fares were paid. The churchman left after saying goodbye to the one redbeard passenger.

Then Boss Joe beckoned to me.

"Get aboard." He spoke loud enough for all to hear. "You do a good deed. Be kind, receive kindness. *One hero knows another.* How can I let this pig demon ride to Yale while you and the boy walk? I paid your fares."

In an instant, I was kneeling and kowtowing. If he toasted me once, then I toasted him ten times. I would be in Yale by sundown and in Victoria tomorrow.

Then I felt the men laughing at me and jumped up to ask about Mary's creek.

"Wasteland," said Boss Joe. "Too hot and dry in the summer. In the winter, herds of cattle freeze to death. What a stink the carcasses leave in the springtime."

"The Natives fare well?"

"Are you stupid? They get bits of land while a redbeard rancher takes a tract that stretches to the horizon. Their men go tend the redbeard's cattle."

The driver whistled a warning. Boss Joe told his workers to meet him the next day in Yale, where he planned to talk to the Council.

The coach reeked of cigars, hair oil, shoe polish, and horse dung while the windows let in swirls of dust. I tried to grip the seat but its cushions had flattened long ago. Among the nine of us were two escorts, a store clerk, another rail hand, a ranch cook, and the redbeard. First to have boarded, now he sat tight in the corner, keen to get off.

"Anyone recall this one?" Seven shouted over the din of wheels and hooves. "Was he in the parade?"

"Those men had messy beards," said the lead escort. "This one is high class."

"Why not scare him a bit?"

"You learned nothing?" The escort rammed an elbow so hard into Seven that he grunted and doubled over. "We don't want trouble."

I turned away. *Don't kill the hen that lays eggs.* One wheel rumbled through a crater and the stagecoach lurched. Seven crashed into his escorts and then fell to his knees. He managed to right himself but stayed on the floor. The escorts kicked him.

"Why not untie him?" I asked.

"He burns buildings," said the escort. "You should thank Boss Joe for doing this."

"He guards his own prospects," said Seven.

"His store burned. Didn't you see?"

"He'll buy the other shops. He wants to do business, that's what he wants."

After a while, the ranch cook passed around dry cakes and cold tea. I declined but the brat ate happily. When the clerk passed around crunchy apples, they talked about the fire.

"I fetched the churchman. He came running but did nothing."

"We moved the safe. The boss dropped the keys and lost them, so three of us pushed and dragged the iron box outside."

"Those boxes can't burn," someone said. "You could have left it there."

"No, fires can roast everything in an iron safe into black ash. Papers don't even need to burn."

As mountains slid across the horizon, I mulled my choice from last night. A few mix-blood children, boys usually, were taken to China from here. No news of them ever drifted back to Gold Mountain, as if they dropped down a deep well the moment they set foot in the frenzied pushing and shoving of China. Had they attended school or guarded flocks of noisy geese? Were they speaking Chinese and using chopsticks? Were they happy? Or had angry kinsmen pressed heavy quilts over the children's faces and smothered them in the dark? Had family members awoken to a death dismissed with: "He never got used to our water and soil"?

Grandmother had no views on the local Chinese who gave up their friends to follow the redbeard Jesus men, translating their speeches and singing hymns in the streets. Grandfather clung to the idea of respect: he lashed out at the rowdies who hurled insults and soft fruit at the Jesus men.

"Live to a hundred, learning doesn't halt," he said.

One day Grandmother bought British cotton at one-third the price of Chinese cloth. Grandfather flew into a rage and denounced her until she agreed to exchange it for local material, even though by this time she had lost her bargaining advantage. She vowed that Grandfather wouldn't get new trousers that year.

In town, Grandfather and his cronies mocked the teenage son that the rice merchant had brought home from the north. The lad spoke with a slight accent but the men insisted they couldn't understand him. They hooted and dubbed him with rude names. Yet when the brothel keeper imported a northern woman who hardly grasped our local dialect, Grandfather and his friends rushed to see and praise her.

The village wags would sneer at how I had aped Ba's brazen ways and spawned offspring abroad without any family blessing. "Like father, like son," they would crow, "all badly taught, not a speck of respect for traditions."

If matters worsened in the village, then I would take Peter to Hong Kong and work there. I had pulled heavy loads alongside mix-bloods on those docks. Chinese women who slept with redbeard men had been raising such children since the days of the first Opium War. Those with well-to-do patrons got stipends and sent their children to English schools. Those with shabby connections to sailors or common workers, or no ties at all to the fathers, reared the children in their own families and sent them to work. Hong Kong was a free port. If you made decent money, then you were a decent man.

Taking Peter home would be easier if I had my bankroll. That would let him become part of my golden success, where I not only earned money but created sons wherever I went. Sons born abroad foretold of sons to be born at home. A first-born male led the way, opened the path for long lines of boy children to follow. I prayed for the gods' help: if I climbed onto this tiger's back, then it would be very hard to get off. Sam and China men like Lam wanted me to take the boy to China. Their talk was cheap; the heavy work fell to me, to win goodwill for the boy after my colossal failure overseas.

The redbeard nodded off to sleep and threw off anguished snores. I looked across the river and saw the fallen mountain already draped over the railway. Screw, we had already passed Sophie's camp. Now I couldn't ask Lam for money. I had wanted to point out the camp so that Peter could see that his father too knew a thing or two about this landscape and could track down people when needed. With Sam gone, I grew taller. Peter poked his head out the window, waiting for curves in the road ahead that would show the six horses thundering by. I looked too but the dust scratched my throat and made me cough.

Seven nudged me with his foot. "You lump of shit, you should have spoken earlier," he muttered. "We could have made things right."

"I need to watch the boy."

"What China do you go to? If we don't fight the redbeards, then we should cut off our pigtails and stop calling ourselves China men."

"You should have acted on your own."

"Shouldn't men fight for their honour?"

"They want to go home. Don't you?"

"They do nothing but talk."

It was time to teach Peter some Chinese: surely that would win him toothy grins of approval in China. I chanted from *Three Word Classic*, rocking from side to side in time with the rhythm.

People at birth, pure and kind.

Alike in nature, not in mind.

If not taught, one's nature falls.

Get a master, learn to focus.

"He can't learn that!" The men slapped their thighs, laughing. "He doesn't understand."

"That's classical Chinese!" cried Seven. "No one speaks it!"

"His mother taught him Chinese," I insisted. "He speaks Chinese. I heard him!"

But no matter how I pressed the boy, he refused to call me Baba and left me looking like a fool and a liar.

14

PROMISES OUGHT NOT TO BE DODGED (1885)

A loud thud caused the coach to lurch and tilt. Curses rang out as those facing the front crashed into a corner while those across the way slid at them on the floor. The horses galloped on, but the carriage had hit the ground and was scraping and bouncing along, causing them to whinny in fear. The car was slanted so steeply that no one could stand, no matter how we tried. I hugged Peter's head and screamed for the driver to stop before the horses swung around a tight corner and flung us to the rocks below.

The horses thundered on. We heard the driver shouting and then the squeal of the brakes against the wheel rims.

Should have gone north to Mary, I scolded myself. I should have asked His Holiness which way to go.

The animals trotted to a stop that let us tumble out. One big rear wheel was gone, leaving the coach lopsided. The driver hurried to unharness the horses and lead them to the side of the road, which was little more than a narrow ledge chiseled out of the cliff. We stood at its edge, shaking our heads, watching the rapids below crash over rocks. That heaving river was still threatening me, Water to batter the sturdy Earth until it crumbled. Getting off the mainland wasn't going to be easy. The passengers jabbered away as if only loud voices could keep them alive.

"Thank Heaven, thank Earth."

"*Survive a disaster, good luck comes faster.*"

"His Holiness is robust, his power stretches far. Wait until Boss Joe hears."

"I'm the saviour!" Seven raised his hands once they were freed. "My virtue saved us. If not for me, you'd all be dead."

"You're a stinking piece of dog shit," I said.

"If not for you," added the escort, "we'd be safe in Lytton."

The boy clung to me and whimpered. I squeezed him to see if he winced, checking for broken parts. As I stood up, he grabbed my shirt and spewed vomit onto it. I backed off but he hung on, head bent. The slush contained cookies, apples, and rice porridge.

"On the ground!" I slapped his face away.

"He's sick," Seven said. "You want blood?"

The escorts were laughing. "He vomits the words you were stuffing into him," said one. "They don't suit his appetite."

"I say Hok won't take his boy home," the other said. "He fears the wife!"

The boy wailed and stamped his feet, his face a smear of tears, vomit, and saliva.

"Can't you stop the crying?" demanded one escort. "He weep-ruins us."

I slapped him again.

Seven pulled the boy away. "*Oxen don't step on ants.*"

"*No spanking, no growing.*" I was brushing slop from my shirt.

The brat kept his clothes clean but left me stinking for the rest of the ride.

"For sure he'll die in China," said Seven.

"What, do dogs chase mice?" He should tend his own affairs. "I can protect him."

"You couldn't even pretend to be a scary ghost."

The redbeard passenger went looking for the wheel but returned empty-handed. Boss Joo's man spoke to the driver and reported to us, "The roadhouse at the bridge is a few miles away. We'll walk there, stay the night, and wait for tomorrow's coach. The driver needs a man to lead each horse."

First we lifted the broken corner and half-carried, half-pushed the coach to the side of the road. Holes and cracks had punctured every surface of the carriage even before this accident. The unhitched horses refused to stand still, eyes bulging and muzzles swinging side to side. As we tried to calm them, the brat came running to help. I wanted to swat him away until he showed me some respect. The driver heaved a padlocked strongbox onto his shoulder and led the way. I recalled the convoys my bandit gang in China had attacked. Good horses always fetched fine prices.

Seven and his horse came behind the boy and me. He called out to our fellow passengers, "This fool takes a mix-blood boy to China. Wouldn't you say he's crazy? Wouldn't you say he lacks family teaching?"

To my surprise, the conversation ran away from Seven.

"Families at home are always adopting boys," the ranch cook pointed out. "What difference is there? A boy is a boy."

"Screw you, the difference is as big as Mount Tai," Seven insisted.

"No man adopts until it's his last choice. If his wife cannot bear him a son, he can take a second wife, even a third."

"What if those wives are barren too?" retorted the cook. "For the rest of their lives, they will still get fed by their husband. *Wah*, wouldn't they revel in luxury with no children to raise!"

Seven pressed his case. "The man could marry his daughter to some beggar who will take his wife's surname."

The other rail hand said, "But the beggar can run off at any time and take the children. He's still the trueborn father."

"Best thing is for the man to take his brother's son as his own," said the cook.

"What if he has no brother?"

"Go to his grandfather's family."

"But remember, as long as the boy has trueborn family around, the new father's claim can fail."

"Buying a stranger's son is best. You pay the cash and sever all ties to the birth family."

I knew all these schemes. My pig brain never thought they had anything to do with Peter. He was my firstborn son, just as I was to my father. But Grandfather had picked my father's wife, while nobody had chosen mine. I had a son but no mother for him. Stupidly, I had done things backward.

※

The two-storey roadhouse sat in the midst of a thick clutter of tree stumps. The ground at the front door had been worn into a rounded pit of hard earth, a sign of steady customers. A China man wearing an apron hurried out and introduced himself as the kitchen helper Fung. He was a small man, the size of Fist, so he was quite brave to be working here alone among the redbeards. When Boss Joe's men described last night's fire, right away he asked about His Holiness. When he heard about the loss of our wheel, he shook his head and remarked, "First comes a leaky roof, then heavy rains at night."

In a low voice, he added, "Avoid the roadhouse. It's full of red-beard rail hands. They look for work but get drunk and fight among themselves."

"There are jobs?" I asked, surprised.

"A few. Ranchers need grazing cattle brought in. Farmers need crops harvested." He advised us to go stay with the Native people. "You have money, no? The village is not far. They will cook rice and feed you. It's not cold; you can sleep outside. No need for trouble just when you head home to China."

He was a bit too timid, too helpful for my liking. I wouldn't mind seeing a no-holds-barred battle between China men and redbeards.

We passed a mining site like many others that Sam and I had skirted along the river, a huge stretch of overturned land with pits deep enough to bury scores of corpses. Puddles of water reflected the sky. Clean and dirty sides of boulders showed they had been flipped over. Trees and bushes had fallen, exposing their roots. Except for the neat walls of rocks stacked by the ditch where they had been washed, it was an untidy mess, as if giant hands had seized the surface of the land and shaken it like a dirty rug. Many sites had been abandoned to weeds and ruin, but this one was still being worked.

"My people could grow crops here," Sam had grumbled to me,

"but your people washed away the topsoil and left the rocks."

"Redbeards did it too," I had reminded him. "If you're constipated, don't blame the hard ground."

One China man broke the ground with a pickaxe, thrusting his back and arms into every swing of the sharpened tip. A second fellow used a shoulder pole to carry pails of debris over the rough ground to dump into the sluice. A low wooden trough brought water from a distant stream to flush away the dirt and leave the gold. A third man chopped at a tree to expand the claim into the forest, where a ragged tent was pitched cockeyed under the trees. You could barely see the three miners, so well did their grimy presence blend into the woods.

"Have time to stroll?" The digger's scornful tone labelled us as idlers who ought to be working instead.

"Redbeards evicted us from Lytton," replied the escort, "so we go home."

The miners frowned to hear about the fire, but only Spade Head spoke.

"Railway workers make trouble for everyone. The sooner you go home, the safer we will be."

The men protested that they were not all rail hands, and Seven retorted, "Screw you. You miners make plenty of your own trouble. Whose land is this?"

"We paid money for this," exclaimed Spade Head. "Redbeards were mining here when we saw a ditch in good shape. We have papers."

"Were they real?" Seven snorted. "You can read English?"

This stir-shit-stick picked fights with everyone, no matter what they stood for.

"These men are working hard," I said. "Leave them alone. They don't bother you."

"They bother the peace and the Native people."

I asked the miners, "How far will you dig?"

"As far as it takes to find gold."

"Water is low." Seven pointed to the flume. "Redbeards sold you piss and shit."

"Come spring, it will rise."

"Did you find much?" I asked.

"Nothing."

Every miner I had ever met answered that question the same way as if one holy sutra could protect everyone.

"Go home," Seven said. "There's no gold left here."

"Go bother the redbeards," Spade Head replied. "You take the road while we cross the bridge."

He cursed us and turned away. We walked on.

"In Lytton you wanted to go beat the redbeards," I said to Seven, "but here you have three mouths and two tongues. If China men don't help China men, then who will?"

"Heaven, if they are good men."

❈

At the Native village, we were sent into the forest to cut pine boughs for bedding. Our beds were on the ground, under lean-tos made of woven mats. Giggling children called out to Peter, and they raced into one of the great round houses built into the ground. Each structure had a wooden ladder emerging from the cone-shaped roof. The village looked clean, and its people were well fed. They tended dusty fields of potatoes. I wished Mary lived in these forests rather than the desert lands of Lytton. Big meaty animals fed among the trees and could be hunted for food. After we came back, we started a fire in a pit of rocks. An elderly woman brought over tea leaves. We sniffed and found them to be a superior grade to what was served in teahouses. To have China men accepting tea from a Native woman was to be eating shit and excreting rice: the ways of the world were reversed.

Then the brat ran by, with Sam chasing him. What was that? I shook my head, thinking that my eyes had gone flowery from lack of sleep. Sam was with his woman and his child, back in Lytton. But the mix-blood guide scooped up Peter and hurried over.

"Yang Hok, we sail to China together!" He gave me a wide smile, and his voice was real.

"What are you doing here?" I felt my bones shrink. Bad luck was snaking up my shit-hole. The last thing I wanted now was to go to China with him and the boy. I may as well bring an entire village of eager Natives. "Was your child born?"

"A girl. The mother insists I am not the father." He did not mind my fellow travellers hearing all his shame. "You won't go to Mary?"

"Didn't you see the fire?" I poured him some tea.

"I was ahead of you! The mother's people didn't want me there. They wouldn't even let me see the baby. I left yesterday, boarded *Skuzzy*, and reached Boston Bar last night. I didn't hear about the fire until I saw Fung at the roadhouse. He mentioned a China man with a mix-blood boy from Lytton, so I came to see if it was you. It's the right thing, changing your mind."

"I need money to buy his passage." I waved at the brat. "You have money for your own ticket?" Surely this would thwart his plans for China.

"Those two boys sold my bootleg." He laced his fingers around the mug and sipped the tea. "And I gambled last night. In China I can help you watch the boy. I can translate for your boy, make his life easier. He won't be so scared."

"Did you stop in Boston Bar and get my money back?" I reminded him that he too had once been too weak to piss.

"I caught a ride on a wagon. I planned to wait for you in Yale."

"People in China will tell you to limp off with your rotted corpse," I said.

"I promised my father I'd go home."

"Kinsmen will smother you and bury you and no one will look for you. The countryside has its own laws."

"My father's ghost and mine would haunt them."

"Village people don't trust strangers." I spat out some tea leaves.

"You wanted to see me recite the family tree to my relatives."

"People in China kill each other over land. They slaughter entire families. No one has enough. That's why we work abroad, to buy more land at home."

"A fellow with a wagon is waiting for me." He handed me the empty tea mug. "You can come with me now."

"I go to see Fist." My mouth saved me before I could think. In truth, the fire had devoured One Leg and his troubles and cast them out of my mind.

Sam's eyes narrowed and his voice was accusing. "You weren't planning that."

I looked away. "In jail, I asked Heaven to help me escape. I promised to help Fist, so I went to the temple."

"You change your mind all the time. Ever stand on both feet?"

"It's the truth."

Sam stalked off, shaking his head. The boy ran after him, calling his name. Sam spun him around, spoke a few words, and sent him stumbling back to me. By the time he arrived, he was wailing again, and the men blamed me for getting weep-ruined.

How dare that Sam presume that I would go with him to China? Yesterday's fire in Lytton had changed everything. How could that stupid cockhead not see that? I had to look after my son now, the same way he was caring for himself, pushing his way into China.

Seven spoke up. "If you don't want that mix-blood man in China, then why take your boy there?"

Luckily for me, the rail hand threw out a handful of dice and started a game for all the men. I said the boy needed to nap and took him away with my cup of tea.

❊

When we returned to the roadhouse next day, the stagecoach had arrived and the horses were being replaced with a new team. The boy ran toward them. Fung stood chatting with Boss Joe, who held a large bundle in his arms. A thick knot showed several layers of stiff new cloth rolled together. Sharp corners poked out to indicate a box.

"Is that His Holiness?" Seven demanded.

Boss Joe nodded.

"You got nothing from Red Tie," Seven went on, frowning and shaking his head, "and now you leave Lytton for good."

"*A homesick heart is a speeding arrow.*"

"You should have let me stay there," snapped Seven.

The lead escort stepped up and greeted his employer.

"Couldn't sleep last night and kept thinking about the temple," said Boss Joe. "Good thing I didn't let you take His Holiness yesterday. What if you dropped the statue?"

"If His Holiness was on the stagecoach, we would have reached Yale yesterday. The wheel wouldn't have gotten loose."

When I told Boss Joe about my plans to go see Fist, he cried out, "Don't waste time with those fool pigs. They will never leave. What His Holiness said won't make any difference to One Leg."

"I cannot not go."

"Then you should have told me earlier, in Lytton," he snapped. "Don't play me for a fool. I would have paid your way just to this bridge. We get no refunds here."

"Hey, Boss." The other escort had spoken to Fung. "So you revenged yourself against Red Tie."

"Where's that fool Seven?" Boss Joe looked around. "He should hear this."

They dragged him over and the story started. "Yesterday I went nosing around my store, looking for melted gold dust. I heard a squealing, very faint, like the mewing of kittens. I stood still and listened. It came from a corner of the floor that had escaped the fire, where water from the overturned barrels had seeped in. Under the boards was a nest of baby mice, just big enough to start running on their own. I scooped them into a bag. Then I went to Red Tie's store and asked for him. When his clerk went to fetch him, I opened the bag and released the mice, ten or so of them. They scampered under the counter. When Red Tie came, I gave him the keys to my safe, which was sitting on the street, and said, 'It's yours.'"

I pictured Red Tie's store stretching long and narrow so the light from the front windows weakened at the back. The mice vanished, wriggling, into narrow cracks in the wall, their tails whipping behind them. A clerk's eyes widened. He chased them, his long apron flapping, with a broom. A woman flung a brown-paper packet of raisins onto the counter. When an oil lamp was lit, it showed black pellets of mouse shit nestled amidst the dried fruit. The woman and her friends marched from the store in a huff. My stomach was suddenly warm with fresh-cooked rice.

"So, only you can take revenge, is that it?" asked Seven. "You're the big hero?"

Boss Joe arched an eyebrow. "My deed harmed no China man."

"You play with mice, you hide like mice. That's no great deed. No redbeard will hear about it."

"You want your hands tied and your mouth gagged?"

"May I bring His Holiness a question?" asked Fung.

"Here?" The lead escort frowned. "Don't be stupid."

"Why not?" Boss Joe clapped Fung on the back. "His Holiness serves his followers wherever they are."

"We have no incense or wine," protested the escort.

"I have everything," said Fung, offering a cloth bundle.

"This place is too exposed, too dark."

"Fung came twice to the temple this year," said Boss Joe. "He has urgent matters."

"It's nothing." Fung reddened at the sudden attention on him. "I keep thinking to go home. I asked His Holiness if the time was right, but both times he told me no. If His Holiness is leaving Gold Mountain, then this is my last time to seek his advice."

The escort untied the knot and opened the crate. The box was lined with more red cloth. He knelt, bowed his head, and whispered a short prayer before lifting the statue out and placing it on a flat tree stump. The escort was right: His Holiness was dwarfed by the trees and the clearing around him. The temple in Lytton had been a tight space where it was possible for His Holiness to assert his powers in a room of familiar trappings. Fung fetched the worship items, lit the candles and incense, and poured wine. Then he knelt and brought his forehead to the ground. Boss Joe handed him the charms, which he cast onto the ground. Everyone crowded in to see. The answer was no. He cast them again, and received the same answer.

Fung sighed. "Still not the right time."

I shook my head at this cockhead. If he wanted to go home, then why not just leave? That lucky bastard had none of my stupid problems. Why seek advice from His Holiness? Could there ever be a wrong time to head for home? Didn't home and family trump all other considerations, even money? What did he fear?

※

From the road-house, the boy and I walked to the bridge. The canyon narrowed here, which had allowed a crossing to be built long ago. The tightened river gave advantage to fishermen, and they crowded the banks with spears and nets. The boy poked his head through the railing and called. The men and women below waved and shouted back.

The boy gave a whoop of joy on seeing the railway, as if the shiny beams were his old toys. At first he tried to walk along one track, his arms spread wide to balance himself, but then he darted ahead. When I hurried after him, the boy thought we were playing chase and ran faster, laughing and screaming. I ran too but let him stay ahead until we both ran out of breath.

A chase from long ago came to mind. A feast of the food left from the annual rites had just ended. My pals and I had just caused our arch-enemy, the spoiled grandson from the richest family among us, to slip into the muddy bank of the river. A sampan bearing coloured banners had drawn us to the water.

Then the grandson's furious minder chased us, waving a bamboo switch. We sprinted by the vegetable plots on the sunny side of the village. We raced through the stone laneways between the black brick houses. We split up to force the minder to choose one quarry.

The minder bore down on me, a set look on his dark face. I stopped. The men of the village squatted in front of the ancestral hall, fanning themselves and smoking tobacco.

The men looked up. Children running always meant trouble. My father summoned me just as the minder ran up and complained about the muddy insult. My name in his voice made me shudder. To my surprise, my father put on a startled look and said, "Such a small matter? You can beat the boy and make him cry, but if that summons bad luck on such a day, don't say I didn't warn you."

The minder backed off.

Every time that memory arose, I wondered if Father had really spoken up for me. Or had he given me a severe spanking later that night? I would ask Grandfather.

꽃

The river and the railway were steadfast guides; there was only one trail to follow, where man had clawed and smashed his way through nature. I strode along as confidently as Sam, hoping the boy would think that I knew this land equally well. Some mountain ridges held bold distinct shapes: a saddle, the fan tail of a fish, an even bowl-shaped dip. No doubt the Native people told stories about each site. At home, all landmarks and their stories were known to me. I planned to climb White Wolf Hill with Peter, taking the short route up and the longer one down. I would point out the curves of West River, the two rocky outcrops that formed Await-the-Husband peak, and the busy port of Sun Chong.

I peered into the forests, wondering if we were anywhere close to that camp where I'd been four years ago, where Poy and Onion had died. It would be honourable if I could find those two graves. I had come all this way and paid respects to strangers instead of my own comrades. Could those grave-sticks that I had carved back then still be standing? Could they still be read? Unfortunately I had no name for the camp, and could not recall where along the river it had stood. Everywhere the rocks and river and trees looked alike to me. To find the camp would be hard; it would be far harder to find the graves. I should have drawn a map. But even then, I had known Poy's bones would never go to China. He had no family.

The brat and I came up behind an elderly couple, bent over, with cloth bundles tied to their backs. The boy called out, and they replied in cracked but cheerful voices. The boy dawdled and chatted with them.

I walked ahead and resisted the urge to shout for the boy. I watched the road to avoid the dung of wild animals. There was little time for him to spend with his own people. Maybe this couple, both with kerchiefs tied around their heads, would leave a strong impression on the boy. He should see that when Chinese and Native faces grew loose and wrinkled with age, they looked very much alike, with fleshy puddles under the eyes, yellowed teeth, and speckled skin. Maybe China would not feel so strange. Maybe he would feel no difference between these people who all despised the redbeard.

When that washman Yang and that miner Lam hinted that they might stay here instead of going home, I thought they were farting brave words and blowing hot air to impress me. To not go home was like chopping off one's own foot to hobble about as One Leg did, all bitter and twisted. At home I would stroll through the paddy, letting my feet sink slowly, deep into the mud with each step. When I lifted my foot, water would rush in to fill the hole, water that had travelled great distances from the lofty mountains of central China. The well of my footprint, China's turgid rivers, the squishy soil underneath: these were my natural world, my only home. Best to follow Grandfather, watching his skinny brown legs, scarred and studded with red insect bites, do the same. Later, there would be fresh rice cooking in the kitchen, rattling the lid, sending up sweet steam. On such a rare occasion, Grandmother would sit and hold my hand, wrapping my fingers over hers, but only briefly because she did not want me to see how the soil and water of the paddy had hardened her flesh.

When at last I went to fetch the boy, the couple looked up in surprise. The woman pulled a bulging kerchief from her pocket. She pointed to my hands, and poured dried berries into them. Then she motioned for us to move ahead.

Building the railway had flattened all the tangled, mature bushes, so berries were hard to find by the tracks. That summer and fall when we were together, Mary often went berry-picking, sometimes with her boss's children. One Sunday, she and I took a pail up into the mountains. We climbed through forest groves, and I chased Mary from tree to tree. A log with a flattened side let us cross a brook. We saw hills of ancient timber, thick with ridged trunks and green with moss. Her white apron became stained with many colours.

When the forest darkened under a leafy roof, the narrow trails vanished from my sight. When heavy rains started, I turned back. But Mary was intent on going higher, to a secret trove of berries. She wouldn't listen to me so we stomped ahead. When I turned, she was gone. Suddenly, every gap between trees seemed to be my last path. I shouted her name. Birds flew up. I thought that any downward slope would lead home until one led me to the edge of a cliff. I tried to retrace my steps. I found the vantage point where we had stopped earlier, but it was impossible to see through the rain.

I turned, and there she stood with face and hair streaming wet. She grabbed my hand and ran. We struggled uphill. I fought her until we reached a cave. Prior occupants, whether animal or human, had left behind rank smells, and I feared the darkness inside. We were cold but safe from the rain. I doffed my jacket and wrung out my handkerchief to mop our faces. We sat on a rock near the entrance, leaning against one another, and watched the dark clouds go by. I felt safe, even though I had no idea where I was or how to get home.

15

A SUPERIOR MAN MERITS A SECOND CHANCE (1885)

The boy ran to the trough with the centipede legs and trotted along-side with a stick, tapping it like a drum. I followed him to the soggy pit where water dripped from the break. I shoved the trough with both my hands, and then gave it another push, this time with my heels dug into the ground. It didn't topple. The legs were braced by a cross beam, buried under the soil. It would take more than one man to push this over.

At the big graveyard ahead, someone was bent over the ground. Perhaps a rail hand on his way home was paying respects to a com-rade. How noble. Sam had bypassed many graveyards due to our bad luck on this trip. The Chinese Council in Yale should demand a refund from him. Maybe then he would stop hounding me to take him to China. He got paid for a job he didn't finish. Our deceased didn't get their incense and whisky. As for those fools who had stolen our packs, I hoped they had found good use for the spirit money, maybe for each other.

Inside the fence, the man glanced up. To my surprise, it was Fist, but he had shaved and dressed neatly, with a re-braided pigtail and clean shirt, as if ready for a clerk's job in town. On seeing his scarred and scowling face, I almost remarked that when a beggar donned the king's dragon robe, he didn't become a prince in the next instant. But I needed Fist to invite me to eat and sleep here.

The graveyard looked different but familiar, like someone's face seen after several years' absence. It puzzled me, because little could change in such a place and this was no season for new flowers. Besides, who—

The rows of grave-sticks were gone.

I looked again. The bones had lost their names.

The site was flattened, as if a dark cyclone had churned through. The fence stood intact but the grass had been crushed and flattened. One corner post was charred; someone had tried to burn it. My first thought was: *run far and fly high*. It was bad luck to have come back here.

"Seen enough?" Fist scowled. "Now get out."

I must have looked bewildered.

He took his time before speaking. "Morning after you left, we found everything yanked out. Maybe it was one shit-hole fiend, maybe it was a gang of them. They could have burned the markers but they didn't. They tossed them aside like chewed-through bones, to laugh at us."

He kicked a rusty pail; it rolled ahead. I recalled Sam attacking the kettle from Boss Soon's gang outside Big Tunnel. That was the day I lost my money roll.

Peter ran at the pail, nudging it along, glancing behind with a hopeful look, wanting Fist to chase him.

"You came back," he said. "What for?"

"Can't the markers be replanted?" What a stupid question. If repairs were possible, then they would have been done already. One Leg was a capable fellow who had taken splendid care of this place.

Fist glared. "You tell me, which name goes where?"

"Not even a few spots? Didn't you tend even one person?"

"I can't read."

I squatted. Surnames and home districts rushed at me, a swarm of raging bees. In China, even the most hardened and bitter of criminals would not wreck a graveyard. Bandit leader Cudgel refused to attack processions taking food to hilltop graves. All people had parents and ancestors, all people needed their blessings and protection. Here, friends and kin of the dead workers had written names on markers, doing their duty as best they could. But now, these nameless bones could receive neither respect nor assurances from kinsmen or co-workers. Now the men's final remnants couldn't be sent to families waiting to mourn them. These were corpses without faces, bones without homes, all adrift without past or purpose.

A crow cawed and flapped high into the air over the trees. I shuddered. Lost souls were watching from the brooding forest. If not for the daylight, they would leap shrieking from the shadowy woods and hurl themselves at this site, clawing to cross over for revenge.

A brisk wind moved grey clouds over the canyon. Rain and nightfall were coming. The loss of the grave-sticks upset the murky balance between living and dead. Saintly priests with clean bald skulls and yellow robes were needed here to chant and restore order. The outraged spirits must be freed to hunt down the guilty redbeards, coil themselves around their necks, and squeeze until those human tongues hung out black and stiff.

"Will you and One Leg leave now?" I couldn't run off too quickly; that would reveal a coward.

"Revenge first."

"You?" I never expected to hear that from this worm. "You're one man! You don't even know who did this."

"The redbeards raged about China men working at the landslide. It was the night before the Lytton fire. Boss Soon came by yesterday. He'll help."

"Was it the Native people?"

"We lived here a year and never had trouble."

"The China men in Lytton argued about revenge there, did you hear?" I mentioned the scuffle between Seven and Boss Joe, as well as the baby mice.

"Stupid fools. We can do better."

I squatted, head between my knees, fingers at the back of my neck. The stubble there had grown long and smooth to the touch, but my pigtail was hard and firm. It was time to wash myself and get a shave in Victoria, before setting off for home. I needed a hot bath, to scrub off all this filth and anger from the other world. Crushed weeds, pebbles, and dirt lay under my battered boots. Nothing decent could grow here.

The boy jumped on my back, wanting to play, wanting to be carried. I growled and shrugged him off. He clambered onto the fence to ride it like a horse, his reins some old rope left there.

I hurried to reproach him; too much dignity had been ripped from this place already. He leaned back and pulled at his pretend reins. Then I saw myself on a horse too, galloping over a hardened path, leading a war party and raising a cloud of dust.

Had Heaven slid me into play here, like a chess piece?

If Fist and I took revenge, then I would become a hero to railway coolies and to all of China. People would praise my name to the skies, petition the mandarins in charge of rites to add me to the ranks of gods, and start to dedicate stately temples to my name. I could go home with head upright, bearing the most valiant of tales to tell. Gentry and high officials would bow to me, sweep their sleeves to the ground. Court artists would bid to paint my likeness, and reveal me to royal princesses. The stinking low-lifes in my village would soon forget about my father. That bastard might even hurry home to bask in my glory.

Fist kicked the pail around tree stumps and bushes, letting it rattle over the broken ground. He asked about His Holiness in Lytton.

I gave him honest answers and saw him relax. "Will One Leg leave?"

"He will obey His Holiness."

"And revenge?"

"Boss Soon said to tell no one. First, we plan what to do."

"I can help."

"You hate railway coolies."

"Not so."

"You called us 'big fools.'" He snorted. "Now you want to stay the night."

I swallowed hard. "Only if it's no bother." It was the only way to learn his plans.

He walked away but then turned back. "Don't have anything to do?" He pointed at the grave-sticks. "Sort these by names and home districts. One Leg wants to write down everything. We should have drawn a map earlier. The old bugger thinks he's smart, but he's not."

I squatted. The markers were two times longer and wider than a schoolboy's ruler. Damp earth and strands of yellow roots clung to the bottom ends of the sticks. One Leg's brushwork was graceful, even for the complicated words with many strokes. He must have followed a talented teacher long ago, or practised a great deal on his own. Names from the Lee, Wong, Ma, and Chan clans were most numerous. No doubt they possessed cosy ties to the agents who raced through the Four Counties, trawling for fools. Those peasants and their families had laughed and rejoiced at landing plum jobs on the railway. Now they were gutted and lost.

Many of the small surnames—Soo, Fong, Woo, and Kwan—were on hand too, just one stick in each pile. Those men must have been lonely as broomsticks, left outside the noisy circles of larger clans unless they could claim ties through marriage or myths of alliance. I spotted a Yang name and let out a breath of relief. That gave me a solid reason to join any mission for revenge. The fellow's home district was far from the Four Counties. I muttered his name and village, but it was a fool's dream to think that I would ever meet his kinsmen in China. Still, I could readily toss his name at Fist and Boss Soon.

Peter yelled and jumped off the fence, but the sorting wasn't finished. I darted back and forth between hard-to-reach piles instead of tossing each marker like a stick of kindling. I murmured each man's name and home village, as if it might somehow soothe him. This was the last show of earthly concern these men would receive. If I gained their favour, then they might help me enlist in Fist's mission.

He came by when I stood and brushed dirt from my hands.

"Done." I pointed to the biggest pile. "You Chans are most numerous."

"Go scrub off the killing airs."

From around the cabins came chopping sounds, dull thuds broken by pauses for loosening the axe head from the wood. Fist still wasn't helping with chores. One Leg swung the long-handled axe as his crutches leaned against a high-back chair. After each blow, he reached out to steady himself. No Brain freed the axe head and re-centered the block of wood on the stump. One Leg looked haggard. Beard stubble covered his face and dark shadows ringed his eyes. Too bad he couldn't help with the revenge.

Fist brought me soap and a pail of water.

One Leg saw me. "Hok, you stinking bastard, you dare show your face? After calling us 'big fools'?"

"I was in a hurry. I was angry when you saw me with Sam."

He lifted the axe, let his body drop back, and swung. The blade bit the wood and No Brain went forward.

"Visit the temple?" One Leg asked.

"His Holiness tells you to go home."

"Just in time too," Fist chimed in. "That night, redbeards burned the temple. We need to leave now. Even Boss Joe is heading back to China."

"Hens and chicks are squawking and fleeing the wolves."

His next swing landed precisely and cut deeper.

Fist reached out to stop No Brain. "No need for more firewood."

No Brain shrugged him off, but One Leg said, "Gather your things. We go home."

No Brain's face crumpled, like Peter's when he was about to unleash a fit of wailing.

Fist pulled him away and the boy followed. I stayed to help One Leg. His axe had bit so deeply that I had to thrust my foot against the chunk to free it.

"Feeling clever?" He hopped around to grab his crutches. "His Holiness agreed with you."

"Will you leave?"

"Never thought redbeards were so low bred." He swung over the crutches, heading to the cabin. "Thirty years ago, foreign gunboats attacked the forts along Pearl River. They landed and we fought them for four days. Five hundred of our soldiers died. The redbeards let us remove the bodies. We dug graves that were never disturbed, even though the redbeards flattened the forts with black powder. Those walls were seven feet thick."

"You were lucky to live." I made sure he saw me toting his chair and axe.

"And carry shame on my back for a hundred lifetimes?"

"I sorted the grave-sticks for Fist. Shall I do the writing too?"

"What do you want?" His eyes narrowed. "You weren't coming back here."

"Fear of His Holiness." I mentioned how the god had prevented deaths in Lytton.

"Screw you. You don't fear him." He took the axe and ran a whetstone along it.

"Why is Fist all cleaned up? I didn't recognize him. Did you shave him?"

"He wants revenge."

"What's his plan?"

"Ah, you want to join him. Don't. I warn you. Don't."

I rubbed at my fingers, sticky from spruce sap. No other sap was so hard to remove. "Revenge is messy, isn't it?"

"That's why smart men avoid it."

I went inside. The smell of opium smoke was still sharp. That man was too afraid to go home and face the jeering in his village, but also too fearful to support a brave deed here. If he didn't want to return home, if he didn't see any purpose in his life, then he should put his life to noble use here. He had worked on the damned iron road. He had seen it kill and maim. Why not bring glory to his clan? Otherwise he would be forgotten forever.

Fist had lit a lamp and dumped No Brain's belongings onto a bed. A pile of clothes lay on a carrying cloth.

"You don't need heavy socks," said Fist. "Not for China."

"Packing so early?" I asked. "You're not leaving yet."

Fist tugged at the socks in No Brain's grip.

"What's that?" I pointed to the bed. Peter pushed his way in, keen as a hungry dog.

"Garbage. He wants to take everything."

White and green pebbles. Scraps of string and soiled blue ribbon. Thick and skinny nails with bent heads. A shiny suspender snap, toothless and loose.

Fist tossed items into two piles. No Brain called, "I want that. I want that."

Fist slapped away the brat's hand.

"As soon as you talk revenge," I said, "China men will try to stop you."

"Like One Leg. He's scared."

No Brain hurried away, still ready to burst into tears.

"In China, I was in a bandit gang, a famous one," I said. "I can do many things."

He jerked away. "You think I'm afraid to kill?"

"In Victoria, I guarded the door at a game hall, the biggest one in town. I fought all the time."

"You think only big fellows can get things done? Not this time."

※

We ate stringy greens that had gone to seed, steamed fish, a fragrant soup, and rice. I needed to get Fist and One Leg talking about plans, but the brat chose this time to turn away his face and refuse to eat. Never before had he dismissed food, not even when we had taken several meals a day in Victoria. The brat should have been hungry; our last meal had been this morning in the Native village. He sipped soup but kicked his feet and shook his head whenever I poked rice at him.

I mixed fish juice into the rice, a wet slurry that had been my childhood favourite, but Peter made a face and rejected it.

I made a grand show of taking food to my mouth and chewing with gusto. Peter still shook his head.

Eat! I wanted to shout. Luck provides a meal now, not tomorrow, not the day after. No telling when we get food again.

"What are your plans for the boy?" asked One Leg.

"The bottom dropped out. With no money, I can't go to the mother. I have no choice but to take him to China, although the men from Lytton called me stupid."

One Leg nodded. "Here, redbeards will kick him around like an old dog."

"He'll get kicked around in China too," said Fist. "Want to know what my older brothers called me? Fried tofu *pok*. Roast pig skin. Pin-cushion nose. They never stopped laughing."

"Crocodile fingers," added No Brain. "Pebble face. Tree-bark cheeks. You never went anywhere with them."

"If boys don't tease you about one thing," I said, "they mock you for another."

Someone pounded the door. I looked for my stick. Fist grabbed the rifle. One Leg snuffed the lamps. No Brain pulled Peter close to him. A spoon clattered to the floor.

"It's Boss Soon," a voice called.

Fist put away the gun, and we had relit the lamps by the time he reached the table. "*Wah*, if dried tree leaves landed on your head, would you all scream?"

This time he was a worker in dusty overalls and heavy jacket. He loosened a bundle from his back and threw aside his cap. A pigtail was coiled and pinned atop his head. The last time I saw him, his fancy western hat had hidden it.

He glanced at me. "Weren't you looking for the boy's mother? You sure quit fast."

"He takes the boy to China instead," Fist said with a sneer. "Not sordid yet, but he'll make it sordid."

"We came down the other side of the river," I said to the book-man. "Your crew is making progress. Did you hire some strong men?"

"Look at this." The bookman showed his sack to Fist, who brought more rice and chopsticks.

"Is it enough?" he asked.

Boss Soon jerked his thumb at me. "You trust this one?"

I busied myself feeding the boy.

"He passed through once," said Fist. "Never saw him before. He's from the island."

"Want to land in jail?" One Leg asked. "Be careful."

"I worked on the railway too," I said. "What those redbeards did to the graves was barbaric."

"Any China man can say that," One Leg declared. "But give him five cents and he'll betray you."

"Kick him out," said Fist. "He hates rail hands."

"I had different plans, that's all," I protested.

"He wouldn't go to the temple for us," Fist said. "Said he wasn't coming back this way."

"But here he is." Boss Soon nabbed a large piece of fish and turned to me. "What's the worst insult you ever threw at a railway man?

"I didn't help bury—" I stopped myself and paused. "I killed one."

"Not an accident?"

I looked away, into the dark. "Shorty was hurting from a bad injury. He smoked opium for the pain. He had no money to send home. He told me to smother him, make it look like he had died during the night."

"A friend?"

"Hardly. But he had saved my life. I owed him a favour."

When I glanced at Boss Soon, he said, "So you want to help?"

My mouth opened, but he stopped me with one raised hand.

"Wait, I know, you want to avenge our late comrades. I know, you want to restore China's faded honour. I know all that. Can't you say something new?"

What shit was he fishing for? The men at the table showed no distress. Fist dug out the glassy salmon eyes and chewed them.

"In my crews," Boss Soon said, "some men quit after a week, others stayed for years. Some coolies hid all day where they couldn't be seen, others did the work of ten men. How can we trust you?"

"You trust this worm Fist?" I demanded. "Did he work for you?"

"I know all about him. People call him a coward. He failed his co-workers. His father lost face and the clan is shamed. He has to regain respect."

"This one said he ran with bandits," Fist said. "Who believes him?"

Boss Soon asked me where.

I gestured that we go outside. He shook his head. "These men watched the graves."

"No one is braver than me," I said, "but I won't lose face before strangers."

He took several mouthfuls of food before changing his mind. We went to the front door. In a low voice, I told him about my parents' shame and the need to restore Grandfather's honour.

"Tell me about the bandits," he said, "but not just hit-hit-kill-kill."

My mouth went dry.

"We were not all killers," I said. "One day, a few of us ambushed a wedding delivery. We usually let such parties go past. This time, we hadn't eaten for days and both sides were startled. We weren't armed and didn't expect them to have weapons. The porters must have been promised a bonus for a completed trip. Or they were embarrassed to be caught wearing gaudy red vests and headbands. When we charged at them, they dropped the roast pig and the baskets of cakes. To our surprise, they didn't turn tail and run. Instead they shouted and pulled out cudgels. Their leader slammed his shoulder pole into me. The porters chased us, screaming to behead us, to skin us alive. This was the first time we had to run away.

"My friend Poy and I were laughing, as if drunk from too much wine, as if running a race between rival clans. We yelled to each other. We didn't believe this was really happening. There wasn't any danger; we knew the trails better than our names. My friend and I ducked behind a bush and then jumped onto a fellow. We crashed to the ground. The porters surrounded us and kicked and beat us. In the next instant, our fellow bandits caught up, waving knives that had been hidden in the forest. So then the tables were turned, the porters ran away, and it was our turn to chase them, shouting like drunks."

"Kill anyone?"

"Not that time."

He shoved the bag at me. "Take a peek. Be careful."

Stubby brown tubes of dynamite were tied in bundles, coiled by their own long fuses.

"We can explode their gravestones," I said.

Yale's redbeard cemetery stood on flat land overlooking the river. Trees still blocked the field but a large cross, taller than two men, watched over upright markers, tower-like stones, and plots enclosed by fences of wood or wrought iron. The redbeards held slow-moving parades to bury their dead, but we China men always avoided them. We weren't curious about their funerals the way they liked to trail after ours.

"What's the biggest building in Yale?" Fist leaned against the wall.

"Engine house," replied Boss Soon, "where locomotives get turned around."

"Just a big shed. How about the Company offices?"

"Too small."

"There's the fancy house where the Top Boss lived."

"China men took the servants' cabin." The bookman shook his head. "They will get blamed."

"We explode the railway," said Fist.

"Isn't it too long?" I spoke without thinking.

He turned to Boss Soon. "There's enough to bring down a trestle, isn't there?"

He nodded.

"Screw!" cried One Leg. "Why not make a circle, noses to each others' backs, and kick the man in front? Our blood and sweat is on that road."

"That road killed China men," said the bookman. "Now we fight for dregs of work."

"Go burn churches!" said One Leg. "Every town has at least one."

"Three fires have reduced Yale to ashes, yet the town's church still stands," said Fist. "Their god is strong too."

"China men wanted to torch a church in Lytton," I said. "But they didn't. The redbeards would have shrugged and said, 'Ah, those China men don't like Jesus and don't like missionaries in China,' and then turned around to build a new one. No, we must make them wonder, 'Why are the China men so angry about the iron road?'"

No one heard me.

"We tie ropes to the tracks," Fist said, "climb down, and lash dynamite to the bracing. Then we climb back up, light the fuses, and run!" He reached for the bag. "How long are the fuses? How much time is there before they explode?"

"Enough," said Boss Soon. "If one section gives way, then the entire bridge may fall. North Bend has a long trestle."

"No, further south," said Fist. "We need to get away quickly."

"Below Spuzzum."

"Straight one or curved?"

"The straight one is higher."

"Very high," I said. "I crossed it recently."

"Then we jump on a boat at Yale and sail away. We'll be home in China in no time!"

"Drinking whisky!" We clapped each other's backs and banged the table.

Again I urged Peter to eat. Once the dishes were removed, he would lose all chance of filling his stomach. I wanted to slap him. If he starved tomorrow, there was nothing I could do.

"You can write to the redbeard newspaper," Fist said to Boss Soon, "saying clearly-clearly that we avenge the fire and the grave-yard. That way, everyone knows everything."

"I'll do that while singing a happy song!" he replied.

"But you need to stay with your crew," I told Boss Soon. "Once this happens, the Company and the police will look for where the explosives came from. They'll question you right away."

"Then you go with Fist," Boss Soon said to me.

Exactly what I wanted to hear!

"Can't trust him," Fist declared. Then he sneered at me. "Besides, what will you do with the boy? Bring him along?"

"He's no trouble."

"He might start bawling or shout to his people. You see them everywhere along the river."

"I'll figure it out." I would do anything to join this mission.

"You're the stupid ones." One Leg struggled to stand up and then leaned against the wall. "This is madness."

"Only crazy China men will side with the redbeards!" declared the bookman.

"I helped build that road."

"So did the men in those graves."

"Then go get their consent. The railway is their grave-stick. It honours their passing."

"Each man had his own marker," Fist said. "You repainted them."

"This iron road is so high and long, it is a marvel for the eye to see," said One Leg.

"It swallowed your leg," said Boss Soon.

"Some mornings," One Leg said, "I go look at the iron road. It's a river of steel, heavy but even. It runs level and smooth. It soothes the mind. Still, I wonder, wouldn't it be faster to move things by the river instead of by the railway? Do you know?"

"Very beautiful." No Brain went to the stove for more rice.

"You want redbeards to raid more graveyards?" said the bookman.

"When you kill people here," One Leg said, "the police will chase you to China. They will join forces with the Emperor. You will never know a night's good sleep until you die."

"No one need die," said Fist. "We can explode the trestle after the train passes."

"Or we can do it early," I said, "before the southbound train arrives. Then it can't reach the coast. It'll be delayed for weeks. The Company loses money. All Gold Mountain will know what we did. "

"We should be better than the redbeards." One Leg slammed the table. "Otherwise, we deserve their disdain."

"You're angry because you can't join in." The headman's chopsticks rattled in his bowl, chasing the last grains of rice.

"I won't leave," said One Leg. "I will stay here."

I cursed under my breath. Fist was a quick thinker but not fast enough for One Leg.

"Redbeards will come to kill you," said Boss Soon.

"Then you avenge me," said One Leg.

"You agreed to leave," Fist cried out in dismay. "You promised to follow His Holiness's advice."

"Not so." One Leg brandished his axe. "I guard this place. Redbeards may return, unearth the corpses, and set them aflame."

"Fist, it's simple." The bookman turned to one side and spat out a bone. "You must leave these men behind."

Fist opened his mouth to reply, but nothing came out.

"I told you many times to go home," One Leg said to Fist. "You never listen."

"You never listen to me!"

"These people should see clearly that I'm not the one stopping you," One Leg added.

"Stinking bastard, you don't want villagers laughing at you."

"Your uncle plays you like a cricket," Boss Soon sneered and goaded him.

"This is a good opportunity." Fist tugged One Leg's sleeve. "I win honour for our clan."

"I agree. You must go."

Fist shook his head. "We came together, we leave together."

"You should stand up for yourself," I said.

"Shit-hole fiend, you don't need his consent." Boss Soon took his sack to the door. "I'll get my men to do it."

"No!" I shouted. "It's easy to trace the explosives to you."

"Leave the bag here." Fist quickly grabbed it. "Give us time to talk."

The bookman shook his head. "You'll never change the old fool's mind."

Fist looked into the bag, and then up. "Maybe I'll kill these two old things tonight."

The headman stormed out. No Brain started stacking the dishes.

I cursed One Leg, the brick apple. No one could get a bite of him, not even a headman who spoke English.

If I didn't take revenge, then I went home a failed man. And it would be a thousand times worse with the boy at my side.

16

THREE HANDS ARE BETTER THAN TWO (1885)

Next morning, a gunshot awoke me.

Bright mid-morning light filled the window. Another sudden bang, then a crisp ping on metal. The boy's bed was empty.

I stumbled outside and saw birds circling overhead, afraid to land.

Sitting on a chair with his thighs wide apart, One Leg aimed his rifle over a cluttered patch of tree stumps. White smoke leaked from the gun barrel. His target was a row of tin cans on top of a tower of wooden crates. No Brain stood by him, hand on the boy's shoulder. The brat covered his ears but his eyes shone with pleasure. One Leg fired again and missed. The boy pounced on the spent cartridge.

I hurried over. "Up so early!"

"That stupid thing, Fist, has run off." One Leg did not look at me. "Let's see if this old cat's whiskers get singed or not."

"Run off where?"

"Spuzzum, to find someone he can trust." He put the rifle on his lap and sat back.

My mind was already on the mission. One of us, Fist or I, needed to stay atop the tracks to pull up the other man. Whoever it was, he needed to be strong. Fist was too scrawny. Or, we could both climb down and up on opposite sides of the trestle in order to save time. But I would be faster and he, on looking slow and weak, would lose his temper and do something stupid.

"You two must go now!" I said to One Leg. "Redbeards will come, wanting revenge."

"Screw! Fist won't do a thing. You watch; he'll be back in time for dinner."

I wanted to smash the rifle into his face. "No, he'll take revenge and run for China."

"He cried like a newborn babe when he left," said One Leg.

"Hindered by your silliness."

"What do you know? Our crewmen took turns burying corpses. Fist's father handled one, but then he got killed. Fist got scared and refused his turn. When we replaced the grave-sticks here, Fist wouldn't touch them until I threatened to get help from Spuzzum. What a spineless coward."

"Plenty of men won't touch those things."

"No crewman refused. Not even No Brain."

"I'll go to Spuzzum." I reached for Peter, who watched One Leg raise the rifle.

"Ah, let him be," he said, squinting through the sight. "Get your things and then fetch him."

I wouldn't let go. The brat screamed and dug his heels into the ground. When I lifted him, his thrashing body arched into a taut bow as his fists and feet pounded me. I twisted away, but his fingers jabbed my eyes. I yelped and slapped him. The more he screamed, the louder I yelled. I held him with one hand and spanked him with the other. No Brain tried to free him.

"Don't smack the head," One Leg scolded. "You'll wreck his brain. You're so big; don't you know your own strength?"

※

The boy refused to walk. He pulled the other way, as if drawn to the north where Mary lived. He lay on the ground, arms and legs spread out, and stared at the sky. When I stood him up, he flopped down. I sang, "*Come, come sit, eat sweet bits*," but failed to amuse him.

I threw him over my shoulder like a sack of rice and staggered along the railway. When I released him, he darted away and shouted to people at the river. The words were gabble to me and I doubted that anyone could hear him over the wind and rushing river. Still, I clapped a hand over his mouth and dragged him away. The last thing I needed was a worried fisherman hurling a spear through me.

It took all morning to return to the bridge. We spent our energy bickering, not making time. The brat dawdled to poke at bugs, pick wildflowers, and collect round pebbles. When we entered the forest to squat, I finished first and shouted for him to hurry. As he ignored me, I thought again of my original plan to dump him here. Fist didn't want him on the mission, he had made that clear. But this time, I would act with more thought, as a superior man should. This time the hand of Heaven was stroking my back, egging me on.

At the bridge, the boy knelt and watched the whitened river shoot through the narrow chasm of high rock. Dark bullets of fish fought the current, driven upriver to spawn and ensure the survival of their line. I was just as determined to charge ahead on this task. It was more important than life itself: it provided honour to otherwise meaningless lives. I saw myself under the trestle, dangling by a rope with nothing but death below. Were Fist and I strong enough? By now, that fool could have reached the trestle. Would he know where to install the dynamite? He could go to the middle of the bridge, or stay close to one end. An explosion meant confronting angry redbeards. Better hurry to Yale, where more Chinese lived.

Good thing Fist had finally left One Leg. If not, nothing would happen—not for me, not for the bones churning in that graveyard. Maybe Fist had pounded his pillow and wept all night. Maybe his father visited him in a dream. Maybe the idiot finally realized that an ugly face such as his required more dressing up than just a few years of work in Gold Mountain. Too bad he had no use for me. If he got caught, then he would bring disaster to the bookman and everyone, and have only himself to blame. His dislike of me was childish, worse than silly. I had brought him the very answers he wanted from His Holiness, yet he turned against me.

In the afternoon, we reached Spuzzum, where I visited the Chinese stores and asked in a carefree manner for Fist. Wary eyes stayed on my back. Any China man who was still kicking around after the railway needed a strong reason to stay. And if he was seeking others, then some plot must be in the air and everyone wanted to know more. People said they had not seen him.

Good, he had left no trail. But I was stupidly drawing attention to his name. I was the fool who might betray Boss Soon. At the cookhouse, the owner put out a chipped porcelain vase filled with yellow and purple wildflowers. The boy reached for it, but I knocked away his hands.

"Didn't you and Sam go to Lytton?" The cook recognized me. "You saw the fire?"

I nodded.

"The stagecoach stopped here with Boss Joe. Then the local men who were thinking of home decided to go too."

"Didn't I tell you?" exclaimed Blue Smock. "Sam is as useless as a fart."

"Is he here?" I hoped to hear "no," and relaxed on hearing that very answer.

The two customers from before were sitting as if they had never left. They rolled three small dice between them, using pebbles for cash.

"In Lytton, didn't you ask Old Yang for help?" asked Knitted Hat. "He knows people."

"No Yangs lived there."

"Where does the boy go?"

"You want him?"

The men snorted, not caring if I was serious or not.

"Did Fist pass through?" I asked. "The one who brings wild meat to sell."

"He ate here. He was looking for a kinsman but couldn't find him."

"When was that?"

"Mid-morning. Those three donkeys talk in circles. Won't they ever go home?"

I breathed easier. If Fist hadn't found a helper, then I still had a chance to join him, unless the fool had run ahead by himself. In that case, a blast could go off at any time.

"Is the washman still here?"

"Of course, his daughter came back. What, you need a bath?"

A small hand-pulled wagon stood by the washhouse door. The air inside was thick with the smells of cooking as Yang served a Native woman at the counter.

"Eat rice!" Peter called out in Chinese, grinning.

I slapped the back of his head for being rude. When Yang paid us no attention, I recalled how he talked against himself. He would waste my time, but I needed help.

The woman, likely a servant in a redbeard household, was pulling laundry from a big cloth bag. Her hair was coiled behind her neck, and a white apron covered her dark skirt. She counted the pieces along with Yang, mouthing the numbers silently.

As the washman wrote out a ticket, she called to Peter, who bantered shyly with her. Then she ran her fingers through his hair and waved goodbye. I wished she was his mother.

"Boy still follows you!" remarked Yang. "Four days aren't enough to find someone."

"I got robbed and had nothing for the mother."

He shrugged. "A woman would rather have her son than a pile of cash."

"It's worse. With no money, how can I feed another mouth in China?"

"Get a job."

"China men are finished here." I leaned in close. "Is there a Native family that can take him?"

Yang shook his head. The boy was trying again to set the toy soldiers upright. This time, Yang wasn't helping.

"The boy can strengthen his people," I added. "Isn't that what you said?"

"He needs at least one trueborn parent. I raised my Jane after her mother passed." Yang squatted to watch the boy, which gave me faint hope.

"Your daughter came back! You raised her well. Do I get to see her?"

"She went to help with the fishing. Those ghost-rat China men called her a demon when she was really a goddess. She and Wee-yum didn't cheat me. Jane went to her people, to a young man there. She wanted me to take the bride money from Wee-yum and go to China. I returned it to him."

"You were right all along." I squatted and slapped his back. "How about raising a boy?"

"This old thing? I'm going home."

He led us to the back room. The table and high-back chairs were gone, replaced by wooden crates. He brought out potatoes cooked with fatty pork and bean sauce, saying, "I cooked enough for several days, so there's plenty."

"Where's the fancy table?" I asked.

"I spent part of the bride money so had to sell the furniture to make up the difference."

Peter reached for a metal spoon, but I thrust chopsticks into his hand. Time for him to use them.

"Isn't there anyone who would take a child?" I was a child begging for an adult favour. "Uncle, the only reason I dare ask again is because we are kinsmen."

We ate for a while before Yang spoke. "Sally the whore, she could take care of him. She saves her money."

"But will she send him to school? Anyone else?"

"Sam's grandmother will know."

"Last time, she made the boy cry," I muttered. "All he did was run to her. He fears her."

"Jane went to her all the time. Girls need the guidance of women."

"Sam isn't here, is he?"

He shook his head. "But you should talk to his grandmother. Want me to help you talk?"

I shrugged. Earlier, on the way into Spuzzum, I had thought about asking Sam to take Peter. But Sam wanted to go to China and find his own family. He didn't want to be dragging Peter around the world. If I could stop Sam from going to China to be humiliated by the people there, then that would be my grand gift to him; indeed, it would repay all my debts to him. Too bad my words were fleas to him. Couldn't he be a better man than me and take Peter from me? They had, after all, the same mix of blood. Surely Sam felt a kinship to the boy and knew exactly what to teach him. The brat had laughed far more with Sam than with me.

What was that old saying? "*Through laugh and talk, all are equal.*" Me, I never tried once to make the boy smile. When Grandfather used to cite that proverb, I always snickered to myself. He was trying to get Mother and Grandmother to be nicer to each other, which was as likely as a rooster laying an egg.

⁂

Yang, Peter, and I set out for the Native village. The railway swerved to higher ground and crossed a stream over logs made into a cricket cage. In clearings among the bushes, great boxes and ragged banners stood in fenced graveyards. Wooden statues, carved as humans and painted in bright colours, wore western hats and clothing. I shuddered, recalling the life-sized paper servants that were burned at funerals in China to join deceased human masters. Those servants were always painted with the rosy cheeks of children.

We took the old wagon road to the village, past meadows of cattle and horses. Dusty rows of crops looped around log cabins where plump chickens scuttled for safety. An old man carried a rack of jiggling dried salmon through the maze of animal hides stretched taut on frames. My boy recognized someone and tugged to escape. A thin woman with white hair and a red blanket on her shoulders sat on the steps of a cabin, chatting with a younger woman holding a basket of potatoes.

The porch was crowded with crates, tools, and empty tin cans. Metal traps for catching animals, large woven trays, and nestled baskets were piled high. Coils of stiff rope hung from the wall. By the door was a waist-high stack of kindling and firewood. Yang squatted and spoke to the boy in Chinook. The brat kept his gaze on the ground, kicking a rock back and forth between his feet. At one point, it rolled toward me and I kicked it back. The boy looked up at me in surprise.

When we approached the old woman, the younger one hurried off. I too wanted to leave. Another China man with a mix-blood child would only remind the grandmother of her errant son-in-law, Sam's father. No doubt she despised China men for causing her daughter's ruin. That daughter would not have had such trouble in China. When a man ran away from his wife, as my father had done, her proper place remained with his family. She would never think to return to her birth home. But Sam's mother had brought her children to this village, a burden for her own mother.

When Yang spoke to the grandmother, she listened intently. I caught words of Chinook: father, home, money, and hard work.

Home. Wasn't that what everyone wanted?

I was supposed to have provided that: plastered walls around a cooking fire, clean straw for the livestock, and a stone courtyard where chickens pecked for food and where the grandparents' scolding brought each day to an end. Withered oranges sat on the ancestral altar, awaiting an event for fresh replacements. Great urns of rice were sealed with heavy, tight-fitting wooden covers to foil the mice.

Yang's words made Sam's grandmother chuckle and she returned the favour. Then he pulled the boy forward and told him to speak to her. The brat pulled back, shaking his head. She took the furry hat from his head and brushed the fur as she spoke.

The boy answered her, and she asked some short questions.

At the end, she shook her head. Yang tried to reason with her, exaggerating his frowns and gestures, but she was firm.

"What does she say?" I demanded.

"China men must take care of their own. Their children need money for school."

"What did the boy say?"

"He liked it when Sam carried him."

"Let's go." I thanked her and bowed stiffly.

"Sam had told her that the boy liked him better than you."

I yanked my son away.

She called out words that Yang translated. "She wants to know if Sam is with his woman in Lytton."

"Tell her a girl was born," I said. "But the mother rejects Sam as the father and her family drove him away."

The grandmother must have repeated her question, because Yang asked me again and repeated his answer. Her jaw quivered. She struggled to stand, but the washman urged her to sit.

"She asks, where is Sam now?"

"On his way to China, to see his father's people."

"Crazy fool," muttered Yang.

When the grandmother heard my news, she cried out in dismay.

Yang glared at me. "Couldn't you stop him?"

"He thinks his life will be better there."

"You let him believe that? You stupid thing."

Yang and the grandmother spoke at length before the three of us returned to town.

"You're in luck," said the washman. "She thought it over and may take the boy. Her thinking is that if Sam becomes a father, then he won't go to China. But someone will need to find Sam quickly."

I was worse than vermin. If I offered Peter to Sam, he would never take him. Far too much bad blood ran between us. He would do me no favours, and I expected none from him. Between men, that was fair. What was not fair was getting a kinsman to sneak me through the back door to approach Sam's grandmother and gain this leverage. It was like kicking a sleeping man in the mouth, smashing his teeth, and letting him bleed. It was not what a superior man did.

⁂

Fist leaned by the door of Yang's laundry, chewing tobacco. "Cookhouse man said you asked for me," he said.

I put on my gambling face and quelled my excitement. "One Leg sends you good wishes: obliging winds all the way."

"Stinking bastard said no such thing." He walked off. "Let's not talk here."

I went with Fist along the railway. Neither of us carried tools, store goods, or baggage. When a horse pulling a wagon rumbled by, I averted my face from the driver and its riders. Two China men, strangers in a rough town, were strolling in the afternoon like scholars pondering a poem. We should have tried harder not to be noticed.

I asked where the explosives were.

"Safe."

"Did you get ropes?"

He nodded.

"Strong ones?"

"You're not the boss!" he snapped.

I folded my lips in to keep quiet.

The town broke apart at the edge of the forest where the wagon road and railway emerged. We avoided the trees that hid nosy spies and climbed the ridge over the river. Fishermen had driven a line of wooden stakes into the water and now men crouched on shore with spears and nets. The roiling river thrashed the bushy tree branches tied to the stakes. Many times Sam and I had seen men in the middle of the river replacing the branches, but I never asked about them.

"Know what that is?" Fist pointed. "Branches churn the water into foam so that fish can't see the net."

"But their eyes are on the side, not the front."

We stood like mourners at a funeral.

"You changed your mind about One Leg and No Brain," I said.

He spat out brown tobacco juice. "One Leg had many chances to leave. This is my big opportunity."

"Now you trust me?"

"The man I wanted, he left town. He got lucky at the game table."

"My boy and I are going to China."

"You saw the Company bigwig in Lytton, no?" Fist grabbed my arm. "He arrived here yesterday, and tomorrow he takes the train to Yale. The station master's cook heard them talking."

"You told him everything?"

"I'm not stupid!"

A sudden whistle raked the air. An eagle with a white head and white tail feathers plunged from a high branch and spread its wings. It swooped to the river, legs outstretched, talons open, then hung in the air between sky and water with no effort at all. The fishermen shouted and pointed. The bald eagle flew away without a fish, cawing with sharp, shrill sounds, as though annoyed. I recalled Grandmother telling me that once she had seen a black eagle fly off with an entire nest of baby birds in its clutch.

Fist's gaze followed the eagle. "When you were small, did you play Eagle Fights Mother Hen?" he asked.

"Yes. I was always the eagle." I recalled playmates shrieking and running from me. "I ran and grabbed the chick all the time. Nobody could beat me."

"They never let me be the eagle." He took a breath. "What will you do with your son?"

"Sam's grandmother will keep him." If she didn't, then I would tell Yang everything and leave the boy with him. He was an upright man.

"You said you were taking him to China."

"This is more important."

A sly smile crossed his face. "I saved you from taking him to China. You should pay me."

"Shut your mouth before I change my mind."

We returned to town, each walking on a different side of the railway.

I kicked a pebble and watched it roll ahead. Fist had done nothing to prove his mettle; he had no righteous claim to lead. By chance, he lived near the graveyard; only that happenstance had brought him here. He held that bag of explosives only by default: his kinsmen were both crippled while Bookman Soon needed to stay safe.

Me, I had been sent here by the gods. One Leg and Fist knew I had not planned on returning to his camp. But odd events had led me there. The stagecoach had an accident. Then, by another miracle, Sam had travelled quickly enough to catch up and give me the news that had swayed his grandmother. I was by far Fist's best chance for success. I had trekked extra miles to his camp, after a week travelling up and down this canyon.

I shut my eyes. The trestle had evenly placed ties. Late-afternoon light flashed between them. The heavy steel gleamed like a silver roof beam but stretched higher and longer. Fist needed to tie ropes to the iron track, the strongest part of the trestle. But knotting the rope required dropping it and then pulling it up. One of us needed to bend over the edge of the track and reach for the dangling length. That involved looking at the ground below. I hoped Fist had strong ropes that had been used lately, even though they had been cast off from other work and salvaged for re-use.

We agreed to leave as early as possible the next morning. I told Fist to lie down and get some sleep. I sighed at his departing back. Fist was a strange one. What if he changed his mind again?

In the washhouse drying room, the boy was sitting on the floor by the open door with a deck of playing cards, sorting them by colour. Every now and then he held up a card and called out to Yang, who was busy hanging wet clothes onto the lines. Yang came over and pointed to one of the piles, either red or black. It was one of the face cards; its colours weren't clear to the boy.

I told the boy to stop bothering Yang's work, but he paid me no attention. He kept calling for the washman. Even when I pointed out the right stack to the boy, he insisted that Yang come over. Having noticed that Yang kept his boots clean and brightly polished, I asked to borrow his brush, cloth, and blacking. He obliged.

I went to work briskly to ensure that if I died tomorrow, then at least the people who recovered my body would find something to admire about me. The caked mud dropped off in clumps. The tear in the leather was longer. I rubbed in generous amounts of blacking. My shoes were the only things of value that I would take back to China.

When Sam's grandmother entered the laundry, then I knew for sure that the gods were watching over me. As she and Yang spoke, I heard Sam's name and the word "China." The boy stared at the floor and fidgeted. He mumbled a few times. The washman told me that the boy said he didn't want to go to China. He wanted to stay here. They would send word to Mary in Cache Creek about the boy's new situation. She might want to do something.

"Did he ask why I was going away?" I asked.

The washman shook his head.

※

On the way to Tai Yuen store, Yang and Sam's grandmother took the boy's hands between them.

I trailed behind. My letting-go helped everyone. Now Sam had a son who was just like him. The boy wouldn't be a water buffalo driven from the temple. And he would likely see his mother again.

Yang said I needn't enter the store. The manager knew both him and Sam's grandmother. He added, "To sell your son, don't touch his head. Touch it and you'll weep a ton."

"Don't worry about me," I snapped.

I almost hurled myself into the air and somersaulted. This was the earlier me, relieved of fatherly duties, free to dance, released to dash in whatever direction I wanted. Every man in the game hall feared me. The hands of the clock had been magically turned back by a week. I was in Victoria, where Rainbow opened her soft white arms to me.

Mary never found me in that teahouse.

That mix-blood named Sam Bing Lew? Never heard of him.

Had there been a fire in Lytton? Don't ask me.

Giddy with glee, I reached into my stockings, hoping that my bankroll was still there. But they were empty, so my gloom returned. I crossed the road and crouched behind some crates. I had to clutch my shoulders and press my arms into my chest to stop its sudden heaving.

What had my father felt when he saw me that last time at our final parting? He had spent hundreds, maybe thousands more days with me than I had spent with Peter. Hadn't he gripped my fingers tight in his rough hands to pull me through a temple crowd?

Could he recall my face or a shared meal? He had scolded me for spilling rice on the table, for failing to brush the mud off his clogs, and for dragging my spoon bottom against the lip of the soup bowl.

He had walked away and sailed far beyond my reach so now I could do the same to Peter. *Father steals a steamed bun, son does arson.*

Two days ago, I had decided to take the boy to China. That made me a superior man. Now a new way to change my fate had sprung up, something far better than entering America.

I hardly knew the brat. We had spent six, seven days together, squabbling the whole time. I was sure he hadn't wailed so much in a long while, stuck with a cheerless fellow who spanked him and threw him about like a bushel of potatoes. I was gruff and impatient. In Victoria, I ignored Chinatown's few children. I sneered at men who fawned and crooned lullabies to call over the little darlings so they could pinch their cheeks and then press sweet treats into their hands.

I never knew this boy when he was a baby.

When did he take his first steps? Had they been on a dirt floor or on some smooth stones?

What blessings were received at his full-month banquet? Did he get any tokens of gold?

How was his name chosen?

When the boy emerged from Tai Yuen, he and Sam's grandmother licked happily at sticks of hard brown sugar. An envelope with a broad red strip on it poked from Yang's pocket.

A tear slid down my cheek. The boy and I couldn't even speak to one another. He never obeyed me and had no inkling how a son ought to behave. *A sampan and a war junk sailed at each other, strong winds behind each.* They could crash and drag each other to the ocean bottom.

The washman took his leave from the others and headed toward me. I scrambled back but hit a wall. How did he know where I was? He must have seen me from the window.

"Why squat there?" He held out the letter. "What do you cry for? You're not a woman."

I didn't go back to the washhouse. I had seen a China man with a lopsided grin stroll from a shack, a hodgepodge of salvaged planks and boards with no windows. I found its door heavy, but it had an oiled hinge that let it swing quietly. The sweet burnt smell of opium hung in the air. Small lamps flickered on the floor where customers muttered and dozed.

The owner asked if I wanted to lie on something solid or soft. Solid meant less risk of fleas and mites. The fumes warmed my chest and relaxed my stomach.

Birds are chirping in the tree. Underneath, Grandmother and Mother squat at a portable clay stove and dish out rice and flavourings. They give me chopsticks and a covered bowl and send me to deliver it to Grandfather. I skip over cobbled paths that survived battle and fire. Now I can see the distant hill. Before the war, the walls of the perimeter houses used to block my view. Those burned buildings were knocked down, so the village is being reconstructed.

A sense of hope warms the springtime air. Everyone who survived the wars came back. Everyone says I'm lucky because Father is working abroad. His money lets us build a new house.

At the site, men pound the earth into a hard floor. Grandfather perches on a high ladder, setting a beam into the frame of the house. He tells me to wait. I sit on a pile of bricks under some shade. My friend Kai has a cage with two crickets. I poke at them but keep looking up at Grandfather. On one of those upward glances, I find him gone. I scramble to my feet, panicked.

"Where's my Grandfather?" I shout.

"At the dike."

I hurry off, clutching the bowl. At several turns, I find my path blocked by the rubble of fallen houses. Several detours later, I'm on my way to the river.

"Hok, taking food to your Grandfather?" Granny Three asks. "What a good boy you are."

Men use ropes to pull old boulders from the water. During the war, the enemy toppled the dike and let the river wash away the road. Now the wall must be rebuilt and the water drained. Grandfather is in chest-high water. I call to him and he tells me to wait. I squat and keep an anxious eye on him. After I come back from peeing, he's gone.

"Where's my Grandfather?" I ask the rock men.

"Went to town for roof tiles."

I run without watching the road. Sharp rocks cut into my feet. I stumble but hold the bowl. If I drop it, then Grandfather will rap his knuckle on my head.

"Hok, your Grandfather just went by," Fourth Uncle yells. "You're a good boy."

At the tile factory, a crowd plugs the entrance. Many people are rebuilding. Grandfather tells me to stand aside and wait. I vow to pay attention until he eats his food. Street vendors pass, touting sweet treats and dried plums. I ignore them.

Grandfather pushes a wheelbarrow heaped with the clay tiles. I beg him to eat. He says to wait. We take the shortcut along the river. But the wheel sinks into mud and the wheelbarrow tips over, spilling the tiles into the water. Grandfather jumps down to retrieve them: gulps air, ducks under the surface, and then hands them to me. I want to join him. Grandfather says it's too deep. He goes under for another load. I wait, but Grandfather doesn't return. I look for bubbles in the muddy water. I call out. Louder. I scream and slide down the muddy bank, but I don't jump in. My body trembles. Then Grandfather leaps up, grabs me, and pulls me into the water to play. We are both laughing, a sound that is rarely heard.

It will be good to see him again.

17

An Unused Road Is Not Smooth (1885)

Fist entered the laundry and bid us a loud good morning. He was late. Through the door I saw railway workers with lunch pails hurrying to the station and travellers standing outside the hotel, waiting for horses and buggies. A man walked by, shaking out a heavy apron.

"Ropes and explosives?" I demanded.

"Not going," he said.

I glanced outside. No packs were there.

He was pointing at Yang. "Does he know?"

I nodded, having told him everything when he demanded to know about my ties to Fist. "Did you wet your bed all night?"

"The road is new and strong. You can't bring it down."

"*A new latrine is fragrant for three days.*"

"Then it's time to go home." He reached for the door. "As you told me."

"Die now!" I grabbed his neck and slammed him to the wall.

"Screw!" His eyes bulged as he clawed in vain at me. "You're dead too."

I expected him to crumple to the ground and weep like a girl.

"I'm a bandit chief." I squeezed his throat harder. "Your life is nothing. You will never see China."

Yang must have climbed onto the counter and leapt, because he crashed from above and knocked us over. We hit the floor and I lost my grip.

He pressed an axe into my chest. "Stop this."

Fist was curled into himself, taking deep breaths. Yang dragged him away. I barred the front door and kicked the bench against it.

In the back room, Fist leaned on the wall, rubbing his neck.

I hefted the axe. "You run and I'll chop your head."

He looked away as I spoke. "On my way home I thought, 'Why not do a nice thing? Let me take His Holiness's words to Fist.' So I made a detour and went all the way to your camp. For this, I even dumped my son."

"You wanted the brat gone," he spat out.

I slammed the axe into the table. He jumped.

Yang brought battered mugs with steam rising. "Drink tea and talk slowly."

"Why can't I leave?" Fist cried out.

I stretched out my arms. "I'll beat you softer than cake. We agreed on this; we're just two men doing a job."

"My uncles shouldn't get fragrant so early."

"You don't care about them; they've run off already. Wrecking the trestle was your idea."

"It was talk, stupid talk."

"One Leg is laughing right now. He's waiting for you to crawl back, head bowed, tail between your legs. You gutless dog."

"No one can fix things here. Men are stiff or gone home. Or crazy as One Leg."

His body was shaking. At any moment, he would start to weep.

Yang draped an arm around Fist's shoulders. "Young man, walk away and your name will stink forever. People in China will hear about the ruined graves; your entire family will be shamed."

"Screw you. They're so far away, nobody will know." Fist shook him off. "It was idle talk, a man letting off steam."

"You could go home where cheering crowds lift you to their shoulders as if you single-handedly kicked all the redbeards out of Hong Kong."

"I could fall off the trestle and get nailed." He stared at the floor.

"Do this for your sons and daughters." The washman poured more tea. "When your children crowd at your feet and ask what you did in Gold Mountain, what will you say? You will lower your head and mutter, 'I was a coolie.'

"'What's a coolie?' they'll shout.

"'Redbeards kicked me around,' you'll mumble.

"'Did you kick back?'

"'I ran away,' you'll moan."

Yang thumped the crate and added, "If your own children don't respect you, you'll get fragrant at a young age."

"There won't be children," snapped Fist. "No woman will marry a pock face."

"You go home a hero, and matchmakers will fill your door like beggars at New Year. Gentry families use famous sons-in-law to make great profits."

We heard the eager clucking of chickens as the neighbour cooed and started to feed them.

When Fist shook his head defiantly and looked away, I said, "Give me the explosives and ropes. I'll go myself."

"Indeed," exclaimed Yang. "If Fist can't do it, then let him back out. This cage has no lid; men come and go as they want. Why stop others from doing what must be done?"

"You're not going to be the rock brain who blocks the way, are you?" I said.

When Fist failed to reply, I sensed his mood shifting. "You're right," I said, "no one knows about you. You can go back to One Leg this very moment. You will be safe forever. Your mother will be pleased to see you."

He shook his head.

"Go ahead to Yale, then," I said. "What about this? You come along and be my sentry."

Fist looked up.

"You think we can do this?"

"I'm going home alive," I told him. "My grandfather and I, we're very close. We have much unfinished business."

He stood. "I'm crazy to follow you."

I clapped him on the back. "I saw how you shaved and cleaned up after seeing the damaged graves. You thought clearly then; do the same now."

❋

The sky was grey and dark; the air hung cool and damp. Rain would slow our trip and stop the fuses from doing their job. We needed to walk fast. The clouds were sliding east, a good sign. The packs were bulky but not heavy, tied with ropes stretched helter-skelter. I watched Fist closely. Without knowing which sack held what, I had not moved fast enough to grab the explosives.

As we trekked away from town, trying to look unhurried, he said, "Know what I was thinking last night? What if Bookman Soon betrays us?"

"He gave us the explosives!"

"He's a Company man. You think he really wants to damage the iron road? That bastard is a boss, through and through. He tells the Company that you and I stole the explosives. He says he heard our plans to explode the iron road but doesn't know where we hid the explosives. He sets a trap for us at the trestle."

"Isn't he your friend?"

"He wants to be a hero to the Company."

"You aim your piss at your own stupid stories."

"Don't say I didn't warn you."

I didn't know what to think. Was he crazy or was he trying to turn me around? There was no time to ponder. I was a Buddha with a stuffed nose, one who couldn't smell lies. It was easier just to keep going.

We walked in silence to Spuzzum village. At our parting, Yang had handed me a cigar box full of Chinese domino tiles. "For your son," he said, rattling the package. "Give him something to remember you by."

I had wanted to kick myself for not thinking of a memento. I should have taken time to figure out his Chinese name.

"Go visit your little precious." Fist squatted by the path. "I'll wait here."

"Not going." If he ran off with the explosives, then I would be a fly with no head.

"You have a gift for your son."

"He doesn't know me."

"Don't trust me, do you? And you think you're such a big stick. Go! You want to see him; otherwise you would have left the dominos with Yang."

I hadn't paid full attention when Yang had led me here earlier, so I stumbled around in a panic looking for the cabin. Even away from the damn forest, I was lost. Good thing Sam's family had that messy, crowded porch that I could recall.

When I banged on the door, it opened quickly. Sam's grandmother stepped forward and pulled the door shut, as if she had been expecting me. Could she have known I was leaving this morning? She wasn't dressed for the day yet; her long white hair was tousled, uncombed. Before I could speak, she pressed her palms together and raised them to her right ear, tilting her head to mimic sleeping. And then she flicked her fingers at me, ordering me to leave. Her eyes were firm.

I paused before giving her the cigar box. "For boy."

She nodded and turned away.

I wanted to storm into her house.

I backed away, scolding myself: I should have gone home with them yesterday for an inspection. Did she have a stove inside? A fireplace? How far away was the latrine? Did Peter have his own bed? How many windows let in the light? I should be a better man than my shit-hole father, who hadn't spared a thought about me. The village in China had plenty of kin to look after its children.

I could always send money here. *Eat dung, shit out rice!*

Fist wasn't where I had left him. I spun around, peering into the bushes and cursing. There hadn't been time for him to get far, even if he ran like a deer. But which way?

The ropes on my back were useless now. I should have insisted on carrying the explosives.

I turned and Fist was there, panting and looking scared.

"Someone walked by," he said. "So I ran to hide."

"Nobody was here," I snapped. "I would have heard."

"Native people move like wind. You see your son?"

"He was sleeping."

I walked away. They said a man wasn't an adult until he had raised a child. I thought that crossing the ocean was a far bigger step. At home, women gathered happily around a child: mothers and grandparents, sisters and aunts. I had a son here, but no one wanted him, as if he had been born a diseased bastard who brought shame into the clan. But he was no such thing. I was his father, but I had walked away from him. He was a dream of the future, thrust into my face. But dreams made in Gold Mountain could not be real. Wet snot leaked from our noses; I turned and emptied mine onto the ground.

That stowaway ride on the train had sped me through this region; now nothing looked familiar. On both sides of the track were rock walls, so close that they formed a second skin, like that of a snake, for the passing trains. My eyes followed the two lines of telegraph cables, rising and falling like a railway in the sky. The redbeards laid claim to everything—land, water, and now the air. Building the railway had felled millions of trees, yet the Company had replanted a line of shaved tree trunks, all the same size. The cables ran high above the tracks, but at some spots drooped near the ground when poles were planted below grade. We knew of telegraphs in China, where lines had been strung between the chief cities of the north. Here, words moved instantly from one station to another, telling of trains going and coming. News of our blast would travel quickly, so we needed to do the same.

"You want to be a big hero in China, don't you?" said Fist.

"In China, we go separate ways. We won't see each other again."

"Fine by me."

"Don't want you at my side, telling people who did what or how things happened. I'll tell the story any way I want."

"Even lies."

I saw excited teahouse diners banging their fists on tables and fighting for the honour of paying my bills. Clerks in the Gold Mountain shops that handled our remittances dropped their pens and abandoned their ledgers in favour of hearing me talk. I brought the truth about the men that they had dispatched across the ocean, the men whose families came to town each month to get the cash sent to them. Even in death, those men in Gold Mountain enjoyed no peace, not when their bones were stripped of names and home destinations. Clerks would bow to me with respect, for they had never heard a tale like mine. I wanted to get fussy welcomes to high-class brothels where, this time, the fawning women urged me to amuse them. We would go to bed later and linger far longer.

"What if someone arrives while we are on the trestle?" asked Fist.

"We say we're railway workers."

"I'll be sentry and stay atop the trestle while you go down."

"Fine. Few people go north today. We need to be quick, that's all." So far we hadn't met any travellers.

"What time does the train leave Spuzzum?"

"Noon. We have lots of time. People fishing will hear the bang and stop the train."

"What if the explosives don't go off?"

"Then Boss Soon will laugh so hard that he'll die."

After a while, I took out some food. Yang had chopped leftover meat, put rice around it to make a ball, and rolled oiled cloth around it. Fist didn't eat. I almost called out for the boy but recalled that he was gone. Peter would have enjoyed the rice balls; the white grains would have stuck to his chin like snow. Old Yang had flavoured the rice with soy sauce and vinegar, and the boy's people liked the strong sour tastes of China.

※

We reached the high trestle, the one that I had sneaked across on a train.

Fist went ahead. I reminded myself of how easily the trains rolled and how heavy they were, made from tons of iron and steel and pulling carloads of coal. I emptied my mind of worry, gazed at the distant mountains, and marched like a soldier, thinking ahead to my triumphant return to China, hearing drums and *di-da* horns inside my head. I almost slammed into Fist, who had suddenly stopped at the middle.

"Go to the edge, bend over, and look underneath the trestle," he said.

"You're insane."

"Show me."

"Let me pass."

"You're afraid." His eyes hardened. "Push me aside."

"Don't be stupid." I wanted to slap him.

"One Leg is wrong. I'm no coward." He went to the edge, dropped to his knees, leaned forward while gripping the ties with his hands, and tucked his head under.

It looked as if he wanted to roll forward and somersault into the air. He looked off-balance. His hands and shoulders had to be strong, to hold on while the bag of explosives rested on his back.

I hurried off the trestle, cursing all the way. He could turn around and go back, for all I cared. The fellow was a three-legged chicken. If he got himself stuck in the middle of the trestle, I wasn't going to help him.

When at last he strolled forward, I raced away, feeling much lighter. It was hardly odd that he had a troubled soul. I had yet to meet a rail hand without one. Some bore open injuries; they limped and dragged one foot. Dark scars gouged their faces. Cloth patches covered lost eyes. Other men swaggered to conceal their loss of fingers, hearing, or power to laugh. They cursed the bosses, damned the Company, and went home with no savings. People whispered darkly behind those men's backs: the rail hands had signed on for the job of their own free will. Not one of them had been coerced, not like the coolies kidnapped and taken to South America. The only ones to blame here were their own stupid selves, and that pained the railway men the most. They just wanted to forget.

Fist had fallen behind. I called out, waited, and fretted, and then returned to the bend in the road. No one. I cursed and hurried further back. I should have tied a rope to him as I had done with the brat. Fist was sitting on a log, his sack at his feet. I sat and handed him a rice ball.

His eyes were downcast. "Last night, at the store, they used dominoes for fortune-telling. I played too."

"Someone had the book?" I wanted to grab the explosives. With them in hand, I could leave behind this shit-hole fiend.

"My reading wasn't good. Played three times, all were bad."

"A man I knew had a reading. It predicted a long life. The man died two days later. It's the truth, I swear."

He pulled the sack onto his lap and wrapped his arms around it, a toddler hugging the family ox.

"You stay here," I said. "Give me the explosives and the ropes. I'll go alone."

Fist shook his head.

"Why stop me?"

"I'll go with you. Just give me time."

Birds chirped in the trees. Leaves and branches rustled. From a distance came the low rush of the river. I needed a rumble of thunder, and then a bolt of lightning to strike Fist and jolt him into action. Where was the fire, the one blazing in his eyes when I saw him yesterday?

After a while, he asked, "Did One Leg tell you? We moved earth and rock to change the slope of the land. Big horses dragged weights to flatten the ground. One day a horse cried out. I turned and my workmate fell onto me. A horse had reared up and struck his head. We hit the ground together."

I stayed silent and let him continue.

"I didn't see that he was dead until I stood up. There were no bruises, no blood. He looked asleep. I called and shook him. I never went near a horse again. People laughed at me."

"Horses here are bigger than oxen. We're not used to them, that's all."

"A man fell off a cliff and landed on rocks. I was small, so they dropped me down by ropes to fetch the body. I got dizzy. My arms went stiff. I couldn't move, halfway between heaven and earth. The men yelled and yanked my ropes, but I clung to the bushes. Finally they lowered another man to fetch me."

"We all get scared. No one flees that."

"No one flees his own memories."

"Make new ones." I stood. "Wreck the trestle, and you'll be reborn. The past won't matter. I promise you, we can succeed."

I reached for the sack of explosives, but he swung it away.

I grabbed his arm. "I can flip you over and crush you. I can put you in so much pain that you will want to die."

"Why don't you go without me?"

"Then give me the explosives."

"No." He clutched the sack even more tightly.

"See? You do want to do this. Let's go." I pointed to the sky. "It's going to rain."

He heaved the bag onto his shoulder and took a few steps. Then he scurried back to sit on the log, head over his knees as if squatting to shit.

"Didn't you smoke any opium last night?" I demanded.

We heard the clanking and rumbling of iron wheels approaching, but it was the light, fast sound of a handcar. Whenever one of those cars passed me on the tracks, I always thought of Monkey's ghost story from years ago. I wanted to believe that two men cranking at four wheels could out-run angry ghosts.

"Keep your head down," I said. "Don't show your face."

I glanced up after it passed. Three redbeards filled the handcar's tiny deck. Two workers pumped at a seesaw lever. The third man wore a suit, gripping the car frame while clutching a small box with three long wooden legs. It was the take-picture man.

I pulled Fist to his feet, jabbering with new fervour. "Heaven has sent us a big chance. That man will go take pictures of the trestle, and then take even more pictures after the blast. He will sell them everywhere and get famous. If they printed drawings beside Boss Soon's letter in the newspaper, the whole world will hear of us."

"Take pictures?"

"The Company took pictures of every tunnel and bridge. They took pictures of the trains, the bosses, and the cliffs. But no pictures of us China men."

"I heard of that," he replied. "Screw the Company."

I hustled him along and tried to boost his spirits. "What will you do in Yale?" I asked.

"Visit Goddess."

"Be careful of people asking where you came from."

"Nobody knows about us."

"You might see Sam Bing Lew. He knew I went to see you."

"You owe him money?"

"No."

"Then what?" He pestered me until I said, "He wants to go to China with me."

Fist burst out laughing. That gave me hope.

At the trestle, the handcar and take-picture man were nowhere to be seen. They had coasted through. Damn them. The grey sky left the iron road looking dull and solid. The beams and logs still carried a scent of fresh-cut wood. It was a steep drop to the beach below, littered with planed timber and debris. Luckily, no fishing stations occupied this stretch of the river, so no one was watching.

"It's as solid as a fortress wall!" Fist pulled back. "This won't work."

"Wooden stilts, that's all." I grabbed him. "When one log falls, it brings down everything else. Don't you remember trees falling in the forest?"

"Redbeard workers fell to their deaths building these trestles."

"They weren't afraid. Are you guarding the way or going down?"

He didn't move, so I added, "Redbeards built this, but it won't stand forever. Even the Great Wall at home was breached. You know that, don't you?"

He swallowed hard. "I'll go down."

I stopped him from heading out. "We don't unpack out there. Too risky."

We uncoiled the stiff ropes and tested their strength. I didn't ask where they had come from. Never disturb rice that's bubbling and half-cooked; you will ruin it. I made a noose at one end and tied the other end around my waist. Fist did the same. We tied the dynamite into bundles of six, loosely coiled their long fuses on top, and fastened them to our backs.

"Once we reach the middle," I said, "loop the noose over the end of a tie. The steel rails sit over the ties, so they won't pop up. At the other end of the tie, let yourself down along the outer leg. I will be two legs away, on the same side. Watch me and do what I do. We each fasten explosives to three legs. Down-up, down-up, three times. Can you do it?"

Fist nodded, his face pale.

"Before you go down," I said, "tie one end of the fuse to the steel and let it unwind as you go down. That way we know how far to go. Simple, no?"

The rush of the river seemed louder as Fist's voice faded.

"We have to be fast," I reminded him.

"Where's the middle?"

"No time to measure."

"What if the rope breaks?"

"Why would it break?"

Fist shrugged.

We lugged the sack of explosives onto the bridge and hurried forward. At least two more men were needed, one to stand at either end to keep people off. *No good plugging leaks when the boat is midstream.*

I dropped over the side and fought to get a grip on the under structure. Luckily, the bridge's legs were angled out and we could clamber onto them. But their slopes were steep, and the Company had used planed timber at the top, not rough logs. Each time I slid my hand down, slivers pierced my flesh. I felt the rope at my waist. I knew better than to look down. Fist hugged his beam, trying to slide down. Given his slow pace, I would need to do most of the work. There was a tug on my back; the fuse stretched no further. I was still very high up, having come down less than a quarter of the leg's length.

"Hey!" someone shouted. It was a voice we hadn't heard before. It wasn't friendly.

I looked up to where my rope met the steel. A man's bushy head and wide shoulders hovered there, dark against the sky, darting back and forth. We hadn't seen anyone all morning, and now this.

"Go up!" I screamed. Fist should have stood sentry.

He reversed and scurried up, arms flying hand-over-hand up the rope, feet fighting to grip the wood. Now we were lucky that he had dawdled closer to the top.

I clawed upward too and saw a glint of metal flashing around the ties. The man was trying to sever my rope. He must have looked into the sack. I wrapped my arms and legs around the beam. Just in time. Something whisked by my face and then the rope around my waist tugged from below. I tightened my grip around the wood and looked for Fist. He wasn't under the bridge. I prayed he had climbed over the top.

"Be careful!" I yelled. "He's got a knife!"

The wind dissolved my words. I heard voices but saw nothing through the underside of the trestle.

A short scream of terror.

"Fist, are you there?"

Had someone fallen over? Who? Should I go up?

I glanced at the sky above. Our gods had abandoned us, halfway between Heaven and Hell. Damn them.

At last Fist peered over the edge.

I couldn't see his face. "Get your rope. Drop it down," I called.

It took forever. I thought to climb on my own but one glance below changed my mind. Finally, the rope came bouncing down. It dangled out of my reach.

"Swing it," I shouted, "back and forth."

The rope jiggled feebly. I lunged several times before grabbing it. I pulled myself up and clambered over the edge.

Fist stood on the other side of the tracks, head down. I hurried over and looked over the edge. A body was sprawled below, a man wearing a brown jacket and dark pants. White flesh showed between the top of his boot and the pant leg. Fist and I were both panting.

"He ran at me. I rolled onto my stomach. He tried to jump aside. Then he screamed."

He tugged at the explosives tied to my back. A blade flashed in his hand as he cut away the ropes. I was trembling, too dazed to see what he was doing. Then he hurled the ropes away. They flew like uncoiling serpents into the river.

"No!" I shouted.

"This was my idea." He grabbed the sack of explosives. "And I say it is finished."

I lunged at him, but his knife was at my throat.

"Fist, you don't need to climb down again." I dropped my hands and spoke in soothing tones. "I can do everything. You keep watch, make sure no one tries to stop us."

"His ghost will follow me forever," he said.

"The spirits of China men will protect you."

"They didn't come earlier!"

I thought he would break into tears. "Give me the sack." I glanced over my shoulder. "Before people arrive."

"I told you not to do this."

"He ran at you. He would have thrown you off the bridge."

I sprang forward as he turned and swung the sack, gripping it with both hands, his entire body behind it. The canvas flew by me. I stumbled and fell back to grab at a wooden tie. The sack sailed into the air toward the river.

He crouched and held out the penknife. "This was that man's. Want to kill me too?"

I snatched it from him. It was heavy; the handle was made of bone. I wanted to plunge it into his face.

He turned and sprinted off the trestle.

I wanted grab his head and pound it into a tree trunk. He had caused the redbeard to fall, not me. He should go to jail, not me.

I took a step but stopped. A whimper wheezed out of me. The wind whistled past my ears and I felt suddenly off balance, unsure. Screw, screw, screw. I had caught a flash of the ground below. I looked away to the distant mountains and tried to walk, but my legs were stiff and heavy. I stretched out my arms, but only felt even more unbalanced. I pulled them in and clenched them to my chest. Turning sideways, I took baby steps, one at a time, with long pauses in between. My teeth chattered from the cold. I cursed Fist for ruining my strengthened feet, for destroying a skill I had fought hard to attain.

By the time I got off the trestle, he was long gone.

An eagle floated over the river, looking for fish. Was it the same one we'd seen the day before? I looked down. The dark bag poked out from the milky brown of the water. Fist was like that sack of dynamite, waiting to explode. He would be a nuisance in China, not me.

He might still be on the railway line or have gone to run by the water. Only a fool would try the beach. The Native fishermen there would surely tell the police who had gone by. And Fist with his pocked face would be an easy mark.

I left the railway tracks and walked in the drainage ditch below the roadbed. If thick bushes grew nearby, I clambered through them.

I should have pushed Fist off the trestle. I could have reported seeing him fight the redbeard before they both fell. China men and redbeards were longstanding enemies; it made sense that they taunted and challenged each other. People could imagine the two men stomping toward each other on the trestle; neither one, being full of pride, would yield the way. They shouted and then shoved and grappled. But then the police would demand to know what I was doing there with those two.

The redbeard's body might never be found. How many people on the railway walked so close to the edge of the trestle? Maybe the corpse had fallen behind rocks and couldn't be seen from the water. Even if it was found, people would conclude that he had fallen on his own. He was drunk. Maybe he was a madman. No explosives had been left behind. And even if someone found the bag of ropes in the bushes, it meant nothing. There was no reason for anyone to think that China men had been involved in the death. When I reached Yale, I would send a letter to Bookman Soon urging him to try again. Fist's plan had been a sound one.

I thought ahead to Yale. I prayed that Sam would not meet Fist, who would tell him that I was coming soon. Sam couldn't go to China with me. He had to go to Spuzzum and be a father to my son. Sam could throw whatever shit he wanted at me and China men. We could not be trusted. We were the same as redbeards, looking down on Native people. We were smart only on the dark *yin* side. Later he would hear from the washman why I had left. He might even cheer my efforts at this revenge, even though they had failed.

But what if Sam looked at the boy and cursed loudly and smashed his fist into a wall? Perhaps a mirror image of himself was too painful to see. He might refuse to take the boy onto the dismal trail where he had been donkey and pack-ass all these years. He clearly yearned to go to China. Yet he had boasted that his child in Lytton had more Native blood than Peter. Men were fickle: my father had left his family without a word or backward glance. Of course, Sam should treat a stranger's son worse than his trueborn child. That was normal for any man, and certainly for a China man.

If Sam had gone ahead to Victoria and waited for me there, then another disaster loomed. I would need to keep hiding and be unable to see my friends.

A horse and wagon approached. I ducked behind tall grasses and waited for it to pass.

Closer to Yale, there was no helpful cover, but dusk was falling. The forest had been chopped down long ago. Then wildfires devoured the new saplings. I needed to keep a hefty distance from the main road to stay safe. I forded the creek and then looped around the town's back to enter it from the west. If anyone saw me, I would be coming from Emory, not Spuzzum. This route also brought me close to the empty house where Sam and Peter and I had stayed.

I approached warily, afraid to find Sam there. It was empty but smelled foul. Passersby had used it as an outhouse.

I planned to avoid Chinatown but needed a warm place to stop my shivering. Good thing Yang had given me some cash this morning. I kept my face down and hugged the shadows of the buildings. The buzzing of night insects was loud. I passed by Clouds Clear Tower and glanced at the windows, low lights glowing behind flimsy curtains.

Someone played a tune on a bamboo flute. The high, pure notes sent a shudder through my body.

I slipped into a dimly lit cookhouse and went to a corner. I called for hot soup and rice. I slurped the food, forehead to the table, my spine to the other diners. A man was scraping every last grain of rice into his mouth with a spoon. At another table, three men were playing with ivory point-sticks, used in place of cash. Only failed sojourners were left in Yale, the ones who had not killed themselves.

Now I was one of them.

18

No Light Inside an Inverted Bucket (1885)

The passage downriver from Yale was quick, but the waters between the mainland and Victoria rose and fell, driven by strong winds that slowed and rocked the sternwheeler. I had boarded with a woozy head, having smoked one pipe of opium too much the night before. I recalled vaguely that Poy and I had resolved long ago never to smoke two nights in a row.

Still, there was less to complain about on this part of my trip: no cow dung to inhale and no redbeards on the upper deck laughing at a clumsy China man failing as a father. It was much easier to keep one's dignity when alone, with no child running wild at one's feet. On that trip, I had a simple plan to get rid of that brat. No wonder he had trusted Sam. Even I knew the line: *People at birth, pure and kind.* Heaven had been watching: I was duly humbled and punished.

At the railing, I pulled up my collar and gazed at the thin line at the water's far edge. All morning my fingers and gut had felt cold and stiff as if the chill of a corpse had infected me. I wanted to throw up. There was no getting warm until I reached China. If I had ginger to chew on, my stomach might settle down.

Fist had boarded too but fell in with some China men throwing dice in a rowdy circle. I had been surprised to see such a large group clutching boat tickets. Its leader, a clerk from Victoria's Bow Yuen store, told me that the Lee clan had pushed hard to raise funds to bring their kinsmen from Yale to Victoria, where they would be less likely to starve and more likely to get help returning home. He knew me from the game hall and tried to make small talk, but I pinched my face and claimed to be seasick, so he left me alone.

I stared at the boat's edge from which Peter had dropped into the water. That tumble had launched this grand disaster, turned me into a snake scheming to swallow an elephant. A superior man would have searched for Sam last night without fear of being noticed in Chinatown. He would have gone through every back-alley game house until he found the guide and warned him again how very dangerous it was for him to go to China. And if Sam said he didn't want Peter, then a superior man would have gone back to Spuzzum for his son.

Too bad I wasn't that man.

Sam and I had been at each other's throats even before we'd been introduced. He demanded that I take the boy to China. Maybe he only wanted to argue, to provoke China men, make them feel small and stupid over every little matter. Even now we didn't know where Peter would find a better home, but here, at least, he would be closer to his mother. If Sam went to Spuzzum and adopted Peter, then Sam and I could have become sworn brothers, sharing a son. We would kneel before the God of War, avowing a blood oath that could never be broken. Family was as sacred as landholdings, but redbeards had claimed all of Gold Mountain for themselves and made Sam a fool for chasing after it. Neither of us had a father, yet we both tried to become better men ourselves. Surely that made us worthy humans.

On the ship to China, I planned to gamble and win myself a small sum. But I would have to show restraint; otherwise someone sore from his losses would knife me as I slept and steal my winnings. Maybe there was work to be had in Hong Kong, though I doubted it, given the glut of railway workers there. At least I would be free to visit the game halls. There would be time for me to embrace Buddha's foot and polish his sacred toes with a soft cloth. Then I would board a slow ferry and head upriver. Hopefully, the girl's family would not change its mind when they learned about my turn of fortune. There were plenty of losers in China, but I didn't belong in their ranks. All night long, I had silently recited the cheerful proverbs used to comfort the less fortunate:

Even ducks drown in the river.

Cast a net ten times, nine times it rises clear.

Lose a chess match; the chessboard remains.

"Lend me something?" Fist held out his hand. "Lucky winds aren't with me."

I shook my head. The last time we had spoken, it was on the trestle. He fiddled with his tobacco and handed me a roll. It took several tries before he struck a flame for us.

"Can you get to China?" I asked, feeling grateful.

"I'm going to America," he proclaimed.

"Bad time now."

"Can you write a letter for me? To tell One Leg what happened."

"Good news or bad?"

"Good for us, but bad for you."

Back in Victoria, I went to Uncle See's store to get a bed for the night and to ask about Sam. The shelves were still full. Few buying customers had come to the store. At this rate, this storekeeper would never go home. Maybe he was doomed to tend the Chinese graveyard here. No wonder he was in a foul mood. He asked about the boy, calling him a piece of dog shit.

"You didn't know," I said. "His mother taught him to speak Chinese. He called me Baba and yelled at me to wait for him. He's a clever boy. He could have called you Grandfather."

"Never heard him say anything. Didn't you say he was a deaf mute?"

"You scared him. I started teaching him *Three Word Classic*."

"You're lucky my cat came back. Otherwise I'd charge you for all the food the mice ate." He paused. "The boss at New World game house asked if you were looking for work."

"No."

"He'll pay well. All you have to do is stand there and the vermin will behave. They're getting rowdy. When it rained last, they refused to leave the place and slept on the floors. The boss begged them to go because his enemies could inform the Health Inspector, who would shut him down. He was as frantic as a woman, but nobody listened to him."

"I already have my two-dollar receipt," I said.

"So you saw the Council office?"

We chuckled.

The fancy rosewood furniture and calligraphy scrolls were

gone from the storefront, leaving it bare and empty. Even the long-case clock with its gleaming brass weights, which passers-by relied on for telling the time, was gone. Two sets of the chairs and side tables had been taken during an overnight robbery. The rest of the furniture was now in locked storage.

"Mister Secretary can't figure out why anyone would steal it," I said. "It can't be sold. Everyone in Chinatown knows everyone."

Uncle See leaned forward. "They say if you go deep enough into the tent city, you'll find the fancy chairs."

Finally I asked about Sam. No, no new mix-blood faces had been seen. I relaxed. That stupid Sam was still waiting for me in Yale.

⚹

Wet Water Dog was closing shop when I arrived with my Council receipt. The office was piled high with carrying cloths, tightly bound around people's goods, and sturdy western-style trunks. Since my last visit, he had pinned on his wall a large coloured picture, printed by a steamship firm, of the great vessels that sailed the Pacific. Sails puffed out like great curtains, clouds gushed from smokestacks, and the skies and seas were soft shades of blue. I doubted that such calm seas lay ahead for me

The rich aroma of Wet Water Dog's cigar made my mouth water. "You returned just in time," he said.

"Didn't think I would, did you?" I said.

"Thought you had climbed into a warm bed with the mother of your son. People in Chinatown bet money on the outcome, did you know? Me, I wagered you wouldn't find her. The odds were supposed to be on my side."

"A guide helped me find her. He was mix-blood, half-Chinese and half-Native."

"What's his name? I want to go to the mainland and ride the train. My woman wants to see the iron road; she heard so much about it. My little boys too, they want to see it before we go home."

"Sam. Sam Bing Lew. He's in Yale or Spuzzum. Go now and you can lay with Goddess before Soohoo shuts down Clouds Clear Tower."

He grinned. "Can I see her without the wife knowing?"

"Don't mention my name to Sam," I said.

"You owe him?"

"Not money. I agreed to help him on a small matter."

"You going home? Didn't you lose all your money on the mainland?"

"Of course I'm going home. Twelve years have passed. My people want to see me; they don't care about money."

"Won't you stay and work a while? The chicken ran off, but you can catch a duck."

"Only steamships are doing well."

"How many rail hands are left in Yale? What's your guess?"

I hadn't told a soul about the loss of my money roll, but it didn't surprise me that people knew. The bandits who stole our packs would have bragged. Boss Joe and the men from Lytton were certain to have talked about me on their way to Yale in the stagecoach. I couldn't wait to escape all this useless talk.

The next afternoon, fragile men overpowered by eagerness crowded the docks as the burly Council guards stopped them from boarding the ship ahead of time. A cluster of shabby, barefoot railway men were travelling on funds donated by the Chinese merchants of San Francisco. Too bad the Lee men from Yale had not arrived here sooner. The travellers looked as if they had been thrown into baths as well as oversized shirts and pants that couldn't get sold. I hoped their pigtails were free from fleas and ticks. Their sponsored departure called for lengthy speeches, giving credit to our fellow Chinese south of the border, a few of whom had come to witness the event.

I carried mostly fresh food that could be eaten before spoilage started. Roast pork would be good for four or five days, but my sack of local apples would last the longest, even though I couldn't afford the sweetest ones. Hawkers mingled through the crowd, touting snacks and small jugs of wine. Dockhands wheeled large crates up the gangplank and large baskets of fresh vegetables arrived for the kitchen. The sooner the ship got underway, the sooner I could start to forget about this place. No one was keen to go down into the gloom of the steerage hold.

Someone pulled my arm. I turned. Fist held out a jug of rice wine.

"What's this?"

He shrugged. "You helped me out. This will keep you warm."

He wasn't referring to the letter I had written for him. "If I hear of you making lots of money in America," I said with a smile, "I'll track you down."

"Did you go to the temple?"

I shook my head. Wet Water Dog had asked the same thing, if I was going to pray for a safe voyage.

A familiar smell slid through the air. Wet Water Dog came behind me, his cigar in one hand and a newspaper in the other.

"Yang Hok," he called, shaking his head. "Your man is in trouble."

The daily paper from Yale had just arrived. Wet Water Dog translated from the English as Fist and I listened. Native fishermen had found the body of a Calvin John Shepard, farm labourer, thirty-one, under one of the railway trestles between Yale and Spuzzum. The constable in Yale had no suspicions until Shepard's friends urged the lawman to arrest Sam Bing Lew, the guide. They said that Lew and Shepard had been gambling until late at night, a few days before Shepard's body was found. Lew had been winning, and Shepard covered his losses by staking his fancy penknife, which he lost to Sam. But as it was a family heirloom that had belonged to Shepard's father and grandfather, he asked for it back, planning to borrow money from his employer to pay Sam. Witnesses saw Sam and Shepard leave Yale together.

According to witnesses, Sam returned to town alone later that day and resumed gambling. When police questioned Sam, he claimed that Shepard had repaid him and regained his penknife. Yet it was not found on the body.

"Wasn't this your man?" Wet Water Dog was shaking his head. "They'll hang him."

I was breathing through my mouth, trying to take in the news. The story had far too many twists of fate to be believed. How could it be that Sam, of the hundreds of people in Yale, would have been gambling against the man who would come across us on the trestle? I cursed Heaven as I touched the penknife, heavy in my pocket. I had thought it would make a fine gift for Grandfather.

I dragged my sack to the other side of the dock. Fist followed. Across the harbour, clapboard houses painted in bright colours dotted the green hills that rose from the shoreline. A scow drifted by, riding low with a heavy load of crates. Two Native men paddled a dugout from the village across the way toward the city. Seagulls hurtled by so close that the flapping of their wings vibrated in my ears.

"You're safe," Fist said. "Nobody knows about you."

"I should kill you," I said. "You know. I know. As do Heaven and Earth."

I braced my legs and shut my eyes and tilted my head back. How many damned ghosts were following me?

"Isn't this good news?" Fist was cheerful. "No lawman will ever ask about us. Everyone is safe, everyone can sleep, even Bookman Soon."

I didn't answer. Fist tugged at my bottle and told me to take a drink.

I shook my head.

"Are you still thinking about that son of yours?"

I jerked away, but he grabbed me. "Don't go back." The smell of his tobacco was strong. "They will hang you."

"Sam is blameless."

"You didn't kill that man," Fist said. "It was me."

"I forced you onto the bridge."

"Don't you want to see your people?"

"Of course."

"Even if you save Sam, what life can he have? He is mix-blood."

I shoved my ticket and receipt into Fist's pocket. I thrust the jug of wine and my sack of food at him and ran from the docks.

If only I had looked for Sam that night in Yale. If I had found him, then we might have left together the next morning on the sternwheeler. Sam could have been standing on the docks beside me. We could have sailed off as two free men.

⚜

It was raining when the sternwheeler reached Yale. I went to see Soohoo at Clouds Clear Tower. Only the brothel keeper would have enough clout to get me into the jail. He greeted me warmly, thinking I wanted more time with Goddess. He had no idea where I had been. I told him I'd come to see Sam.

"Not involved in that fall, are you?" he demanded

I chose my words with care. "Sam could not have killed anyone. He is a good man."

"The story goes against him."

"Will the Council help him at trial?"

"Why? He's no China man."

"He's half—. He helped me on my trip."

"What if the police arrest you too?"

"They have no reason for that."

"You are Sam's friend. They can say you helped him."

"Has anyone visited him?"

"Only his grandmother."

Soohoo took me along as he spoke to bigwig redbeards at stores and offices. Finally we went to the sturdy log cabin that served as jail. The constable was not there, only his Native helper. Soohoo spoke to him and then to me.

"Be careful. If anything happens to you, it may be hard to get you out."

Sam's cell had a heavy wooden door with a tiny barred slot. I lit the candle that Soohoo had given me and peered in. It was daylight outside, but the small room had no windows. The stink reminded me of our time in Boston Bar's jail. When I called Sam's name, the figure on the ground stirred.

"Yang Hok," he murmured. "Going back to China?"

"Sam, come here."

"Limp off."

"Did they beat you? Do you need liniments?"

"Limp off."

"I came from Victoria. I was boarding my ship when the news came."

"You have money to waste? Didn't you lose everything?"

"I brought water and food for you."

There was the clank of a heavy chain as Sam shuffled over.

I shoved a slim bottle of cold boiled water through the bars. He drank eagerly. Then I passed through rice and meats wrapped in cloth.

"Go piss against those walls." I brought the candle close and showed him the penknife. His eyes flickered for a moment.

I shoved it back in my pocket. "You didn't kill that man," I whispered. "I did."

Sam's eyes were dull. "What does it matter?"

"I'll tell the police. Then they will free you."

"You think they'll believe you? You're a China man!"

"The knife proves I did it. I'll show it to them."

"You stupid shit-hole fiend. They'll say we killed that man together. They'll put a rope around your neck and hang you too. People saw us together, here, at the start of the trip." He pulled at the blanket around his shoulder and turned away.

"This isn't right," I said. "You didn't kill anyone."

"You hear the shit leaking from your mouth?"

"I want to help you."

Sam returned and clutched the iron bars. "Go help Peter. Who's his father?"

"You," I said. "He likes you better than me."

Sam shook his head. "You fool, you can swear by all your ancestors' names that you killed that man, but the redbeards will never free us. One of us killed one of them."

"Peter isn't mine any more. He's with your grandmother."

"I heard. She said she took him for me. But I will die soon, and same for her."

I reached for Sam's hands, but he walked away. The iron bars were warm where he had clutched them. My hands were wet, from tears.

"Do what you want," Sam said. "You never listen to me, but this time you should."

"Should I take him to China?"

"Do whatever you want."

"And you? What do you want?"

"What I want has never mattered." He paused. "Don't weep like a woman. Do you want to be the boy's father? Yes or no? After that, thinking about China will be easy."

Then he vanished into the darkness.

From:

Provincial Archives of British Columbia

Connaught Library

Parliament Buildings

Victoria, British Columbia

Blanshard 5 - 0672

For Immediate Release

Mr. Willard Ireland, British Columbia Provincial Archivist, and Mr. Kong Hay Wong, President of the Chinese Consolidated Benevolent Association of Victoria and Chair of the Chinese Subcommittee of the B.C. Centennial Committee, will unveil a pioneer Chinese treasure at the Provincial Archives on April 16, 1958.

This is one of the Provincial Archives' extensive program of events marking the centennial of the birth of the province.

Mr. Hok ("Hank") Yang of Boston Bar was a pioneer immigrant to B.C. and worked on the building of the Canadian Pacific Railway, which took place from 1880 to 1885. For years he ran the Tai Hing General Store in Boston Bar. Before his death in 1938, Mr. Yang presented the Yale and District Museum with his 300-page memoir.

Since that time, the memoir has not been read. The gift came with a restriction: it could not be opened until 1958, 100 years after his birth.

"I only know that it's written in Chinese," says Mr. Ireland. "It's invaluable; we don't have many records from the Chinese."

Mr. Wong will do on-the-spot translations during the unveiling, which will also feature colourful dances from China's 2,000 years of tradition, performed by the Chinese Public School dance troupe.

Confirmed guests at the unveiling include Lieutenant Governor Frank Mackenzie Ross, CMG, MC; Mr. Lawrence J. Wallace, Deputy Provincial Secretary and Chairman of the B.C. Centennial Committee; as well as Mr. Hok Yang's son Peter and Peter's children and grandchildren. Members of Mrs. Peter (Jeannie) Yang's extended family from the Kopchitchin Indian Reserve will also attend.

When queried about his father's memoir, Mr. Peter Yang revealed, "Pop wanted to tell the truth of why he stayed here and didn't go home to China, but he didn't want to embarrass anyone."

####

ACKNOWLEDGMENTS

This author acknowledges that the story "The Transformer" belongs to the Nlaka'pamux First Nations people of British Columbia's Fraser Canyon and that unresolved issues remain around the use of traditional Native stories. First Nations assert that such stories told by their people may not enter the public use domain the same way as stories told or written by white people.

The version of the story used here was collected by James Teit, an anthropologist working from Spences Bridge in the early twentieth century. As pointed out in *Our Tellings: Interior Salish Stories of the Nlha7kápmx People*, compiled and edited by Darwin Hanna and Mamie Henry (UBC Press, 1995):

"Without the aid of a tape recorder, however, he [Teit] had to rely on his memory. As a result, his records are mere sketches of the original telling. He also had to submit his collections to the editorship of his mentor, Franz Boas. Because Boas was more interested in composite than in individual stories, he eliminated many of the names of the individual tellers and communities. On reading Teit's published collections today, one is left wondering exactly whose works and whose stories are being represented." (p. xiv)

I urge readers of this book, and of "The Transformer" tale, to recognize the many outstanding issues confronting the First Nations of British Columbia and to lobby their political representatives to move toward addressing these matters to the full satisfaction of all parties involved.

In writing this book, I received help from friends, family, and colleagues. Wayson Choy, SKY Lee, and Jim Wong-Chu commented on earlier portions of the book. Prabha Khosla, Dr Keith Lowe, and Dr Lisa Yun provided insights on the term "coolie." Susan Safyan, editor at Arsenal Pulp Press, noticed the glitches in my manuscript and proposed solutions. My brother Vernon and his family hosted me on my research trips to Vancouver. Dr. Andrea Laforet provided advice on traditional First Nations stories. Most important of all, my partner Mohamed Khaki had unshakeable faith in this writing project despite its long gestation. His sister Jenny provided delicious meals far beyond the call of duty. I gratefully acknowledge funding from the literature programs of Canada Council for the Arts and the Toronto Arts Council.

PAUL YEE was born in Saskatchewan but grew up in Vancouver's Chinatown. He is the author of nearly thirty books, including the Governor General's Award-winning novel for young people *Ghost Train* and *Saltwater City: An Illustrated History of the Chinese in Vancouver*, winner of the Vancouver Book Award. He lives in Toronto. ***paulyee.ca***